S0-ART-947

PASSION'S CAPTIVE

Sebastian spread his hands on the wall on either side of her head, making escape impossible. He bent his dark head and nuzzled her neck. Tory's skin shuddered from the touch of his mouth on it. Ineffectually, she shoved against his rock-hard chest.

"Stop it," she hissed furiously. Heat flooded her body. "What do you think I am?"

"But I *know* what you are, *gatinha*—a liberated female, a woman unafraid to take what she wants from life and damn the consequences."

Tory had never considered that freedom for women might mean *this*—allowing a perfect stranger to make her feel things she didn't want to feel. She opened her mouth to scream, but he didn't give her the chance. His hand moved to her chin and held it steady while his mouth came down upon hers. She felt the hot pressure of his lips. Their breaths mingled. Her senses flooded with the scent and taste of him, and she felt as if she were drowning. . . .

LET ARCHER AND CLEARY
AWAKEN AND CAPTURE YOUR HEART!

CAPTIVE DESIRE   (2612, $3.75)
by Jane Archer

Victoria Malone fancied herself a great adventuress and student of life, but being kidnapped by handsome Cord Cordova was too much excitement for even her! Convincing her kidnapper that she had been an innocent bystander when the stagecoach was robbed was futile when he was kissing her until she was senseless!

REBEL SEDUCTION   (3249, $4.25)
by Jane Archer

"Stop that train!" came Lacey Whitmore's terrified warning as she rushed toward the locomotive that carried wounded Confederates and her own beloved father. But no one paid heed, least of all the Union spy Clint McCullough, who pinned her to the ground as the train suddenly exploded into flames.

DREAM'S DESIRE   (3093, $4.50)
by Gwen Cleary

Desperate to escape an arranged marriage, Antonia Winston y Ortega fled her father's hacienda to the arms of the arrogant Captain Domino. She would spend the night with him and would be free for no gentleman wants a ruined bride. And ruined she would be, for Tonia would never forget his searing kisses!

VICTORIA'S ECSTASY   (2906, $4.25)
by Gwen Cleary

Proud Victoria Torrington was short of cash to run her shipping empire, so she traveled to America to meet her partner for the first time. Expecting a withered, ancient cowhand, Victoria didn't know what to do when she met virile, muscular Judge Colston and her body budded with desire.

Available wherever paperbacks are sold, or order direct from the Publisher. Send cover price plus 50¢ per copy for mailing and handling to Zebra Books, Dept. 3595, 475 Park Avenue South, New York, N.Y. 10016. Residents of New York, New Jersey and Pennsylvania must include sales tax. DO NOT SEND CASH.

KATHARINE KINCAID

TROPICAL CAPTIVE

ZEBRA BOOKS
KENSINGTON PUBLISHING CORP.

For Cel Suszek
A dear friend as well as a relative,
With thanks for your support.

ZEBRA BOOKS

are published by

Kensington Publishing Corp.
475 Park Avenue South
New York, NY 10016

First printing: December, 1991

Printed in the United States of America

Prologue

Estãncia de Fãlcao
Bahia, Brazil
1882

The smell of smoke awakened the boy. Gasping for breath, he sat up in bed. His eyes stung, and his throat hurt. A crackling sound came from outside. Through the cracks around his shuttered window, smoke curled in thick, gray wisps. He slipped out of bed, the floor tiles cool and familiar beneath his bare feet, and made his way through the darkened house to the bedchamber of his parents.

In front of their closed door, he hesitated, having been taught not to barge in on them in the middle of the night. Timidly, he opened the door and peered into the inky depths of the room. He had to squint in order to see his parents, lying close together in the big four-poster. *Papai*'s arms were around *Mamãe*. Both appeared to be sleeping. Their room was as smoky as his own.

Again, he debated whether or not to risk his father's anger. "You're a big boy now," *Papai* had said the last time. "You can sleep through the night alone and not come running to your *Mamãe* every-time you have a bad dream."

But this was no dream. The smoke and the crackling sounds were real and frightening. *Papai* wouldn't like it that a fire was burning so close to the house. Everyone had to be extra careful these days, because there had been no rain for a long, long time. The trees were all dying, and the grass had shriveled. The cattle were dying, too, because a wicked man named Mundinho Cerqueira wouldn't let them cross his land to drink from the São Francisco River.

Quelling his misgivings, the boy walked over to the bed. *"Mamãe,"* he whispered, reaching out to touch his mother's shoulder. "Wake up. There's a fire outside."

His father snapped upright and reached for the long-nosed *pistola* he always kept on the nightstand. "What is it? What's happening?"

The boy stepped backward. The look on *Papai's* face frightened him. His mother stirred and sleepily called his father's name. "Manuel? Is everything all right?"

Both adults noticed the smoke at almost the same moment. With startled cries, they leaped from the rumpled bed. His mother screamed. *"Mamãe* de Jesus! The *sertão* must be burning!"

"And I know who set it afire—damn his black soul!" Pistol in one hand, *Papai* grabbed for his trousers with the other. He was stark naked, the boy saw in amazement. As his father hurriedly dressed, his mother wrapped herself in the bed linens from off the bed. She must be naked, too, he realized, but she did not allow him to see her body.

"Meu Deus! Where are you going? What will you do?" *Mamãe* sounded close to tears. Her voice quivered as she pushed a strand of long, black hair out of her eyes.

6

"Kill him . . . But first we must get to safety. Hurry, there's not a moment to lose. Bring the boy. We must flee the house."

"But the servants! We have to rouse the servants first."

"I'll wake the servants. Wait for me near the front door . . . Don't go out until I come."

"Manuel, I'm so frightened!"

Mamãe started to cry, and the child did, too, but a fit of coughing overcame them both. It was becoming harder and harder to breathe. The boy's chest burned. A giant fist seemed to be squeezing the air from his lungs. His mother took his hand, and he immediately felt better. Clasping it tightly, she followed his father from the room. They hurried down the long tile hallway and soon reached the heavy, wooden front door.

"Wait here . . . I'll return in a moment."

As soon as *Papai* disappeared in the direction of the servants' quarters, *Mamãe* released his hand and began pacing back and forth. Three steps down the hallway. Stop. Turn. Three steps back again. "Dear God, I knew it would come to this," she moaned. "Cerqueira means to destroy us, then the land will all be his."

"Did Cerqueira really start the fire, *Mamãe?* Why would he do such a bad thing?"

She paused near him and stroked his hair with gentle fingers. "You are too young to understand, my little *falcão*, my innocent fledgling. Land is gold. Land is wealth. Land is what every poor peasant wants, and every rich man will die to protect . . . Cerqueira wants all of it."

The boy thought he understood well enough. His father's love for the harsh scrubland where they made their home had been drummed into him over and over. "This land is yours, *mon filho*, your birthright,

7

your heritage," *Papai* often reminded him. "But you will have to fight to hold it . . . When that day comes, fight proudly. You are a *Falcão*, and the *Falcãos* never admit defeat."

Papai would kill the bad man, Cerqueira, then the land would be safe again. The cattle could drink. The boy hoped he would get to witness the murder—only it wouldn't be murder. It would be a *"crime de vingança"*, which he already knew was the way things were done here on the *sertão*.

Moments later, *Papai* came rushing back to them down the smoky hallway. "Those worthless servants! The cowards have already fled. Come, we must leave now. I'll go first, to make sure it's all right. Then you follow. Have the boy come last."

His mother nodded. "Be careful, Manuel. It may be a trick to force us out of the house."

"Don't worry. I have my *pistola*. If they think to find me unprepared, they are mistaken."

Papai unbolted the front door and threw it open. The boy blinked and peered through the smoke. A line of fiery scrub and cactus confronted them. Someone had rolled the dry, thorny underbrush into a pile in front of the house and set it ablaze. The grass was burning, crackling as the flames consumed it and raced toward the house.

"I don't see anyone," his mother quavered.

"It is nothing—only a little brush fire meant to scare us. But we *Falcãos* do not scare easily. Stay here while I check."

Holding the *pistola* in two hands, aiming for whoever might be outside, *Papai* stepped from the house. A loud clap, like a crack of thunder, made the boy jump. At the same moment, *Papai* spun around, his eyes opened wide. An ugly red flower blossomed in the center of his chest, then dripped down his flat belly onto his white trousers.

8

"Manuel!" The boy's mother rushed forward.

Another crack sounded. *Mamãe* stumbled and fell. The bed linens came unraveled, and she sprawled half-naked across *Papai*. Her hands clutched frantically at his arms, then stilled. The boy stood rooted to the spot, too horrified to move. He could see them, now—shadowy figures on horseback, moving back and forth on the other side of the flames. Their voices carried to him on the smoky, night wind.

"Got them both, eh, Mundinho? Might as well get the fledgling, too. Then all the arrogant *Falcãos* will be dead."

Something ricocheted off the doorjamb and whizzed by the boy's ear. His legs felt too stiff to run. Hardly aware of what he was doing, he dropped to the floor and hugged the cool tiles as if they might protect him.

"That does it, my friends! *Estância de Falcão* is mine!" a man cried triumphantly.

No, the boy thought, the Falcon Ranch belongs to me now. He clung to the thought as he cowered on the floor, waiting for the men to leave. And he clung to it after they had gone, and the full weight of what had happened that night descended upon him. Years later, he was still clinging to it, living a lie and biding his time until he was old enough to seek revenge. The day would come when the ranch would be his again. On that day, he would destroy Mundinho Cerqueira and make him suffer for all the pain and suffering the man had caused. Vengeance will be mine, the boy told himself as he grew. Each day he repeated it to himself like a litany: *Vengeance will one day be mine.*

Chapter One

Castle Acres Farm
Lexington, Kentucky
1906

"Tory! Tory King! What in hell do you think you're doing?"

The cry rang out like a pistol shot, and Victoria Amanda King had no difficulty detecting the anger in her brother's voice. Jordan was furious, as she had very well known he would be, if he caught her doing what she was doing now. It was time, however, for Jordan to learn that he did not own her, could not dictate to her, and had no business even *trying* to tell her how to live her life. Ignoring him completely, Tory concentrated on keeping her seat aboard the prancing, snorting horse beneath her. The big bay was ready to explode, which was exactly the way *she* often felt. If ever horse and rider were meant for each other, she and Renegade were—and Jordan could take his wearisome over-protectiveness and go straight to perdition with it.

"Tory!" The angry summons came again. "Damn my Aunt Milly's corset! Have you no sense at all?

11

That horse could kill you."

Sensing that his bad manners were being discussed, Renegade bunched his muscles and tossed his head. Anticipating a rear or a buck, Tory tightened her reins and sat deeper in the saddle. She was an excellent rider—better than Jordan, but Renegade had defied every known method of training to make him an obedient, docile mount. He refused to be ridden or driven and always managed to dislodge whoever dared climb on his back or get in a cart behind him. It wasn't that he didn't know what was being demanded; he'd had ample opportunity to learn, but he was a rebel. Like Tory herself, he resented being told what to do and when to do it.

Determined to escape her brother, Tory signaled for a canter. The big bay responded by spinning in a tight circle in a futile effort to evade the pressure of her trouser-encased leg. As he did so, Tory caught sight of Jordan's face. His green eyes were twin pools of fire, his mouth a grim slash. Jordan was the very image of enraged masculinity. A light breeze ruffled his blond hair, flattening his shirt against the taut muscles of his broad chest, and Tory knew a moment of bitter frustration and envy. She and Jordan looked enough alike to be easily identifiable as brother and sister—but Jordan had been born a male. Therefore, he could do what he pleased *when* he pleased, while *she* had to endure the constraints of a society that thought a woman should have no more on her mind than how much lace and ribbon ought to adorn her latest tea gown.

A quaintly-ruffled Gibson girl Tory wasn't, and neither was Jordan's wife, Spencer, who shared many of Tory's unorthodox, inflammatory views. Both were ardent supporters of female emancipation, but despite his own wife's outspokenness, Jordan still seemed to think he had the right to forbid his younger sister to do certain things—such as riding Renegade, whom he regarded as unfit for any duty except siring sturdy, fleet-footed foals.

Tory tried again to urge Renegade into a canter, but the horse stubbornly pranced sideways, almost trampling Jordan as he came abreast of them. Jordan swore under his breath and grabbed Renegade's bridle, nearly tugging the reins from Tory's hands.

Grimly, she held on. "Leave me alone, Jordan! I can handle him. I don't need you or any man to come dashing to my rescue."

"You're damn lucky he hasn't killed you yet! Didn't I tell you to stay away from him? You can ride any other horse on the whole damn farm. With a choice of several dozen, why do you insist on choosing *this* one? He can't be trusted, and you damned well know it."

Tory glared down at her tall, angry brother, wondering why *he* had also been the one to receive the heart-stopping good looks, while she and her two younger sisters paled in comparison. Bold, blond, and ruggedly handsome, Jordan turned people's heads wherever he went. She, on the other hand, almost never drew anyone's notice—until she opened her mouth. Then everyone frowned in disapproval.

"Is 'damn' the only word you know, Jordan? You ought to expand your vocabulary. At the very least, you should cease condemning Aunt Milly's corset. I can't think why you cling to that juvenile epithet. It doesn't even make sense, since we've never had an Aunt Milly, and . . ."

"Get off that damn horse!" Jordan reached up

with his free hand to grab her arm and drag her out of the saddle.

She half-fell, half-slid to the ground. As soon as her weight left his back, Renegade stopped prancing and became meek as a lamb, which only infuriated her further.

"You stupid, uncooperative hunk of flea bait!" She tilted back her head to meet Jordan eye to eye and turned her ire on him. "How dare you manhandle me like that, Jordan King! I said I don't need your help, and I don't!"

"I dare because I care about you! Much more, apparently, than you care about yourself! I've told you time and again to stay away from Renegade. Are you trying to kill yourself?"

When she didn't answer, but only stood scowling, thinking the idea had merit, he frowned and said in a softer tone: "That isn't *really* what you were trying to do, is it, Tory? I know you've been miserable since you came home, and we've all been wondering why, but things can't be as bad as all that, can they?"

She had to swallow hard against the sudden lump in her throat. "I haven't told you how bad they are, Jordan," she admitted, dropping her gaze. "You think I only came to Castle Acres to spend the spring break with you . . . Well, I did, but there's something more you should know."

She took a deep breath before blurting the awful truth that shamed and humiliated her more than anything that had happened to her in the past twenty-six years, the last five of them spent teaching at an East Coast boarding school, from which she herself had graduated and was now being tossed out on her ear.

"They're letting me go," she whispered. "They've

14

asked me not to return in the fall. When I come home for the summer, I'll be coming for good—that is, if you want me . . . If you don't, I'll stay in the East. I have money saved, and I can find another job besides teaching . . ."

"*Want* you? Of course, we want you! But what do you mean, 'they let you go'?" Jordan paused long enough to hand Renegade's reins to Abelardo, his son by adoption, who had silently come up beside them. "Abelardo, put Renegade away, will you?"

He tucked Tory's hand beneath his arm and started walking toward the house with her. "Why would they not desire your return? You're a wonderful teacher. *Too* wonderful, I sometimes think. You've dedicated your whole life to that damn girls' school. Those pompous old fools . . . Don't they realize what a treasure you are?"

Tory smiled tremulously. "I don't think treasure is a word they consider when it comes to me, Jordan . . . They—several members of the school board—think I'm a hussy, a jezebel, an agitator . . . a soap-box orator bent on ruining the minds of their impressionable young daughters."

"*What?*"

"They couldn't invent names bad enough to describe my wayward behavior. They held a special meeting over it, even criticized the fact that I live alone and ride my bicycle—wearing knickerbockers—to work every day. Said it was unnatural for a woman to be so independent."

"Your bicycle wears knickerbockers?" Jordan teased, but when he saw she wasn't laughing, he instantly sobered.

"I don't know why the board members were so upset. I change into a skirt as soon as I arrive at school. With the number of women now embracing the new fashion, knickerbockers can hardly be called scandalous."

Jordan shook his head, and she rattled on, trying to make light of her misery, but it was a raw open sore in her breast. "You should have heard them, Jordan. What it all comes down to is that they don't want me teaching their daughters to think for themselves. They want them to marry, have babies, and leave all important decisions to their husbands. In their misguided opinion, reading a fashion magazine—*Harper's Bazaar* or the *Delineator*—is the most taxing thing a woman should do with her mind. We're a half dozen years into a new century, on the brink of liberation for women, but those old *walruses*, those conceited, pea-brained hippopotamuses . . ."

"Wait a minute." Jordan came to a sudden halt. "You didn't call them that, did you?"

"Of course, I did! Right to their faces, not behind their backs. I never met such a flock of puffed-up peacocks determined to live in the past and keep women forever subjugated. You're right to call them pompous old fools! They were only upset because it was reported in the newspapers that I took part in a public demonstration on behalf of the right to vote . . ."

"What sort of demonstration?"

"Oh, it wasn't so very awful . . . We merely marched to the courthouse, lit torches, and gave speeches . . ."

"You gave a speech?"

"An excellent speech! It inflamed every female within hearing distance. They cheered and waved the American flag and pledged undying support to the

16

cause . . . True, a few onlookers did become unruly and had to be led from the scene by police, but . . ."

"Oh, God . . . And you never guessed that the board members of that very wealthy, extremely conservative boarding school might take issue with your actions?"

"Well, I did suspect they might not like it that I had my entire class attend to swell the crowd and hear for themselves the compelling arguments being presented . . ."

"You didn't invite your students!"

"Not exactly," Tory hedged. "Actually, I made it a homework assignment."

"Tory! . . . What did you expect the parents of those young girls to do? They aren't paying a fortune in tuition and boarding fees in order to have their daughters turned into rebels and radicals."

"I'm not trying to turn them into rebels and radicals! I'm trying to mold them into full, functioning human beings—creatures who can think, reason, ask questions, and contribute something to society, instead of merely decorating it! I want them to be real people, not just . . . paper cut-outs or shadows of real people."

"So they suggested you not return next year . . ."

"And relieved me of my teaching duties until the end of *this* year. I may work in the library, but not speak to my students, nor fill their heads with any more suffragette nonsense, nor . . ." Tory hiccupped on a sob and could not go on. She fumbled for a handkerchief, but as usual, couldn't find one.

"Oh, Tory . . ." Jordan squeezed her hand comfortingly, then resumed walking. "So that's why you've been so gloomy and withdrawn, not at all your usual ebullient, charming, opinionated self."

17

"Is it so obvious? I didn't think anyone had noticed."

"No, of course we didn't notice. But we did wonder if your cat had died or your dog bit you."

"Felicity and Beauregard are both doing well, thank you." Tory grinned through her tears. "But I did need to ask if it would be all right if I brought them back with me when I come at the end of the school year."

"You have to ask?" Jordan shot her a glance of exasperation. "This is your home, too, Tory. When I bought it with the money I made on rubber, I meant for it to be not only my home and Spencer's, but also yours and your sisters. I didn't spend all those years in the Amazon jungle working for myself, you know. I did it for you, Eleanor, and Grace. Castle Acres belonged to all of us once. We all experienced the grief of losing it to father's creditors after he died . . . It's only right that we should jointly experience the joy of living here once again, breeding and raising the finest standardbreds in all of Kentucky."

"Eleanor and Grace don't *need* to live here. They're leading happy, fulfilled lives of their own. They aren't forced to intrude on their brother and his family because they've made a proper mess of things and have nowhere else to go at the moment . . ."

"Don't say such things!" Jordan gave her arm a shake. "You're insulting me and Spencer. She'll be delighted to have you live here. And so will I— provided you don't disobey me again and try to ride Renegade when I'm not looking."

Tory stopped walking and swung around to face him. Renewed anger made her tremble. "Jordan . . . If you ask me sweetly not to ride him, I may consider your feelings on the matter and desist, but if you

18

forbid me, then I'll *surely* ride him every chance I get."

Jordan drew in another long breath, then expelled it wearily. "Tory, I'm not the enemy. I swear to you I'm not. If I were, would I have married a woman like Spencer? Would I permit—no, encourage—her to practice her profession and support her every way I can? Be fair, and give me a little credit, will you? I try not to be condescending toward females, and I think I've succeeded at being less so than most men."

Considering his arguments, Tory felt a stab of chagrin. Spencer was a doctor who traipsed all over the countryside at odd hours, yet Jordan was remarkably lenient and ignored all criticism regarding his wife's activities. It was a virtue that had *not* endeared him to many of his male acquaintances whose wives were kept closer to home.

"All right, you're *not* the enemy," she conceded. "But, Jordan, please understand . . . If I come to live here, you won't be responsible for me in any way. I plan to *earn* my keep. Just think of me as another employee—preferably *male*."

"Oh, I doubt I could think of you as anything but." His green eyes mockingly swept her boy's trousers, muddy boots, carelessly tucked-in shirt, and dusty cap. "If you plan to wear Abelardo's clothes everyday, I may begin to call you Vic, instead of Victoria. Would that suit you better, my little rebel of a sister?"

She laughed. "It would suit me better if I'd been *born* a Vic, instead of a Victoria."

"Tory, Tory . . ." Jordan heaved his third deep sigh of the afternoon. "You've almost made me forget why I was coming to find you in the first place. We have guests, and they're going to be extremely

19

shocked to meet you dressed as you are now."

"Then I'll change first. Are they prospective buyers? I may be a rebel, Jordan, but I promise not to embarrass you in front of your friends and business acquaintances."

Jordan's eyes strayed up the hill to the house behind her. "I'm afraid it's too late for that—I mean, for you to change clothes before you meet them. They're coming down the path to meet us."

Turning, Tory glanced toward the lovely, red-bricked, two-story house fronted by four white pillars. Behind it loomed the round, castle-like tower from which the farm took its name, and in front of it, two men were striding down the flagstones toward them. One was a short, plump, balding fellow dressed in a friar's flowing brown robe with a rope for a belt, and sandals on his feet; the other a tall, dark-haired, dark-skinned gentleman, clad head to foot in black, except for his snowy white shirt.

Studying the second man with flaring interest and curiosity, Tory felt her heart unaccountably miss a beat. She narrowed her eyes. Even at a distance, the taller gentleman was the most striking male she had ever seen. As dark as she was fair, he was foreign-looking, almost exotic, definitely not the sort normally found in the vicinity of Castle Acres. As he drew closer, she saw that his eyes were the most peculiar shade of clear, bright amber, so bright they almost leapt from his bronzed face.

Suddenly, she regretted being caught with her hair stuffed beneath a boy's cap, looking like some scruffy groom with her dirty boots and ill-fitting trousers. On impulse, she snatched the cap from her head, then realized she'd made a dreadful mistake. Her hair tumbled down around her shoulders, revealing her for an unkempt female. Both men's eyes widened in surprise. The amber ones, especially, fastened upon her with keen intensity, searching her thoroughly from toes to crown. She flushed ten shades of red and wished she'd had the good sense to keep her cap on and pretend she really was a groom. Certainly, her curves wouldn't have given her away; they were barely noticeable. But the amber eyes seemed to notice, scorching across her slim, boyish figure as if memorizing every peak and valley.

Boldly, she stared back at him, giving *his* body the same blunt appraisal, and finding it a most satisfactory and intriguing body, indeed.

"Ah, Mr. Black," Jordan said. "And Padre Osmundo . . . We were just coming up to the house. I finally located my sister, and I'd like to introduce her to you, now. Gentlemen, this is the eldest of my three sisters, the only one at Castle Acres right now, Victoria King . . . Tory, this is Padre Osmundo and Sebastian Black. They've come all the way from Brazil in search of good breeding stock. Padre Osmundo, I understand, is originally from the United States—or at least his family was at one time."

What sort of 'good breeding stock'? Tory wondered, and felt her cheeks turning even redder. Quickly, she tore her gaze from Sebastian Black and concentrated on his companion. Padre Osmundo reminded Tory of a dimpled Humpty-Dumpty. She immediately warmed to his merry grin and twinkling black eyes.

"Pleased to meet you, my dear," he said in perfect English.

"And I, you, Father . . . You must forgive my attire. I've been riding and didn't know we had guests."

21

"We saw you on that magnificent horse." Sebastian Black had a low, husky voice, vibrant and provocative, that somehow reminded Tory of velvet sliding across bare flesh.

She shivered slightly. Looking up into Sebastian Black's clear amber eyes, she could think of absolutely nothing to say in response. Up close, the man was even more striking than he'd been at first glance. His hair was the color of rich, glowing sable, his skin the shade of honey or golden molasses. His nose was straight and regal-looking, his teeth blinding white, his lips full and sensuous. But it was his eyes . . . those clear, light eyes in that dark, dark face, beneath the slash of sable brows . . . that seemed to rob her of breath, not merely speech.

"Let me amend that. I thought the horse was magnificent, until I saw *you*." Sebastian Black took her hand and raised it to his lips. "You are even more magnificent, *moçinha*."

Tory had no idea what *moçinha* meant, but Sebastian Black made it sound like a caress. His English was slightly accented, exotic and foreign like he was, and Tory shivered again, drowning in his unique, amber-colored eyes. Her mind stupidly and exasperatingly refused to function.

"Tory will want to change before dinner." Jordan's tone was a bit hostile as he watched the tall Brazilian take an absurdly long time to relinquish her tingling hand. "Won't you, Tory? We'll have some liquid refreshments while we wait. Hopefully, my wife will return soon and can join us in time for the evening meal."

Sebastian Black shifted his penetrating gaze to Jordan. "You *Americanos* are most amazing," he purred in his velvet voice. "I would never allow *my*

22

wife, if I had one, to go off tending the sick, while I waited at home alone with my guests."

So he isn't married, Tory thought breathlessly, then she noticed Jordan's reaction.

Her brother stiffened, every muscle shouting insult. Before he could respond, the little priest broke in. "*Sebastião,* you forget where you are. This is not the *sertão,* where danger lurks behind every bush and tree. Women are treated differently here. They don't need escorts in order to move about safely."

"I can see that, Padre," Sebastian Black replied silkily, his amber eyes again sweeping Tory. "In my country, it would be unheard of for a woman to dress like Senhor *Rei*'s sister."

Tory's flush deepened. Distractedly, she fastened upon the fact that Sebastian Black was calling Jordan by his name in Portuguese. Senhor *Rei* meant Mr. King. Foreign languages came easily to her, and because Jordan had spent so many years in Brazil, she had endeavored to learn a word or two, in addition to her fluent Spanish and French. "It's almost unheard of here, Senhor *Prêto,*" she informed him. "Please don't judge all American women by what I do. I assure you I'm not a good example of the average *Americana.*"

His brows lifted at her translation of his name into Portuguese. *Prêto* meant black. It pleased her to note his surprise that she knew something of his native language. "Do you speak Portuguese, *moçinha?* I thought it was only your brother who'd been to my country."

"I don't actually speak it, but I can manage a few words. What, pray tell, does *moçinha* mean?"

"It means 'little woman'. A term of endearment or familiarity."

23

"And inappropriate for my sister, in as much as you've only just met her," Jordan clipped.

"Ah, but I intend to get to know her much better . . . And I also intend to buy that horse she was riding."

"We shall see," Jordan said frostily. "Come, let's go up to the house."

Chapter Two

Following Jordan King up the hill toward his house, Sebastian found himself the recipient of a frowning look from his friend and traveling companion, Padre Osmundo. The priest glowered at him and shook his balding head, communicating displeasure at Sebastian's behavior toward their host and his sister. In response, Sebastian carelessly shrugged his shoulders.

If a man didn't want his sister to be treated disrespectfully, he ought not to permit her to go about dressed in men's breeches, riding unsuitable, half-wild horses. The freedom women had achieved in this country—the land of his grandfather's birth—was scandalous. Sebastian rejoiced that no such reforms had yet arrived in Brazil. Unbeknownst to anyone, even Padre Osmundo, Sebastian's grandparents had migrated to Bahia following the defeat of the South in the Civil War. If they had not, Sebastian might still be living in Kentucky, breeding horses or growing tobacco, and pondering the depths to which the United States had sunk, allowing the weaker sex to do whatever they pleased.

In Brazil, there were only two kinds of women: good and bad. The good ones never went anywhere—even to church—without a chaperone, and they certainly didn't dress in men's clothing, ride spirited horses, or argue with the men in their families. The feisty, little *Americana* with the beautiful blonde hair, huge gray-green eyes, and delicate body was obviously one of the "liberated females" Sebastian had heard so much about. That meant, he assumed, that a man could obtain her favors without having to marry her to get them—a prospect he relished, for all he disapproved.

Since he didn't plan on ever returning to Kentucky, he decided he might as well make the most of this visit; he would purchase Jordan King's best stud, and also go to bed with his wanton sister—when Jordan King wasn't looking, of course.

His eyes sought Senhorita King's well displayed figure as she walked in front of him into the house. It was considered daring for a woman to flaunt an ankle, yet the girl wore slim-fitting trousers that revealed everything below the waist! Her waist itself was so narrow he could almost span it with one hand. Her hips were daintily fashioned and moved with a graceful, feminine sway of which she was probably unaware, never having viewed herself from the back. And her legs—or "limbs" as polite society called them—were as pleasing and provocative as the rest of her.

Long a connoisseur of women, Sebastian decided that Victoria King had the sweetest little bottom he'd ever seen. Inhaling appreciatively, he lifted his gaze to her hair—that glorious, golden, sun-streaked hair! It spilled down her back to her waist, and the urge to run his fingers through it was nearly irresistable. A

26

woman's hair was her crowning glory, the most sensuous thing about her, and Miss King had been blessed with a gorgeous abundance. He wanted to see how her golden tresses would look spread across his own dark skin—an image that greatly excited him.

As if reading his thoughts, Padre Osmundo moved closer and hissed in Portuguese: "Stop looking at her like that! You're sinning in your mind, my son."

"Then I might as well sin in the flesh, hadn't I, Padre?"

Sebastian's appreciation of lovely women had long been a source of friction between him and his childhood friend. It made no difference that Sebastian never callously tossed aside a *namorada* when he was finished with her. Rather, he always provided for the woman until another man came along, and he stood ready to claim and support any children that resulted from his liaisons. Thusfar, he'd fathered two that he knew of; one had died at birth and the other in infancy. He sincerely mourned the loss of both of them, but none of that seemed to impress Padre Osmundo. Nor did it matter that Sebastian could point to parish priests with their own little broods of indiscretions.

Padre Osmundo flat out deplored the healthy exercise of an unmarried man's virility, warning Sebastian he might one day burn in hell for it. But Sebastian could no more ignore a pretty girl than he could refuse to eat when hungry or sleep when fatigued. The priest was always urging him to marry, but he couldn't see the sense of it. He could never share his secrets with whomever he married, and anyway, he was perfectly happy with the way things were.

A wife would only nag, demanding that he be

faithful. Dogs should be faithful—and horses, too, but men? Sebastian wasn't sure it was possible, and he could see no reason to deny himself one of life's great pleasures. A man was a fool if he didn't take what God had so graciously created for his enjoyment. Sebastian avoided cuckolding his friends and neighbors, and also shied away from scheming virgins bent on marriage, but all other women were fair game . . . and Victoria King, shamelessly flaunting both hair and body, begged to be mastered and tamed. All he needed to do, it seemed, was find a way around her vigilant brother.

Ushering Sebastian and Padre Osmundo into a wide, spacious library furnished with leather sofas and chairs, Jordan King turned to them and said: "May I offer you gentlemen a drink?"

Sebastian nodded. "Bourbon, *por favor*. Some of your good Kentucky bourbon."

"Bourbon for me, also," Padre Osmundo said, not considering drunkenness as bad a sin as fornication.

Gesturing for them to be seated, the tall blond *Americano* strode to a cabinet set amidst the many bookshelves and returned a moment later with two small goblets of a clear, golden-brown liquid that made Sebastian's dry mouth water in anticipation.

"Obrigato," Sebastian thanked him, lifting the glass to his lips. He savored first the aroma and then the warm burning sensation as the fine bourbon slid down his throat. Setting his glass on a nearby table, he regarded Jordan King through slitted eyes, waiting until Jordan had fetched his own refreshment before opening negotiations on the horse.

"That was a beautiful animal your sister was riding . . . a bit cow-hocked, perhaps, but otherwise well-conformed." In his usual fashion, Sebastian attacked his opponent where he least expected it.

Sitting down opposite Sebastian, Jordan King measured him with a chilly gaze, his green eyes darkening. "Renegade is not cow-hocked; his conformation is perfect . . . He's one of my prime sires."

"Too much for a woman to handle, I noticed. Does he pass on his bad temper to his get?"

"No, he doesn't. We think he must have been abused or improperly broken before we bought him. We've seen no sign of intractability in his foals."

"I would of course wish to see several before I made an offer on him."

Jordan King inclined his head politely. "Of course . . . I'll show you around tomorrow. We have many fine horses besides Renegade. If he doesn't suit, I've other promising young colts you might consider. We expect great things from our youngsters on the race track, and later, in the breeding shed . . . I take it you intend to race the animals you purchase, though I didn't realize harness racing had become fashionable in Brazil."

"Racing is not why I want him," Sebastian admitted. "Let us just say I wish to strengthen my herd. My horses are small and wiry, excellent for use on the *sertão*, but not exceptionally fast . . . Lately, I've had need of more speed in my horses. That is why I came to Kentucky—to get the best."

"I offer the best, but if you live on the *sertão*, you must use your horses mainly to herd cattle."

"*Sim*. My *estância* is near the border between Bahia and Sergipe. Bahia is known for its sugar cane and cocoa. I plant some of my land in cane, but on most, I run cattle. For that, I need good, fast horses."

"Not necessarily race horses." Jordan King looked puzzled. "And certainly not standardbreds. Although they can be ridden, they are mainly trotters bred for the racetrack.''

"That horse your sister was riding did not look to be a trotter."

"He isn't, and neither are a dozen others I have for sale. However, the majority are. Our reputation was built on our standardbreds. While Renegade may not be a trotter, neither is he a range or stock horse. He's unquestionably hot-blooded and built for speed, probably with Thoroughbred bloodlines. We bought him on impulse at auction, and he possessed no registration or breed papers. To be honest, he's something of an experiment for Castle Acres. I'm sorry to discourage your interest, but he's not a horse I would recommend for your purposes, however much he may have caught your fancy.''

"He's exactly what I want," Sebastian insisted, impressed by how adroitly Jordan had put *him* on the defensive. "Trust me, Senhor, to know my own needs. I am not a fool when it comes to horses.''

Padre Osmundo cleared his throat and leaned forward. "He did not say you were a fool, *Sebastião*, though I sometimes wonder . . . Please forgive my young friend if he seems overly persistent about this horse, Senhor *Rei*. I fear he has the most pressing reasons for wanting to buy the fastest horse he can acquire.''

"Jordan . . . Please call me Jordan." Jordan King's eyes and voice warmed when he looked at the priest.

In return, Padre Osmundo beamed a beatific smile. "Very well, Jordan . . . Now, what *Sebastião* isn't telling you is that speed has become an absolute necessity in recent years on the *sertão*.''

"Why is that?''

Sebastian wished Padre Osmundo would stay out

of it, but his friend plunged ahead undaunted. "In recent years, *Sebastião* and many others have been subjected to raids and thievery by roving bands of *cangaçeiros*, who steal everything they can lay hands on, then disappear across the *sertão*."

"*Cangaçeiros?* You mean bandits?"

"Bandits and cut-throats," Sebastian curtly translated. "My *vaqueiros* and I of course give chase, but we rarely catch them, since the *cangaçeiros* are mounted on the best horses in the region—the ones they stole from us."

"I see," Jordan said.

No, you don't see, Sebastian thought to himself. No one—not even Padre Osmundo sees, though he might possibly suspect.

"The greatest *cangaçeiro* of all," Padre Osmundo confided, "is a man called the *'Falcão'*, or Falcon, who robs from the rich to give to the poor . . ."

"And rapes and pillages and murders people in their beds," Sebastian added in a scathing tone.

"No! No! There's no proof it was he who did that!" Padre Osmundo protested. "Indeed, I rather think it was someone who wanted everyone to think it was the *Falcão*, in order to discredit him and further infuriate his enemies."

"Bah!" Sebastian scoffed. "You only defend him because he gives you money to help the peasants."

"And so do *you*, *Sebastião*, though neither of you give in sufficient quantity to make my efforts successful—which is why I had to come along on this trip."

Padre Osmundo's eyes were gently reproachful, and Sebastian wearily shook his head. If he had the funds, which he didn't, he couldn't donate more without arousing suspicion. Padre Osmundo must never discover that *he*, Sebastian Black, a member of the ruling aristocracy, was also the Falcon, a man who robbed his own neighbors and even himself, in order to feed and shelter the desperate, hungry peasants, who had once sheltered and fed him. Banditry was the only way possible to help the poor *caboclos,* while at the same time protecting his own identity as he slowly but surely engineered the downfall of his worst enemy: Mundinho Cerqueira, the monster who had killed his father and mother but unknowingly left alive the only witness to the crime, their small son, *Luis Sebastião Falcão*.

"You came to America in order to raise money to aid the peasants?" Jordan King inquired of Padre Osmundo.

Sebastian eyed him speculatively. Not many rich *Americanos* were interested in the work of a fat old priest in the wilds of Brazil. For Padre Osmundo's sake, Sebastian hoped that Jordan King *was* interested and would convert that interest into cold, hard cash.

"Sim, Senhor," Padre Osmundo replied. *"Sebastião* kindly invited me to accompany him to the United States, because I'm trying to raise money to build a school and some sort of medical post in a poor rural area where none exist."

"I know of the poverty in the arid Northeast," Jordan King said. "I used to travel to Ceará and once even to Bahia to hire workers to tap my rubber trees. My wife and I would be happy to make a substantial donation to your cause."

"Ah, Jordan! *Obrigado!* Your promise is sweet music to my ears." Padre Osmundo turned enthusiastically to Sebastian. "Did you hear that, *Sebastião, mon filho?*"

"I heard," Sebastian growled, being careful to hide

32

his elation behind a look of displeasure. "I only wish I had not promised to match the donations you receive in the *Estados Unidos.*"

"The *Falcão* will match them also, I have no doubt—then I'll have enough to get started, at long last."

"If the Falcon will match them, there's no need for me to do so." Sebastian scowled harder than ever. It was ridiculous, but he felt jealous of the esteem in which the priest held a mere bandit, even though the bandit was himself. "I don't know how you can live with yourself, Padre, taking money from a thief and murderer such as the Falcon."

"Judge not lest ye be judged." Padre Osmundo chuckled. The little priest leaned toward Jordan and lowered his voice conspiratorially. "All of the big landowners in Bahia hate the Falcon. And all of the other priests preach against him and condemn his wickedness . . . but I do not believe him to be evil. On the third Sunday of every month, he leaves large donations in my collection basket. How they get there I do not know, but someone always brings them . . . and always they are wrapped in plain, brown paper stamped with the likeness of a falcon, flying free in the sky."

"Why has this modern-day Robin Hood singled out *you* to receive his charity?" Jordan King inquired. "A man like that isn't usually willing to part with his ill-gotten gains."

"I suppose it is because of the work I'm doing. Undoubtedly, he was once a poor peasant himself."

No, Sebastian silently disagreed, it's because *you* were the one who took in that lost, frightened child the peasants found wandering alone on the *sertão* . . . You saw to it that he was educated in a Franciscan

33

monastery and given every advantage. And later, when he was grown, you lent him church money to buy land to start an *estância*—for which generosity you would undoubtedly have been defrocked and excommunicated had that greedy, old archbishop, Cerqueira's cousin, discovered what you were doing.

"Padre Osmundo is the champion of poor *Sertanejos*," Sebastian drawled with just the right touch of sarcasm. "I keep asking him why he does it, when he could lead a happier, more comfortable life if he'd only serve the rich *fazendeiros*, like the majority of his fellow priests . . . and he keeps reminding me that God sent His only son to be a carpenter, not a king."

"That's true!" Padre Osmundo exclaimed. "However I do consort with *you*, my son, so you cannot say I *never* serve the rich—or at least, the almost rich."

"*Cristo! I would* be rich had I not supported you and your poor peasants these past ten years."

"Do not take the Lord's name in vain, *mon filho.*"

"Tell me about your family here in the States, Padre," Jordan King invited. "Do you still have relatives here?"

For a moment, Sebastian wished he could mention the possibility that he, too, might have relatives living in the area—another reason why he had chosen Kentucky to look for the perfect stud to breed strength and speed into his horses. Jordan King might know of a family named Falcon. Meeting people of his own blood would be wonderful, a consolation for having grown up deprived of a family. Other than Padre Osmundo, there was no one he cared about except the poor *caboclos*. Only an old, half-blind peasant and his ailing wife even remembered him as the child they'd found on the *sertão*,

34

crying for his murdered Mama and Papa, afraid to tell anyone his name . . . But he could never claim his heritage, never search for his blood kin, so long as Mundinho Cerqueira lived.

"My mother's family came from North Carolina," Padre Osmundo said. "Their name was Benedict. I don't suppose you've heard of them, Jordan."

"Sorry, but I haven't."

"They used to be prominent cotton planters, but they've dwindled down to a single old maid aunt. I correspond with her regularly, and she sends small donations to help further my work."

"Padre Osmundo will take money from anybody, even old maid aunts who probably can't afford it," Sebastian drily pointed out.

"Then you write English as well as speak it," Jordan observed. "I'm impressed by how effortlessly you both converse in my language."

Setting down his empty whiskey glass, Padre Osmundo sat back in his chair and steepled his fingers. "Ah, my aunt is responsible for that. When she learned I wished to become a priest, she insisted I come to the States to study. I took my vows in New Orleans, then returned to Brazil where I was truly needed. Twas I who insisted *Sebastião* be educated here, also. He was orphaned very young, you see, and I could learn nothing about his parents. The peasants brought him to me when he was five or six years old. Because of his brilliance—he could count and already knew his letters—they thought he should receive further instruction. I thought so, too, and hoped he might become a priest like me."

"Poor Padre Osmundo was doomed to disappointment, because I refused to take the priestly vows at the end of my schooling," Sebastian explained. "By then, I'd discovered women."

"That's my one regret in life," Padre Osmundo sighed. "Your roving eye, *Sebastião* ... You obviously have no priestly vocation, but you could at least marry and get yourself a proper heir."

"A *proper* heir?" Jordan King echoed.

"Well, you know what I mean." Padre Osmundo raised an eyebrow meaningfully, and Sebastian groaned softly to himself. Now, Jordan King would be even more vigilant when it came to his sister.

"Yes, I think I do know what you mean." Jordan cast a wary glance at Sebastian. "Will you gentlemen excuse me while I see what's keeping my sister?"

"Of course," Padre Osmundo said.

As soon as Jordan had risen and left the room, Sebastian rounded on his sly, old friend.

"You did that on purpose," he accused. "He's probably gone to warn his sister to watch out for me. He'll say I can't be trusted."

"Can you?" Padre Osmundo's black eyes were unrepentant.

"No," Sebastian conceded. "But I was looking forward to the chase, and now you've ruined it for me."

"I certainly hope so." Padre Osmundo got up and waddled over to the cupboard where the bourbon was kept. "Here," he said. "Hand me your glass. I'll not let you compromise Senhor *Rei*'s sister, but another drop or two of his bourbon won't hurt ... He'll never miss it."

Sebastian grinned, never able to stay angry with Padre Osmundo for long. "In that case, hide the remainder of the bottle in one of those deep pockets of yours. If I can't have his sister, he at least owes me something."

Upstairs in the maize-and-cream-colored room that had been hers as a young child, Tory had just finished struggling into the first round of clothing considered proper for a young lady. Her underwear consisted of a chemise, worn next to the skin with a little drawstring ribbon that went round her neck, then over that came the tight corseting which created the "S effect" of full bosom, flat stomach, arched back, and prominent derriere. Next, came the camisole, sleeveless and elaborately trimmed with lace, which would form a bodice beneath her outer clothing.

Below the waist, she wore "drawers"—actually knee-length knickers—followed by a flannel petticoat, several cotton petticoats, and a silk underskirt to make a smooth underlining for the gown she was ready to don. Already exhausted, she still had not selected the gown. It would have been far easier and more comfortable to have worn one of her simple shirtwaists, but since she had embarrassed Jordan once today, she was determined not to do so again. If anything, she wanted to make him proud by dressing in the height of fashion, no matter how much she had to suffer in the process.

Rifling through the gowns in her clothes closet, she finally selected one, assuring herself that Sebastian Black had absolutely nothing to do with her decision to wear a frilly, lacy concoction of willow-green crêpe de Chine. The gown was the very epitome of the feminine apparel so beloved by ladies these days and equally adored by gentlemen. It also brought out the color of her eyes, not that she cared a bit about getting Sebastian Black to notice her eyes.

She did have to admit that she had never met a man quite like the tall Brazilian—so strikingly dark and handsome, yet also so predatory. Jordan had once described Brazilians as being smaller than Americans, the men rather thin and wiry by comparison, but Mr. Black was every bit as muscular as Jordan and topped him by an inch or two in height.

Indeed, Tory thought, she couldn't recall any American male of her acquaintance as attractive as this Brazilian, and that included Jordan himself.

She wasn't one to judge a man by his looks, however. No man yet had made her swoon and giggle like some silly school girl, and she doubted any man ever would inspire her to such foolishness. What she hoped to find one day—and was beginning to despair existed—was a retiring, thoughtful sort of male, a scholar perhaps, with whom she could share her love of learning and from whom she would not have to hide her intellect. Of course, he would have to be tolerant of her views on emancipation. If he couldn't join her in fighting for a woman's right to vote, he must at least allow her to participate in the battle. And he mustn't criticize her bicycle or knickerbockers, nor refuse to allow her to ride any horse of her choosing.

She had long since tired of waiting for such a miraculous creature to appear, but she didn't intend to settle for anything less. Peering at herself in the full length mirror that stood in the corner of the room, she tugged and pulled at the crêpe de Chine to make it lie properly. When she stood sideways, she had the perfect S-shaped silhouette, but when she faced frontwards, she looked like a balloon being squeezed in the middle and threatening to explode top and bottom.

Why did women do this to themselves? Or allow fashion to do it to them? Just because an hour-glass figure was considered desirable didn't mean that every woman in the country should subject herself to torture in order to achieve one. Since her bosom was not particularly voluptuous, Tory had to squeeze her waist extra tight in order to make her chest look bigger. Now she could hardly breathe and was considering changing into a flour sack when a knock sounded on her door.

"Tory? . . . Are you in there? What's keeping you? I'm hungry, and I want to eat."

Jordan was nothing if not direct. Turning from the mirror, Tory crossed to the door and opened it. "Honestly, Jordan . . . Has Spencer come home? I thought you wanted to wait dinner until she arrived."

"No, she hasn't, but . . ." Jordan's eyes lit when he saw her. "Damn my Aunt Milly's corset! You look beautiful, Tory . . ." Then he spoiled it by frowning. "Too beautiful. That damn Brazilian won't be able to keep his eyes off you."

Tory felt a rush of excitement and anticipation before she thought to quell the reaction. "I'm not beautiful, Jordan, and you know it. My figure's too thin, my nose is crooked, my mouth's too big, and my eyebrows are so light you can hardly see them."

"They are?" He squinted at her face. "I never noticed that until you mentioned it . . . Also, you have a very determined jaw—like a man's, actually."

"I never noticed *that!*" she wailed, anxiously feeling her chin with her fingers.

"But tonight, you're beautiful . . ." Jordan assured her, laughing. "So watch out for that oily Brazilian. Padre Osmundo came right out and warned me he can't be trusted around women."

"Oh? Just what did he say? Beware my friend doesn't rape your sister?"

"In so many words . . . I mean it, Tory. Brazilian men aren't like Americans. Their culture is very different. You could get into trouble flirting with a man like Sebastian Black."

"Flirting! I've never flirted in my entire life."

"Then don't start now." Jordan grinned, knowing he was being impossible.

"I should think you'd be pushing me at him," Tory snorted, departing the room ahead of him. "If you don't get rid of me soon, you and Spencer may be saddled with me for life."

"Don't start that again . . . Believe me, we *want* you at Castle Acres."

But I don't want to be here, Tory thought to herself. This is *your* home now, not mine . . . I want . . . I don't know what I want . . . except that it isn't here.

As they descended the staircase together, Tory's spirits sank. Suddenly, she felt awkward and ugly, trying to be something she was not. She belonged in a prim, high-necked, shapeless blouse and dark skirt, slapping a pointer across her palm as she debated how best to inspire her students. She was, after all, a teacher—a role in which she felt comfortable and needed, if sometimes bored. What was she going to do at Castle Acres? For that matter, what was she going to do with the rest of her life?

What I need, she thought bitterly, is for a knight on a white charger to come galloping up the hill to Castle Acres and carry me away to a life of adventure and romance.

That was what every woman was supposed to

want, but somehow Tory couldn't picture herself riding off into the sunset behind a white knight. She had been born the wrong sex, in the wrong time, at the wrong place ... Even in her childhood daydreams, *she* was always the one who slew the dragon and rescued the terror-stricken villagers. How God must have been laughing when he created her a female!

Feeling distinctly sorry for herself, Tory followed Jordan into the dining room.

Chapter Three

"Pass the butter to Mr. Black, Marta," Tory said to the little red-haired, green-eyed girl sitting beside her at the table. "Then give your Daddy the peas."

"Yes, Aunt Tory," the child obediently responded. "When will Mama be coming home?"

"Soon . . . Be quiet now, so you don't disturb Daddy and his guests."

On Tory's other side, Abelardo was wolfing down his dinner, his dark eyes fastened on Padre Osmundo and the devastatingly handsome Mr. Black. These were the first Brazilians the boy had seen since coming to the United States with Spencer and Jordan; he was naturally curious about the visitors, although the *sertão* was more than a thousand miles from the Amazon, where Abelardo had been born.

Spencer and Jordan had adopted the black-haired Indian boy before leaving Manaus. Marta had been born after they returned home. Now in his teens, Abelardo had totally adapted to the American way of life, but seemed as hungry for information about his homeland as he was for the thick slices of roast beef on his plate.

Between bites of mashed potatoes and gravy, Padre Osmundo was describing the plight of the poor peasants. "They live in thatched roof hovels, eating rice and beans when times are good, and only *manioc*, a kind of root, when times are bad . . . Babies often die before they are a year old. The peasants call them 'God's little angels', and don't even celebrate their births until they've reached their first birthdays . . . It's a common sight to see the children carrying a little white coffin down to the cemetery for burial. That's the custom—children bury children, and I sometimes think the lucky ones are those who die young and don't grow up to suffer like those who survive infancy."

Tory was appalled. "Don't the big land owners take care of their workers? Don't they help feed and clothe them?"

"Oh, yes . . ." Padre Osmundo nodded. "To a certain extent. But the peasants are like serfs, working the land as did their counterparts in feudal times. During seasons of drought, food becomes scarce, and the peasants are ignored."

"I always feed my workers—drought or no." Sebastian Black's amber eyes sought Tory's. "Not all the *fazendeiros* are cruel and heartless, though many are worse than Padre Osmundo says."

"Do the peasants go to school?" Tory pursued, growing oddly warm and breathless beneath the Brazilian's penetrating gaze.

"There are no schools in the middle of the *sertão*," Padre Osmundo sadly informed her. "Some of the larger towns have them, but the poorest of the poor do not attend. Where schools for the poor have been tried, it is difficult to find and keep good instructors. Sometimes, the teachers have as little education as

43

the students. You see what a problem it is. I will soon be able to build a school for the children of the *caboclos*, but then I'll have no one to teach in it . . . Good teachers cost money, and they don't want to live so far from the amenities of civilization."

"That's terrible!" Tory firmly believed in education for everyone. "Why doesn't the government or the church *do* something?"

"Tory . . ." Jordan gently interrupted. "The *fazendeiros are* the government and the church in most cases. They are all intertwined. Isn't that so, Padre?"

"I'm afraid it is. Indeed, it's the custom in wealthy, landed families for at least one son to enter the priesthood and the others to be involved in politics. Whatever riches don't belong to the *fazendeiros* belong to the Church."

"In Salvador," Sebastian Black drawled in the husky, sensuous voice that made shivers run down Tory's spine, "there is a church for every day of the week, and one of them—the *Igreja de São Francisco*—has walls covered entirely in gold."

"Salvador?" Unaccustomed to having a man stare at her so intently, Tory felt flustered and embarrassed. "Where is that?"

"It is the largest city on the southern coast of Bahia—four days' journey on horseback from my *estância,* a place I hope you will one day come to visit."

"*Sebastião,* you exaggerate, *mon filho* . . . Salvador has many churches, but I doubt there's one for each day of the week. It is, however, a most beautiful, fascinating city, which served as the capital of Brazil from the time the Portuguese first landed in 1500 until 1763, when the capital was moved to Rio de Janeiro."

"No history lesson, Padre." Sebastian's smile was both lazy and aggressive. "Once you get him started, there's no stopping him. He'll go on all night."

Tory could not look away from his mesmerizing eyes. His eyes seemed to compel her to look at them. "But I *want* to hear about your country's history . . ."

"I want to hear more about the peasants," Abelardo unexpectedly spoke up. "Are they mistreated as badly as the Indians on the Amazon?"

Everyone glanced in surprise at the good-looking youth. Tory remembered that Abelardo's father had been a chieftain of the Huitotos, a tribe nearly wiped out in the quest for rubber. Before adopting Abelardo, Jordan and Spencer had fought against a powerful rubber baron responsible for annihilating many Indians—fought and won. Only last year, they had gone to England to testify against him in the House of Commons at a hearing arranged by another American who had worked with them to stop the massacre.

"I have never been to the Amazon, young man," Padre Osmundo said. "So I can't draw any comparisons between the Indians and the *caboclos*. All I can say is that the peasants live in poverty from the cradle to the grave. They need food, clothing, and medical care. Most of all, they need schooling, if they are ever to escape the dreariness of their lives . . . *Sebastião* is a prime example of what education can do for a person. Had he not learned to read, write, and cypher, he could never have gone so far in life. I saw to it that he went to school, and thus he was able to become a *fazendeiro* himself, instead of always having to work other people's land."

"Then there's land available for a peasant to buy, if he does become educated." Tory forced herself to concentrate on the conversation, rather than on Sebastian Black's hypnotic gaze.

"There are many ways to obtain land, Senhorita." Sebastian's handsome face hardened. "Buying it is only one. As for the others, a man must have a degree of learning even to be able to think of them. *Caboclos* are born with brains, of course, but their minds soon become dull and sluggish, due to poor food, illness, and the monotony of their lives. Most of the *caboclos* cannot conceive of owning land, much less figure out how to get it."

He waved his hand dismissingly. "But let us change to a more cheerful topic. Beautiful young women shouldn't bother their pretty heads about problems so far away. Your brother has already promised to donate funds to support Padre Osmundo's efforts; there's no need for you to concern yourself."

"Why shouldn't I concern myself?" Irritation sharpened Tory's tone. "I have a mind, too, Mr. Black, and I know how to use it."

"No doubt you do, *moçinha*, but men are rarely interested in a woman's *mind*."

For a moment, there was an awkward silence around the table, then Jordan burst out laughing. "He has you there, Tory! And what he says is true, I'm afraid—at least, in general."

Tory's irritation mounted when Padre Osmundo, Abelardo, and the infuriating Mr. Black joined in Jordan's amusement at her expense.

"What's so funny, Aunt Tory?" Marta piped up.

"Nothing, darling . . . It's just that sometimes gentlemen laugh themselves silly over things in which no one else can find the least bit of humor. In that, they take after hyenas."

"What's a hyena?"

"I guess you could say it's a dog with a personality problem," Tory snapped, catching Sebastian's mocking eye.

For the remainder of the meal, she refused to take any more part in the conversation. As she sat fuming, she began to formulate an idea. When Louisa, the King's cook and housekeeper, served coffee and tiny iced cakes for dessert, Tory sprung it on Padre Osmundo.

"Tell me, Padre. Could an American teach in the school you're planning for the peasants?"

"I suppose so, my child—providing he could master the language."

"I wasn't thinking of a he, Padre. It's a *she* I have in mind, namely myself. I'm a certified teacher, and I'm extremely adept at languages. I'm sure I could learn Portuguese in no time."

Sebastian Black lowered a forkful of cake en route to his mouth, and Jordan set down his cup with a clatter. "Tory, I hope you're joking, because I could never permit you to return to Brazil with Mr. Black and Padre Osmundo."

"I'm not planning to return with them . . . And whatever I do, Jordan, I don't need your permission."

"Now, Tory . . ." Jordan began, but Tory didn't give him time to finish.

"I have to complete the school term before I can do anything. However, when summer comes, I'll be free to leave for Brazil or wherever else I choose."

Jordan glared at her across the table. "I don't care to discuss this in front of guests, Tory."

"Good . . . Because there's nothing for *us* to discuss. This is between me and Padre Osmundo."

47

Turning to the priest, Tory continued. "With the exception of the language problem, I'm probably over-qualified for what you want, Padre. But I'd love a chance to teach simple subjects to people who really want to learn ... A year or two in Brazil would be a wonderful adventure for me. I'm quite envious of my brother and his wife, because of all the things they've seen and done on their travels, and I ..."

"Tory!" Jordan's shout rattled the chandelier overhead.

"Yes, Jordan? You aren't going to have a temper tantrum in front of guests, are you?"

Jordan gritted his teeth. "No, dear sister, I'm *not* going to have a temper tantrum. Unlike you, I'm not a child who resorts to extreme behavior to get her way." He bestowed a brief cold smile on the silent onlookers, then continued in the same infuriatingly patient tone, as if addressing a simpleton. "My dear Tory, you have no idea what you're suggesting. Padre Osmundo may indeed need a teacher for his school, but a young unmarried female would never do in such a rough place."

"Please stop referring to me as a child, Jordan. I'm twenty-six years old, and I need a job, since I'm not fortunate enough to have a husband. Not that I want one, since he might turn out to be as bossy as you."

Sebastian Black's brows lifted at her bluntness, but Tory didn't care if she had shocked him or not. Maybe it was her age that had shocked him. People were usually surprised to find out how old she really was. "Don't forget," she added, "Spencer—your own wife—was about my age when she traveled to Brazil to find work as a doctor. So I don't see how you can possibly object."

48

"Spencer is precisely the reason why I can and do object. If not for me, God only knows where she would have wound up—probably dead in the jungle. Brazil can be a dangerous place for an unprotected female . . . Tell her, Padre."

Padre Osmundo leaned back in his chair. "Well, now, my friend . . . you . . . ah . . . put me in a difficult position. If your sister is willing to donate her services, say for a year, I'd of course be willing to accept them—and to keep her from harm while she is there."

"What are you *saying?* You aren't actually offering her a job, are you?"

"Did you say *donate* my services?" Tory cut in.

Padre Osmundo threw up his hands. "Dear me, I'm just trying to answer your questions. This is all so sudden, and I've had no time to think about it. But yes, your help would be most welcome, my child. However, you would have to donate your services. I've no money to pay a salary. I could perhaps manage a modest living allowance for a year or so; that should give me enough time to find a permanent teacher and a way of funding the position . . . Yes, the idea strikes me as very possible."

"You mean I'd be like a missionary," Tory clarified.

"Out of the question!" Jordan roared.

"Oh, be quiet, Jordan. It's not your decision to make, and Brazil sounds most appealing to me at the moment. Tell me more, Padre."

"More about what, child?" Padre Osmundo shrugged his round shoulders. "I need a teacher, and you, apparently, need a new position. Compared to what you are used to, the facilities would be quite primitive. I have a hut that could be used as a school

49

until the new building can be constructed, and I'm sure I can find you a safe place to live with one of my parishioners. If you're serious, I'll start making arrangements as soon as we return to Brazil. No one would be happier than I to have my little peasant children start learning as soon as possible."

In a matter of seconds, Tory made up her mind. "It sounds exactly like what I've been looking for. I'll do it, Padre!"

"Damn my Aunt Milly's corset, Tory! You can't . . ."

"Wait a minute," Sebastian Black growled.

Tory glanced at him in surprise. For the past few moments, she'd forgotten he was there. Now she wished he wasn't; from the look of him, he intended to side with Jordan.

"Padre, having a teacher drop out of the sky must seem like a miracle to you, but *Senhor Rei* is right to be fearful about his sister . . . Have you forgotten the *cangaçeiros?*"

"They've never harmed me, *mon filho*. It's only the rich who need fear them, and Miss King will be working for practically nothing."

"There are other considerations, Padre, as you well know. Miss King is unmarried."

"True, *mon filho*, but I could ask my housekeeper, Carmelita, to take her in. Carmelita can also act as her chaperone, should she need one."

"I won't be needing a chaperone."

"Oh, yes, you will," Sebastian Black disputed. "If you don't have one, the peasants will rightfully think you're indecent."

"Enough! This is clearly impossible!" Jordan banged his fist on the table. "You can't go, Tory. I've been to Brazil. I know what it's like. And it's the wrong place entirely for an innocent young woman like you."

"I agree," Sebastian Black said.

"I do not," argued Padre Osmundo.

"Nor do I." Tory eyed her brother with stubborn insistence. "Don't try and stop me, Jordan."

"Oh, Aunt Tory, I don't want you to go so far away!" Marta wailed.

"Go, Aunt Tory . . . If the peasants are like the Indians, they need all the help they can get." Abelardo's black eyes were shining.

"For the love of St. Brigid!" a woman said from the doorway. "What's happenin' in me own dinin'-room?"

Tory looked up to see Spencer, Jordan's red-haired Irish wife, standing in the doorway. Slender as a reed, but with a bosom that put Tory's to shame, Spencer Kathleen King entered the room as if she owned it, which she did. Not pretty in the conventional sense, she was nonetheless a compelling woman with her snapping, blue-green eyes, splendid figure clad in a dark blue shirtwaist, and vivid coloring.

"Jordan, ye dinna tell me we were havin' guests this evenin', or I'd have tried t' come home sooner," she said in her lilting brogue.

The brogue alerted Tory to the fact that her sister-in-law was upset. Spencer only lapsed into it during moments of stress. The rest of the time she spoke as clearly and precisely as anyone else. Reading the same storm signal, Jordan rose and went quickly to her side.

"Spencer, love, I'm sorry, I didn't know we were having guests when you left this morning . . . Come, sit down. You're just in time to tell Tory why she can't go running off to teach the poor peasants in

51

Brazil how to read and write."

"Maybe she's just in time to tell you why I can."

"My goodness," Spencer said. "This sounds serious. Why dinna ye introduce me t' these fine gentlemen, and then tell me what this is all about?"

Twenty minutes later, Spencer had heard it all—but she refused to render an opinion one way or the other. "I believe we should all sleep on this," she said with a cautious smile. "In the mornin', we may see it differently."

"An excellent idea," Padre Osmundo agreed. "I certainly never meant to start a war within your family, Jordan. It's just that your sister's offer is too good to pass up. I desperately need a teacher for my little school."

"For you, I'm sure her offer is most advantageous. But for Tory herself . . ." Jordan began. "Why, I can't think of anything worse for her to do."

"Tory, love," Spencer intervened. "Will ye show our guests upstairs t' the guest chambers? I'm sure Louisa has had time t' make up the beds by now."

Glad of a chance to end this abominable discussion which shouldn't even be taking place, Tory rose from the table. "Padre Osmundo, Mr. Black, follow me, please. I'll show you where everything is, then you may retire if you wish, or else join my brother in the library for a brandy to round out the evening."

"Of course, of course . . ." Padre Osmundo pushed back his chair, and so did Sebastian Black. "The dinner was most delicious, Mrs. King. Please tell your cook I said so. I believe I'll retire early and forego the brandy in the library. I'm not as young as I used to be."

"I'll join you later for brandy, Senhor *Rei*," Sebastian Black offered. "Aside from these diverting

52

personal matters, you and I still have business to discuss."

Little Marta dropped a polite curtsey to the two departing guests. "Good night, sirs. I'm pleased to have met you."

"Well done!" Spencer hugged her daughter. "Now, you and Abelardo must help Louisa clear the table before you are excused."

"Good night, Padre, Mr. Black." Abelardo bowed stiffly. "I look forward to seeing you again at breakfast."

"Charming children, Senhora *Rei*." Padre Osmundo smiled. *"Boa noite*, Senhor *Rei*."

As Tory mounted the staircase ahead of Sebastian Black, she could feel his gaze on her back, and her heart began to pound in loud, erratic thumps. When they came to the first guest chamber, she almost knocked Padre Osmundo down in her eagerness to show him the room. "I hope this will be satisfactory, Padre. The bed is very comfortable, and you'll find towels, soap, and whatever else you might need on that little stand in the corner."

"Dear girl, this will be lovely," Padre Osmundo assured her. "Such luxury will spoil me unmercifully."

Tory wondered what luxury he meant. The upstairs was simply furnished with plain, sturdy wood furniture and braided rugs on the hardwood floors. It contained few of the knick-knacks and decorative items usually found in the homes of the well-to-do. Spencer and Jordan had put all their money into horses, not the house, and Spencer's tastes tended toward the simple anyway.

"Good night, then, Padre."

Only after Padre Osmundo had closed the door,

did Tory realize that she ought to have given Mr. Black the first room and saved the second for the plump little priest. Now she was alone with Sebastian Black as she led him further down the long hallway, which was lit only by a single, inadequate electrical fixture—the second lamp being burnt out.

"This will be your room, Mr. Black." She stopped in front of the open door and gestured for him to enter.

He never so much as looked through the doorway. Instead, his clear amber eyes locked with hers. *"Moçinha,* let me take this opportunity to tell you that you are not only the most beautiful, but also the most outspoken young woman I have ever met. I am unaccustomed to hearing females state their opinions so openly. I find it difficult to get used to, but in some ways, it is quite refreshing."

Tory didn't know what to say. "I fear my outspokenness sometimes offends people," she murmured noncommittally.

"Undoubtedly . . . but your beauty must enchant them at the same time." He moved closer, and she instinctively backed away, colliding with the wall behind her. "However much I'd like to show you my country, *moçinha,* I must warn you that your brother is right—Brazil is no place for a young woman alone, especially for one like yourself who has never known hardship or danger."

Moving closer still, he dared to spread his hands on the wall on either side of her head—making escape impossible. It occurred to her that she was experiencing danger right now, and *he* was the cause of it.

"Must I fear attracting undesirable masculine attention?" she asked pointedly, eyeing her prison with a shiver of nervousness.

"You must fear it with your every breath," he purred. "Though if you come to Brazil, and anybody touches you, he'll never live to boast about it. I promise you that."

Her heart was hammering so loudly she thought he must surely hear it. If not her thundering heart, he would hear her knees knocking together. "What will you do?" she whispered hoarsely.

"Tear him limb from limb—*after* I geld him."

Tory couldn't quite conceal her shock. "That seems a rather violent reaction in defense of a woman you don't even know."

He lifted his hand from the wall, and with one finger, traced the curve of her lower lip. "By then, I *shall* know you, *moçinha*. I assure you. I'll know you most intimately."

Did he mean "know" in the Biblical sense? Tory feared he did, and she trembled with the sudden certainty that he was going to kiss her. She could read his intention in his eyes. Her knees felt rubbery, and her stomach somersaulted, but somehow, she found the courage to keep her voice from quivering. "You're quite sure of yourself, aren't you, Mr. Black? Quite sure I would welcome your interference in my life . . . Well, I don't. I don't welcome it at all—either here or in Brazil."

"*Sebastião* . . . You must call me *Sebastião*, and I shall call you Tory, as your brother does."

"I don't want you to call me Tory. So I won't call you *Sebastião*."

He flashed his perfect white teeth. Damn! Was there nothing *im*perfect about this man? Tory wondered. Smile, teeth, body, charm . . . He was perfection personified, and she almost hated him for it.

"How stubborn and scrappy, you are!" he exclaimed. "Like a kitten showing its claws. Instead of *moçinha,* perhaps I should call you *gatinha,* little kitten . . . Yes, that sobriquet better suits you. You even have the mysterious, gray-green eyes of a little blond cat, and I don't doubt that you feel as soft as one."

"Perhaps I should call *you cachorro,* dog, for backing me against this wall and saying such outrageous things to me."

"Ah, *gatinha,* what I say is nothing compared to what I wish to do . . ." He bent his dark head and nuzzled her neck. His breath blew hot down her bodice, and her senses spun.

"Senhor *Prêto!*"

Her skin shuddered from the touch of his mouth on it. Ineffectually, she shoved against his rock-hard chest, but there was no moving him to a safer distance. Lightning-quick, he seized her wrists and pinned them to the wall. Then he nuzzled first her neck, her ear, then her hair.

"*Cristo!* Your smell of roses, *gatinha.* A man could go mad from your scent."

"If you like it so much, I'll gladly break a bottle of rose water over your head! Let me go, Mr. Black, or I'll scream down the house."

"No, you won't." His certainty infuriated her as he leaned into her, his big body pressed along her length. "I can feel you trembling. You want me to touch you, *gatinha*—to pet and stroke your softness."

Securing both wrists with one hand, he brazenly fondled her breasts through the crêpe de Chine. "Like a little dove you are, soft as down . . . Yield to me, *gatinha,* and I'll pleasure you better than any man you've ever known."

"Stop it!" she hissed, enraged by his boldness. Against her will, her breasts were tingling, her nipples budding. Heat flooded her lower abdomen. "What do you think I am?"

"But I *know* what you are, *gatinha*—a liberated female, a woman unafraid to take what she wants from life and damn the consequences."

His logic frightened her; could he read her innermost thoughts? But she had never considered that freedom for women might mean *this*—allowing a perfect stranger to fondle her and make her feel things she didn't want to feel. She opened her mouth to scream, but he didn't give her the chance. His hand moved from her breast to her chin and held it steady while his mouth swooped down upon hers. First, she felt the hot pressure of his lips, as they easily subdued her protests.

Then his tongue shamelessly forayed with her tongue. Their breaths mingled. Her senses flooded with the scent and taste of him. His body was hot and hard. Fascinating ridges of muscle and an enormous, inescapable protrusion pressed against her own soft flesh. She felt as if she were drowning or being swallowed whole by him. The kiss went on forever, so long and devastating that it really wasn't a kiss at all, but more an invasion of her total self.

When he finally lifted his mouth from hers, she would have puddled at his feet had he not held her up.

"Ah, *gatinha* . . . I knew that kissing you would be like this."

"L—like what? I didn't feel a thing!" she desperately denied. In point of fact, the kiss had shaken her to her very core, but she knew instinctively that to admit that was to invite another one.

"Come into my room with me . . . only for a moment. We must talk—and kiss some more."

"I—I *can't!*" She was horrified, more by the fact that she *wanted* to go into the room with him, than by the invitation itself. "This is *unseemly*, Senhor *Prêto!*"

He laughed softly, richly, his amber eyes gleaming. "Unseemly? What a quaint way of putting it. What is unseemly is that you should pretend to deny that you enjoy kissing me."

"I do deny it! I didn't like it at all! And if you don't let me go this instant, I promise you I'll scream!"

"*Cristo!* You try my patience, *gatinha.* Tell me honestly, if that is possible. What do you *Americanas* want before you permit a man to remove your clothing and make love to you?"

"What do we *want?* Are you mad? I would never allow a man to touch me before marriage."

"You don't expect me to believe that," he scoffed. "Anyway, I've already touched you, haven't I? And will again, *gatinha.* Only the next time I caress your sweet softness, you'll be naked beneath my hands and mouth."

Just then, they both heard a door open. Sebastian Black casually stepped back, while Tory cowered against the wall. She was trembling from head to foot. Padre Osmundo poked his head out of his room, saw them, and made a clucking sound with his tongue.

"*Sebastião*, you should be ashamed . . . and you, Senhorita King, should know better than to permit a lusty *Brazileiro* to get you alone with him. Perhaps you would not do well in my country, after all. Haven't you learned by now that men will always try and take advantage of a woman foolish enough to

58

listen to flattery and trust the rogue who utters it?"

"How did you know he was flattering me?" Her voice came out in a squeak. Utterly mortified, Tory longed to sink out of sight into the floor.

"Because I know *Sebastião*." Padre Osmundo winked. "Now be gone from here both of you, before you embarrass yourselves any further."

Tory did not wait to see what Sebastian Black would do; she fled for the staircase as if her gown had caught fire. And she did not stop running until she reached the kitchen, where Louisa and Spencer both gave her curious looks as she seized a towel and began drying dishes faster than Louisa could wash them.

Chapter Four

The next morning, Jordan invited Tory into the library before breakfast, then carefully closed the door behind them and turned to her with a mixture of calmness and brotherly solicitude that made her wonder what he was up to now.

"Tory, sit down," he said, nodding toward the sofa. "I want to talk to you."

Perching on the edge of the sofa, she smoothed her skirt over her knees and hoped that Jordan wouldn't notice the rings around her eyes from sleeplessness. She had lain awake for hours, scolding herself for not having punched Sebastian Black in the eye the previous night—or kneed him in the groin, which she had once advised her students to do if ever a man should get too familiar with them. She'd read in a biology book in the school library that a man's groin was a particularly sensitive and vulnerable part of his anatomy. Having no personal knowledge of a man's anatomy, she had to take the book's word for it and could only wish she had remembered the information last night.

"What is it, Jordan? I hope you aren't going to be tediously overbearing again, before breakfast yet. I don't think I can stand it on an empty stomach."

He glowered at her, then surprisingly grinned. "Is that what I am—tediously overbearing, when all I want is to protect you from harm?"

"All right, I take that back. You're a sweet, loving brother, who simply needs to learn that I'm all grown up now and entitled to make my own mistakes."

His grin disappeared. "It *is* a mistake for you to go to Brazil, Tory . . . However, Spencer has convinced me that I should state my case, then support you in whatever you decide to do. So that's what I'm doing, stating my case."

"I already know your case . . . Believe me, I do. But it isn't as if I won't have someone to look after me and make certain I'm safe. If it weren't for Padre Osmundo, I don't think I'd go . . . It *would* be too dangerous."

Jordan looked heartened. "Well, I'm glad to hear you say that, at least. I certainly wouldn't trust Mr. Black to protect your virtue."

"Nor would I."

Jordan's eyes narrowed. "He hasn't *done* anything, has he? By God, if he has . . ."

Tory quickly waved her hand. "No, no . . . My virtue's quite intact, thank you . . . I just don't like his manner, that's all."

"He's a typical Brazilian male, Tory . . . Very predatory toward women. In the Brazilian culture, men don't even speak to decent women until they marry one . . . The sexes simply don't mix."

"I don't intend to mix with men in Brazil either, Jordan. I'm going there solely to teach children— and only for a year. It will give me time to figure out what I'm going to do with the rest of my life . . . I feel I'm at a crossroads. I don't know which direction to take."

61

Jordan sat next to her on the sofa and reached for her hand. "You'll find the right path, Tory. I'm sure you will. You have so much to give! You're so clever and articulate. Spencer and I both admire you far more than you know."

Tory smiled ruefully. "So far, my cleverness has only gotten me into trouble . . . but I do thank you and Spencer for being so dear and supportive—and for not trying to stand in my way."

"Last night, I fully intended to stand in your way. But as usual, my wife persuaded me to rethink the issue."

"Thank God for your wife! She's a wonderful woman, Jordan. I don't know what she ever saw in *you*."

"If I didn't think you were teasing, I'd be offended, Victoria King. I didn't have to break her arm to marry me, you know."

Withdrawing her hand, Tory playfully poked him in the ribs. "I *am* teasing, dear brother. Spencer was equally fortunate to have found you . . . Can we have breakfast now, before you change your mind and start lecturing me again?"

They went arm in arm to the dining room, where Spencer, Padre Osmundo, Abelardo, and Marta awaited them. Sebastian Black was conspicuously absent.

"Where's Mr. Black this morning?" Tory casually inquired as she sat down at the table. She was both relieved and disappointed not to have to face him, just yet.

"He hasn't appeared," Spencer answered. "Does he usually sleep this late, Padre Osmundo?"

"Not usually." The priest was beaming as he looked over the array of dishes Louisa had set before them. "If he doesn't show up, I'll gladly eat his portion."

"I'm not surprised he's not here," Jordan said. "We sat up late. He wouldn't let me go to bed until I'd promised to sell him Renegade, providing he likes his colts when he sees them."

"No wonder you look tired." Somewhat guiltily, Tory noticed the circles under Jordan's eyes—*and* under Spencer's. They must have stayed up even later discussing *her*. "I just hope you didn't agree to sell Renegade too cheaply," she sniffed. "As you know, I'm rather fond of him."

"That's reason enough to give him away. However, I told Mr. Black that if he wants him, he'll have to pay full price for him."

"I want him," rumbled a deep voice.

Tory looked up from filling her plate to see Sebastian Black striding into the room. A shaft of morning sunlight fell across his dark face, turning the amber eyes golden. He was, she thought, indecently handsome, and the only one in the house who looked well-rested, with the exception of Padre Osmundo and the children. He might have been the devil himself all decked out for seduction in his impeccably-cut riding clothes, which included fawn-colored breeches that fit like a second skin and tall black boots that emphasized well-proportioned legs and calves.

"I see you have a number of Renegade's foals down in your paddocks," Sebastian Black drawled. "They're stamped with his look of sturdiness, strength, and speed."

Jordan calmly slathered a biscuit with honey. "I told you he was an outstanding sire. Now you must realize why I can't come down on his price."

63

"You may have your price—outrageous as it is. Now, about that colt with the white blaze on its face . . ."

"Come eat breakfast, Mr. Black," Spencer interrupted. "Business can wait until afterwards."

"Business can never wait, Senhora King. But if you insist, I'll try and be patient."

"I do insist." Spencer smiled graciously but her voice hinted of steel.

"No one argues with my wife." Chuckling, Jordan gave Spencer an unabashedly warm and devoted look. "She tells everyone what to do, even guests."

Sebastian's glowing amber eyes met Tory's. "This country strikes me as more and more amazing. When I attended school here, no one mentioned a word about the power of women in the *Estados Unidos*. Of course, I was educated in a Franciscan monastery, and that was many years ago. Maybe women only recently learned how to dictate to everyone around them."

"If you think we have power and influence now, wait until we gain the right to vote, Mr. Black," Tory couldn't resist goading. "I believe that day will come in my lifetime."

"How fortunate that I live in Brazil then, where such dangerously liberal ideas have yet to taint womens' minds." Seating himself at the long table, Sebastian accepted the plate of ham Spencer handed to him.

"I wouldn't be too complacent if I were you . . ." Spencer warned. "When Tory goes to Brazil, she'll be bringing her liberal ideas with her."

"Ah . . . You are coming then?" Padre Osmundo gleefully turned to Tory.

"Yes," Tory affirmed. "And Jordan has finally

64

consented to give his blessing to the venture, I'm happy to say."

"*Maravilhosa! Sebastião,* how soon can we leave? I must make arrangements for Senhorita King's arrival."

"That depends on her brother and how soon he agrees to sell the colt with the white blaze." Sebastian Black picked up his fork and stabbed a piece of ham, at the same time giving Tory an intimate look that unsettled her stomach as much as if he'd stabbed *her.* "I do not approve of you coming to Brazil, Senhorita King, but I will naturally aid and assist you any way I can while you are in my country."

"I'm sure I won't need your assistance." Remembering his behavior of the night before, Tory kept her tone cool and distant. "I intend to spend all my time either in school teaching or otherwise helping Padre Osmundo with the peasants."

"Then perhaps I can at least advise you on your travel plans."

"Oh, yes, my travel plans . . ." Tory wished she could state what they were, but she hadn't yet made any. She wasn't even sure where in Brazil she'd be going. "Padre? What is *your* advice?"

"Well, now, this is what you must do, my child . . ."

Tory spent the remainder of the morning discussing travel routes and accommodations with Padre Osmundo, while Sebastian Black went off with Jordan to negotiate the sale of the colt with the white blaze. Tory didn't see him again until late afternoon, when Spencer sent her down to the stud barn in search of him and Jordan.

"Jordan? Mr. Black?" she called, hurrying into the shadowy brick building which stood apart from the rest of the complex. "Are you two in here? Spencer sent me to tell you that supper will be served promptly at six."

Sebastian Black stepped out of Renegade's stall right in front of her, but Jordan was nowhere in sight. "*Gatinha*, you are looking for me?"

"And my brother. I'm looking for both of you." Tory craned her neck to see behind Sebastian, but the barn appeared deserted. Neither Jordan, Abelardo, nor any of the stablehands were about. "Where's Jordan?" she demanded, not about to be caught alone again with this man, if she could help it.

"He's gone to the mare's barn to see about a problem there. One of the stableboys came to get him."

"Oh . . . Then I'll just go find him."

"Wait a moment, *gatinha*." Sebastian's strong brown hand grasped her arm.

Already knowing it was useless to fight his greater physical strength, Tory slowly turned to face him. "Take your hand off me, Mr. Black. There will be no repetition of the liberties you took last night."

"No, *gatinha?*" His lazy, provocative smile turned her insides to jelly. "What if I were to pull you into a dark corner of this barn and kiss you senseless? How would you feel about that, I wonder?"

As he spoke, he was tugging her toward a stall partially filled with hay bales. "Let go of me, you . . . you big Brazilian baboon!"

He laughed deep in his chest. "Yesterday at dinner you spoke of hyenas; today you mention baboons . . . I take it you are a student of animals?"

"I know a snake when I see one! You are the lowest of the low, Mr. Black—trying to seduce me in my own brother's house—his barn, I mean!"

66

"Well, he isn't *my* brother, *gatinha*. I owe him no loyalty."

"You're a guest at Castle Acres! Doesn't *that* mean anything to you?"

He paused, considering. *"Sim,* I suppose it does. Such rudeness on my part would be unforgivable if you didn't want this seduction as badly as I do."

"I don't want anything, you conceited lout!"

"What you say and what you do—the way you behave, *gatinha*—speaks louder than your empty protests." He pulled her struggling into the stall, then pushed her back against the stacked bales of sweet-smelling hay.

Tory was shaking with anxiety and agitation. She also felt a jolt of raw excitement. The very air around this disturbing man seemed charged with electricity. "Explain what you mean by that! What did I ever say or do to invite ravishment?"

"Ravishment? Who intends to ravish you, *gatinha?* Certainly not I." He drew back in mock horror, but without giving her room to dart past him and escape.

"Just what do you call *this?* Dragging me into this stall today—and . . . and kissing and fondling me last night."

"I'd call it remarkable patience on both our parts to wait until this afternoon to do what we wanted to do last evening."

"Ooooh, that's no answer at all! Ravishment is when a man does things to a woman that she doesn't want. Rape is another term for it. You *have* heard of rape, I presume."

"Sim, but I give you my word, I've never done it." He cocked his head, eyeing her with amusement. "I think you are one of those women who will always say no, even when she means yes, are you not?"

"No! I always say exactly what I mean. And you still haven't answered my question: What did I say or do to make you think I want to be pawed and manhandled?"

"Do you know that your eyes are growing greener by the moment?" he asked irrelevantly. "And your cheeks have sprouted roses. Anger becomes you, *gatinha*. Perhaps you should endeavor to lose your temper more often."

"Answer me, damn you!"

He burst out laughing. "Ah, *gatinha* . . . What am I supposed to think when you go about dressed in tight trousers, with your hair falling down your back as if you just rose from a rumpled bed? And what should I think when you refuse to obey your brother—and spout nonsense about women voting and not needing chaperones before they are wed? . . . Decent women don't behave like that. So you must be the other kind—the sort who enjoys being pawed and manhandled, as you so indelicately put it."

"You're even worse than the school board! I suppose you don't approve of knickers, either."

"Knickers? Now you confuse me, *gatinha* . . . Anyway, we are wasting time. I only want another kiss from you—just to see if it's as rousing a kiss as you gave me last night."

"I gave you nothing—nor will I ever!"

"Yes, you will, little firebrand . . . Indeed, you'll soon be begging for my kisses."

He crowded her into the hay bales, but this time she was ready for him. With fist and knee, she let him have it. He grunted in surprise and pain, then doubled over. One hand clutched at his eye, the other at his groin, that sensitive, vulnerable portion of his anatomy described in the school's biology book. She was gratified to learn that the book hadn't lied.

"Cristo!" he groaned.

"Next time, I'll geld you—then tear you limb from limb!" she spat.

Cursing him under her breath, she ran from the barn.

At dinner an hour later, Sebastian had to explain his blackening eye. He conjured a tale of stepping on a rake in the barn and having the handle fly up and hit him in the face. Then he waited to see if anyone would call him a liar. No one did. Instead, they made sympathetic noises, and Jordan King vowed to box the ears of whoever had left the rake lying on the ground. Tory herself did not dispute his story; she couldn't because she wasn't there. Jordan's sister had suddenly, inexplicably come down with a headache, Jordan's wife explained. Tonight, she would be eating alone in her room—with the door barred, no doubt, Sebastian thought to himself.

He was inordinately glad he didn't have to account for his hidden bruises, but part way through the meal, he forgot himself and squirmed uncomfortably on the chair, prompting Spencer to ask if anything besides his eye was bothering him. It crossed his mind to inquire if she had ever treated a *half*-gelded man. Valiantly, he assured her that nothing other than his eye had been injured in his encounter with the rake.

All through dinner, Sebastian seethed quietly, furious with himself for allowing a little hellion of a she-cat to get the best of him. Victoria King wasn't fooling him one bit; all her pious protestations could never convince him she was pure as an angel and worthy of his respect. In his experience, innocent little virgins resembled shy, timid mice scurrying to and from church in the company of their chaperones. They did plenty of sideways glancing and giggling, but were afraid to look a man in the eye.

Not so Victoria King. She far more resembled the *other* kind of woman—those who boldly gazed at men through their open windows and invited them to come inside. How could Padre Osmundo be so foolish as to permit this scandalously brazen *Americana* to teach in his school? Within days of her arrival on the *sertão*, men would be shooting each other over her . . . and if she truly *was* a virgin when she arrived, which he seriously doubted, she *wouldn't* be when she left. Sebastian could just picture her with her belly swollen with some nameless *cangaçeiro's* sprouting seed . . . She would be weeping and repentant, disgraced exactly as she deserved.

Cristo! He hoped he would be around to see it . . . Victoria King had far too much pride and arrogance for a mere woman. Doubtless, she would be looking around for someone to marry, even willing to consider *him,* the only man besides Padre Osmundo for hundreds of kilometers in either direction who could write his own name. What pleasure he would feel in rejecting her! He would spit on the ground at her feet and walk away. . . .

"Mr. Black . . . I understand you'll be leaving shortly, now that you've settled your business with my husband . . . Mr. Black?"

Sebastian started. "What? Oh, yes, Senhora King . . . We'll be leaving as soon as I've made arrangements for transporting the animals I've bought."

"Where will you ship them—into Salvador?"

Jordan King's red-haired wife was difficult to ignore. Like her sister-in-law, she commanded a man's attention whether he wanted to give it or not.

A plague on all these upstart *Americanas* who didn't know their places!

"Yes, Salvador is where they'll be going. From there, it's only four days journey to Paraíso, my *estãncia*."

"Paraíso! You named your ranch Paradise?"

"*Sim*, though that's not a very accurate description. I fear it in no way resembles heaven."

"Neither did my husband's rubber plantation on the Amazon. What a coincidence that you both chose the same name . . . Jordan, did you hear that?"

Deep in discussion with Padre Osmundo, Jordan King glanced up distractedly. "What is it, Spencer?"

Spencer King's eyes sparkled as she looked at her husband, causing Sebastian to notice for the first time that she was actually quite beautiful. On first meeting her, he had thought her striking, but nowhere near as compelling as the petite, blonde Victoria. The younger woman still outshone her, but Senhora King did possess an arresting face and a figure to match her powerful personality.

"Mr. Black has just told me that the name of his ranch in Bahia is Paraíso."

"Really," Jordan commented. "I hope your ranch is more worthy of the name than my rubber plantation."

"At the moment, it isn't—but one day, it will be."

As Jordan returned to his discussion with Padre Osmundo, Spencer King smiled, looking prettier by the moment, almost as if she had discovered a wonderful secret or made up her mind about something. "Paraíso . . . Somehow, that strikes me as a good omen, Mr. Black."

"I'm pleased you approve," Sebastian said dryly. "I chose the name with the future of the place in mind."

"Speaking of futures, Mr. Black, I'm hoping you will help Padre Osmundo keep an eye on Tory when she comes to Brazil."

Sebastian coughed in the midst of sipping coffee, the weak American imitation which in no way resembled the strong brew of his own country. Such a request coming from Victoria King's sister-in-law struck him as ludicrous, but he could hardly explain why. Recovering, he dutifully murmured: "I'd be delighted to, Senhora, but she may have other ideas."

"I'm sure she does, Mr. Black, and so did I when I went to Brazil. Tory is sure she can take care of herself, just as I was. Unfortunately, though I hate to admit it, there are times when a woman needs a man's protection. If Padre Osmundo should ever be . . . unavailable . . . I hope we can count on you to help Tory in the event she needs it."

Sebastian stared at this presumptuous woman, understanding better now where Tory had gotten her presumption. "I've already offered to do what I can for her, Senhora. If she doesn't want my assistance, I can't force it on her."

"Not force perhaps, Mr. Black—but something tells me you can be irresistably persuasive when you desire."

"I can?" Sebastian raised his brows at her astuteness, then winced at the throbbing in his bruised eye.

A smile played about Senhora King's mouth. "You did convince my husband to sell you Renegade, and then a colt he was determined to keep."

"*Cristo,*" Sebastian muttered under his breath. "All right, Senhora . . . I swear to you on my honor that I'll help protect your husband's sister from harm."

"That includes all harm from *you,*" Spencer King dropped her voice so that it was barely above a whisper. She looked straight into his eyes, her smile suddenly vanishing. *"Especially* from you."

Sebastian couldn't help wondering if Jordan King's wife and Padre Osmundo were in league with each other. "Of course, it includes all harm from me," he politely agreed.

"I know you'd never lie, Mr. Black. Anyone educated in a monastery can surely be trusted to keep his word."

Amazing! The woman had neatly cornered him. *"Sim,* Senhora. I can be trusted . . . How I should hate to have to buy horses from you, when you're so clever and persistent."

"What I am is observant, Mr. Black. It comes from being a doctor."

"And what have you observed, Senhora?"

"Only my sister-in-law's bruised knuckles . . . They look as if she's been in a fist fight, though she assures me she's done no such thing."

There's no sense denying it, Sebastian thought. Were all *Americanas* so smart? He sighed and shrugged his shoulders. "I thought my story about the rake very convincing. Too bad it was not."

"'Twas a fine bit o' blarney, lad . . . But any Irishman would've seen through it."

He found the brogue she sometimes affected charming. "What a pity you're already married, Senhora King. You'd make a man a most interesting companion. I can see now why your husband took you to wife."

She glanced at him sidelong. "So would Tory make an interesting companion and wife. But whoever Tory marries will have to be man enough to handle her. You yourself haven't made a good first impression, I'm sorry to say, though perhaps that's exactly what you intended. In any case, for reasons

73

we won't discuss at the moment, Tory despises you. I can't say I blame her."

Sebastian sat back in his chair, stunned by the woman's perceptiveness and audacity. In a polite but telling way, she was chastising him as if he were an errant schoolboy caught stealing apples. Spencer King and her sister-in-law, Victoria, were unlike any women he had ever met. A man would have to be bewitched to marry either one of them. He didn't know why he had even mentioned the subject, considering that marriage was the furthest thing from his mind. Beautiful women always seemed to make him say things he didn't really mean. Telling women what they wanted to hear was a kind of game with him. But these two *Americanas*—who could ever understand them? And who would want to?

In the future, he resolved to steer clear of both of them. Tory King, especially, was a complication he didn't need in his already too-complicated life. Padre Osmundo would just have to take care of her—if and when she arrived in Brazil. The Falcon had better things to do with his time.

Chapter Five

Salvador, Bahia
Five Months Later

The blue-green waters of the Bay of All Saints, or *Bahia Dos Todos Santos*, gleamed in the early afternoon sunlight as Tory disembarked from the steamship which had brought her to Brazil. She did not know where to look first: at the *Cidade Baixa* or Lower City, which seemed to be one vast marketplace teeming with animals and people, or at the *Cidade Alta*, the Upper City perched high on the cliffs overlooking the bay, where church spires and pastel-colored houses with red-tiled roofs competed with palm trees and a brilliant blue sky.

Standing on the unloading platform, clutching an over-stuffed carpetbag, Tory waited for the guide who was to escort her to the *Igreja de São Francisco* with its adjacent Franciscan Monastery, where Padre Osmundo had told her to come upon her arrival. Captain Belinda had said he would make all the arrangements to see her safely to the famous landmark, since she was a stranger to the city and might get lost en route. He had also promised to make

75

certain that the rest of her baggage was delivered there as soon as possible.

She didn't mind waiting, though she was terribly thirsty and felt half-suffocated by the heat. The tropical sun beat down mercilessly, the sweet breezes which had cooled her aboard ship having vanished. Still, there was so much to see, smell, and notice that these discomforts seemed minor. Everywhere she looked, alien sights met her eyes—oxen pulling a huge cart heavily laden with unidentifiable fruits, a man balancing a basket filled with still-flopping fish on his shoulder, another man shuffling down the street to his own private melody. Curious scents assailed her nostrils: the repugnant odor of rotting fish and floating garbage, but also the tang of spicy cooking mixed with the fecund smell of earth and blooming flowers.

It felt wonderful to be on land again after the long sea voyage, and her excitement at finally having arrived in this strange, exotic country spiraled to a fever pitch. Ships from every conceivable country crammed the beautiful Bay of All Saints, and all manner of cargo was being loaded or unloaded on the busy docks. Dray wagons, donkeys, horses, mules, and people jammed the narrow cobblestone streets, and the sound of Portuguese being spoken too rapidly for her to translate assaulted her ears.

From the ship, she had been able to see only high cliffs, endless white sand beaches, and palm trees along the lush, green coastline; it seemed incredible that such a vibrant, large city could suddenly appear out of nowhere, but a city this was—sensually opulent and fascinating.

Nearby, an enormous Negress sat on a crate, cooking something on a brazier in front of her. She wore a white turban, a white blouse pulled down to reveal plump ebony shoulders, and a voluminous white skirt. Beads and bangles adorned her neck and wrists. Catching Tory's eye, she flashed a white-toothed grin, then called to her in Portuguese.

Having spent every waking moment of the last five months studying the language and history of Brazil, Tory knew she was being invited to try the woman's wares, some sort of pastry, fried in oil. Tory politely shook her head. Best to wait here for Captain Belinda; after seeing her safely off his ship, the bewhiskered captain had warned her not to wander off or speak to anyone until his return with a reliable guide.

Next, Tory directed her attention to a man carrying a huge crate of wriggling crabs atop his head. This man's skin was nut-brown in color, darker than Sebastian Black's, but not as dark as the woman street vendor's. Every shade of brown, black, and white could be found in the skins of the people on the docks. In America, Sebastian Black had looked dark to Tory, but here in Brazil, he was unmistakably an upper-class white man. Irritated with herself for allowing him to dominate her thoughts again after five months of trying to forget him, she wondered why he had popped into her head at this moment.

Following their last encounter in the barn at Castle Acres, Sebastian Black had departed without saying another word to her. She was hoping she'd seen the last of him. With any luck, his *estância* lay nowhere near the school Padre Osmundo was building. She intended to avoid Mr. Black if at all possible, and was determined to overcome this distressing tendency to recall details of his appearance, speech, and manners that she would prefer not to remember.

She supposed it was inevitable that she should think of him now. After all, this was his country, and she would soon be plunging into the culture which had produced him. Obviously, his nationality had shaped his views on women, but the women she could see on the docks gave no clue as to how they were treated or regarded in Salvador, Bahia. The female street vendor seemed happy enough; she laughed often as she called out to passersby, enticing them to try her cookery.

The only other women in the immediate vicinity were either buying or selling fruit, fish, or other items at the open-air stands crowding the docks. Most were poorly dressed, possessing Negro features and dark skins; none appeared to be landed gentry, of whom Sebastian Black was such a prime example. But even as she was thinking this, Tory saw an elegantly-gowned young woman accompanied by one apparent servant and what could only have been a chaperone—an older, prune-faced female who frowned at everything and everyone.

The young woman was strolling among the market stalls, examining fresh produce and pointing out this or that to her servant, who then began arguing over prices with the merchant. Tory admired the lacy, white gown the young woman was wearing—and admired her beauty even more. She had sparkling brown eyes, raven-black hair, and smooth golden skin, but what really set her apart was her grace of movement. Every gesture showed refinement and delicacy. Her slender hands fluttered like butterfly wings, and Tory couldn't help wondering if those hands had ever done any work. Somehow, she doubted it. Nor could she imagine this exquisite creature donning knickerbockers and riding a bicycle.

The young woman disappeared from sight, and Tory found herself once again thinking of Sebastian Black. Instinctively, she knew that the chauvinistic

Mr. Black would approve of the sort of coddled femininity the lovely stranger represented. And he would *not* approve of Tory standing all by herself in a public place waiting in the hot sunshine for a guide to appear. Maybe Captain Belinda had forgotten her in the worry of unloading his cargo and arranging to purchase cocoa and sugar for the homeward journey.

Straightening her shoulders, Tory reminded herself that she had come here to teach poor peasants, not to win Mr. Black's approval, though she was getting nervous about the attention she had begun to attract. Every man who passed, whether young or old, black, white, or brown, eyed her curiously, and she thought, a little too boldly. Some of them made comments to their companions, but she couldn't quite hear what they were saying.

Not far from where she stood, a group of people had gathered, and now she realized with a start that they were talking about *her*. She caught the word *loura* in their conversation and recalled Jordan telling her that he had often been referred to as a *louro*, which meant blond. Her straw bonnet, sensible brown shirtwaist, and high button shoes would not have been out of place anywhere in America, but here, they were conspicuous . . . The women in the marketplace all wore long, dusty skirts, faded blouses, and sandals—or else they were barefoot.

She was obviously a foreigner, and that word, too, *estrangeira*, reached her ears. Suddenly, a youth of about twelve or thirteen materialized in front of her and began speaking in rapid-fire Portuguese.

"More slowly," she begged, annoyed at herself for not understanding the rush of foreign words.

Impatiently, he repeated what he had said, then grinned widely—a charming grin that stole her heart. "Come," he said clearly. "My name is Antônio, and I will take you to the *Igreja de São Francisco.*"

This, then, was her guide. She was about to ask what had happened to Captain Belinda, but the boy reached for her carpetbag and set off at such a jaunty pace that she feared losing him in the crowd.

"Antônio, wait!" she cried, hurrying after him.

Nimble as an elf, Antônio ducked into an alley, which proved to be a cobblestone street so narrow that Tory could practically touch the buildings on either side. The sun didn't even reach into the dark, malodorous, steep passageway. Huffing and puffing, Tory followed the boy up the narrow, winding road, fronted on both sides by dirty, white-washed buildings with worn shutters and wet laundry strung between them. They made many twists and turns, squeezing past pedestrians and donkeys with precarious loads. Finally, the angle of ascent lessened, and they came out on a wider street, with nicer-looking homes and shops, and better dressed people.

Tory gawked at a passing group of black women garbed in bright-colored skirts and blouses, and carrying various jugs and baskets on their heads. The women were strikingly beautiful and animated, reminding her of brilliantly plumaged parrots. Many of the passing men were as picturesque and colorful as the women; some wore strings of beads around their necks and wide straw hats to ward off the sun. But nowhere did Tory see white women dressed as she was, though a number of elegantly-attired gentlemen strolled by, bearing gold-headed canes and walking sticks.

The architecture of the buildings also drew Tory's notice. Their rich ornamentation spoke of the original Portuguese settlers, whose influence was everywhere apparent. Blue and white tiles adorned numerous buildings, and almost all had tall windows that could be closed with shutters. Some of the windows opened onto tiny balconies, causing Tory to wonder if the inhabitants didn't lack privacy. Where one house ended, another began. Here and there, a long, solid wall hid the structure behind it. The buildings probably all had inner courtyards, she decided, a place where people could relax and take their ease away from prying eyes on the street.

Antônio led her up one meandering street and down another, until eventually they came out on a large square, then passed into a smaller plaza fronted by not one, but three churches.

Here, the boy suddenly stopped. Flinging wide his hand, he identified each of the ornate buildings. Two were 17th-century structures: the Cathedral Basilica, and the Church of the Third Order of St. Dominic. The remaining was St. Peter's of the Clergy, built in the 18th century, according to her young guide. A fourth church caught Tory's eye. Rising majestically from an adjoining square stood an impressive edifice built of stone, to which another building was annexed, with yet a smaller, richly ornamented church beside it.

Seeing where she was looking, Antônio affirmed her guess. *"Igreja de São Francisco!"* he grandly announced, then began reciting some of the history of the old church.

The Church of St. Francis was built during the 18th century of stone imported from Portugal. From floor to ceiling, its walls were covered with intricate carvings thickly encrusted with gold leaf. *"Real gold!"* Antônio assured her. On one of its side altars stood a statue of St. Peter of Alcantara, carved from a single tree trunk by Brazil's most famous baroque artist, Manoel Inácio da Costa.

Next to the church was the Franciscan monastery she was seeking, but before Tory could ask why he'd chosen to wait so long before pointing it out, Antônio held out his hand, palm upward. "I will tell you more about these buildings, Senhorita, but first you must pay," he gravely informed her.

Tory felt a sinking sensation. She'd had no time or opportunity to exchange her American money for Brazilian currency; indeed, she was counting on Padre Osmundo to tell her how to do that—but here was the boy waiting to be paid for having brought her to the right place and eagerly imparting information she might find interesting.

"I'm sorry," she explained in her awkward Portuguese. "I have no money, yet—I mean, no Brazilian money. But if you'll come with me to the monastery, I'm sure my friend who's awaiting me there will lend me some."

The boy regarded her doubtfully for a moment, then gave a startled cry: "Aiee, Senhorita! Look behind you!"

Tory spun around, expecting she knew not what. Several old women were going into one of the churches, and three beggars sat on the steps, calling out to them. Nothing seemed greatly amiss. Puzzled, she turned back to discover that Antônio was nowhere in sight. Then she spotted him, running as fast as his thin legs could carry him down a narrow, twisted street. In his hand, he still carried her carpetbag.

The carpetbag held many things: toiletry items, a change of underlinen, several precious books—one a Portuguese-English Dictionary—and some of her money. She had packed it with care and could ill afford to lose it, especially if her baggage wasn't

82

delivered by tonight. Realizing that the thief was making good his getaway, she sprinted after him. But there was no catching Antônio. He knew the streets, and she did not. Moreover, her feet were hurting from the long climb to the Upper City. Losing sight of him, she finally gave up and limped back to the square where the monastery was located.

By now, the enchantment had gone out of her arrival. Her mouth felt dry as cotton, and perspiration dripped between her breasts. She hoped Padre Osmundo would immediately offer her something to drink and a place to rest and recover from the headache now pounding in her temples. There was no restaurant or lodging nearby where a person could take refreshment, she noticed, and in any case, the American money she still had in her reticule wouldn't buy anything.

Remembering Padre Osmundo's instructions that she should approach the gate and request to see him, then wait in the church until he came, she walked to the monastery's main entrance and rang the bell beside it. Women were not permitted inside the monastery itself, he had told her, but her message would be conveyed to him, and he would come directly. There had to be at least a visiting room located somewhere in the annex.

When no one answered the bell on the first summons, Tory rang it again. Several long moments later, someone finally came, but Tory couldn't see his face—only his beady black eyes as he slid back a grate and peered through the tiny opening. "*Sim?*" he inquired. "Who is there?"

"My name is Victoria King," Tory started to say in English, then sheepishly switched to Portuguese. "Will you please tell Padre Osmundo that I have arrived?"

"Padre Osmundo?" The man repeated the name as if he'd never heard it before. "Wait in the church, please. Someone will be out to speak with you shortly."

"He *is* here, isn't he?" Tory sought assurance that Padre Osmundo was indeed in residence, passing the entire month of September on retreat as planned. It was only the middle of the month now, so he should be awaiting her arrival.

"Go to the church, daughter. Go and pray . . . It will make the time pass quickly."

Tory didn't like the sound of that, but she had no choice but to do as commanded. Sighing with impatience, she headed for the imposing church. Inside the thick stone walls, it was cool, dark, and quiet. She paused to allow her eyes to adjust and noticed the exquisitely-painted blue and white tiles on the walls of the vestibule. They depicted the life of St. Francis of Assisi who had given away all his worldly goods and preached the value of simplicity.

In the church itself, she found everything to be exactly as Antônio—and before him, Sebastian—had described. Not an inch of wall or ceiling remained unornamented. All were intricately carved and sheeted with gold, gleaming warmly in the glow of votive candles. Struck with awe, Tory inhaled deeply of the stuffy, incense-laden air, then walked up and down the side aisles, examining the amazing display of wealth and riches. Even the statues of the saints— except for St. Francis himself—wore fine silks and velvets, sewn with precious jewels. She spent more than an hour contemplating the workmanship and skill of the unknown artists who had created this house of worship, for it was truly magnificent, even ostentatious.

When she finally tired of walking, she knelt down

in a wooden pew and bowed her head, praying she might do some good in this country. She also prayed that her uncertainty about her future would soon be resolved. Candles lit the gorgeous altar, illuminating its golden artwork, but Tory found it difficult to think of God residing in this opulent church, when the land He had created outside held so much natural beauty. Did the Almighty really prefer gold to the blue of His brilliant sky and the glorious green of His trees?

So much gold was oppressive. Instead of lifting her thoughts to heaven, it made her think of conquest— of men toiling deep in mines beneath the earth or sweating under the lash to build such a splendid monument. Surely, slaves had helped to haul the stones and mine the gold, and poor artisans had labored to carve the wood. If these walls could speak, she wondered, what would they say?

She sat down in the pew, but kept glancing around, watching for Padre Osmundo. One hour stretched into two, and as the third slid past, she grew more and more annoyed. What could be keeping him? She got up, left the church, and went back to the monastery, where she rang the bell three times without success. No one came to the grate. Perhaps the monks were at prayer now, or it was their dinner hour. Whatever the reason, they should have sent *someone* by now.

Returning to the church, she resumed her seat in the pew and tried to decide the proper course of action if Padre Osmundo failed to appear . . . But he *must* appear, she thought desperately. It was growing late in the day, and she faced a night alone in this strange city, without money to rent a room or buy a meal . . . She could always go back to the ship, of course, but the thought of traversing the narrow, twisting streets again filled her with apprehension. She wasn't sure of the way, and it would be dangerous to be caught after dark down on the docks. If she hadn't been able to trust the boy, Antônio, how could she trust the men of the area not to accost her?

The minutes crept by with agonizing slowness. One by one, other visitors to the church departed, until only two old women with squares of black lace on their heads knelt before the sanctuary. When they, too, rose and left, Tory became truly alarmed. She stood up, glancing around the silent building with dismay and rising anger. She was *not* going to spend the night in an old, dark church. She would go back to the monastery and ring the bell until someone came and told her what had happened to Padre Osmundo.

She was half way out of the pew when a familiar voice stopped her in her tracks. "*Gatinha* . . . So you came to Brazil, after all, didn't you?"

She whirled about, just as a tall dark figure emerged from the shadows of a side altar and came toward her. She knew who he was even before she could see the sardonic smile curling his lips. His deep, velvet voice would forever haunt her memory.

"Mr. Black!"

"Sebastian . . ." he huskily corrected.

"How did you know I was here? Where's Padre Osmundo?"

"So many questions, *gatinha*—and without even a proper, polite *boa tarde*."

He came into the pew, took her by the shoulders, and pressed his smooth-shaven cheek to hers in greeting. The clean male scent of him filled her nostrils. For a moment, she stood perfectly still, sniffing appreciatively, then recoiled in shock at herself and pushed him away with both hands. "Why do you say

86

good afternoon? This isn't afternoon anymore. It's evening. I've been waiting in this church for hours."

He grinned down at her, mocking her with his amber eyes. "I'm so sorry about that, *querida*, but I came as soon as I could. The moment I received word of your arrival, I dropped everything to come to you."

Wasn't *querida* a form of address used between lovers, Tory wondered. Frantically, she tried to remember all the Portuguese she had studied for so long. Unable to think coherently when he was so close to her, she returned to her most immediate problem.

"Where's Padre Osmundo?" Her voice came out unnaturally loud, echoing in the vast cavern of the church. Shouting was probably sacrilegious in this holy place, but she needed answers, and she needed them now.

"Detained at Paraíso with an injury, I'm afraid. He was so eager to get the new school built before you arrived that he foolishly climbed a ladder to help tile the roof, took a step backward, and fell to the ground . . . Fortunately, he only broke his ankle, not his neck."

"Why didn't they tell me at the monastery when I inquired? They never said a word about *you*."

"Ah, the good friars spend as little time as possible conversing with women—tempts them from their vows, you understand. Also, I told them not to. I wanted to surprise you; I knew how delighted you'd be to see me again."

Tory fought to keep a smile from emerging. He was so outrageous she could hardly take him seriously. "I'm not in the least delighted to see you again, Mr. Black."

"Sebastian . . ."

"So what do we do now, Sebastian? I take it you are charged with delivering me safely to Padre Osmundo."

He made a mock frown. "Alas, I had to swear to treat you with the utmost courtesy."

"Then it would be a mortal sin if you disobeyed."

"I wouldn't mind eternal hell if I could enjoy a few brief moments of paradise on earth," he drawled suggestively.

His gaze lingered on her mouth, then strayed down her figure with unconcealed interest. The fine hairs rose on the back of Tory's neck, and she found it exceedingly difficult to breathe properly.

"You'll have no moments of paradise with me," she snapped. "If you think differently, you might as well leave me right here. I'll take my chances alone in the city over accompanying you anywhere tonight."

"Ah, *gatinha* . . . You wound me to the quick with your sharp tongue . . . Don't worry so. You're entirely safe with me. Tonight, you will spend in my townhouse, and tomorrow, we'll leave for my ranch. Then, as soon as Padre Osmundo is on his feet again, the two of you can go to Espirito Santo, the little village where he's building his school. It's a good distance from Paraíso, and I don't want him going anywhere until he's completely healed and can better tolerate the long journey."

Tory was relieved to hear that the school was *not* at Sebastian's ranch, but she didn't at all like the idea of spending the night at his house in town. Anything could happen—and probably would, given his character. What she had seen of this man so far indicated that he would *make* something happen.

"Perhaps you can recommend an inn or hotel, Mr. Black," she primly suggested. "I've no intention of staying at your house tonight."

"Alas, you must, *gatinha,* or else Carmelita will be furious."

"Carmelita?"

"Padre Osmundo's housekeeper . . . he sent her to keep you company while you are here in town—and also on the long journey to my *estãncia* . . . Alas, we will not be alone together, *gatinha.* Padre Osmundo has seen to that."

Tory wondered if he was telling the truth. She didn't trust him one bit. Yet Padre Osmundo had certainly sent Sebastian Black to get her, and the priest knew better than anyone how lacking in morals and manners Sebastian Black could be. In all probability, he *had* arranged for Carmelita's presence. Despite her misgivings, she would have to trust Sebastian, at least this one time.

"If I arrive at your house and find no one there but us, I'll leave immediately," she warned in her coldest, haughtiest tones.

His sudden laughter rolled through the empty church, making her cringe with embarrassment. It was bad enough they were talking; no one should laugh like that in a church. His lack of respect scandalized her. She scowled at him in disapproval, but that only seemed to add to his amusement.

"*Gatinha,* if you could see yourself! My poor abused little kitten. Never have I witnessed such dark suspicion on such a pretty face."

"Have you no shame?" she hissed. "This is the house of God."

He stopped laughing and gazed scornfully about them, his eyes suddenly hard and distant. "This? A house of God? . . . No, *gatinha,* you are mistaken. This is a monument to greed and oppression. If I could, I would tear it down stone by stone and give the gold to the poor beggars who sit outside on the steps."

His vehemence caught her by surprise. She would never have expected this arrogant, rich *fazendeiro* to make such a comment. Hadn't he scoffed at Padre Osmundo's dedication to the poor? She had not been present at all of the conversations between Sebastian and her brother, but Jordan had told her that Sebastian Black supported the priest's projects grudgingly, if indeed, he supported them at all.

"Come," he urged. "Let us leave this place. It makes my blood boil even to stand here."

There was obviously more to this man than first impressions indicated, she decided. Intrigued and curious, Tory permitted him to take her arm and lead her from the church.

Chapter Six

Sebastian Black's house was barely a ten minute walk from the church. It stood behind a white-washed wall on one of the narrow, twisting streets where the houses all looked alike: pastel-colored with red tile roofs. The gathering darkness prevented Tory from getting a good look at the building, but she noted that it was the color of cream and stood between a pink and a blue house. Then Sebastian was whisking her inside the wrought-iron gate and up a staircase overhung with trailing magenta blossoms from a nearby tree. He flung open the door, and she stepped onto a softly gleaming parquet floor in a narrow hallway that bisected the center of the house. The first room to the right appeared to be the main salon for entertaining guests, and Sebastian steered her straight to it, bellowing over his shoulder as he did so.

"Carmelita! *Vem cá!*"

Tory briefly noted the room's contents. It was austerely furnished with a minimum of dark wooden chairs, a large round table, and a long, low sofa of brown leather. A huge, heavy wooden cross—life-size in its proportions—dominated one wall. Opposite it hung a collection of weapons, pistols, and whips, such as might be used to herd cattle. A leather hat with a turned-up brim hung next to the collection, and framing the whole was a large rosary with enormous carved silver beads.

While she was gaping at the pistols, knives, whips, and rosary, a short, fat woman who could have passed for Padre Osmundo's sister waddled into the room. Dressed in a voluminous red skirt and white, off-the-shoulder blouse, Carmelita was as round as a ball of butter and had merry black eyes, black hair parted in the middle and skimmed back to form a bun at the nape of her neck, and a grin that could melt stone. She enfolded Tory in a rib-cracking embrace, then leaned back to look at her.

"Too skinny!" she pronounced, shaking her head and pursing her lips. "The *professôra* is too skinny, Senhor *Sebastião*. We must fatten her before we take her to Espirito Santo, or else she will fade away before she can teach anybody to read and write."

Professôra meant teacher, Tory knew. She was pleased with herself for understanding the woman's Portuguese and emboldened to test her own mastery of the language. "You must be Carmelita," she said. "I'm so pleased to meet you, especially since I wasn't certain if Sebastian was telling the truth about your presence here."

"Oh, that one . . ." Carmelita rolled her black eyes in the direction of Sebastian. "Never trust a thing he says, *Professôra*. He's a notorious liar when it comes to pretty women. That is why I am here. Padre Osmundo has charged me with protecting your virtue and reputation."

"Ah, but who will protect *your* virtue and reputation, Dona Carmelita?" Sebastian smoothly inquired.

"Surely, if I'm such a rogue, you yourself must beware. I might sneak into your hammock this very night while you are sleeping."

"Humph!" Carmelita snorted. "If you do, you'll be surprised by a few tricks I learned years ago, when I was young and pretty. I know how to handle over-eager young men like you."

"You're still young and pretty, Dona Carmelita," Sebastian gallantly assured her. "And you cook like an angel. You ought to wed again; you're depriving some poor man of a wonderful wife."

A wide grin split Carmelita's round, happy face. "I had one husband, that was enough—God rest his soul. Why should I marry, when I work as hard as any wife looking after Padre Osmundo?"

"Why, indeed?" Sebastian teased. "At least, with Padre Osmundo, you can leave if he bosses you around too much. However, I'll bet he doesn't try . . . You probably box his ears if he gets too pushy."

"No, what I do is burn his dinner."

Listening to their easy banter, Tory decided that staying in Sebastian's house might not be so terrible, after all. She had no doubt that Carmelita could hold her own with Sebastian and then some. And she was even more reassured when the woman took her arm and steered her toward the hallway. "Come, *Professôra* . . . I will show you where you are to sleep. The room can easily accommodate both of us. You shall have the bed, and I will take the hammock."

"Oh, I'd be happy to sleep in the hammock," Tory protested, but Carmelita vehemently shook her head.

"*Professôra,* I am accustomed to sleeping in a hammock, while you are not. You see, I know a little about the habits of *Americanos*. Padre Osmundo told me that in your country, no one sleeps in hammocks. Such a rich place, with beds for everyone! Here, beds are luxuries used mostly by the wealthy, like Senhor *Sebastião*."

"Padre Osmundo also sleeps in a bed, Carmelita," Sebastian reminded the woman. "And perhaps Senhorita *Rei* would like something to eat before you hurry her off to bed. You *did* say she was much too skinny."

"First, the *professôra* will see where she is to sleep, and she can freshen herself, if she likes. *Then* I will feed her," Carmelita announced, brooking no arguments.

Sebastian helplessly spread his hands and said in English: "Padre Osmundo has sent a tyrant to protect you from me, *gatinha* . . . But I will find a way around her vigilance, never fear."

Tory could not suppress a grin as she followed Carmelita down the hallway and into the depths of the long, narrow house. It opened onto a charming inner courtyard, choked with palm trees and flowering plants. Starlight filtering through the tree branches lit the enclosure, and crossing it, Carmelita led Tory to a sturdy wooden door, which she opened with a push of one pudgy hand.

A kerosene lamp on a table illuminated the medium-sized room, revealing the bed, a large wooden clothes cupboard, two chairs, a trunk, and a hammock slung almost directly across the entryway. Carmelita indicated the hammock with a satisfied nod.

"No one will be able to disturb you without disturbing me, *Professôra*. I myself supervised the hanging of that hammock . . . And I will accompany you anywhere you wish to go in Salvador and also on our journey to Paraíso and after that, to Espirito Santo. I take my duties as a chaperone very seriously. Young women cannot be too careful of their reputations, and as Espirito Santo's new teacher, you must be even more cautious and proper."

Tory's relief mingled with a sense of dismay over her sudden loss of freedom; she wondered if she had gained a jailer, rather than a chaperone. No one in her entire life had supervised her this closely. She liked this cheerful, bubbly woman, but wasn't prepared to spend every minute of every day with her. She valued her privacy too much to sacrifice it, even in the interests of her reputation.

Noting the existence of a bare light bulb hanging over the bed, she distracted herself from these grim thoughts by asking about electricity.

"Oh, yes!" Carmelita exclaimed. "Salvador is a modern city. It has electricity like Manaus and Rio de Janeiro."

Curious to see if the exposed wires really carried power, Tory snapped on the wall switch. Nothing happened.

Carmelita grinned sheepishly. "It doesn't work all of the time. We keep lamps and candles about, just in case . . . Now, let me get you a basin of water and some soap and towels. Do you wish to change clothing? Can I help you in any other way?"

Remembering her stolen carpetbag, Tory grimaced. "Could you find a brush, comb, and mirror? I'm afraid I have nothing with me. Everything is still aboard the ship on which I arrived . . . I did bring along a few necessities inside a small carpetbag, but I'm afraid I lost it earlier today."

"You lost it?" Carmelita blinked inquiringly.

"Well . . . My bag was stolen by the young boy who

95

acted as my guide . . . I should never have given it to him in the first place. I think he only ran off with it because I had no Brazilian money to pay for his services. I should have thought to exchange some of my American dollars for cruzeiros before I left the ship, but unfortunately, I didn't.''

Carmelita frowned, her round face indignant. "I will speak to Senhor *Sebastião* about this."

"Oh, no, don't bother! When my baggage arrives from the docks, I'll have everything I need . . . Really. The bag wasn't worth much. I'll hardly miss it." Tory did *not* want Sebastian to learn that she had been victimized on her first day in his country. He would probably give her one of his superior looks and say "I told you so."

"Wait here, *Professôra*. I will return with everything you need for tonight."

Tory sat on the edge of the bed, aware of exhaustion for the first time since she had arrived. She could hardly keep her eyes open, and the prospect of facing Sebastian over dinner seemed less and less attractive. He might note her weariness and remark upon it. The last thing she wanted was for him to detect any fragility in her. Even the slightest hint of weakness would convince him he had been right all along about her inability to cope with life on the *sertão*. Still, things weren't nearly as primitive as she had been led to expect—why, Salvador even had electricity!

Lying back on the bed, she gazed up at the bare bulb suspended from the ceiling. What could it hurt to relax a few moments and rest her eyes? The sweet, heavy air must be what was making her so sleepy; Spencer had cautioned that it might take time to adjust to all the changes in weather, food, and culture. Empty though her stomach was, Tory felt less hungry than she did tired. Yes, a brief rest might revive her, making it possible to endure Sebastian's disturbing company with more equanimity. How that man puzzled her!

If he didn't like churches and wasn't religious, why was such a heavy wooden cross hanging on the wall of his living room? And a rosary? It was the last question she asked herself before closing her eyes. When she opened them again, she was lying on her side, and slants of sunlight were probing the tile roof, revealing gaps between the tiles where water was likely to enter when it rained. Her door was closed and the window shuttered, but she knew it was morning. She sat up with a snort of self-disgust; she'd slept the whole night through!

Carmelita must have taken off her shoes and covered her with a light linen sheet. Carmelita herself had already arisen; the hammock was empty, and on the back of the door hung the woman's red skirt. A pair of sandals stood near the wall, and the promised basin of water, soap, and towels, along with grooming articles, lay neatly arranged on the small table beside the bed.

Tory could hardly breathe for mortification. She had missed dinner and possibly breakfast, leaving no doubt in Sebastian's mind that she wasn't equal to the tasks before her. Jumping off the bed, she started scrubbing her face with a vengeance. Halfway through her efforts to make herself presentable, a smart knock sounded on the door.

"*Gatinha,* are you alive in there?" The mockery in Sebastian's voice was unmistakable. "Should I fetch a doctor? Or do you plan to spend half of every day lying on your back in bed? . . . Not that lying in bed is

97

bad for a person. Indeed, in *your* case, spending more time in bed might improve your disposition—especially if you have company. I'm thinking of myself, of course, as the compa . . ."

"I'm not ill!" Tory shouted, cutting him off mid-sentence.

Heedless of her hair, still in disarray, she yanked open the door. She meant to give him a good set-down for his impertinence, but suddenly face to face with him, she couldn't think of one. He stood there smiling his mocking smile, looking handsome as a Greek god in a white, open-necked shirt, skin-tight black trousers, and boots, which seemed to be a kind of uniform for him. His amber eyes swept her with keen appreciation of her tumbled hair and partially unbuttoned shirtwaist. Angry with herself for having opened the door to him, she clutched at her blouse in an effort to hide the fact that several buttons were undone, but the wicked glint in Sebastian's eye left no doubt that he had already noticed.

He leaned into the doorjamb and folded his arms across his chest. "Do you need any help dressing, *gatinha*? Carmelita is occupied in the kitchen, but I'd be more than happy to help you do—or undo—your buttons."

Tory shut the door on him, but his foot was in the way. She would have stamped on it with her own foot, except she hadn't yet donned her shoes. Sighing, she opened it again. "Mr. Black . . ."

He grinned more widely, showing off his dazzling white teeth. "I thought we were past that, *gatinha* . . . It's Sebastian, remember?"

"*Cochorro*," she said pointedly. "Senhor Dog . . . Aren't you embarrassed to keep trying to seduce me where Carmelita can surely hear you?"

The amber eyes sparkled. "If she does hear us, I will tell her I was merely asking what you wished for breakfast. Have you forgotten? She does not, I'm afraid, understand English."

"I expect she knows what you're saying from your tone—and the knowledge of your sorry character," Tory countered. She raised her voice. "Carmelita? Where are you? Can you hear me?"

There was no response, prompting Tory to inquire: "In which direction might I find the kitchen?"

Sebastian seemed most amused by her eagerness to be reunited with Carmelita. Before she could guess his intent, Sebastian leaned forward and dropped a quick, familial kiss on her nose. "Finish dressing, *gatinha,* and I'll escort you to the dining room and see that you get some breakfast. I wouldn't want to starve you. Carmelita already thinks you are too skinny."

Despite herself, Tory's nose tingled. She also began to wonder if her thinness bothered *him.* "There's no need for you to take time from your busy day to look after me. I'm sure I can hunt down the dining room without your assistance."

"All right. If you insist on being churlish, I'll leave you to your own sense of direction. I myself have already broken my fast . . . But then I rise with the sun. No one in Brazil sleeps past the crowing of the cocks. Obviously, your journey exhausted you. If you find Salvador so fatiguing, I can't imagine how you will survive the *sertão.*"

Tory tossed her hair back over her shoulder in a consciously defiant gesture. "A good night's rest is all I need to survive anything. Don't underestimate me, Mr. Black. I'm much tougher than I look."

The corners of his mouth quirked into a sly grin. "What you look is adorable, *gatinha*—so flushed, radiant, and fresh from your long sleep. Are you sure I cannot help you dress? Perhaps, I could brush your long golden hair. I've been wanting to touch it since the moment I first saw it."

He reached out to twine a strand of it around his finger, but she slapped his hand away. "When I see Padre Osmundo, I'm going to tell him about your bad behavior, so you'd better keep your hands to yourself."

His brows lifted. "What bad behavior? As yet, I've done nothing! Surely, you wouldn't condemn a man merely for his thoughts."

"From the thought to the deed is a very small step," Tory retorted. She had a sudden image of him touching her hair, her waist, her bosom . . . between her legs. A hot flush climbed up her body.

He laughed softly. "I think your thoughts are no more innocent than mine, *gatinha* . . . Our trip to the *sertão* should be very interesting."

"How fortunate that Carmelita is accompanying us when we go," Tory said primly. "And the sooner the better. Will we leave today?"

"Not yet . . . Your baggage has not arrived. Perhaps tomorrow. Today will be a day of rest. Go back to bed if you wish. I'll try not to think less of you for it."

She snorted with annoyance. "I knew you wouldn't let me forget I slept through dinner last night and breakfast this morning."

He tilted his head to one side and regarded her somberly. "I still think you do not belong here, *gatinha*. But I promised Padre Osmundo I'd deliver you safely to his side, so I will do it—no matter what I think."

"Just remember the word 'safely' . . . Will you remove your foot, now, so I can close the door?"

"With regret," he sighed. "With utmost regret."

A half hour later, hungry and curious, Tory left her room. People were chattering beyond the courtyard, and she discovered that a second courtyard adjoined the first through a heavy gate in the back wall. A cooking shed attached to the house overlooked the second courtyard where a score of dirty, smelly people—men, women, and children—sat on long benches or on the ground, avidly eating fresh bread and thick yellow porridge in wooden bowls. A tall black man, better dressed than anyone else in sight, walked among them with a slight look of disdain, his nostrils flaring, as he distributed the fragrant loaves.

Carmelita looked up from a huge black pot as Tory entered the second courtyard. *"Professôra!* What are you doing out here? How did you sleep? Are you hungry? What can I get for you?"

Tory answered the barrage of questions with a few of her own. "Who are all these people, Carmelita? Where did they come from? What are they doing here?"

Carmelita ladled porridge into the wooden bowl of a scrawny child with an enormous, swollen belly. The child wore only a pair of tattered trousers that came to his knees. He was shirtless and barefoot. Sores and scabs covered his stick-like arms and legs. He took the bowl eagerly, retreated a few steps, sat down on the sun-washed cobblestones, and dug into the porridge with his fingers.

"Ah, these poor souls are a few of Salvador's beggars . . ." Carmelita finally said. "I am helping Amâncio to feed them. When they finish here, they will probably go to the churches, sit on the steps, and

101

beg alms of the worshippers. Or perhaps they'll go down to the marketplace."

"Amâncio? Who is Amâncio?" Tory's gaze swept the crowd. More beggars were entering by a gate in the back of the second courtyard. They pushed in urgently, their eyes fastened upon the bread the tall Negro was distributing.

Carmelita nodded toward the black man. "That is Amâncio. The bread he bought this morning is almost gone, but I saved some for you. I was going to bring bread, coffee, milk, and some of this *couscous* to the dining room for you. You do not need to eat out here among the beggars; it isn't healthy. Many of these poor creatures are ill."

"I can see that," Tory said, eyeing the many sores, fever-glazed eyes, crippled legs and arms, and other deformities. These people were the flotsam and jetsam of humanity, yet still they chattered among themselves, greeted one another, and exchanged often toothless grins. They also belched, broke wind, and scratched their filthy bodies. Tory was repelled, even as she felt sympathy for them.

She saw a woman holding a tiny baby to her bared breast for nursing, but the infant looked too sick and weak to suckle. It mouthed the woman's breast for a moment, whimpered, then tossed its head restlessly from side to side. Tory strode over to the pair and sank down to her knees beside them.

"What is wrong with your baby?" she asked.

The woman stared at her a moment, as if she didn't understand. Tory repeated the question, and the woman answered stiltedly. "She sick."

"How long has she been sick?" Tory persisted. "What are her symptoms?"

The woman shrugged, seeming more interested in Tory's blond hair. "Pretty *loura*," she murmured,

102

reaching up a clawed hand to touch it.

The baby whimpered again. Tory held out her arms. "Give her to me. If you don't mind, I'd like to look at her. Perhaps she needs a doctor."

Just then, a shadow fell across Tory and the woman, blocking out the bright sunlight. *"Gatinha, do not touch that child. Come away from here. This is no place for you."*

Tory looked up to see Sebastian looming over her. Shading her eyes, she saw that he was scowling. "This baby is sick," she informed him, wondering why he should be angry. "In fact, half the people here have something wrong with them. We must help them, not just feed them."

"These people are not your problem, *gatinha*. You came to teach the peasants at Padre Osmundo's school. These beggars are no concern of yours."

Tory stood, thinking he hadn't heard her properly. "Sebastian, this baby needs a doctor. Everyone here needs a doctor. Why haven't you done something to get medical care for them?"

"Don't lecture me on my responsibilities, *gatinha*." Sebastian's amber eyes were hard as glass. "Leave this courtyard at once. I should have told you before not to come out here."

Tory was astounded, then furious. "Why shouldn't I come out here? What are you trying to hide? I'm pleased that you feed the beggars; I only wish you'd fetch a doctor for them as well."

"I *don't* feed the beggars. This is all Carmelita's doings. She does not have my permission. She and Amâncio have taken it upon themselves to waste my food on the city's scum."

"The city's scum! Is that what you think of these poor people?" Tory could not believe her ears.

"I will show you what I think of them, *gatinha*."

They had been speaking to each other in English, but now Sebastian began shouting in Portuguese. Moving away from her, he startled everyone with his booming voice. "Out! Get out of here! Leave my courtyard at once! Tell your friends and relatives: *Sebastião Prêto* feeds no more beggars. You're not to come here again!"

Utter silence descended on the courtyard. At first, the beggars looked stunned and disbelieving. But as the words sunk in, they bowed their heads in a collective attitude of defeat, and sullenly, fearfully, began to depart, taking the bread with them, but leaving the wooden bowls on the cobblestones.

When the last one had scurried out through the back gate, Tory confronted Sebastian, hands on hips. "I can't believe you did that."

He stared back at her as hard as she was staring at him. "Believe it, *gatinha*. And be sure to tell your friend, Padre Osmundo."

"He won't believe it, either. Why do you help the peasants, but send the beggars away hungry? I *know* you help them; some of the money used to build Padre Osmundo's new school came from you. Or so my brother told me. You are not exactly enthusiastic about your charity, but you *do* donate to the cause."

"It's Padre Osmundo I help, not these poor scraps of humanity who are better off dead than alive. This is a harsh land, and only the harsh can survive. I have no time nor inclination to personally look after peasants or beggars. Believe me when I tell you that what happened here this morning will not be repeated."

Tory's eyes stung; she felt on the verge of tears but was more angry than sad. He couldn't really be as heartless as he sounded—could he? His behavior simply didn't make sense. Maybe his male pride prevented him from openly showing compassion in front of others. Or maybe he really did despise the peasants and beggars. She would have to ask Padre Osmundo; the priest seemed to know him better than anyone, maybe better than he knew himself. She would also ask Carmelita—and the Negro, Amâncio, who was silently picking up the wooden bowls.

"I will see you this evening at dinner." Sebastian bowed slightly and slanted her a mocking glance as he turned to leave. "Unless of course, you're too tired to join me."

Chapter Seven

It took two hours for Sebastian to make the rounds of the beggars' stations throughout the city. At each one, he slipped handfuls of *cruzeiros* to those needing medicine or a doctor's attention, then reassured each person that they were welcome to eat their meals at his house for as long as he remained in town. He did, however, insist upon two things: They must enter and depart the back courtyard silently, staying only as long as necessary, and they must tell no one of his generosity.

If asked, they were to claim that his servants had been feeding them without his knowledge. In exchange for their cooperation, he promised to distribute small sums of money to tide them over until his return to the city when he left for his *estância*. Their expressions of gratitude indicated that this was an unnecessary incentive to insure their silence, but Sebastian couldn't take any chances that word of his charity might leak out. Also, he wanted to ease their minds that they wouldn't go hungry, if begging brought in too little money to enable them to survive. As he well knew, the line between survival and starvation was a thin one indeed.

All the while he was tramping the city, Sebastian cursed himself for allowing Tory to find out that he was secretly feeding Salvador's poor and homeless. The last thing he wanted was for her to tell Padre Osmundo or anyone else she might chance to meet. He had already sworn Carmelita and Amâncio to silence, and he had confidence that they would never betray him. But Tory was an unknown quantity. She might blab the truth to all and sundry, alerting his enemies that he wasn't what he appeared to be—a hard-hearted, rich man who hated the Falcon every bit as much as they did.

Once his sympathies for the poor became common knowledge, someone was bound to connect him to the Falcon. The only reason he had started feeding the town's beggars in the first place was that Salvador was big enough, the gap between rich and poor wide enough, that he could be reasonably certain no one would ever find out. At his ranch, he never took such risks. All his efforts to help the poor peasants on the *sertão* were channeled through Padre Osmundo, either from the Falcon in the form of anonymous donations, or from his grudging contributions as Sebastian Black. Even the peasants in Espirito Santo could only guess at the extent to which he had helped to build the new school. In order to further confuse everyone, he was careful to speak and act as other *fazendeiros* did, as if he had no time or patience with the problems of those beneath him, never having experienced crushing poverty himself.

Nothing taught a man compassion for the hungry like hunger pains in his own belly, he bitterly mused.

When Sebastian completed his rounds of the beggars' stations, he made one last stop at a small booth in the marketplace, where a handsome Negress was frying *acarajé*, a batter of beans mashed together

107

with shrimp and onion, in hot dende oil. A descendant of the African slaves brought in by the Portuguese to work the cane fields, the woman was a prime example of the striking *Baianas* who made the city so diverse, colorful, and interesting. The necklaces draping her ample bosom identified the African gods she still worshiped, and he knew from past experience that very little in Salvador escaped her watchful eye. If anyone could help him locate Tory's stolen carpetbag—which Carmelita had told him about—it was Florzinha, who also happened to be a high priestess of *macumba,* the religion practiced by many of Salvador's ex-slaves.

"Florzinha, I need your help. . . ." he said without preamble.

At sight of him, Florzinha's ever-present smile widened into a huge grin. "Of course, Senhor *Prêto.* I'm always happy to help a man who does so much for the city's poor."

Sebastian frowned. Florzinha never came to his house to eat—she made a living selling not only her pastries but also charms, love potions, and religious rites. He didn't like it that she spoke so openly of his generosity.

"Whatever I do will cease immediately if certain people in the city find out about it. They would consider my modest attempts to be charitable as a sign of weakness. I'm a rancher and businessman; in my position, I can't afford to appear too tenderhearted."

"Charity shows a man's strength, not his weakness," Florzinha argued, her black eyes darkening. "But do not fear, Senhor *Prêto.* Not a tenth of what I know passes my lips. I keep secrets men would kill to learn."

108

Sebastian studied her silently for a moment, wondering if she knew who he really was, and if this was her way of telling him. But how could she know? The Falcon was only a legend in the city; Sebastian confined all his activities as a bandit to the *sertão*. He never stole from the rich in town—not even from Mundinho Cerqueira, who kept a house here the same as he did. *Cangaçeiros* never left the *sertão;* they lived and died on the dry, arid ranges, born in the cloying red dust and dying with their mouths and eyes full of it.

"Perhaps you know a secret about a carpetbag stolen from a guest of mine," Sebastian prodded.

Florzinha cocked her head. "No, but I'm sure I could find out."

"Please try. I'll reward you well."

"Where you are concerned, no reward is necessary, Senhor. If I recover the bag, I will send it to your house . . . Now, tell me about this bag."

Sebastian told her what he could. Never having seen the item, he could not describe it, but as soon as he mentioned that his guest was an *Americana,* Florzinha knew who she was. Her eyes lit with recollection.

"I saw the girl waiting on the docks yesterday morning. She's a pretty *loura,* is she not?"

Sebastian nodded. A *very* pretty blonde, he thought, with the sweetest body he'd ever lusted after. "She arrived by ship yesterday afternoon," he confirmed. "The boy who guided her to the *Igreja de São Francisco* ran off with the bag when she couldn't pay him."

Florzinha sighed and tossed her turbaned head. "That would be a young scamp named Antônio. I know him well—an enterprising lad. He's managed

109

to wheedle *aracajé* from me in the past . . . I thought there might be trouble when I saw him lead her away from the docks."

"Can you recover the bag, Florzinha?"

"It should not be too difficult—providing Antônio has not yet disposed of it. I will see what can be done. The boy's afraid of evil spells, so I think he'll be most cooperative when I threaten to make his toes shrivel and fall off if he doesn't hand it over."

"I thought you never used your powers for evil, Florzinha." Chuckling to himself, Sebastian pressed a few worn bills into her hand. "Take this, and use it for some good."

Florzinha grinned and tucked the money into the bodice of her white blouse. "If God wills, the bag will be in your hands by tonight."

After he left Florzinha, Sebastian strolled the noisy, smelly marketplace purchasing supplies for the journey to his ranch. Amâncio could come later with the wagon and pick up everything—along with Tory's baggage, if it wasn't delivered before then. When he had completed his business, he made his way up a narrow, twisted street to a house he visited frequently whenever he was in Salvador.

The door opened on his first knock, and he was engulfed in a flower-scented embrace by a tall woman of faded, voluptuous charms who exclaimed with delight the moment she laid eyes on him. "Senhor *Prêto!* How wonderful to see you again . . . I'll tell Otália you are here! She'll be so pleased."

Already knowing that Otália would take a half hour to make herself more beautiful than nature intended, Sebastian requested that a bottle of *cachaça* be brought to him in the inner courtyard. While the woman scurried away to fetch both bottle and Otália, he sat down on a wrought iron chair in the

110

lacy shade of a large banana tree. An hour alone with Otália should make it easier to endure Tory's irresistably seductive company on the long journey to Paraíso; Otália's lush body could ease any man's frustrations.

As Salvador's leading prostitute, Otália entertained only a select few clients—Sebastian among them—in her own house overseen by the ex-madam of the lower-class establishment where Otália had first gotten her start in the business. Sebastian had once tried to make her his own private mistress, but she had refused. He spent too much time on his ranch, she had prettily pouted, unaware that much of his time was spent robbing Mundinho Cerqueira and other rich, powerful landowners who also enjoyed her favors.

When the bottle of *canchaça* arrived, Sebastian poured a glassful and took a sip of the fiery cane liquor, letting it slide down his throat with deep appreciation. The ex-madam hurried off to help her mistress dress, and Sebastian leaned back in the chair to let his muscles relax. He had been wound tighter than a watch spring ever since Tory's arrival—indeed, since he'd seen her standing in the dimly-lit church, the very picture of false innocence, which in no way concealed her blatant provocativeness and sensuality. For reasons he couldn't fathom, the mere sight of her made his blood rush through his veins, so that all he could think about was seducing her—loosening and rumpling that long, golden hair, kissing those tender lips until she collapsed against him in complete surrender, and finally, undressing and exploring every inch of that slender, delicate, refined, feminine body.

She affected him in ways he hadn't felt for a woman in a long, long time, if indeed he had ever felt

111

this slow, burning fever to possess and ravish a female he otherwise hardly knew. Before Otália, Sebastian had known many women, including some from whom he was lucky not to have caught the pox. Fortunately, Otália exercised rigid standards of cleanliness and insisted that her lovers be free of disease. She did not, however, touch him emotionally. Nor had any of the women with whom he'd enjoyed his previous carnal associations.

Only his mother had ever owned an integral part of Sebastian; the reality of her violent death still jolted him occasionally from a sound sleep or caused nightmares in which he became a child again, crying and calling out for her, sobbing because she could no longer comfort him in the dead of night . . . Of course, he mourned his father, too, but somehow, the loss of his mother struck him where he was most vulnerable. Only the deaths of his illegitimate children had come close to affecting him so profoundly, but their deaths had been easier to overcome, probably because he had cared so little for their mothers.

Never again did he want to experience such searing pain and loneliness. So never again would he let *any* woman get that close to him. Otália suited him perfectly; she scorned personal commitment every bit as much as he did, taking her pleasure when and where she found it, and demanding only money in return. Best of all, she seemed unable to conceive children. Had she borne him a child, that would have given her a power over him, whether he wanted it or not.

He reviewed her many charms while he waited. She was the very opposite of Tory King—dark where Tory was fair, curvacious where Tory was slender and delicate-boned, honey-voiced where Tory was

112

rapier-tongued and critical, pliant and willing where Tory resisted her own desires and thwarted him at every turn . . . Why was he wasting time thinking about Tory King when he was about to experience every man's erotic fantasy? he wondered disgustedly.

It galled him that he should lust after the feisty blond woman with an intensity that Otália had rarely aroused in him—Otália who was everything Tory King was not. Otália could—and would—do things that Tory only hinted at, then primly refused. Tory's primness greatly exasperated him, especially since he knew it was all an act. Who did she think she was kidding? Maybe her foolish, naive brother believed she was still a virgin, but . . .

"*Sebastião!* How are you, *meu amado?*"

Sebastian looked up from his *cachaça* to find Otália standing before him in a long diaphanous gown that floated enticingly away from her breasts and hips as she sank to her knees before him.

"Too long you have not been to see me, *Sebastião,*" the lovely young woman pouted, running her pink tongue along her lower lip. "Too long have you denied Otália the exquisite pleasure of making love to you."

Moving as languidly as a cat uncurling itself in the sunshine, she dipped her dark head and nuzzled between his thighs. At her touch, Sebastian groaned and opened his knees, trapping her between them. Then he leaned back and regarded her through slitted eyes. When he looked at her that way, with the filtered sunlight bathing her black hair, he could almost imagine that she was blonde—almost picture Tory King locked between his legs, her breath hot in his lap, her eyes promising untold delights . . . *Cristo!* Now, the impudent *Americana* was intruding upon his idyl with Otália!

113

He pushed back his chair and stood, almost knocking Otália over. She lifted her head and gazed at him in surprise. The color on her lips was too red, he saw, too garish to be real. And her face no longer seemed quite as beautiful as he remembered it. The nipples of her full breasts protruded through the sheer fabric of her gown, but rather than attracting him, he suddenly found both her attire and her manner crass and calculated. She was nothing but a cheap little whore, the plaything of any man who could pay for the privilege, and she was way over-priced, at that.

"Sorry, Otália, but this time, you've kept me waiting too long," he snapped. "I've just remembered an important appointment."

She reached up and boldly grasped him where only a moment before he'd been hard and ready for her. "What could be more important than *this, Sebastião?*"

There had been a time when nothing could have persuaded Sebastian to leave at such a moment. Now he could think of a hundred pressing reasons why he couldn't remain. He would never admit that Tory King might be one of those reasons, but neither could he deny that she seemed to be there in the courtyard, watching everything with her clear, gray-green eyes.

"I'll be back," he promised, breaking away from Otália. "Don't worry, I'll most definitely be back."

But he wondered as he left the house whether or not he would be, ever again. He didn't think so.

Tory's baggage arrived in the late afternoon. Joyfully, she changed into cool, clean clothing—a soft, feminine shirtwaist blouse, and a lightweight linen skirt—before dinner. She brushed her hair until it

114

gleamed like yellow cornsilk, then gathered and pinned it into a simple, yet elegant pompadour, after which she went to the dining room for the evening meal. Carmelita was there, looking disgusted and disappointed.

"I don't know where Senhor *Sebastião* is," the plump little woman huffed. "He should be home by now. The meal is ready."

Tory didn't know whether to be glad or relieved. She eyed the two solitary place settings at the big wooden table with some annoyance. "Why don't we forget about Senhor Sebastian, and you and Amâncio come sit down and eat with me? I'd love some company." *But not necessarily Sebastian's,* she added silently.

"Oh, no, *Professôra* . . . Amâncio and I have already eaten. We take our biggest meal at noon and only a small one in the evening. That is the custom here. Senhor *Sebastião* requested this dinner especially for you, since you eat differently in your own country . . . But perhaps he forgot about it."

"*Ordered* it is more likely, you mean. And from now on, I'll follow *your* customs. No more special dinners for me, Carmelita."

"*Sim, Professôra,* if that is your wish. Will you eat without Senhor *Sebastião?* I have made *feijoada,* a favorite dish in this part of the country."

Tory pulled out a chair and sat down. "I would love some *feijoada.*"

She dined alone on the delicious dinner, a kind of stew combining black beans and various unidentifiable meats served over rice. There were side dishes of chopped tomatoes, onions, and green peppers in vinegar, and a grainy, powdery substance that reminded her of sawdust. Mixed with the chopped vegetables, the sawdust-like dish was palatable, though less agreeable than the main course. With the meal, Carmelita served what she called a *bebida*, a sticky, sweet juice from a fruit Tory had never before tasted.

Sometime during the meal, someone came to the front door, but Carmelita did not announce who it was, so upon completing the meal, Tory left the table and headed for her room. Since she hadn't seen Sebastian at dinner, she hoped to avoid him altogether. She still felt angry over what he had done that morning—sending the beggars away untended, before they had even finished eating. Neither Carmelita nor Amâncio had been able to shed any light on this perplexing, cruel behavior.

Carmelita had only said: "Senhor *Sebastião* is a strange man, *Professôra*—one moment kind and teasing, making everyone laugh, and the next, quiet and brooding, full of mystery and silence. Amâncio was making the *couscous*, so I helped him this morning, but whether he feeds the beggars *every* morning, I do not know."

When Tory had asked Amâncio about it, the tall Negro had been too shy to answer. He would only grunt, and all his grunts sounded like the answer, no, or, I don't know. Tory had been very frustrated. Opening the door to her room, she saw that Carmelita had already lit the lantern on the table—the electricity apparently not working tonight, either—and something was lying on her bed.

Recognizing her carpetbag, Tory uttered a startled cry and snatched it up. She opened it and discovered that not a thing was missing, not even her American money. "Carmelita?" she called, exiting the room at a fast walk with the carpetbag in her arms.

In the dimly-lit courtyard, she almost ran into Sebastian. He grabbed her by the shoulder to keep her

116

from flying past him. *"Gatinha,* what is it?" His eyes went to the carpetbag. "Ah, I see that your bag has been returned. I'm glad. I did what I could to get it back for you. Was everything still intact?"

Tory eyed his knowing grin suspiciously. "Yes, everything is here. But how did you find it? How did you even know it was missing?"

"Carmelita told me... How I found it is, of course, none of your business. Let us just say that I can find anything in the city within a matter of hours."

"Then I'm indebted to you once again, first for rescuing me from the church and inviting me to stay here, now for finding my bag ... I suppose I must get used to being indebted to you, since you'll soon add to the list by taking me and Carmelita to Padre Osmundo."

He stepped closer to her, backing her into a small potted palm tree. He always seemed to be backing her into something, she thought distractedly. "Since you feel so indebted," he purred, "why don't you show your gratitude? I'd be happy to accept a kiss in payment."

Tory felt suddenly breathless, as she usually felt in his presence. "Why is it that I much prefer giving you kicks instead of kisses, Senhor *Prêto?"*

"I wish I knew, *gatinha."* He shook his head and expelled a long, exaggerated sigh. "Probably it's for the same reason that you insist on calling me Senhor *Prêto,* instead of *Sebastião* or Sebastian ... I'd almost prefer you call me *cochorro* permanently; at least it's not so formal."

"All right ... I christen you Senhor *Cochorro,* dog, a fitting name for someone who snatches food away from hungry people."

"You're still angry about this morning." He

117

cocked a well-shaped eyebrow and regarded her quizzically.

"Yes, and puzzled . . . puzzled most of all."

He lifted his hand and ran a finger down the side of her cheek. "Forget about this morning, *gatinha*. It wasn't important. Forget everything but permitting me to kiss you. I kissed you once, and I haven't been able to erase that kiss from my memory. Surely, you haven't forgotten it either. It was a most wonderful experience."

His amber eyes held her prisoner, and the memory of that first kiss flooded her like a burning tidal wave. "I don't remember that kiss at all."

"Yes, you do . . . Here, let me remind you of the deep emotions it stirred." He leaned forward and brushed his lips gently across hers.

She stood transfixed, every muscle frozen in place. His lips were warm and firm upon hers, gently coaxing, urging her to return the kiss. She parted her lips the merest fraction—in order to breathe better—and he took advantage by making small nibbling motions along her lower lip. The nibbles could not be called rough or harsh, but they awoke a fluttering feeling in the pit of her stomach. How well she remembered that wild fluttering!

He nibbled his way all around her mouth. She tasted whiskey or brandy on his lips and inhaled the wonderful male scent of him—an enticing mixture of soap, leather, and sunshine. Then he touched his tongue to hers, and the intimacy jolted her clear to her toes, just as it had the first time. He used his tongue playfully at first, darting it into every corner of her mouth. Then he thrust it rapidly back and forth, at the same time moving his hips so that she felt his arousal, hard and throbbing, against the juncture of her thighs.

She swayed against him, filled with the familiar treacherous weakness engendered by his first kiss five months ago. This was how it must feel to drown, she thought, to sink down, down, down into nothingness. But it wasn't a void into which she was falling; rather, it was a pulsating whirlpool of pleasure in which his tongue, his kiss, and the hardness of his body called forth responses within her own body that she struggled helplessly to control.

Every nerve ending seemed on fire. Several layers of cloth separated his flesh from hers, but she felt every movement as if they were both naked. His hands encircled her waist, then slid lower to cup her bottom. He pulled her into him, pressing her against that hot, hard part of himself that was purely, animalistically male ... Her breasts ached and tingled; moisture dampened her underdrawers. She moaned in the back of her throat. To her great embarrassment, he raised his head, broke the contact of their mouths, and chuckled softly.

"Come, *gatinha* ... I will take you to my room. There, we can be sure of privacy while we continue this delightful interlude."

Aghast at herself, she pushed away from him. "No! ... I'm going to my own room, and you aren't coming with me ... Carmelita! Carmelita, where are you?"

"*Professôra?*" called a muffled voice from inside the house. "One moment, and I will be there with you."

"Ah, *gatinha* ..." He sighed mournfully. "How long do you intend to keep fighting this attraction we have between us?"

"This isn't an attraction! It's ... it's a sickness, that's what it is!"

"Perhaps, you are right ..." Sebastian solemnly

119

agreed. His lips twitched as he glanced down rue-fully at the huge bulge in the front of his snug trousers. "Kissing you certainly leaves me in a most painful condition. I can hardly endure the discomfort."

Tory flamed from head to foot, amazed that he would dare call attention to . . . to . . .

He laughed when he saw her expression. "Is that shyness that reddens your cheeks, *gatinha?* How can that be possible—a sophisticated female like you? . . . You know precisely what you do to me; it's useless to pretend otherwise. Enjoy your power, *gatinha,* but one day I promise you, I'll demonstrate the power I have over *you* . . ."

Tory didn't know exactly what he meant, but she could make an excellent guess. Under the influence of his kisses, she couldn't seem to resist anything he wanted to do to her. Whirling on her heel, she sought the safety of her room as fast as her trembling legs could carry her.

Chapter Eight

Tory was awakened early next morning by Carmelita shaking her shoulder. *"Professôra,* wake up! Today, we are leaving for Senhor *Sebastião's* ranch."

"Wonderful," Tory mumbled, yawning and rubbing her eyes. "I'll be glad to see Padre Osmundo again and to finally start teaching."

"Hurry and dress, *Professôra.* I'll bring your breakfast to the dining room."

Once on her feet, Tory washed, dressed, and did her hair with a speed that set a new record for her. She didn't want to keep Sebastian waiting. Maybe he was already eating his breakfast, eager to get started and chafing at delay. She hurried to the dining room, encountering no one on the way. The table held only a single place setting, and Carmelita was not in sight.

Too anxious to wait, Tory went looking for her in the cook shed. As she approached the gate in the wall of the courtyard, she heard muffled sounds on the other side. This time, instead of barging in unannounced, she tiptoed to the gate and furtively opened it a crack. The same beggars who had been there yesterday were there again today—eating quickly and quietly, obviously making an enormous effort to keep their presence a secret.

Tory put her eye to the crack and watched Amâncio distributing not bread this time, but small pouches that jingled and clanked, as if they held coins. Fearful of discovery, Tory spied on the scene for only a moment before retreating to the dining room to await Carmelita . . . She had no wish to get Carmelita and the tall Negro in trouble. Sebastian would be furious if he found out that they were continuing to help the beggars in blatant disregard of his orders.

As she remembered Sebastian's callousness of the day before, Tory's anger sprouted anew. Why should his servants have to sneak around in order to feed the poor from his great abundance? She was ashamed of her fascination for such a cold-hearted man—and for allowing him to treat her with so little respect. She didn't even like the arrogant Brazilian, yet she had permitted him to take shameless liberties with her! Well, if he thought he was going to steal any more kisses on the journey to his ranch, he could think again. She wouldn't give him the opportunity.

By noon, they were ready to leave—Sebastian, Carmelita, Amâncio, and Tory herself. Tory was pleased that Amâncio would be accompanying them. The presence of one more person on the trip would make it doubly difficult for Sebastian to get her alone. She marched confidently out of the house but came to a skidding stop when she saw how they were going to travel. A heavy-laden cart pulled by two oxen awaited her outside in the street. Amâncio and Carmelita were already aboard, sitting side by side on the single seat. Carmelita was arranging her blue skirt to make room for Tory.

"Where are *you* going to sit?" Tory asked Sebastian who was waiting to help her into the cart. "That seat isn't big enough to hold two more."

"I'm riding Renegade," Sebastian smoothly informed her.

He nodded to the big bay horse tied to the back of the cart. Tory's eyes widened. She had forgotten all about Renegade—hadn't even thought to ask how the horse was doing. It had simply not occurred to her that Renegade and the colt Sebastian had bought from Jordan might be here in the city, instead of at Sebastian's ranch. The colt, however, was nowhere in sight.

"Renegade won't behave for you," she warned. "He'll throw you off before we get out of Salvador."

"No, he won't, *gatinha*. Renegade and I have reached an understanding. I don't abuse him if he doesn't abuse me."

"My brother and I never abused him," Tory snorted. "But he still never gave us a decent ride. On these narrow, busy streets, you'll be lucky if he doesn't kill you—or some poor bystander."

Sebastian regarded her smugly. "You and your brother did not know how to handle him. He's a very special horse who requires an abundance of discipline mixed, of course, with an equal amount of affection. In that, he resembles some women I know."

Tory wanted to smack the smirk right off Sebastian's face. However, she restrained herself, knowing she could depend on Renegade to humiliate him soon enough. "I'll be interested to see how you handle him when he dumps you on your backside on the cobblestones," she coolly responded.

Tory climbed into the cart without Sebastian's

assistance, Sebastian mounted Renegade, and Amân-cio got the oxen moving without further delay. As the huge beasts lumbered through the narrow, twisting streets, heading out of town, Tory tried to keep her attention on the sights, smells, and sounds of Salvador, but her eyes kept straying to Sebastian astride the big bay. Renegade exhibited perfect manners, behaving as docilely as an old plug mule. To her amazement and chagrin, he paid no attention whatever to the traffic, noise, and congestion of the streets.

Tory wondered if he was the same horse she had known at Castle Acres. Several times, Sebastian caught her eye and grinned, at the same time giving Renegade an indulgent pat on the neck as a reward for his flawless performance. Much impressed, Tory refused to show it; Sebastian could wait forever if he expected compliments from her. She noted the gleam of Renegade's coat, the excellent condition of his hooves, and the play of sleek muscles that indicated supreme fitness. She hated to admit it, but Renegade had never looked better in his life. She supposed she would have to write Jordan and tell him how well the horse was doing—but she would die before she would ever praise Sebastian himself for producing these remarkable changes in the once stubborn, unmanageable beast.

Fastening her eyes on the slow-moving rumps of the cream-colored oxen, Tory schooled herself to maintain a neutral expression. Hours later, she was still staring at the oxen's rumps and about to fall asleep from boredom and exhaustion. Ignoring Sebastian had proven more tedious and difficult than she had anticipated.

"We'll stop and make camp here for the night," Sebastian announced, riding up beside Amâncio.

"We've gotten a decent start on our journey. Tomorrow when we're fresh will be soon enough to tackle the *sertão.*"

Tory jerked fully awake and blinked at her surroundings. The land was still lush, green, and hilly, dotted with palm trees, not at all the wasteland she had expected. Here, the red earth still offered sustenance in the form of scattered, wild fruit trees yielding bananas, mangoes, and large, round fruits with bumpy, greenish-black exteriors. The golden light of evening bathed everything in a radiant glow, producing a rare beauty, as Amâncio stopped the cart beneath a cluster of palm trees some distance from the rutted track that served as a road.

"Good thing this isn't the rainy season," Sebastian commented, lightly dismounting from Renegade. "It's almost impossible to travel the countryside during winter. The roads are too muddy and in some places, washed away entirely."

"I didn't realize we'd been traveling on a road," Tory sniffed, not about to reveal her admiration for the country to this rude, arrogant Brazilian. "What you call roads hereabouts hardly qualify as paths back home. Will we stay on this track all the way to Paraíso?"

Sebastian shook his head. "Once we reach the *sertão,* there are few roads as good as this one. Enjoy the land's benevolence while you can, *gatinha.* The *sertão* doesn't offer palm trees for shade."

Tory thought he was just trying to scare her, and she regretted having mentioned the poor condition of the road. "Well, it will be winter soon anyway, and then it should be cooler on the *sertão.*"

Sebastian snorted. "Winter? No, *gatinha.* Soon, it will be summer. Our seasons are the reverse of yours.

125

Christmas heralds the hottest, driest time of year, while June, July, and August bring heavy rains—except during times of drought, of course."

Tory stretched her stiff legs and crawled down from the cart with as much dignity as she could muster. "Oh, yes, I had forgotten," she admitted sheepishly.

She wiped a film of perspiration from her forehead with the palm of her hand. It seemed hotter already—especially beneath Sebastian's mocking, amused gaze.

"Amâncio and I will have dinner prepared shortly, Senhor *Sebastião*," Carmelita chirped, scrambling down behind her.

"I'll help . . ." Tory offered. She was willing to do anything to keep busy so she wouldn't have to make conversation with Sebastian.

"No, no, *Professôra* . . . You must rest from the journey. Amâncio and I will see to everything. Here . . . let me get a basin of water so you can bathe your face and hands."

"Carmelita, I can get it myself. You must stop treating me like an invalid. I've been meaning to talk to you about that ever since I arrived."

Carmelita looked affronted. "I do not treat you like a sick person, *Professôra* . . . I am showing respect. You are a *professôra*, not a simple *empregada*, like me. I will not try to do your job if you will not try to do mine."

Carmelita began rummaging in the back of the cart, leaving Tory to deal with a slyly grinning Sebastian.

"You've insulted her, *gatinha*," he softly informed her. "Don't you realize it makes her feel important to be taking care of you?"

126

"Well, it makes *me* feel useless and inept. What does *empregada* mean? I don't know the word."

"Servant—or perhaps, maid, you would call it. Amâncio is an *empregado,* with an 'o' instead of an 'a' at the end, meaning a male servant . . . Shall I instruct you further in my language? I fancy myself a teacher, too—though you probably think you already know all there is to learn. Certainly, you've made great progress in mastering Portuguese since we first met in the United States."

"My vocabulary and my accent are improving daily, Senhor *Cochorro,* but there are still many words I don't understand. If you teach as well as you boast, I should be as fluent as Padre Osmundo by the time we reach your ranch."

Sebastian burst out laughing. "I teach even *better* than I boast. If I really put my mind to it, I'm sure I can have you sounding like a native by then . . . and doing other things as well."

Tory decided not to ask him what *other* things he had in mind. She thoughtfully measured him. As much as she tried to fight her attraction to this man, every inch of Sebastian Black delighted her eyes, and his laughter sounded most pleasant. "Why don't we begin improving my Portuguese right now?" she challenged. "Every time I make a mistake, you must correct me."

"All right . . . What do you call the washbasin Carmelita has readied for you?" Sebastian indicated the metal pan Carmelita was holding out to Tory. It held water taken from a barrel on the cart.

Tory said the word she thought meant pan, and Sebastian nodded approvingly. "Very good, *gatinha.* Now, what do you call water and towels?"

"That's easy. *Agua* and *toalhas.*"

127

"Ah, you have translated correctly, but your pronunciation could use improvement." He repeated the words with the proper inflection and made her do the same until she got it right. Then he paused and pointed to the pan. "You'd better wash now, *gatinha*. Carmelita is waiting, and it grows late. We can continue the lesson another time."

Tory hated to quit, but consoled herself that at least he had referred to future sessions. She couldn't help wishing that improving her Portuguese might become the safe topic of conversation she had been looking for, something that distracted Sebastian from trying to seduce her and also provided the opportunity to get to know him better.

While Carmelita held the basin, Tory splashed water on her face and hands. Red grime washed away, suggesting that her blonde hair must by now be titian. Carmelita handed her a towel, and Tory gratefully dried herself. When she was finished, Carmelita offered the basin to Sebastian who began washing in the same water.

"Don't do that!" Tory cried. "You should have clean water."

Sebastian gleefully flicked a few droplets on her before dousing his face with the reddish-colored liquid. "Impossible. We dare not waste water this close to the *sertão*."

"But what you're doing isn't sanitary."

Shaking water from his fingers, Sebastian gave her a look that was most definitely a leer. "Perhaps not, but I enjoy using an element that has first touched your lovely skin. When we get to my ranch, you may take a complete bath—and I shall take one immediately after, unless by some miracle, you prefer to take one at the same time."

Here we go again, Tory thought. Back to what Sebastian does best—being naughty and incorrigible.

She darted a quick glance at Carmelita. "You're certain Carmelita doesn't understand English?"

"Absolutely certain, *gatinha*. Feel free to say yes; she'll never know what you're promising."

Tory smiled her most charming smile, but spoke between gritted teeth. "I'd rather walk naked through Espirito Santo than share a bath with a vile, low-minded, over-sexed ox like you. It's impossible even to carry on a decent conversation with you."

Carmelita caught the word for ox and looked askance at the two big beasts Amâncio was busily unyoking. *"Boi?"* she questioned.

"That's the word for ox," Sebastian helpfully supplied.

"And what are the words for vile, low-minded, and over-sexed?" Tory sweetly inquired.

"Ah, let me see, now . . . Vile means . . . *brioso.*"

"Brioso?" Tory experimentally rolled the word off her tongue. "You are very *brioso,*" she announced.

Carmelita's round face beamed. *"Sīm.* Senhor *Sebastião esta muito brioso."*

"She agrees with me!" Tory crowed. "Now, teach me the words for low-minded and over-sexed."

"You wish to shock poor Carmelita? No, *gatinha,* I will teach you no more words you may use to insult me."

"Then never mind. *Brioso* describes you accurately enough."

"I'd like to teach you other words that apply to me as well . . ." Sebastian taunted in his velvet voice. "Words like tender, passionate, irresistible . . ."

"Don't bother . . . I wouldn't feel right using them to refer to you . . . Unless it's completely unavoidable, I almost never lie."

"Nor do I want you to tell falsehoods, *gatinha*. I prefer that you *lie*—as in lie down with me. It's what you want, too—only you've been lying to yourself about it."

Tory heaved a huge sigh of exasperation. So much for putting Sebastian in his place! Matching wits with him was enough to give a woman a monumental headache. Every word led in one direction, but by the time she divined his intentions, it was too late to change the subject. "Enough!" she snapped. "I'm going to help Carmelita prepare dinner now, and I won't allow you or her to dissuade me."

Her capitulation brought a smile to his full, sensuous lips. "Then I will help Amâncio with the oxen. Also, I must feed and rub down my horse."

Tory paused a moment. "About your horse . . . How about letting me ride Renegade tomorrow? I detest bouncing around on the seat of that cart. A saddle instead of a hard board would be a welcome change."

"Ah, *gatinha*, I'm sorry, but no . . . Riding Renegade is much too dangerous. He is as you say, bad-mannered. In the wild country we'll be entering, he'll dump you in the dust and run away."

"I take back what I said about his bad manners. Obviously, he's changed. Perhaps he prefers life in Brazil to life in America. In any case, I'm sure I can handle him. I didn't do too badly with him even before he came to this country." Tory stopped short of complimenting Sebastian on the horse's reformed behavior; it still galled her that he had been able to achieve what she and Jordan had not.

"Even with his 'new' personality, you cannot ride him, *gatinha*. It would not be proper. Here in Brazil,

130

women don't ride horseback—at least, not often. The few who do, ride sidesaddle. Even then, their virtue is questioned. They are considered overly bold. Riding horseback is a man's sport—and the gentleman is usually wealthy. Poor men either walk or if they're lucky, ride mules, donkeys, or in ox carts. Women walk, ride in some sort of conveyance, or stay at home."

"You can't expect me to spend a year walking everywhere or riding behind a pair of plodding old oxen," Tory flared. "I ride every bit as well as you do. You saw me ride Renegade in Kentucky. You may not like to admit it, but it's obvious that I'm your equal in many things."

"That may or may not be true, *gatinha*. What is true is that you aren't in Kentucky now . . . So you can't ride horses, wear men's breeches, or bully us about as you are accustomed to doing in your own country. If you doubt me, ask Carmelita—or Padre Osmundo, when you see him."

"I don't bully men about! *They* are the ones who bully me!"

Tory bit down hard on her fury. She already knew Sebastian had disapproved of her attire that day—she herself had been embarrassed to be seen in it. But she couldn't understand why she could *never* ride a horse in Brazil, especially if she could find a sidesaddle or alter one of her skirts to permit riding astride. If Sebastian wouldn't allow her to ride Renegade, she would buy a horse of her own as soon as possible. He couldn't stop her—nor could Padre Osmundo. The priest probably wouldn't try; Padre Osmundo was far more reasonable than Sebastian Black.

"Excuse me, while I assist Carmelita," she said haughtily.

"Of course," he responded in a gracious—if slightly mocking—tone. "If you must do something unconventional, cooking dinner with a servant is a much less dangerous rebellion than riding a horse in a country like this one."

Then maybe the country ought to change, Tory thought furiously. Maybe I can force it to change.

But she didn't say what she was thinking to Sebastian Black; he would only attempt to thwart her every step of the way and laugh while he was doing it.

By the third day of the journey, Tory felt as if she'd been traveling for a month on the dry *sertão*. They had passed out of the *recôncavo*, the agricultural area where grain, sugar cane, and cocoa were harvested, along with the fruits of many different kinds of trees. Now the land was relatively flat, the grass sparse, and the earth sandy, cracked, and hard. The only thing that flourished on the *sertão* was the *cãátinga*—a mixture of scrub, crooked trees, thorny underbrush, and cactus.

The heat was searing, making everyone short-tempered and grouchy, or else abnormally quiet. Amâncio, who rarely spoke in the best conditions, ceased speaking even to the oxen. He tied a bandana across his face to deter the dust, hunched his shoulders, and with his old leather hat jammed down on his head, reminded Tory of a turtle—a tall, thin turtle with sad brown eyes.

Carmelita sat huddled under a black lacy shawl that covered her from head to waist. Reddish-colored dirt ringed her eyes and mouth, so that she resembled a raccoon, rather than a woman. Tory could only guess how bad *she* looked in her dusty straw bonnet and the cape jacket she wore to protect herself from the pervasive dust the oxen kicked up as they plodded across the dry plain.

Only Sebastian looked relatively comfortable. He rode Renegade with sensual ease, the big bay snorting occasionally to clear his nostrils but never to challenge his rider. Sebastian wore unrelenting black out on the *sertão*—black trousers, boots, and shirt. Leather chaps and vest protected him from the *cãatinga*, and a leather hat with turned-up brim warded off the hot sun. Dust had darkened all his clothing to the same shade of brownish gray.

It amazed Tory that Sebastian managed to retain his handsomeness even under such challenging conditions. His amber eyes continued to glow with their own inner light, and his lean, strong, perfectly-proportioned body repeatedly drew her eyes, making the breath catch in her throat when he moved in some new, surprisingly graceful, masculine way. Whereas Amâncio was tall, thin, and wiry, Sebastian was muscular, lithe, and fit. Like Renegade, he exuded sleekness and athletic ability. Unlike everyone else except his horse and the patient oxen, Sebastian never seemed to tire.

Sometimes, he was the only one who spoke for hours at a time. He delighted in pointing out various features of the land through which they were traveling, and he related anecdotes and funny stories that made Tory laugh no matter how hot and miserable she was. She learned that Sebastian could be truly witty and informative, when he wanted to be, which was a side of him she hadn't seen before. He pointed out mud and wattle huts—now abandoned—that dotted the range, then told her about the superstitions of the peasants who had very likely once lived there.

"Anything a *Sertanejo* doesn't want to do, he can

find an excuse to avoid, by claiming that it's '*faz mal*'."

"*Faz mal?*"

"It might harm him. It does bad or is bad . . . For example, if he doesn't want to work on a particular day, he might claim that working hard on the eve of a new moon will ruin his health . . . Or if he's afraid to try something new, he can always think of a reason why it's *faz mal* . . . Superstitions govern his life from the cradle to the grave, and the *Sertanejo* has superstitions involving food, sex, religion, planting and harvesting crops, birth, death, marriage, and almost everything in between."

"That's fascinating . . ." Tory said.

"And frustrating, too. The superstitions of the *Sertanejo* and the *caboclo*, indeed of all poor people, are the main reason why they are so difficult to teach. They cling to ignorance out of fear and stubbornness, even refusing to eat properly if a superstition demands otherwise."

"Oh, I can hardly believe that . . ."

"Believe it, *gatinha*. It's true. I've known women to reject meat, fruits, and certain vegetables after childbirth, then sicken and die as a result of poor nutrition. I've known midwives to smear the umbilical cords of newborn infants with cow dung, then wonder why the infants die a week later. I've known healthy men to crawl into their hammocks and not get out of them again upon hearing that they've been cursed. Their belief in the power of *macumbeiros* is so great that they will fall ill and die simply because a *macumbeiro* has told them they will."

"I know what a *macumbeiro* is—a kind of witch-doctor," Tory offered, elated that she could contribute something to the discussion, and elated even more that they were actually *having* a discussion that

134

didn't, for once, involve sex. "When my sister-in-law, Spencer, lived on the Amazon, she was able to treat the illnesses of the native Indians because they thought she was a great *macumbeira*."

"All *macumbeiros* are liars," Sebastian scoffed. "But in Brazil, they hold enormous power. Everyone believes in them—even the rich and educated."

"But you don't?" Tory queried. She was relieved that they were speaking in English so that Carmelita and Amâncio would not be insulted, if they, too, believed in *macumbeiros*.

"Of course not. The Franciscan friars knocked all that nonsense out of my head during the first few months I lived with them. They also destroyed my beliefs in the African counterparts of Catholic saints, whom the *macumbeiros* revere. I'm one of the few Brazilians in Salvador, perhaps in the entire country, who doesn't secretly maintain a little altar to Iémanja, Oxumare, and other gods and goddesses of *condomble* or *macumba*, as it's also called."

Tory wondered why the good friars hadn't made other improvements in Sebastian's character while they had him in their clutches. She was about to say something of that nature when she spotted a cloud of dust fast approaching them from the west.

"Can that be some of your *vaqueiros* riding out to greet us?" she asked, nodding toward the dust cloud.

"What *vaqueiros?*" Sebastian looked where she was looking, saw the small band of galloping horsemen bearing down upon them, and began shouting orders to Amâncio. "Stop the cart! Get the women under it, and grab your Winchester, Amâncio!"

"What's wrong?" Tory cried. "Who are they?"

Carmelita's screams told her everything she needed to know. *"Cangaçeiros! Meu Deus!* They'll rob and kill us—and maybe do worse!"

135

Now, what could be worse than killing us? Tory thought irrelevantly as she clambered down from the cart and crawled between the big wooden wheels at Sebastian's insistence.

"They'll probably rape us before they kill us," Carmelita sobbed, joining her beneath the wagon. "There's so many of them and so few of us. What can we do to stop them?"

"Sebastian will stop them," Tory assured her, hoping she was right. She fervently prayed that Sebastian was every bit the man she thought he was and even half the man he himself claimed to be. For the first time in her life, she felt the need of a good, strong man.

Chapter Nine

Tory could not see a thing through the churning dust, but she could hear horses neighing, men shouting, pistols and rifles firing, and the heavy thud of hooves drumming the dry earth all around the cart. She and Carmelita lay side by side, choking on huge mouthfuls of the cloying dust. It was impossible to breathe properly. At last, Tory could stand it no longer. Crawling backwards, she left Carmelita and huddled beside a wagon wheel where the air was slightly clearer.

"Get back under there!" Sebastian snarled, firing his rifle at one of the mounted men as Tory struggled to stand beside him.

"But I want to help. What can I do?"

Roughly, he pushed her down. "You foolish bitch, you can do what you're told! . . . *Cristo!* At this rate, you will get yourself killed and me along with you."

It was the "bitch" that did it. Defiantly, Tory craned her neck, searching for the tall Negro. "Where's Amâncio?" she demanded. "If you don't want my help, maybe he does . . . He hasn't been shot, has he?" she added, worried.

Sebastian fired again before answering. "He's

trying to keep the oxen from bolting. Don't you hear them?''

At that moment, Tory did hear them. The beasts were bellowing loudly enough to make the cart shake. She wiped her eyes and peered through the reddish haze, catching a glimpse of Amâncio standing near the oxens' huge heads. He had taken the long stick he normally used to prod the oxen and jammed it through the rings on both their noses. By turning the stick, he twisted the rings, thereby controlling them. Unfortunately, he couldn't fire his rifle at the same time. Tory saw the gun lying on the ground near the black man's feet, where it could not possibly do any good.

She dashed to where it lay, snatched it up, and returned to the shelter of the cart. As she raised the rifle, attempting to aim the heavy weapon, Sebastian grabbed it out of her hands.

"Cristo! If you insist on doing something, hold the oxen so Amâncio can take the rifle.''

"So now you think I'm too inept to fire a gun, but strong enough to hold a pair of oxen. That's typical male logic, if I ever heard it.''

"And arguing in the middle of a gunfight is typical feminine foolishness, if *I* ever heard it.'' Sebastian worked while he talked, checking the weapon to be sure it was ready to fire. Then he tossed it back to Tory. "Here! Go give this back to Amâncio . . . All you have to do to hold the oxen is twist the rings in their noses like he's doing. They can't go anywhere their noses won't go. Just try and keep the oxen between you and the *cangaçeiros'* bullets.''

"Why, that should be the easy part,'' Tory quipped sarcastically.

"It's not as hard as it sounds.'' Sebastian hefted his own Winchester back into position to resume firing.

138

"The *cangaçeiros* won't want to lose such valuable beasts. As long as you stay close to them, you've a good chance of surviving this attack. Now, get moving."

With rifle fire roaring in her ears, Tory raced back to Amâncio, leaned the gun against the wagon, and seized hold of the prod. Amâncio was startled to see her there but relinquished the prod after she jerked her head in the direction of the rifle. "Go and help Senhor *Sebastião*. I can do this. What I can't do is load and fire a Winchester."

The tall Negro nodded and hurried away, leaving Tory face to face with two huge animals who could easily trample her into nothingness if she didn't keep her wits about her. She summoned all her strength to hold the prod in position as the oxen fought to free their heads. Their wide, frightened eyes were almost rolling back in their sockets. The insides of their nostrils flamed red, and their hot breath blew in Tory's face. She concentrated on keeping the nose rings twisted, forgetting about the battle, Sebastian, Carmelita, and Amâncio, forgetting everything but holding the oxen in place, if not with strength, then with sheer determination.

One of the oxen suddenly succeeded in tossing his head, and Tory nearly lost him. She turned the prod until the nose rings tightened again—then jumped when she heard a snort of laughter behind her.

"You can let the poor beasts go, *gatinha* . . . Our illustrious attackers have turned tail and fled. Apparently they are unaccustomed to meeting such vigorous resistance."

Cautiously, Tory released the nose rings. The oxen bellowed plaintively and surged forward a short distance, knocking Tory to one side. Strong arms caught her and held her upright. "Are you all right, little one?" Sebastian rumbled in her ear.

Remembering that he had called her a foolish bitch, Tory pushed away from him. "Why, I've never been better, Senhor *Cochorro*. What about Carmelita and Amâncio?"

"Carmelita is only angry, but Amâncio is wounded. If you are sure you aren't dead or dying, I will check his leg now."

"Dear God, please do! I hope he isn't seriously injured."

Tory watched over Sebastian's shoulder as he examined Amâncio's leg. A bullet had creased the black man's thigh, serrating both flesh and trousers. Sebastian probed the wound with the tip of a knife while Amâncio determinedly gritted his teeth. Tears rolled down the Negro's face, but he maintained a stoic silence.

"Looks as though the bullet cut a straight path and missed the bone entirely," Sebastian said. "The wound is painful but not fatal. We'll pour *cachaça* on it and bandage it tightly. That should suffice for medical treatment until we get to Paraíso, and Padre Osmundo can take a look at it . . . Take my arm, old friend, and let's get you into the cart. Try to stand on your good leg, and we'll support you as best we can."

Sebastian got on one side and Tory on the other, while Carmelita clucked in anguished sympathy. "Oh, poor Amâncio! Don't worry. Padre Osmundo has a gift for healing. He'll make it better."

When Sebastian and Tory tried to lift Amâncio to his feet, the black man gave a terrible groan and clutched his good leg, not his bad one. Frowning, Sebastian glanced down, then back up at Tory. "I think his other leg might be broken."

Amâncio confirmed the guess. "*Sim*, Senhor, I think it is. . . . I fell awkwardly when I was shot, and

140

there was a loud crack. Now, I cannot stand, and the pain of moving it . . ." He trailed off, gasping.

Tory had never heard Amâncio say so much at one time. "We'll have to make a splint," she told Sebastian. "I wish Spencer were here. She would know what to do."

Sebastian's amber eyes mocked her. "I'm sure I can manage without her, *gatinha*. Doctor or no, she is, after all, a mere woman."

Tory glared at him. "Amâncio is suffering, and the *cangaçeiros* could return at any moment. Do you really think we should stand around debating your ridiculous prejudices? I don't."

"Neither do I, *gatinha*. All I was doing was stating facts. Wait here while I see what can be found in the cart to make a splint."

In the end, they had to tear up the single board that formed the seat of the cart to make a splint for Amâncio's leg. It took all three of them to lift the groaning man and lay him down on top of the supplies and belongings piled in the vehicle. They tried to make him comfortable by tucking quilts and pillows around him, but it was obvious from Amâncio's ashen face that he was miserable.

Tory had never realized that a person with dark brown skin could look so pale; Amâncio's flesh had taken on a grayish hue, and his features were pinched and haggard. Even his closely-cropped, tightly-kinked black hair seemed to have lost its vibrancy. Tory wondered whether he would make it to Paraĩso, and if he did, whether Padre Osmundo could do anything to help him.

"Perhaps we should return to Salvador," she suggested to Sebastian. "At least in Salvador, he could see a real doctor."

"No, *gatinha*. We are closer to Paraĩso than

141

Salvador at the moment. Besides, the few doctors available in the city would not make a priority out of treating a poor black man."

"You would pay for his treatment surely!"

"Of course . . . Payment is not the issue. Amâncio will be far better cared for at Paraíso than in Salvador. Don't argue with me, *gatinha*. I know better than you what is best for him."

Tory doubted this, but she joined Carmelita in trudging beside the cart, while Sebastian drove the oxen, and Renegade trailed behind, tied to the back end. They stopped early that night to make camp, and this time Carmelita didn't protest when Tory helped her gather firewood and prepare a simple meal of rice, stale bread, dried beef, and coffee. The food was tasteless, but the heavily-sugared coffee revived her and temporarily banished her weariness. Tory helped Amâncio to eat and drink, and thought he looked better afterward. Since breakfast, Amâncio had had only sips of *cachaça*, the cane whiskey Sebastian had used to clean his bullet wound, and as a result, the injured man had sunk into a kind of dazed stupor.

The quilts and pillows that cushioned Amâncio were the only bedding available, but neither Carmelita nor Tory wanted to remove them, so they each sat down on the dry, cracked earth and leaned against a wagon wheel to rest. The setting sun flooded the western sky with a blood-red color, but Tory could not enjoy the beauty of the tropical sunset as she had on previous nights. She was too stiff, sore, and tired—and too worried about Amâncio.

She looked up to see Sebastian swinging into Renegade's saddle, and felt a surge of new energy as indignation flared in her breast. "Where are you going? You can't mean to leave us alone out here!"

Sebastian quirked an eyebrow at her. "I think you'll be safe now. We crossed the border of my land a half hour before we stopped . . . In any case, I must attend to business. I'll be back before morning."

Tory scrambled to her feet. "Before morning! But what if you don't return at all? What do you expect us to do? Two women alone with a severely injured man are prime targets for anyone who happens along— not that we aren't capable of managing perfectly well without you," she backtracked, "But we don't even know where we're going."

Sebastian flashed his mocking grin. "I'm flattered you need me so much, *gatinha*. Coming from you, such an admission is quite a compliment . . ." More soberly, he added: "If for some reason I don't return, keep traveling north. Eventually, you'll run into someone from Paraíso or see the ranch itself. If you encounter a river, you've gone too far. Turn west for a couple miles, then double back south."

"Those vague directions are the best you can do? You should be ashamed to abandon us to our fate like this. What if the *cangaçeiros* come back? I doubt they pay much attention to boundary lines."

"They have always respected mine . . ." Sebastian said darkly. "Now I'm going to teach them to respect me even when I am not upon my own land . . . Go to sleep, *gatinha*. Nothing bad will happen to you now, unless you or Carmelita get stung by a scorpion or bit by a poisonous snake. If that occurs, it won't make much difference whether I'm here or not. My many accomplishments do not include the ability to work miracles. Not even your talented sister-in-law could save you from the painful consequences of being bitten by the wrong sort of snake."

His continued slighting of Spencer's abilities— indeed of all women's abilities, except when it suited him—fanned Tory's fury past the boiling point. "Oh, you are the most unprincipled, conceited, impossible lout I have ever met!" she shouted. "You—you *brioso* pig!"

He laughed and saluted her. "And you are the most alluring, adorable, soft-spoken, delectable little kitten I have ever met . . . *Até logo, gatinha.* That means goodbye until the next time."

"I *know* what it means!"

"Hush!" He leaned down and lay a finger across her lips. "You'll awaken Carmelita and Amâncio. What a pity I can't stay long enough to take advantage of their exhaustion."

A loud snore punctuated the sudden silence. Tory glanced at Carmelita who was leaning against the cart wheel, eyes closed, mouth open, snoring loudly enough to wake the dead. She stood on tiptoe and checked Amâncio inside the cart. He, too, was sleeping. When she turned to look, Sebastian was gone—galloping across the plain in the direction from which they had just come.

She shook her fist at his departing figure. "If you don't return by morning, Sebastian Black, I'll . . . I'll *kill* you with my own bare hands when I finally see you!"

A terrible thought struck Tory; if indeed he *didn't* return, it would be because the *cangaçeiros* had beaten her to it.

Sebastian came galloping back across the *sertão* just as dawn was painting the eastern sky a soft, dusky pink. Tory heard him before she saw him. Rather, she felt the vibration of hoofbeats pounding the earth. Taking cover beneath the cart, she shakily aimed the rifle she had held all night. It sounded like more than one horseman approaching, and she debated whether or not to awaken Carmelita and Amâncio, but finally decided there was no point in it. Carmelita knew less about guns than she did, and Amâncio could never get into position in time to fire one.

Sighting down the gun barrel, she recognized Sebastian by his graceful posture in the saddle and his superb riding skills. He held the reins of three saddled but riderless horses in one hand, while with the other, he controlled Renegade. Tory crawled from beneath the cart to take charge of the extra animals as soon as he arrived.

As the sky brightened, she saw that the horses belonged to yesterday's attackers. She would not have recognized the *cangaçeiros* themselves, but she always noticed horses—their physical condition, level of training, and indications of fine breeding or lack of it. Of the three Sebastian had brought, only one deserved a second glance: a chestnut with a bald face and two white hind hooves. As she had noted yesterday, this one appeared younger and stronger than the other two, though all three were having trouble keeping up with Renegade. The best of the *cangaçeiro's* horses—a tall, muscular black—was not among the captured.

Sebastian rode up without a word of greeting. "These animals could use some water . . . If you can't handle it yourself, awaken Carmelita."

"I can certainly handle such a mundane task without assistance from someone who knows nothing at all about horses!" Tory bristled. "What happened to the *cangaçeiros?* Did you kill them? You must have in order to get their mounts."

Sebastian did not respond. He slid off Renegade, handed the reins of the three horses to Tory, then led the big bay away to be unsaddled, rubbed down, and

145

groomed with the tools kept in his saddle pack. When he had finished, he fetched himself a drink of water, gave some to Renegade, and then lay down with his head on his sweaty saddle and promptly closed his eyes.

Tory studied him with growing consternation: Had Sebastian cold-bloodedly murdered three men? Shooting at bandits during an attack was one thing, but going after them in the dead of night—and killing them—was quite another. She didn't know what to think. Her first reaction was to be appalled. Yet the bandits had wounded Amâncio and would have killed all of them had Sebastian not stood up to them. His gun and his supreme arrogance were the only things protecting them from present and future harm.

Tory waited until the sun was high in the sky before daring to awaken Sebastian. Gently, she shook his arm. "Sebastian, you must get up now. The sooner we reach Paraíso, the better for Amâncio."

"Cristo," Sebastian growled, sitting up and knuckling his eyes like a schoolboy reluctant to abandon his slumbers.

Tory handed him a cup of Carmelita's strong, hot coffee and waited until he took a sip before opening her mouth again. "Aren't you going to tell me about last night?"

"Last night does not concern you. If I tell anyone, it will be Amâncio, but I doubt he's as rude as you are. He'll never ask."

"R—rude! I'm not being rude; *you* are!"

Sebastian concentrated all his attention on the coffee, not bothering to respond until he'd drained the cup. Then he shoved the tin container in her direction. "Is there more where that came from?"

Tory snatched the cup and flung it to the ground

in exasperation. "I want to know if you killed the *cangaçeiros!*"

"That subject is closed, *gatinha*. We will speak of it no more."

"We certainly will speak of it! We'll speak of it right now!"

He tilted his head and regarded her through slitted eyes. "All right . . . I will answer *your* questions, if you will first answer mine. Agreed?"

"Agreed," she said reluctantly, wondering what his questions would be.

A sly smile quirked the corners of his mouth. "Did you sleep well last night, *gatinha?* Did you dream of me? Did you perhaps imagine me holding you close and caressing you until you begged for mercy?"

If she hadn't already thrown the cup, she would have done it now—this time, at his head. Was there nothing on this man's mind but sex? "Never! I'll never dream, imagine, or hope for such intimacies. Especially not with a man like you."

"What a pity." Sebastian shrugged, and a dark, brooding expression crept across his face. "Since that wasn't the answer I wanted, I refuse to answer *your* questions . . . Let's get moving. By tomorrow night, I want to sleep in my own bed at Paraíso, and I want Amâncio under Padre Osmundo's care."

Sebastian brooded all that long, hot, dusty day. If he said two words to anyone as they trudged across the dry *sertão*, Tory never heard them, nor did she herself make any attempt at conversation. She was furious with Sebastian, and he did not seem any too happy with her. His foul mood kept Carmelita and Amâncio silent and withdrawn as well. Only Amâncio's groans could be heard when the movement of the cart jostled his legs. It was nearly dark before they stopped to make camp for the night. By then, Tory

147

could barely stay on her feet. She contemplated the thought of preparing a meal and didn't care if she ever ate again.

Carmelita was equally exhausted. Dabbing at her sweaty, grimy face with the edge of her shawl, the plump little woman collapsed by a wagon wheel. Concerned that the day's exertions had proven too much for the poor lady, Tory fetched her a cup of water and watched anxiously as she drank it. Then she dipped a square of the shawl into the last few remaining drops and gently wiped Carmelita's eyes and mouth.

As she started toward Amâncio, intending to minister to his needs, Sebastian stopped her with a hand on her arm. "I'll do it . . . Rest, or you'll never make it to Paraíso."

Too weary to protest, Tory trudged back to Carmelita. It was Sebastian who pressed the last of the now very stale bread into her and Carmelita's hands, fed Amâncio, helped to take care of Amâncio's personal needs, and then looked after the horses and oxen. After choking down the dry bread, Tory cuddled up to the cart wheel beside Carmelita, and within minutes, fell fast asleep.

She awoke to find Sebastian leaning over her in the sunlight, grinning his old mocking grin. "I never saw a woman sleep so much or so deeply. I could have had my way with you, and you never would have known it."

"I'm sure I wouldn't have missed much," Tory groused, more out of habit than any real rancor. Remembering his kindness of the night before, she couldn't quite muster the anger she had felt toward him all day yesterday.

"I disagree, *gatinha*. I'm acknowledged far and wide as an excellent lover, as you will one day dis-

148

cover for yourself. However, when I finally do have my way with you, I want every inch of you alive and awake."

When he looked at her in that lazy, sensual way, every nerve in Tory's body jangled. Disturbed more than she wanted to admit, even to herself, she scrambled to her feet. "Tell me, Senhor *Cochorro*, will we make Paraíso today?"

"I think so. Barring any unforeseen circumstances."

"Good! I can't wait to see Padre Osmundo." She edged away from the heat and scent of him, which made her nostrils flare with awareness.

"You think he will protect you from me, eh, *gatinha?* Don't count on it too much. He's probably still confined to bed. I hope he has recovered enough to doctor Amâncio, but I doubt that he's capable of the journey to Espirito Santo. I'm looking forward to having you sleep beneath my roof for some time yet."

Tory made a great show of brushing the dirt from her long, rumpled skirt. "Whatever his condition, at least you'll have to stop saying such outrageous things to me. Carmelita may not understand English, but Padre Osmundo comprehends every word."

"Then would you care to learn French, *gatinha?* I have a French dictionary in my library at the ranch. We could learn together, and after that, we needn't worry about anyone eavesdropping on our private conversations."

Wild horses could not have dragged out of Tory that she already knew French, Spanish, and a smattering of German. "Thank you, no. I've had quite enough of these private conversations."

He surprised her by agreeing. "So have I . . . What I really would prefer is to say less and do more."

Tory shot him a scathing look. *"This* particular

149

conversation has gone far enough. Excuse me while I help Carmelita prepare breakfast.''

His soft laughter followed her as she spun away. Without looking at him, Tory knew that his eyes lingered on her. How she hated the way he made her feel! All limp, tingly, off balance, and out of control. She was filthy, her hair, clothes, and body dirtier than they had ever been in her life, and Sebastian was even filthier—in mind as well as body. How could she be so attracted to him? He was arrogant, cruel, and had a terrible attitude towards women. Worst of all, he was quite likely a cold-blooded murderer. At the moment, she couldn't think of a single redeeming quality he possessed . . . But it made no difference. Her heartbeat still accelerated whenever he looked at her, and she was actually beginning to relish the dangerously alluring sensations he aroused in her.

She thoroughly disgusted herself. Her only salvation, it seemed, lay in escaping his presence as soon as possible.

Chapter Ten

With his broken ankle elevated on a stool, Padre Osmundo sat on the verandah of Sebastian Black's ranch house and gazed thoughtfully into the hazy distance. It was early evening, and the heat had died down, a pleasant time for sipping a *cafêzinho* and ruminating on his plans for the future. He couldn't wait for Jordan King's sister to arrive and for the two of them and Carmelita to leave for Espirito Santo. At long last, his dream was coming true; his poor peasants would soon have their very own teacher, and someday, there would be not only a school, but a small hospital or health post, where the *caboclos* could be treated for illnesses and injuries.

It was about time for Sebastian to return with Miss King. For the past two days, Padre Osmundo had been keeping watch for them. He had even sent the boy, Tuísca, out on a donkey, to watch for signs of their approach across the *sertão*. He couldn't help his impatience; he was getting old, and there was so much yet to do and so little time in which to do it.

Unfortunately, his confounded ankle showed no signs of being ready for the long journey to Espirito Santo. He still could not walk on it, and it pained him more than he would have thought possible. He could get about with the crude wooden crutches Amâncio had fashioned for him before he left with Sebastian for Salvador, but he couldn't go far; his ankle throbbed whenever he put weight on it, and his back and arms ached from the unaccustomed strain of using crutches. At times, he found himself blaming the Almighty for placing so many obstacles in his path, but chief among those obstacles was his own stubbornness. He never should have climbed that rickety ladder to help the laborers lay the roof tiles for the new school in the first place. But he had, and so here he was—stuck in one place, where every idle, wasted moment taught him what hell must be like: an eternity of idle, wasted moments.

He finished his *cafêzinho* and sighed. It didn't look as if they would arrive tonight. He might as well prepare for bed. Like the peasants, he kept the same hours as the sun. Candles and oil lamps were costly, and he hated to spend money on any purpose that didn't directly help his people. Removing his ankle from the stool, he reached for his crutches. As he rose on one leg, he caught sight of a movement on the distant horizon. *Yes!* An ox cart was coming toward the house. It *had* to be Sebastian returning with Senhorita King.

"Tuísca!" he shouted. "Quinquina! Miguel! Teodoro! Everyone come quickly—the master of the house has returned."

Chattering *caboclos* emerged from the house behind him and came running from the corral and barn in back of the house. Quinquina, a fifteen year old girl with a sunny smile, cinnamon brown eyes, and long black hair, danced beside him with excitement. "Padre Osmundo! It's the *professôra* from America, isn't it? You will tell her how good I have

152

been, helping Tia Guilhermina with the cooking and cleaning here at Paraíso, won't you?"

"I will if you want me to, Quinquina. But why should she be interested? She doesn't even know you yet."

"I hope to become her *empregada*, Padre. She will need someone to keep house for her and cook her meals when she goes to Espirito Santo."

"No, she won't, child. She'll be living with Carmelita and probably taking her meals with me . . . It's all arranged. There's no reason for her to have a maid. Besides, Dona Guilhermina needs you too much here."

Quinquina made a face of disappointment. "Oh, Padre, you are spoiling everything! I want to go to Espirito Santo with you and learn to read and write in your new school. And how can I do that if I don't have a place to live and a job to support myself?"

Padre Osmundo frowned. Quinquina was old enough to marry, and she was very pretty. A husband was what she needed, and from the looks young Teodoro had been giving her, he seemed a likely candidate. Quinquina's interest in learning to read and write had caught Padre Osmundo by surprise. He doubted that Dona Guilhermina, Quinquina's aunt, would be pleased to hear of the girl's desire to work for Tory King . . . Yet wasn't Quinquina's ambition the very reason why he had wanted the young *Americana* to come—because the *caboclos* deserved a chance to better their lot in life?

"We'll see what can be done, Quinquina . . ." he promised. "Only don't forget that you are needed here. Who will help your aunt if you fly away to Espirito Santo? . . . And who will console Teodoro? You know he'll be sad to see you go."

Indecision flashed in the young girl's eyes. "I don't

know, Padre; I hadn't thought about that . . . But you have always said that everyone should learn to read and write. Am I not smart enough to learn? Perhaps females are too stupid to master the skill, but oh, I should love to try."

"Indeed, you are not stupid, Quinquina. Where did you get such a foolish idea? The *professôra* is a female, and her gender hasn't kept her from reading. . . . Let me think on the matter. Before any decisions are made, I'll have to discuss it with your aunt and Senhor *Sebastião*."

"*Sïm*, Padre," Quinquina graciously acquiesced. "Oh, look! Something is wrong with Amâncio!"

Padre Osmundo turned his attention back to the approaching ox cart and saw that something was very wrong with Sebastian's servant. Amâncio lay flat on his back in the ox cart, while Carmelita, Tory King, and Sebastian trudged on foot alongside it. Sebastian's horse and several others brought up the rear. Grasping his crutches, Padre Osmundo hobbled down the front steps of the verandah and limped toward them as fast as his crutches would permit.

Sebastian waved to him. "Well, Padre, you're looking better than when I left you. Do you feel up to a spot of doctoring?"

Padre Osmundo hurried toward the cart. "What is it? What's happened to Amâncio?"

"We were set upon by *cangaçeiros*, and in the fight, Amâncio was wounded in the leg. When he fell, he broke his other leg . . . We did the best we could to fix it, but I want you to take a look at it."

"*Mamãe de Jesus!* Who were the *cangaçeiros*, do you know?" Padre Osmundo peered over the side of the cart at Amâncio, who nodded wearily in greeting.

Sebastian brought the oxen to a halt and handed his prod to Teodoro. The young *vaqueiro* seemed more interested in watching Quinquina than controlling the oxen, Padre Osmundo noticed.

"Don't worry . . ." Sebastian said. "It wasn't the *Falcão*. Instead, I believe it was the bandit known as Porco. I went after his band, but only caught three. Porco himself escaped."

Padre Osmundo saw the three horses but no men. "If you caught them, then where are they?"

"He killed them," Tory King answered, her glance at Sebastian chilling. A lesser man would have been frostbitten, Padre Osmundo thought, but Sebastian didn't seem in the least daunted. "He refuses to admit it," she continued. "But I'm quite certain he killed those men and left their bodies to rot in the sun."

Padre Osmundo's heart sank. He deplored the lawlessness of the *sertão*, but at the same time realized that Sebastian had only done what any other red-blooded Brazilian would do in the same circumstances—take revenge on his attackers and insure that they would bother him no more. A man who didn't stand up for himself in this lonely land only invited further harassment that usually ended in injury or death, often his own.

"Don't believe a word she says, Padre," Sebastian grunted. "I'd never leave three bodies to stink up the *sertão* . . . Before I parted company with the three gentlemen, I buried them in a shallow grave and said a prayer over them."

"I knew it!" Tory came around the side of the ox cart with fire flashing in her gray-green eyes. There, she confronted Sebastian, hands on hips. "I just knew it. But I didn't want to believe it."

Sebastian slanted an exasperated glance at Padre Osmundo. "She would have preferred that I allow them to sneak back at night and rape and kill her and Carmelita."

"That isn't what I prefer, and you know it! Oh, what's the use of talking to you? You twist everything I say to suit your own purposes." Tory turned to Padre Osmundo. "Dear Padre! You don't know how glad I am to see you! I was beginning to despair that we'd ever meet again!"

She flung her arms around his neck, making it difficult for him to maintain his balance on the crutches. "I'm overjoyed to see you, my child . . ." Awkwardly, Padre Osmundo patted her shoulder, then leaned back to get a good look at her. "My, my . . . You seem to have grown up since I last saw you. If it weren't for that blond hair, I might not have recognized you."

Stepping backward, Tory tucked a wisp of dust-coated hair beneath her dirty straw bonnet. "As soon as Amâncio is taken care of, I'm going to have a bath," she announced. "I know I look a fright. This journey has done much to age me."

Padre Osmundo studied her a long moment—then glanced at Sebastian. The two of them provided ample evidence of the filth, fatigue, and strain of their travels, yet between them, there crackled an unmistakable energy. Neither looked at the other, but the awareness was there, the same as it had been in Kentucky. Padre Osmundo wondered what else besides an attack by the *cangaçeiros* had occurred on the trip. He wished again that he had not been incapacitated and unable to meet Tory in Salvador. He was responsible for the young woman's safety; if she came to harm or was compromised, he would never forgive himself.

"And how are you, Carmelita?" he said to the bedraggled creature coming around the cart toward him.

"Exhausted, Padre . . . Like everyone else, but we dared not stop to rest because of Amâncio. We wanted to bring him to you as quickly as possible."

"Well, let's get him inside then . . . Teodoro! Miguel! Help *Sebastião* carry Amâncio into the house."

Sebastian chuckled. "I see you have usurped my role of authority while I've been gone, haven't you, Padre?"

"I've tried, *Sebastião*, but it hasn't been easy. I'm only a poor priest, not a rich *fazendeiro*. I lack the proper arrogance to intimidate the *caboclos*."

"I can hardly believe that. Dire warnings of hellfire and damnation are far more intimidating than anything I might threaten."

"But I've never threatened hellfire and damnation, *Sebastião*. I preach love and forgiveness. You would know that if you came to church more often . . . and you would also know that I don't approve of crimes of vengeance no matter how great the provocation."

"Then perhaps that's why I rarely come to church, Padre. Some things can never be forgiven or forgotten . . . In any case, I hope you can heal as well as you sermonize."

Padre Osmundo cast a worried glance at Amâncio's splinted leg as Miguel and Teodoro lifted him out of the cart. "I hope I can, too, *mon filho*. Certainly, I will try."

As she followed the little procession into the house, Tory took careful note of the thick walls, red tile roof, and spacious rooms of the white-washed structure that Sebastian called home here on the *sertão*. They had passed several dried-up cane fields on the way in, but the house itself was shaded by luxurious palm and banana trees, and a variety of

157

flowering shrubs. The cattle Sebastian had told her about were nowhere in evidence, but she had seen outbuildings, several neatly-thatched huts, and a large corral containing several horses behind the house.

Everything was spotlessly clean and functional, a great contrast to the poor dwellings they had seen on their journey. A covered well stood on one side of the house—the source, no doubt, of the water that kept everything and everyone at Paraíso alive. They climbed the steps to the pleasant, shaded verandah where a person could sit and enjoy the cool of the evening or seek shelter from the hot noonday sun. In the gathering dark, she could not ascertain any further details of the ranch, but guessed it must be very large, comprising hundreds of acres. Despite her tiredness, she felt an eagerness to explore—but for that, she would first need to rest, and then to find a horse she could use. No more walking for her!

Entering the house, Tory encountered a tall, thin, grim-faced woman dressed much like Carmelita, but without Carmelita's warmth and charm. *"Professôra?"* the woman said, her dark eyes expressionless. "I am Dona Guilhermina. Let these others take care of Amâncio . . . You come with me. Your room is all prepared, and I'm sure you must be travel-weary."

"Oh, but I'd like to see for myself that Amâncio is all right," Tory protested. "The journey hasn't been nearly as hard on me as it's been on him."

"He will be well tended, *Professôra*. Senhor *Sebastião* wishes me to see to *your* needs . . . We who live here are used to the heat and dust. You are not. If you don't rest, you may become ill."

Tory did have a headache. Still, she paused, unwilling to be treated differently than everyone else.

"What about Carmelita? Isn't she going to share a room with me?"

"Carmelita will be along shortly . . . Come, *Professôra* . . . Quinquina! Fetch a lamp and bring it upstairs."

As she followed the tall, thin woman up a narrow staircase to the second floor of the house, Tory hoped that Quinquina, whoever she was, would be less bossy and sour-lipped than Dona Guilhermina. They passed down a long, candle-lit hallway and came to an open door at the very end. It was dark inside the room. Shadows flickered in the corners, making it appear sinister and uninviting. For a moment, Tory didn't want to enter. Just then a young girl came hurrying after them with an oil lamp.

"Here I am, *Tia!* . . . Welcome to Paraíso, *Professôra.*" The girl dropped a shy, awkward curtsey and slanted Tory a bright, eager smile. "I am so pleased to meet you. Padre Osmundo has told me all about you and the country you come from so far away across the sea."

Before Tory could respond to the greeting, Dona Guilhermina took the oil lamp from the girl and ushered Tory into the room. "Fetch a pitcher of water and a basin, Quinquina. The *professôra* will want to freshen herself."

"Oh, yes," Tory agreed. "Actually what I'd really like to do is bathe, but I don't want to inconvenience anyone. There's no need to heat water; I find cold water invigorating, and I'll be glad to haul it myself. All you need do is point out the tub to me."

"Amâncio usually hauls the water for bathing," Dona Guilhermina clipped. "Tomorrow I will find someone else to do it. I trust you can wait until then."

159

"Why, uh . . . yes, of course, if you insist. Tomorrow will be fine. However, I do wish to change my clothes at least. Is someone available to carry my baggage upstairs? If not, I can do it. It's really no bother."

"Tomorrow, *Professôra*. All will be done tomorrow, I assure you."

Dona Guilhermina certainly isn't friendly or accommodating like Carmelita, Tory thought irritatedly. Normally, she would be tempted to argue with such a stubborn woman, but tonight, she was just too miserable. She felt ashamed of herself for her weakness, but suddenly all she wanted to do was go to bed. Tomorrow would undoubtedly be soon enough for a bath and a change of clothing. For now, she would have to content herself with washing her face and hands.

While Quinquina went to fetch water, Dona Guilhermina busied herself turning down the sheets on the two narrow beds. Still curious about Sebastian's ranch, Tory wandered to the large, unshuttered window. There was no balcony, and she couldn't see much in the dark, but stars were beginning to appear in the sky. The air was sweet-smelling and soft upon her cheek. The heat of the day still lingered, and in the night-stillness, each sound seemed magnified. Tory could hear oxen lowing, horses whinnying, and voices drifting up from below in the house. She turned to ask Dona Guilhermina a question, but the woman had silently departed the room and closed the door behind her.

Fortunately, she had left the oil lamp burning on a small table between the two beds. In its rosy light, Tory studied the room's furnishings. They were as plain as they had been in Sebastian's house in Salvador. Only one piece of furniture suggested wealth or opulence—the *guarda-roupa,* a large, double-doored, wardrobe closet elaborately carved from dark, shiny wood. Tory strolled over to it and opened the double doors. It stood empty, save for a large gray cobweb. If this room was meant to serve guests, Sebastian apparently didn't have many visitors to Paraĩso.

A scurrying sound drew Tory's attention to a tiny green lizard darting down the wall. It paused midway to look up at her.

"Hello, little fellow . . ." she murmured, heartened by the creature's company in this strange, unfamiliar, slightly unfriendly place.

The lizard cocked its head and flicked its tail, but a knock at the door sent it dashing for cover behind the *guarda-roupa.*

"*Professôra,* can you open the door for me?" Quinquina called out. "My hands are full."

Tory obligingly did so, and Quinquina hurried inside. She carried a full pitcher of water, a basin, and Tory's carpetbag. "Carmelita said you would want this . . ." The girl nodded toward the bag.

"Yes, thank you, I do." Tory took it and set it down on the bed. "Will Carmelita be coming up soon? I know she's as tired as I am."

Quinquina set down her other burdens next to the lamp on the table between the two beds. "Soon, *Professôra* . . . She is with Padre Osmundo taking care of Amâncio. I'll bring you a tray of food next . . . Carmelita will probably eat downstairs."

"Then I'll go downstairs, too."

"Oh, no, *Professôra!* You must let me fetch your dinner . . . It will be my pleasure. I am so happy to have you here, you see. Other than Padre Osmundo, we don't get too many visitors at Paraĩso."

Tory smiled at the pretty young girl. "Well, I'm

161

happy to be here, Quinquina. While I eat my dinner, perhaps you could sit with me and tell me more about the ranch."

"If my aunt doesn't need me, I'll gladly stay and talk with you, *Professôra*."

"Good! I think I'll wash now, before you bring dinner."

"I'll be back soon, *Professôra*."

But it wasn't Quinquina who brought Tory's dinner a short while later; it was Sebastian. He walked in without knocking, catching Tory in an awkward position. Expecting only another female to enter the room, Tory had stripped down to her chemise and was sitting on the bed, brushing out her hair. When she saw Sebastian, she jumped up and snatched her blouse to cover herself.

"Relax, *gatinha*," Sebastian advised as he breezed into the room unconcernedly. "It's only me—and I've imagined you in far less clothing than you have on now."

"You could at least knock! What are you doing in here? Where's Carmelita and Padre Osmundo?"

"What does it look like I'm doing? I'm bringing refreshments. You went hungry once before in my house, so this time, I'm determined to play the perfect host and see that you are fed before you fall asleep."

"But where's Carmelita? You have no business in this room. As you can plainly see, I'm not decent!"

Laughing softly, he set down the tray on the opposite bed. "That bald admission comes as no surprise to me, *gatinha*. It's what I've suspected all along and have tried ceaselessly to get you to admit. You are *not* decent. Therefore, the sight of a man in your bed-chambers should hardly bother you at all."

Tory kept her blouse in front of her like a shield. "Sebastian, get out of here. You go too far. I insist that you leave and tell Carmelita to come to me."

"Carmelita is occupied, *gatinha*. She will probably sleep downstairs tonight. She and Padre Osmundo are going to take turns sitting up with Amâncio."

This information momentarily distracted Tory from her state of undress. "Amâncio hasn't taken a turn for the worse, has he?"

"No, *gatinha*, but it's best not to take chances. Padre Osmundo cleaned his wound again and adjusted the splint we made, and poor Amâncio is not feeling too well at the moment."

"I'd be happy to take a turn sitting up with him."

"We'll call you if we need you, *gatinha*. But first, you must eat and rest . . . My poor little kitten, you look as if you've been in a fight with a nasty dog twice your size."

Sebastian moved toward her, and in her haste to avoid him, Tory fell backward on the bed. Not wanting to give him any ideas that he didn't already have, she sprang upright like a bent twig snapping back into place. "I mean it, Sebastian. You must leave at once."

"Wouldn't you like a bath, *gatinha?* I have not forgotten you said you wanted one."

"Dona Guilhermina promised to see that I get one tomorrow. I *don't* need a bath tonight, and I certainly don't need your help in taking one."

"You are learning to read my thoughts, *gatinha.* I interpret that as progress . . . Are you sure you have everything you could possibly require?" His eyes slid down her body, caressing her bare shoulders and probing the blouse she still held in front of her.

163

She clenched her jaw and refused to react. "Everything. I have absolutely everything I want, need, or require."

"No, *gatinha*. You only think you do. In reality, you are missing the one thing that makes life worth living . . ."

"And that is?"

"Don't pretend you don't know, *gatinha*. I can see it in your eyes that you do . . . What I don't understand is why you continue to punish and deny yourself, when I am so willing to give it to you."

"Get out!" Tory hissed. "If you don't get out this minute, I'm marching right downstairs to Padre Osmundo and demanding that we leave for Espirito Santo this very night. Dona Guilhermina will just have to take care of Amâncio."

"You can't leave tonight . . . You know you cannot. Where is your sense of humor? I'm not even touching you . . . All I did was bring your dinner, yet you act as if I mean to harm you. You make threats and issue ultimatums. Your ugly suspicions wound me, *gatinha*. I am crushed by your continued hostility."

"What I'd like to do is physically incapacitate you once and for all!" Keeping her blouse in place with one trembling hand, Tory picked up her dropped hairbrush and brandished it under his nose. "How will you explain to Padre Osmundo why I started beating you with this hairbrush? How will you dismiss the welts on your face and head? . . . For that matter, how will you rationalize the fact that I am undressed?"

"All right, you win; I'm leaving!" Laughing, Sebastian retreated toward the door. "Good night, my beautiful, spitting wildcat. If there's anything else you desire while in my house, you have only to ask for it."

Struck by a sudden thought, Tory paused a moment. "There is something I want, Senhor *Cochorro*—a horse. I want to purchase a horse from you!"

His laughter died abruptly. "What would you do with a horse, *gatinha?*"

"Ride it, obviously! What else would I do with it? Oh, I don't mean for you to sell me Renegade. I'll take that chestnut you stole from the *cangaçeiros*."

Sebastian's face darkened. "I've already told you; you can't ride a horse in Brazil."

"Nevertheless, I want one—for starters, to explore your ranch."

"No, *gatinha*. Not only is it not customary for women to ride horses in Brazil, but it would be too dangerous for you to go riding off by yourself. And knowing you, I'm certain that's what you would do."

"It's too dangerous to be standing here talking to *you!*" she shouted. "Yet I'm doing it—fool that I am. I'll pay you twice what he's worth. No one else would make such a generous offer."

"No horses, *gatinha* . . . Learn your place. This is Brazil, not America."

She threw the hairbrush at him then, but he ducked and closed the door in her face. His laughter carried to her ears as he walked away—and she vowed to herself that one way or the other she would have a horse before she left for Espirito Santo!

Chapter Eleven

By the time Tory went down to breakfast the next morning, Sebastian had left the house. Dona Guilhermina informed her that he had ridden out at daybreak and would probably be gone the entire day, checking on the horses and cattle that roamed the *sertão*, and also on the *vaqueiros* who watched over the stock. Tory fumed silently as she drank her *café con leite* and nibbled a mango. She had wanted to take up the matter of a horse again, but this time in a safer setting, with all of her clothing intact. Well, there was plenty to keep her occupied today, but by tomorrow, she was determined to have a horse at her disposal.

The table at which she sat in the spacious, high-ceilinged dining room was very old, fashioned from the same dark, carved wood as the *guarda-roupa* in her bedroom. After she had finished eating, she wandered through the house, learning its layout and searching for someone else besides the intimidating, dour-faced Dona Guilhermina.

As in Salvador, there were parquet wooden floors throughout, heavy ornate furniture to match the dining room table, chairs, and her *guarda-roupa,* tall open windows which could be shuttered in case of rain, and a noticeable lack of ornamentation, except for a plain, wooden cross on the hallway wall which reminded her of its life-sized counterpart in Salvador. The only feminine things in the entire house were the squares of beautiful lace that graced the tables, and the arms and backs of several chairs. Tory suspected that they had been placed there by female hands, rather than Sebastian's, though she found it difficult to credit Dona Guilhermina with such delicate, domestic touches.

The airy front rooms and the verandah were vacant, so Tory headed for the center of the house which most likely contained the courtyard. She found it easily, a large square area dotted with plants and trees, and enclosed on all four sides by the house. In the center was a round structure that looked as if it caught and stored rainwater. Near it stood a bone-dry fountain rimmed by a bench. Tory circled the fountain and walked around the perimeter of the courtyard, examining the rooms that opened off it.

In one of them, she found Amâncio sleeping in a narrow bed, while Quinquina watched over him. The girl smiled and left the room to talk to Tory.

"Where's Padre Osmundo and Carmelita?" Tory whispered. "I've seen no one yet this morning."

"Padre Osmundo is resting in that room over there . . ." Quinquina pointed across the courtyard to a closed door. "And I think Carmelita has gone to my aunt's house to sleep where it is quiet. She did not want to disturb you by entering your room before you had awakened."

"Your aunt's house? Doesn't she live here?"

"Oh, no, we have our own house out back, *Profes-*

sôra. There are also houses assigned to those *vaqueiros* who have families they wish to keep close by . . . Of course, some of the *vaqueiros* are not married, or else their families live somewhere on the *sertão* or in Espirito Santo."

"So no one usually stays in *this* house except Senhor *Sebastião?*"

"*Sim, Professôra.* Senhor *Sebastião* is a very lonely man, with no wife and no children."

"Hasn't he ever seemed interested in marriage?" Tory was ashamed of herself for quizzing this innocent child, but she couldn't quell her curiosity.

"I have never heard that he was. But, of course, there have been women from time to time."

"What women?"

Quinquina looked down at the bare feet peeking from beneath her ankle-length brown skirt. "I should not mention them, *Professôra. Tia* Guilhermina would say I was gossiping."

"Yes, it would be gossip," Tory agreed. "We have no business discussing this . . . Forgive me for prying."

"There is nothing to forgive, *Professôra.* Besides, I am only stating what is common knowledge, so I don't see how it can harm anyone." Quinquina stepped closer and dropped her voice conspiratorially. "I have heard that there were as many as three women who stayed in our house before we did."

"All at one time?" Tory demanded, shocked.

"No, no . . . not all at one time. Three separate women each stayed for a period of time, until Senhor *Sebastião* tired of them and sent them back where they came from . . . While they were here, they also ran the house, like my aunt."

Three mistresses, Tory thought, fighting a stab of

fierce, surprising jealousy. Sebastian had had three mistresses and kept them in a house behind his own house. He probably had a string of illegitimate children, too. Come to think of it, the boy, Tuísca, looked enough like Sebastian to be his son—or maybe she was just imagining the resemblance.

"How did you and your aunt happen to come to work here?"

"Padre Osmundo brought us. We were living in a small village like Espirito Santo—my mother, my father, and my aunt. When my mother and my father died of fever, we were alone and hungry, with no one to care for us. Padre Osmundo learned of our plight and brought us here ... We have been here ever since—about four years."

"And during the time that you've been here, there have been no more women in the houses out back?"

"No, *Professôra*. My aunt would tell Padre Osmundo if Senhor *Sebastião* did that. However, it is said that he sees women when he goes to Salvador."

"I don't doubt it," Tory muttered under her breath.

"But you must not think badly of Senhor *Sebastião*, *Professôra* ... All the big *fazendeiros* keep women. Even after the rich landowners wed, they maintain their *namoradas*. No one criticizes them for it ... It is the nature of men to desire the favors of beautiful women."

"It's not the nature of *all* men to be promiscuous and unfaithful! ... How old are you, Quinquina, that you should know so much about men?"

Quinquina straightened her slim shoulders. "I'm fifteen, *Professôra*—old enough to marry ... But I don't want to get married and have babies yet. First, I'd like to learn to read and write. I want to come with

169

you to Espirito Santo and go to school, but I'm not sure my aunt will let me. I help her do the laundry, clean the house, and cook—then, too, there is a young man who wishes to marry me."

"But you're just a baby yourself!" Tory exclaimed. "Fifteen is far too young to be thinking of marriage . . . I'll see what can be done to persuade your aunt to allow you to accompany us to Espirito Santo. Perhaps you can help Carmelita keep house . . . If your young man truly cares for you, he'll be content to wait until you grow up and become educated. Then maybe you'll be able to teach your own children to read and write."

The girl's eyes shone like twin brown stars. "Oh, *Professôra!* That would be so wonderful! I do care for Teodoro, but if I marry him now, I'll never have the chance to learn anything . . . To read and write must be a wonderful thing."

"It is, Quinquina . . . and you shall have that chance if I have anything to say about it. Indeed, I could start teaching you before we leave for Espirito Santo. It will give me something to do all day . . . Now, why don't you show me around outside, and maybe later on today . . ."

Just then, from somewhere in the depths of the house, Dona Guilhermina called for Quinquina. The girl's face sagged with disappointment. "Excuse me, *Professôra*, but my aunt needs me right now. I must go and see what she wants."

"Of course . . . But come to me this afternoon if you can, and I'll begin teaching you your letters."

"*Sim, Professôra!*" The girl gave Tory an impromptu hug, then ran in the direction of her aunt's voice.

Tory tiptoed into Amâncio's room, and, finding

him still sleeping, tiptoed out again. More eager than ever to explore Sebastian's entire ranch, she headed for a doorway that looked as if it opened into the cookshed. It did, and at the back of the shed, another door led to the outside. Glad of a chance to be on her own, Tory slipped out of the house and headed for the corral where the horses were kept. She counted a half-dozen mares that were nothing much to look at, but did appear sturdy, healthy, and sure-footed. Their conformation wasn't all that bad, she decided, studying them, and crossed with a fine stud like Renegade, the mares might produce nice foals.

A barn adjoined the corral, but it contained no separate stalls like the barns back home. The single, large structure apparently served only to provide shade from the burning sun and shelter from rain. At this hour, a pole blocking the wide doorway prevented the horses from entering, but there was room enough inside for at least a dozen or so animals to mill about.

In a nearby smaller corral, Tory found the oxen contentedly munching a pile of sugar cane stalks. The still loaded cart stood nearby. Seeing no one, Tory wandered through the outbuildings where equipment, harnesses, and saddles were stored. Eventually, she strolled down a well-worn track toward a cluster of neat-looking huts some distance from the main house. From the huts came the sound of women chattering and children laughing and playing. Her appearance drew a small crowd of curious onlookers, among whom the children were especially delightful.

Dark-haired and dark-eyed, brimming with curiosity, they greeted her politely. Tory tried to make conversation, but everyone hung back as if too awed to speak with her. Deliberately, she made mistakes in grammar and pronunciation, drawing laughter and shy corrections. Soon, both women and children were asking dozens of eager questions about where she had come from and why. On inspiration, she invited them all to attend the classes she planned to initiate for Quinquina.

An hour later, by the time Carmelita emerged yawning from one of the huts, Tory felt she had made many new friends. The warmth and generosity of the *caboclos* amazed her; they insisted she accept gifts of fresh fruit, squares of fine white lace and small embroidered handtowels, and a pair of leather sandals that one woman declared were much cooler and more comfortable than the high button shoes Tory wore.

Even Carmelita seemed amazed by the peasants' hospitality. Taking Tory aside, out of earshot of the others, Carmelita exclaimed: *"Meu Deus!* So many presents, *Professôra!* . . . But what are you doing in the servants' quarters? I don't think Senhor *Sebastião* will approve of your coming here."

"Then don't tell him, Carmelita . . . On second thought, *do* tell him. How I occupy my time while I'm here at his ranch is not his concern. I must do something, or else I'll go mad with boredom."

"But what can you have to talk about with these poor *Sertanejos?* You are a rich, educated woman who has traveled the world, and these people have never been off the *sertão.* Most have never been to Salvador."

Tory was surprised, amused, and somewhat disappointed by Carmelita's snobbery. "I came here to teach the *caboclos*, Carmelita, not to prove myself better than they are. Indeed, I'm going to start

172

teaching them this very afternoon. Quinquina wishes to learn to read and write, and I've invited anyone else who would like to attend to do so."

"But, *Professôra* . . . It is the peasants in Espirito Santo you are to teach—not these. These people work for Senhor *Sebastião*. He may not want you to interfere in their lives."

"I can't believe he would not allow a few literacy classes, Carmelita. He's never said a word against my teaching in Padre Osmundo's school—other than warning that life on the *sertão* is too difficult for a supposedly pampered *Americana*."

Carmelita doubtfully shook her head. "If I were you, *Professôra,* I would at least ask Padre Osmundo what he thinks. Soon, it will be time for the noon meal. You can ask him then."

"I'll think about it, Carmelita . . . Though it seems to me you are worrying over nothing."

At the noon meal of the usual rice and beans, Tory did think about discussing the matter with Padre Osmundo, then decided against it. She needed no one's permission to introduce a few willing peasants to the wonder of the written word. She couldn't see how Sebastian could object . . . Instead, she broached a topic about which she already knew Sebastian's opinion and where she needed Padre Osmundo's help to overcome his ridiculous disapproval.

Padre Osmundo was on his second helping of black beans when she smiled at him and said: "Padre Osmundo, it's become increasingly obvious to me that I must purchase a horse. Don't you think that would be a good idea?"

Padre Osmundo swallowed a mouthful before answering. "Well, now, my child . . . Were you not such an accomplished equestrian, I would say abandon that notion because few females venture to ride horses in this country."

"True, but in as much as I *am* such an accomplished equestrian, it seems foolish to deny myself the pleasure and convenience of my own transportation. I can't accept walking everywhere for the time I'm in Brazil."

Padre Osmundo smiled and helped himself to a portion of baked bananas dusted with cinnamon and cane sugar. "You're never one to honor convention and the customs of society, are you, my child?"

"No, Padre, I'm not. If I were, I would never have come here. It's not that I *try* to be contentious; it's just that I can't bear to be a hypocrite. I must live by my own conscience, and where I can, try to right the wrongs I see."

Padre Osmundo's smile grew wider. "Then you are an idealist after my own heart, dear Senhorita King. I sensed that when first I met you . . . So have you discussed this matter with *Sebastião?* He is the only one around here with horses he could possibly sell to you."

Tory took a small bite of banana and found it delicious, but she was too agitated to eat more. Exasperated, she set down her fork. "As you may imagine, he does not approve of my flaunting custom. He refuses to sell the horse I want—or indeed any horse at all."

"And which horse do you want?"

"One of those he stole from the *cangaçeiros.* It's a chestnut with a bald face and two white hind feet. The horse would serve my purposes admirably, and I'd be willing to sell it back to him when I leave Brazil."

Padre Osmundo sipped his *cafêzinho,* then pushed

174

away the small cup. "What is it you want me to do? *Sebastião* pays little heed to my pronouncements. I could argue all day on your behalf, and he would not relent."

Tory leaned forward eagerly. "You could buy the horse for me, Padre. I'm sure he'd sell it to you. You could say you want it for when we go to Espirito Santo—so you don't have to walk on your injured ankle so much."

Padre Osmundo's round Humpty Dumpty belly shook with silent laughter. "You want me—a man of God—to *lie* to *Sebastião?*"

"God will forgive you, Padre. Such a tiny falsehood would serve a good cause . . . After all, you want your volunteer teacher to be happy, don't you? It would be a terrible thing if she became so miserable that she couldn't stay to teach the poor peasants after all."

"Ah, you blackmail me, my child! Such audacity . . . But what if *Sebastião* has a perfectly good reason why he doesn't wish to sell that horse? You assume *you* are the reason—but that may not be true."

"I'm the *only* reason, Padre. Make him an offer for the horse. He'll sell to *you*, I'm sure."

"All right, my child . . . I shall try to buy the beast for you as soon as *Sebastião* returns from the *sertão*. At the moment, however, I must go and check on Amâncio."

"Is he better today, Padre? When I saw him this morning, he was sleeping."

Padre Osmundo reached for his crutches. "He's much better, thanks be to God. It will be two months or more before his broken leg is completely healed, but there should be no complications. The break was clean—unlike my poor ankle that sustained severe bruising as well as a fracture. I sometimes wonder if this ankle will ever heal as good as new."

"All the more reason why you need a horse then, Padre."

Tory winked at him, and he laughed.

Tory was conducting her first class with Quinquina, several other women, and all of the children gathered on the shady verandah when Sebastian rode up on Renegade, accompanied by Miguel and Teodoro, also on horseback and like Sebastian, coated with the dust of the *sertão*. Tory saw the men out of the corner of her eye, but didn't stop to say hello. Instead, she again traced the letter Q in the air, explaining as she did so: "This is the first letter of Quinquina's name . . . If I had a slate and some chalk, I could show you better, but since all my teaching supplies are still packed away in my baggage, you'll just have to imagine what it looks like for now. It's round like an egg, with a little tail on the bottom of it."

"Oh, that should be easy to remember!" Quinquina crowed. "An egg with a tail on it . . . I'll never forget that."

"Now, everyone try to draw one in the air," Tory urged. "Point your finger and trace the shape of it just like I'm doing."

Sebastian rode to the bottom of the stairs leading up to the verandah and sat and watched her. Tory's skin prickled as it always did whenever he was near, and she darted him a nervous glance, fully expecting to find him scowling. To her great astonishment and relief, his face wore a wide, white grin. "Couldn't

176

wait to get started, eh, *gatinha?*" he called out in English.

"Please don't interrupt," Tory primly responded. "There are wonderful things happening here . . . A few minds that have been trapped too long in cages of ignorance are being set free."

Sebastian tipped his leather *vaqueiro's* hat to her. "I can see that . . . Do continue, esteemed *Professôra*. I'm happy to witness such progress occurring on my own front porch."

Tory's heart swelled to bursting; Sebastian did not disapprove! He honestly did seem pleased that she was teaching the wives and children of his workers. However, the two men with him were frowning, and before she could continue with her lesson, the one named Miguel gave an angry shout. "Filomena, go home! . . . I am hungry, and I wish to eat. Take the children with you."

One of the women stepped forward, her face flaming. "Yes, my husband . . . I am going. Come, children."

Two of the little ones with the brightest, most intelligent eyes scrambled to their feet and clutched their mother's hands as she led them away. Tory's happiness shattered. She wanted to protest, but dared not interfere. Even in America, she had never intruded between a husband and wife. It simply wasn't done. Besides, no matter how much Tory hated to see such injustice, she knew she couldn't change things overnight for this woman—or any woman who permitted herself to be bossed and bullied by a jealous, domineering male.

The young man named Teodoro then sat up straighter in his saddle and cleared his throat. "Quin-quina, what are you doing here? Aren't you supposed

177

to be helping your aunt with the evening meal?"

Tory wondered where the young *vaqueiro* had gained the right to remind Quinquina of her duties—especially when Dona Guilhermina herself had not seen fit to call the girl away.

"I am learning to write my name—and one day to read," Quinquina announced with a flash of defiance. "We aren't married yet, Teodoro. You can't tell me what I can or can't do."

"We'll be married soon enough . . . As soon as you cease pretending you're the daughter of a rich *fazendeiro*, instead of a humble *empregada*. What need have you to read and write?"

The young man's challenge caused the women and children to murmur uneasily among themselves. Tory waited for Sebastian to say something—to put this young pup in his place. But Sebastian sat perfectly still, listening but saying nothing.

Quinquina's liquid brown eyes suddenly filled with tears. "Why do you mock me, Teodoro? I know I am nothing special . . . It is just that I have this hunger inside me . . . Can you not understand?"

"Quinquina!" Glowering like a thundercloud, Dona Guilhermina suddenly appeared in the doorway to the house. "Come inside at once. There's work to be done."

"*Sim, Tia.*" The girl choked on her tears, then darted past Tory and went running inside.

Never having expected her modest efforts to produce such devastating results, Tory gazed after her in dismay. How quickly this first sweet triumph had turned bitter as ashes! She caught Sebastian's eye. He did not look at all surprised. If anything, his expression seemed to say: Did you think it would be easy, *gatinha*? I told you it would not.

Pointedly ignoring him, she turned to the remaining subdued little group. "That will be the end of our first lesson for today. We'll try again tomorrow, when I'll teach you the letter for *my* name and then for each of your's."

As women and children left the verandah, Sebastian reined Renegade around and kneed him into a trot. Sensing the tension in the air, the big bay whinnied, and Tory was reminded to encourage Padre Osmundo to speak with Sebastian *today*. She had suffered one setback and didn't intend to suffer another. By tonight, she intended to own the horse she craved, no matter *what* Sebastian thought.

Chapter Twelve

Sebastian poured himself and Padre Osmundo a brandy, and then carried the two goblets out onto the verandah where the old priest sat with his tightly-bandaged ankle propped upon a stool. In the gathering dusk, Sebastian could just make out his friend's smiling features as he accepted the glass and raised it in a wordless toast. There was something on the old man's mind. Sebastian had seen the signs during dinner; there had been an extra twinkle in the merry black eyes, a thoughtful pursing of the full lips, a knowing glance passed back and forth between the priest and Tory King.

Undoubtedly, Padre Osmundo was going to try and persuade him to sanction the literacy classes Tory seemed intent on conducting. His approval would undercut the *dis*approval of Sebastian's own *vaqueiros,* none of whom could read and write, and none of whom appreciated women and children learning something they didn't know and didn't have the time or inclination to learn.

Aware of the value of education, Sebastian had at first been delighted that Tory had undertaken to teach his workers while she was in residence—but as usual, he could never express his true feelings without raising doubts about his character as Sebastian Black. As a *fazendeiro*—or *patrão*, as he was sometimes called—his role was essentially a fatherly one. He must remain strict, even cruel at times, in regards to how his workers used their time. Though rarely unjust, he could not afford to be too friendly or kind, and he certainly could never champion the idea of his *caboclos* rising too high above their stations. He walked a precarious line, one that required perfect balance if he himself was not to fall over the edge.

No, if need be, he would have to curtail the classes. Hopefully, it wouldn't come to that. Perhaps if Tory confined her activities only to the children, his men wouldn't become too restive. Quinquina, especially, should be discouraged from continuing; she was all but betrothed to Teodoro. The girl needed to learn housekeeping and cooking skills, not pursue mental advancements that would bring her nothing but grief in the end. One of the harsh realities of life on the *sertão* was that no man would want her if she put on airs and became too haughty—and without a husband, a woman was doomed to a life of sadness and loneliness. She had no place in society and was looked down upon by everyone.

Sebastian sipped his brandy and sat down beside Padre Osmundo. With Tory off feeding Amâncio the evening meal, now was the time to discuss this sensitive matter with Padre Osmundo. Sebastian could state his opinions without fear of instigating a loud, explosive argument. Whereas, if Tory joined them, he would be letting himself in for an evening of escalating hostility—and hostility was the last thing he wanted to arouse in the very provocative and desirable Miss King.

"All right, Padre, what's on your mind? You've been working up to something all evening."

Padre Osmundo chuckled and rearranged a fold of his brown robe over his elevated ankle. "You know me too well, *mon filho* . . . There is something on my mind tonight, so I'll not keep you in suspense any longer. I'll tell you what it is, and you can say yes or no as the spirit moves you."

"Then tell me. I'm listening."

"I've been wondering if you could bear to part with one of your precious horses."

"My horses! Why, that's a surprise, Padre . . . I was expecting you to say something else. Why do you want a horse? I've never known you to be overly fond of the animals or interested in climbing on their backs."

"Normally, I'm not. But hobbling about on these crutches has given me a new perspective. It will be some time before my ankle heals, and when it does, I expect it will bother me to do a great deal of walking . . . I walk constantly in Espirito Santo, visiting my little flock which is scattered all over the *sertão*, and it has occurred to me that now would be a good time to take up riding—to spare myself discomfort and weariness."

The growing darkness made it difficult to see the old man's face, but his voice sounded sincere enough. Sebastian entertained a fleeting doubt that the priest might be trying to procure a horse for Miss King, instead of for himself, but then set it aside. Padre Osmundo was certainly capable of deviousness, but he also had a valid argument for why he wanted a horse when he had never before desired one. The request made sense.

"So you actually intend to ride instead of walk to make your rounds in Espirito Santo," Sebastian reiterated.

Padre Osmundo nodded. "Yes . . . though we won't be leaving immediately, I assure you. I want to be certain Amâncio is mending well first, and I'd also like to be more mobile myself. In view of your own recent attack by *cangaçeiros*, you must admit that an incapacitated man has no business traveling until he's at least fit enough to defend himself."

"I'm glad we agree on that . . . Which horse of mine do you covet?"

"Well, I'm not much for choosing a good horse, but that red one you got from the *cangaçeiros* looks to be a dependable fellow."

"My, my . . . That's the second offer I've had on that chestnut recently. He seems to be quite popular."

"You mean Miss King has offered to buy him?" Padre Osmundo lifted his brows. "Then I suppose you'd prefer selling him to her, since she's a much better rider than I am."

"On the contrary, Padre. I refused to sell any of my horses to Miss King. You know as well as I that she can't go galloping about the *sertão* as she did on her brother's farm. Such freedom for a woman is unheard of in this country."

"True . . . true . . ." Padre Osmundo took another swallow of brandy, then peered at Sebastian over the rim. "Of course, I can't begin to offer what the horse is probably worth. You know my financial situation."

"I'm amazed that you can afford to offer anything . . . Were you, perhaps, hoping I'd give him to you?"

183

A sly grin illuminated the priest's round face. "Now that you mention it, that's not a bad idea, *mon filho*. I would, of course, be willing to say a few masses for the salvation of your soul in exchange."

"All right then, he's yours, Padre . . . I give him to you for nothing, except a few paltry masses. So long, that is, as I never see Miss King racing him across the *sertão*."

Padre Osmundo shifted in his chair. "*Mon filho*, I told you this horse was for me . . . and while I am correcting your misimpressions, let me also say that a few masses are *not* paltry. You need masses as well as anyone."

"You mean I need them *more* than most . . . But that is another subject altogether. Be happy you have gained your horse, Padre. You can't win everything in a single day."

"Oh, I am happy, and I thank you, *Sebastião*. Once again, you have proven that quite contrary to appearances and public opinion, you have a kind and generous nature."

Sebastian frowned. "Better to believe public opinion, Padre. Don't ever *count* on my kindness and generosity. You may be bitterly disappointed."

"My son, I've been counting on it for years, and I've never once been disappointed. When others mention your name, I am sometimes astounded by their harsh opinions of you . . . For some reason, you seem to go out of your way to hide your basic goodness of heart."

Sebastian drank more brandy to hide his sudden agitation. *Then perhaps I'll have to go out of my way to prove to you once again that I really cannot be trusted,* he thought. *I* can't *have you singing my praises in front of my enemies.*

He searched his mind for a way to demonstrate his wickedness, but the only thing that occurred to him was an idea he had already thought of—being a bastard when it came to Tory King's literacy classes. Yes, he must take a harsh stand and forbid the classes to the women and maybe even to the children. He hated to deprive the children, but protecting his identity as the Falcon was more important at the moment, especially now, when the Falcon was again becoming active. Someday, there would be a better time and place for the children to learn; once Cerqueira was destroyed, all the peasants on the *sertão* would lead better lives. He would see to it.

He downed the last of his brandy and yawned exaggeratedly. "Excuse me, Padre, but I find myself extremely sleepy this evening . . . You won't mind if I say goodnight early."

"Not at all, *Sebastião*. I intend to retire early, too, as soon as I check on Amâncio. I thought Senhorita King would have joined us by now. Since she hasn't, I had better make certain that everything is well."

"She's probably teaching Amâncio to read," Sebastian said drily. "But I wish she would save her zeal for education until she gets to Espirito Santo. She's starting a bit early, I think."

"You disapprove of her teaching your workers?"

There it is, Sebastian thought, the opening for which he had been waiting.

"I disapprove most strenuously, and you can tell her so for me. There are to be no more literacy classes on my verandah."

Leaning forward, Padre Osmundo raised his hand in protest. "But *mon filho!* How can you deny your workers the advantages I myself once gave you? Everyone should learn to read."

185

"I strongly disagree, Padre." Sebastian squirmed inwardly, suddenly hating the duplicity and deceit he practiced. He detested the necessity of inflicting pain on his oldest and dearest friend, but could see no way out of the dilemma.

"The comparison between myself and my workers is hardly apt," he brutally continued. "I was a gifted, unusual child. You have stated this many times in the past. I do not want Miss King raising the hopes of poor, stupid peasants that they can achieve things far beyond their modest capabilities. Given half a chance, she'll soon have them thinking that all they have to do is learn to read and write, and their lives will improve dramatically overnight . . . If Quinquina can write her name, will that attract a better husband for her? Of course not. It will only create tension between her and Teodoro."

"Then maybe Teodoro should learn to read and write! How can you say these things, *Sebastião?* You of all people should realize that education confers power and opens doors."

"Yes, and it also causes great unrest and dissatisfaction. There can only be so many rich men, Padre. Why else does a man seek to better his mind if not to improve his station in life? Teach a man to read, and before you know it, he'll want to live in a big house like I do and lord it over other men . . . It is what *I* wanted when I studied so hard among your Franciscan friars. I saw education only as a means to becoming the man I am today . . . But how many men like me can there be? Who will clean my house, drive my cattle, tend my horses, and cut my sugar cane, if all my workers become educated?"

By now, it was completely dark, but Sebastian did not need light to see that Padre Osmundo was utterly stricken. He could gauge his friend's reaction by the long, heavy sigh he expelled.

"Oh, my son . . . Your words cut deeply into my heart. I never thought to hear you say such things, never dreamed that you were thinking them . . . All these years, you have contributed to my work and helped to make my dream of a school come true . . . Why did you do it, if you truly believe what you've just said?"

I don't believe it, Padre, but I can never admit it to you, at least not now, not yet.

"I'm not without gratitude for what you've done for me, Padre," Sebastian drawled, concealing his remorse in deliberate, hurtful sarcasm. "You took a handful of humble clay and molded it into a man to be reckoned with . . . You mustn't blame yourself if I now wish to protect what I've become and all I've obtained . . . Miss King can teach the peasants in Espirito Santo. She can strive to elevate them to whatever heights you both deem appropriate. But leave *my* peasants at peace in their dark little caves of ignorance, as Miss King calls it. I will see to it that they are fed and cared for. Their lives will have purpose and meaning, limited though it may seem to you. They'll never starve beneath my roof . . . Just don't give them expectations that can never be realized or make them unhappy in my service."

"Stop!" Padre Osmundo pleaded. "Don't say another word, I beg you . . . I see now what mistakes I have made with you, *Sebastião* . . . *Meu Deus*, I have failed you miserably! We Franciscans gave you mathematics and literature. From us, you learned history, logic, and Latin . . . But the things you needed most, we never taught you! . . . You lack charity and compassion. Humility is not a word in

187

your vocabulary . . . And what of justice and mercy? What of simple human kindness?"

"Don't torture yourself, Padre. I doubt that God will judge you as harshly as you judge yourself . . . If I have any saving grace, it is my affection for you. Because of you, I helped build that school . . . And because of you, I'll help build your hospital, though I see little sense in prolonging lives that are bitter and useless . . . Only death can bring the freedom and happiness you desire for the *caboclos*. In life, they must learn to accept what fate has decreed for them. Before they were born, they were doomed to a life of servitude. It has always been thus for the poor, and always will be."

"Oh, *Sebastião* . . ." There was a catch in the old man's voice, and tears glistened in his eyes.

Sebastian almost wept with remorse for having caused his friend this pain, but he remembered who and what he was, and why he was doing this. "Save your sorrow for something or someone more deserving, Padre . . . I have disappointed you. I deeply regret it. But let there be truth between us, if nothing else."

Sebastian stood and put his hand on the priest's shoulder. "I will leave you now. The hour grows late. Do you need help going into the house in the dark?"

Padre Osmundo sat hunched in the chair, his shoulders sagging. "No, *mon filho*. I can manage . . . I just wish . . . I just wish that sometimes you were *not* so truthful."

If you only knew, Padre, Sebastian thought. If you only knew . . . I have *never* been truthful with you.

Tory sat beside Amâncio's bed, patiently tracing

the letter A in the air. "That is the first letter of your name, Amâncio. It's not so difficult, and once you learn all the letters, you'll be ready to start reading . . . Then the whole world will open up for you. Perhaps Senhor *Sebastião* will permit you to borrow the books he has in his library, and you will discover for yourself that books can teach you anything you want to know. They can take you places you've never been and reveal truths you have never imagined."

Amâncio's brown eyes glistened in the lamplight as he watched Tory's hand. She could not be sure he understood what she was trying to tell him—or that his mind was capable of grasping the abstract concept of letters and reading. Since Amâncio spoke so little, she had no real idea of his intelligence, but he could handle oxen, shoot a rifle, and do various other tasks assigned by Sebastian. Surely, that meant he could not be a complete imbecile. If she could teach him to write his name, she would be giving him something on which to build a solid foundation for a lifetime of learning and enrichment.

"Can you say the letter A, Amâncio? It's the first letter of the alphabet . . . a most important letter that is used in many, many words. Your own name has it twice . . . Let's try it, shall we?"

Tory repeated the sound for A, but Amâncio merely stared at her lips, his dark eyes mesmerized. He would not talk to her beyond the simplest sentences and then only when unavoidable. His behavior frustrated and exasperated her. Amâncio was going to be laid up for a long time, a perfect opportunity for utilizing his mind, instead of his hands. But unless he learned to relax and speak more in her presence, they would never get anywhere.

"What I need is writing materials, so I can show

189

you how the letter A looks when it is drawn. Tomorrow, I'll insist that my baggage be unloaded so I can go through it and find some. I wasn't going to unpack until we got to Espirito Santo, but if we stay here much longer, I can see that I'll have to . . . What do you think, Amâncio? Tell me, would you like to learn to read and write?''

Amâncio stared at her a moment, then uttered the single word, *"Sim."*

It was enough to fuel Tory's flagging enthusiasm. "Wonderful! Then I'll give you a lesson every day that I'm here, and when I depart, I'll leave you a copy of the entire alphabet and your name written out, so you can practice each letter on your own until I see you again . . . How will that be?''

Amâncio gave her a shy, uncertain smile and nodded, heightening her elation, so that when Padre Osmundo came into the room on his crutches, she babbled to him excitedly. "Amâncio wants to learn to read and write, Padre . . . I've already started teaching him. Isn't that marvelous?''

The pale, sad features of the priest brought her up short, causing a sinking sensation in her stomach. "What is it, Padre? What's wrong?''

Padre Osmundo made his way to a chair and sat down before responding. *"Sebastião* has forbidden any more classes in literacy, my child . . . He claims they will stir up discontent among his workers for a life they can never have.''

"He claims *what?* But that's nonsense! And I hope you told him so.''

Padre Osmundo regarded her with such a downcast expression that her heart went out to him—and swelled with anger toward Sebastian. "I doubt I can say anything to influence his twisted views, my child.

190

Something—I know not what—holds a greater influence over him than I ever achieved . . . I don't understand it . . . To refuse to permit the literacy classes is blatantly unfair. I have known him a long time, and it is the most unfair thing he's ever done."

"Well, he's not going to deprive people of learning so long as I can do something about it," Tory huffed.

"There's nothing you *can* do, my child. *Sebastião's* word is law here on his *estância.*"

"He can't stop what he doesn't know about! I'll conduct the classes in secrecy, while he's out riding the *sertão.* People have done things behind his back before and gotten away with it, so I don't know why I can't."

Tory was thinking of Carmelita and Amâncio feeding the beggars in Salvador. She turned to Amâncio. "You wouldn't tell on me, would you, Amâncio? Especially since you're going to be one of my prize students."

"*Não, Professôra,* I would not tell," Amâncio agreed.

Tory counted this a great breakthrough in her relationship with the black man. "You see, Padre? If Amâncio won't tell, the only person I really have to worry about is Dona Guilhermina, and I'll get around her one way or another. Since Sebastian's *vaqueiros* usually go with him, who does that leave to protest?"

Padre Osmundo shook his head. "Deceit is a terrible thing, my child. It feeds upon itself and produces more deceit . . . The end does not justify the means."

"Don't worry about it, Padre. You've given me Sebastian's message, now leave everything else to me . . . By the way, did he sell you that horse I want?"

"He didn't sell it, my child, he *gave* it to me . . . But promised to take it back if ever he sees *you* riding it."

"Then that's just another little secret we'll have to keep from him, isn't it? . . . Darn! He's so . . . so prejudiced! I offered to buy that horse for twice what it's worth, and he wouldn't consider it because I'm a mere woman . . . But to you, he'll *give* it away for nothing."

"Not for nothing, my child . . . I promised to say several masses for the good of his soul."

"It would take a lifetime of masses to save *his* soul," Tory scoffed. "That is, if he's even got one."

"Oh, he has one, my child . . . We all do . . . I only wish I knew when his became so endangered. His prejudice toward women I can understand. In Brazil, women have never enjoyed your American freedoms . . . But his prejudice toward the *caboclos* greatly disturbs me. In the past, he's always helped and defended them. Now he seems to think he's better than they are, so much so that he's beginning to remind me of Mundinho Cerqueira, a local *fazendeiro* who exemplifies all the worst traits of his class . . . I am greatly saddened to see this. More, I pity *Sebastião* for what he is becoming."

Tory felt great sympathy for the poor priest. Obviously, he had been blind to Sebastian's faults all along, even though they were glaringly apparent to an objective observer like herself. "Don't feel too badly, Padre . . . Soon, we'll be leaving for Espirito Santo. If you want to pity someone, pity Amâncio, who has to stay here with him . . ."

"Senhor *Sebastião* is not a bad man," Amâncio suddenly spoke up. "In his heart, he is good and seeks good for others. This I have many times wit-

192

nessed with my own eyes."

For the second time that evening, Tory stared at Amâncio in astonishment. The bedridden servant had just been told that his master didn't want him to improve himself. In Salvador, Amâncio had had to sneak around Sebastian in order to feed the beggars, and it was poor Amâncio who got stuck with all the menial, degrading chores. He of all people had reason to be critical of Sebastian—yet still, he defended him!

"It seems to me, Amâncio, that *you* are the good man in this house," Tory countered. "The better I get to know Sebastian, the less I like him. Whereas the better I get to know you, the more impressed I am."

"But it's true, my child . . ." Padre Osmundo sided with the black man. "*Sebastião* is *not* all bad. I am disappointed in him tonight, but I can still recall the many times he has helped me in the past, and I have no doubt he will again do so in the future."

"Well, you two can debate his character all you wish, but I'm going to bed—just as soon as I sneak out to the corral and have a closer look at that horse you finagled out of him. What is he worth to you, Padre? I can't offer to repay you in masses, but I will donate something to the school—or the hospital, whichever you prefer."

Padre Osmundo spread his hands. "I cannot take money for a horse that cost me no money, my child . . . That would not be proper. All I ask is that you do not ride him until we are well away from here, nor ever reveal what I have done . . . I don't want *Sebastião* to catch me in a lie."

"He won't, I promise you, Padre . . ." Thinking that she would find a way to pay Padre Osmundo anyhow, Tory rose from her chair. "Goodnight, both of you . . . Sleep well, and I'll see you in the morning."

When she left Amâncio's room, Tory made her way through the courtyard to the cookshed and then outside to the corral. Overhead, the stars formed a fiery, diamond-studded canopy that illuminated the horses in the pen. She leaned on a railing and studied the animals, easily picking out the bald-faced chestnut contentedly munching fodder beside Renegade. As the only stallion on the ranch, Renegade took it upon himself to show his superiority by occasionally nipping at the geldings and sometimes even at the mares, though he treated the latter with a bit more respect. Of the three geldings in the pen, two were completely intimidated, snatching a mouthful of fodder whenever they could, but otherwise keeping well away from Renegade. Only Tory's new horse kept shouldering into the main group, demonstrating a dogged perseverance that appealed to Tory. She decided to call him Perseverance, or Percy, for short.

It was an apt name for a horse that now belonged to her; perseverance was her own most dominant quality. She hated to retreat from a fight and wouldn't be caught dead giving up or slinking off in defeat to lick her wounds. Had it been possible, she would have remained a teacher at that stuffy boarding school in her own country and continued to broaden her students' minds and challenge their parents, too. But it hadn't been possible, and that was why she now found herself in Brazil, fighting greater prejudice against women and the downtrodden than she had ever imagined existed in the world.

A sudden wave of homesickness washed over her, and she longed to see Jordan, her sisters, and Spencer again. She wished she could seek Spencer's practi-

194

cal, levelheaded advice, eat a slab of rare, juicy steak instead of rice and beans, climb on any horse she wanted and go for a good gallop, romp with her dog and run her fingers through her cat's soft fur. She hoped Abelardo and Marta were taking good care of her pets, and that her students had not forgotten all that she had tried to teach them.

In this strange, alien culture, she suddenly felt very much alone. She wished she understood Sebastian better because then she would know how to counter his objections about teaching his workers. She wished she could like him better; it was agony to physically desire a man for whom she otherwise felt anger and contempt. It bothered her that she was so vulnerable where he was concerned—that her heart leapt whenever she heard his voice, and her breath rattled in her chest whenever he came near.

I won't think about him, she sternly lectured herself. *Soon, I'll be leaving, and I'll never have to be near him or alone with him again.*

When a muscular arm suddenly slid around her waist, and a velvet voice purred in her ear, she almost leapt from her skin—Sebastian! Her forbidden thoughts had conjured the man himself, and all the cutting, furious things she wanted to say to him fled from her mind. Whirling in his embrace, she confronted him eye to eye.

"What are you doing?" she gasped. "Let go of me this instant, you *brioso* cretin."

He chuckled deep in his throat. "A better question would be, what are *you* doing, *gatinha?* You shouldn't be out here all alone after the rest of the house has gone to bed."

"I'm looking at the horses—including the one you gave Padre Osmundo but refused to sell to me."

195

"Ah well . . . What did you expect? He is a man, and you, my sweet, are a desirable, delectable woman whom I cannot seem to stop wanting, no matter how hard I try." His words prickled her flesh with goosebumps, and she shivered uncontrollably, causing his arms to tighten around her. "Are you cold, *gatinha?*"

His body pressed along the length of hers, the heat of his flesh branding her through the light fabric of her clothing. No, she wasn't cold; she was burning up! Dazed and disoriented by his nearness, she noted that he was dressed for riding, in the dark attire he favored out on the *sertão*.

"Are you going somewhere tonight?" she asked.

He smiled down into her eyes, his own eyes reflecting the starlight. "If I were, would you come with me? I might consent to a moonlit ride where no one could see you."

"A moonlit ride? But . . . I . . . there's no moon tonight!"

"We could ride in the starlight," he whispered suggestively. "We could mount our horses bareback and run like the wind beneath the stars."

"I . . . um . . . don't have a horse," she responded thickly, her tongue tripping over itself. At all costs, she mustn't betray Padre Osmundo! But she did desperately want to go for a ride. What Sebastian was offering sounded incredible, in view of his past objections—and if he became too amorous, she could always escape by galloping away.

"You don't need one," he purred. "You can ride with me."

Before she could form a protest, he scooped her off her feet and cradled her in his arms like a baby. "Come ride with me," he whispered. "Tonight was made for flying across the plain like the falcon flies across the sky."

It was too much of a temptation to resist—a chance to gallop beneath the stars! To be alone with Sebastian and get to know him better. He seemed a different person tonight, or maybe *she* was different . . . Why was she permitting this to happen? Sebastian never lost a chance to try and seduce her, and she was more angry with him tonight than she had ever been in the past . . . But suddenly, it didn't matter. Nothing mattered but this moment of recklessness. Somehow, miraculously, Sebastian had changed his mind about letting her ride and had invited her to join him in a wild race across the silvery *sertão*. If he could change his mind about this, maybe he could change it about other things. She *couldn't* say no.

Meekly, she let him carry her through the gate of the corral. He walked straight to Renegade and lifted her up to sit sideways on the horse's back. The big bay whinnied and nosed Sebastian's shirt front.

"Mind your manners," Sebastian told him, slipping a bridle over Renegade's head.

Sebastian must have had the bridle in his hand all along, but Tory hadn't seen it . . . He *had* intended on going somewhere tonight. Or maybe he was just going to put the bridle away in the barn. Sebastian led the horse out of the corral. While he did so, Tory hiked up her skirt and straddled Renegade the way she always had. Her bare legs were partially revealed, but she hoped Sebastian wouldn't notice in the darkness . . . Now that she finally had her chance, she didn't want to fall off!

When they were away from the corral, Sebastian easily mounted behind her, then slipped one arm around her waist. With his free hand, he kept hold of the reins. "Now, isn't this better than riding separately, *gatinha?*"

She hardly knew how to respond. She had *begged* him to let her ride Renegade again, and he had adamantly refused. Whatever the reason for his capitulation, she wouldn't be cheated now. Giving no warning, she squeezed her legs together and dug a heel into Renegade's side. The horse took off; only the fact that they were both excellent riders prevented them from tumbling backwards.

Sebastian's arm clamped tightly about her waist. "Wildcat . . ." He laughed into her hair. "This is what you've been wanting for a long time, isn't it?"

"Yes!" she cried into the wind, urging Renegade into a flat out gallop. "Yes! Yes—oh, yes!"

Chapter Thirteen

Glorying in the feel of the fine horse between his legs and the beautiful woman in his embrace, Sebastian let Tory have her exhilarating gallop beneath the stars. He had no fear of Renegade tripping or falling; the horse was sure-footed and loved to run, and the night was bright enough to enable him to avoid the thorny underbrush and cactus of the *cããtinga*.

Cristo! But Tory was a woman to tempt a man beyond his endurance. She was a wild, free creature no man could tame, doing things she had no business doing, possessing skills—like her riding—she had no business possessing, and driving him half-mad with wanting her. He was supposed to be en route to meet his most experienced, trustworthy *vaqueiros* for a raid on Mundinho Cerqueira's cattle. Teodoro and Miguel had already left to join the others, and they were waiting for him at their usual meeting place near a branch of the *São Francisco* River . . . But tonight, they would have to wait an extra long time.

When he had seen Tory standing in the starlight, her blond hair shimmering like the gold on the walls of

199

the *Igreja de São Francisco*, he had not been able to resist. He wanted her to himself for a short while—wanted her alone and free beneath the stars, and was even willing to offer her something he knew she could not resist in order to persuade her to come away with him. When he had mentioned the possibility of a ride, her face had lit up like a star itself, but this gallop on Renegade was only one of the rides he wanted to give her; the other sort was a very intimate, personal one, and he thought he knew just the right sort of setting for it.

Guiding Renegade north toward the distant river branch, he made certain he was nowhere near the spot where his *vaqueiros* were awaiting the Falcon's arrival. While Tory enjoyed the sensation of the powerful horse straining its powerful muscles beneath them, Sebastian enjoyed having his arm around Tory's slender waist. Eventually, as Renegade tired and slowed to an easy canter, Sebastian began a gentle rubbing motion near Tory's midsection. She sighed and leaned back against him, making his hopes spiral giddily. He inhaled the sweet night breezes and fought to still his pounding heart; he felt as if he couldn't get enough air to expand his lungs properly.

As the horse slowed to a trot and then a walk, Sebastian silently nuzzled Tory's magnificent blond hair, seeking the column of her neck. She suffered him to nibble gently on her earlobe, and he darted his tongue inside her ear while his hand stroked her waist—and then slowly moved higher. An experienced woman would know immediately what he wanted by the boldness of this action; Tory did not stop him, so he assumed that she was at long last amenable to his attentions. She had, after all, been fighting their mutual desire for an absurdly long time.

Draping the reins across Renegade's neck, Sebastian allowed the horse to walk at will while he employed both hands to conquer Tory's crumbling defenses. Kissing and nibbling along her neck and shoulder, he wrapped both hands around her slender midriff and gently massaged the tips of her delicate breasts with his thumbs in a feather-light motion. She grew still as a captive bird, and he could feel her heart hammering furiously. He knew better than to speak or push her too far without having first won her complete acquiescence.

Gently, he turned her towards him, setting her sideways on the horse, in which position he could kiss her mouth, not just her neck. "Sebastian . . ." she started to protest, but he cut her off by enfolding her in his arms.

"Hush, *gatinha* . . . Don't speak. Just feel . . . Feel the night wind rippling your hair. Feel the horse moving beneath us . . . my arms holding you tightly . . . the way you make my heart pound just to be near you . . ."

He lifted her hand and placed it over his racing heart. Her fingers were shaking. Holding them still against his chest, he bent his head and took her mouth. She kissed like an innocent—with her lips primly closed . . . This surprised him, but her mouth was so soft and tender that he hardly minded the slight resistance. He coaxed her lips apart with his tongue and wouldn't let her pull away when he began to gently plunder the warm, moist cavern.

He kissed her long and thoroughly—until she leaned against him in mute surrender. He himself could hardly keep his wits about him, but he

201

cautioned himself to patience. He must not frighten her now. For some reason, she was still wary of him, reluctant to surrender what she had undoubtedly given many men before him. Perhaps her American lovers had been too hasty, crude, and aggressive to woo her properly . . . Well, he would show her what it was like to be loved by a man of his expertise and prowess . . . He wanted her melting in his arms, begging him to take her, her body awash with exquisite sensation. It was no great trial to bring a woman to full flowering and then to prolong the final ecstasy until they were both beyond rational thought. He never had been able to understand why some men rushed things, behaving like rutting bulls instead of experienced lovers. It heightened a man's own pleasure when a woman wanted him with all her being.

Kissing Tory as thoroughly and passionately as he knew how, he slid his hand beneath her shirtwaist blouse, which he had been working free of her skirt by slow degrees. His fingers searched her chemise, found the drawstring, and nimbly tugged it loose. Thank God, she wasn't wearing a corset! He hated corsets, but Tory, in her own practical way, had eliminated that bothersome barrier, probably because it was too hot for one out on the *sertão*. Slowly, silencing any potential protests with his kisses, he bared her breasts, then proceeded to pay diligent court to them.

In his opinion, even the most devoted of lovers often ignored the erotic potential of a woman's breasts. But he had found that if he spent time lavishing attention on them, teasing them to pebbled peaks with his hands and mouth, then the woman was his . . . She would spread her legs eagerly when the time came and welcome him with a honeyed slickness that made penetration easy and painless, a true feast of sensation. He used all his past knowledge and experience to conquer each of Tory's possible objections . . . Her breasts were so delicate and feminine! He loved making love to them.

Keeping a tight rein on his own reactions to the delightful love play, he slid his hand beneath her skirt and up her thigh. He had noticed that her legs were bare—another wonderful concession to the heat—but she still wore underdrawers. He cursed the invention of such a stupid, ridiculous garment, resenting anything that prevented skin from touching skin. Slowly, he massaged her thighs through the sturdy dimity, then clasped her intimately between the legs.

She stiffened when he touched her there, but the evidence of her desire delighted him. She felt warm and damp. The answering response of his own body made him quickly remove his hand; he didn't want to lose control before she was ready for him to take her! Yet he could hardly wait. Patience, he sternly reminded himself. This woman had been taunting him since the day he had first met her. It was worth a bit of self-denial, even a bit of discomfort, to finally be able to possess her totally.

With a ragged intake of breath, he stopped kissing Tory and glanced up to discover that they had reached the small branch of the mighty *São Francisco* River that watered his land. On the distant horizon, a herd of his cattle languidly grazed. The muted voice of a *vaqueiro* singing to the animals to calm them carried to him on the night breeze. Renegade flicked his ears back, patiently awaiting some further instruction.

"The horse . . ." Sebastian whispered in Tory's ear. "Renegade is tired . . . We must rest him here, before we go back . . ."

Tory barely seemed to notice the cattle or the *vaqueiros*, who were, thankfully, moving in the opposite direction. She made a little sound of protest in her throat as he slid his hand from beneath her skirt, quickly dismounted, and lifted her down. She went into his arms willingly, allowing him to slide her body down the length of him so that she could not fail to feel his arousal. He became even more enflamed.

"*Gatinha* . . ." he groaned. "*Cristo*, I burn for you."

"We shouldn't be doing this . . ." she murmured, her eyes dreamy in the starlight. "We mustn't . . . It's not right."

"You mean it's not right to torture ourselves this way . . ." he corrected. "Let me make love to you, *gatinha*. Let me cherish every sweet, beautiful inch of you . . . I'll never hurt you. I swear it."

"Sebastian . . ." Her voice was the merest whisper, hesitant and shy. "Sebastian, I think I'm falling in love with you."

He smiled into the darkness. It was what women always said at such tender moments; they inevitably sought to justify the ultimate surrender. Such fragile admissions demanded that he respond in kind. It was the thing to do. Love talk, as he thought of it, would make her feel better about the whole thing, especially afterward, when she would be prone to guilt—if a liberated woman such as Tory even permitted herself to indulge in that old-fashioned emotion.

"I feel the same," he assured her in the sincere, intimate tone he always used to calm a woman's last minute fears. Amazingly, he experienced a strange little flutter inside as he uttered the words. Maybe this time they weren't a lie, he thought wonderingly . . . Maybe he really was falling in love with this brazen little *Americana*—but that was absurd! It *couldn't* be true . . . could it? Why, Tory herself had probably said the same thing to a dozen men before him! He was surprised she still needed to say it, and to hear it from him.

"Trust your feelings, *gatinha*," he urged, pressing against her. "Test them with me, now . . . If this is *not* love, it must be something very close to it."

"Oh, Sebastian . . ." she said tremulously. "Maybe we should wait . . ."

"No . . . no, *gatinha*. Wait for what?" He hugged her tightly, kissing her long and sensuously, touching her breasts, caressing her thighs. . . .

With a little sigh, she collapsed against him, giving herself utterly to his embrace. He lifted her and carried her to the soft, short grass that grew along the river bank, where the cattle loved to graze. He lay her down on the ground and quickly stretched out beside her, enfolding her in his arms. She was so incredibly lovely! So easy to love . . . He did feel emotions he had never felt before. The strength of his feelings momentarily scared him—but then he convinced himself that he was only experiencing a new variation of lust. He had wanted this woman far too long; tonight, he would slake his passion on her pliant body and free himself from her web of enchantment, once and for all!

"Ah, *gatinha . . . gatinha . . .*" he murmured. "*T'amo muito . . .*"

In Portuguese, the lie was easier. *I love you. I love you.* He whispered it over and over, while his hands removed her clothing and his mouth tasted her naked flesh . . . The words pounded in his brain, and he forgot that he was telling lies, so close to the truth did his false assurances finally sound.

Tory could not believe she was doing this—allowing Sebastian to undress her, reveling in his kisses, caresses, and endearments, trying a few exploratory caresses of her own. She felt bewitched. Like a wanton, she opened herself to Sebastian, granting him access to territory heretofore uncharted by any man's hands. She wanted him so much! In the fever of her desire, she could no longer remember all the things she detested about him . . . Perhaps if he came to love her as much as she had begun to love him, he would change. They could discuss their differences and resolve them . . . Spencer and Jordan had found ways to communicate; she and Sebastian could find them, too!

As Sebastian's mouth claimed hers, Tory ceased trying to understand why she was giving Sebastian what she had never entrusted to any man . . . She focused only on the gift itself. Untutored in the ways of love, she followed his lead in everything—kissing and touching as he did, discovering the marvelous geography of his hard male body by using her hands and mouth to wantonly explore him. She found nothing she didn't like or didn't want to know better.

His chest hair fascinated her; it was so crinkly and wiry compared to the soft, thick hair on his head. She loved the texture of it against her breasts and delighted in the friction when he rubbed against her. Prior to this moment, she had never suspected or imagined that her body was capable of feeling so many wondrous and exciting sensations . . . Sebastian seemed to know precisely how to tease and tantalize her. She sensed that he was leading her toward some ultimate peak of pleasure, but every time she reached for it, he retreated and began some other tactic that ultimately left her panting and quivering with ravenous need.

His hands were everywhere—on her breasts, belly, thighs, and hips. They entwined themselves in her hair to hold her steady while he bruised her lips with demanding kisses . . . They forayed down her body like conquering soldiers, determined to map every hill and valley, to search every hidden cave and crevice. When he sought to learn her most intimate secrets, she responded in kind, but he would not permit her to revel too long in discovering the size, shape, and feel of him.

As her boldness flourished and passion consumed her, he pinned her hands to the ground by her head, then lowered his body onto hers. She craved his sweet weight and the jut of him between her thighs. Their bodies seemed made to fit together, and she arched to meet him, but again, he withdrew—lavishing kisses on her forehead, eyes, mouth, and throat—until she moaned and thrashed beneath him, wanting him with every fiber of her being.

"Sebastian! Oh, Sebastian, please!" she shamelessly whimpered, unable to stop herself.

Still, he didn't take her. He suckled her breasts until she thought she would die of need for him. Then he suckled her navel. When his mouth moved lower, she bucked in surprise and embarrassment. "Sebastian, no!"

He chuckled deep in his throat. "Why deny me now, *gatinha?* I've done nothing so far to hurt you, have I?"

She was too mortified to answer and could only

plead: "Sebastian, what more do you want? . . . I can't bear this sweet, burning torture any longer! Must I grovel to make you end this?"

His voice was a throaty purr. *"Gatinha,* I want everything you have to give . . . I want you to want me as you've never wanted any man . . ."

"Then you have your wish. No man has made me feel like this, I swear it! . . . Oh, Sebastian, please, I beg you. Finish what you've started."

He teased her further with the insistent probing of his hot, hard shaft between her thighs. He belonged inside her, but she wasn't certain how to get him there. Biology books were not particularly instructive on the actual details of the act of procreation. None had warned her about the wondrous feelings that accompanied love-making. A tension was building in the lower half of her body, making her nearly frantic. Raw desire made her arch her back and thrust her body upwards against Sebastian's.

Abruptly, he released one of her wrists. "Hold me, *gatinha* . . . Show me how much you want me. Guide me into you."

Despite her lack of experience and the paucity of her knowledge, Tory suddenly sensed her own power and realized that she could make this magnificent man her slave every bit as much as he had enslaved her. Reaching down, she stroked him gently at first, marveling at the strength and beauty of him. Then her excitement spiraled out of control, and she could wait no longer. Opening her thighs, she guided him into her. He eased into her throbbing passageway, but stopped when he reached the barrier of her virginity. She felt the first twinge of discomfort, but by then, didn't care how much it might hurt; she wanted all of him inside her. She raised her hips—

208

inviting his downward plunge—but he poised above her, his breathing ragged.

"*Gatinha* . . . You are so small and tight . . . I will hurt you."

"No," she denied. "You could never hurt me. I want you, Sebastian."

It was true. Every nerve ending in her body screamed for him to possess her totally. Bounteous pleasure shimmered just beyond her reach. If only he would take her! They could share the pleasure together. He pushed inside a little further, causing a tearing pain. Involuntarily, she gasped. He reacted as if stung, jerking backward until he was free of her.

"*Cristo!* You are a virgin after all!"

She knew a moment of wrenching disappointment, physical and emotional. Then she blurted the first thing that leapt to mind: "Of course, I'm a virgin! What did you expect—that I've done this hundreds of times before?"

He rolled away from her. "I thought you had at least done it enough times to have stretched your passageway to accommodate a man of normal proportions. In my more jealous moments, I had convinced myself that a liberated woman like you must have entertained no fewer than a dozen men between your milk-white thighs."

"*A dozen men?*" She was outraged. Indignation momentarily blotted out the hurt and frustration. Snapping upright, Tory reached for her clothes, which lay scattered all about them on the grass. "Well, if you believe that of me, why didn't you imagine that I had already given myself to a thousand men? Better yet, why not a million? Would I be stretched enough for you if I had entertained an entire army of men between my thighs?"

"You should have told me you were a virgin," he said accusingly. "Since I never would have guessed it for myself. You neither walk, talk, dress, nor behave like one. I thought you must have had vast experience. I thought you were liberated . . . I thought . . ."

"Just because I wear knickerbockers and, occasionally, a pair of boy's trousers, doesn't make me a whore!" she shouted, struggling to climb into her underdrawers and chemise.

"That garment you are putting on now . . ." He pointed to her drawers. "Is that what *Americanos* call knickerbockers?"

"No! Knickerbockers are a kind of pants that women in my country sometimes wear to ride a bicycle . . . *These* are my drawers, and I never would have permitted you to take them off, had I known you were so reluctant to ravish a virgin."

"I never would have taken them off, had I known you were a virgin. It seems to me that drawers are a most useless and unattractive garment. I like you much better without them—but that doesn't change the fact that you misled me concerning your virginity."

"*I* misled *you?* Do you mean to say that I would have been safe from your unwanted attentions if I had come right out at the beginning and said that I had never been with a man?"

"Of course, you would have been safer." He reached for his clothing, his eyes glinting in the darkness. "I'm not in the habit of despoiling virgins, even pretty, desirable ones like you . . . Whatever else I am, I'm a gentleman who protects and shelters decent young women. That's part of my heritage, the tradition of my people."

Tory found it difficult to believe what she was

hearing. "*You*—a gentleman?" she squeaked. "You don't know the meaning of the word 'gentleman'! You haven't been a gentleman from the day we first met."

He dressed with a casual grace that mocked her own awkward, fumbling gestures. "That's because I didn't believe that *you* were a 'lady'. Had you behaved and spoken like one, I would have left you alone."

Tory stepped into her skirt, and jerked it up over her hips. "I believe I *did* mention the fact once or twice . . . Oh, I didn't discuss my virginity in so many words maybe, but I certainly made my lack of experience clear to you. I resisted you from the very beginning."

"I mistook your resistance for invitation . . . Everything you did or said convinced me you were really a trollop . . . an accomplished little tease who enjoys the game of pursuit and plays it until she drives a man mad with jealousy and passion."

"Is that what you call it—being mad with passion? Not falling in love or learning to care for me?" *As I care for you,* she added silently and miserably.

He finished tucking his shirt into his waistband, then planted himself directly in her path. "I admit it; I was mad with passion for you . . . You are a beautiful woman, *gatinha*, and I am a normal, healthy man . . . I thought we could love and enjoy each other, share a few moments of pleasure, then part without regrets . . . I thought you had done the same with many men, so why shouldn't you do it with me? . . . I never meant to hurt or mislead you . . . I deeply apologize for going as far as I did before discovering the truth—that you *are* a virgin and worthy of respect."

211

"You don't really care for me," Tory said woodenly. "You only wanted what you thought other men had already had."

Sebastian regarded her silently for a moment, seeming unwilling to commit himself either way. Finally, he sighed. "A wife isn't in my plans right now, *gatinha* . . . So it matters not what I do or don't feel. I confess that I am not certain how I feel . . . I have wronged you, but fortunately, we stopped before the worst was done. Your virginity is still intact. I didn't penetrate you fully."

Tory had to swallow hard to keep from bursting into tears in front of him. She had *wanted* him to penetrate her fully. Worse yet, she *still* wanted him to do it. She had given him everything he demanded and more—her heart along with her body, and he was rejecting it. "Sebastian, just answer me this. How did you find the strength and self-control to stop when you did? How can you stand here so calmly discussing this? Only a few moments ago, we were . . . we were . . . n-naked and . . . and . . ."

"Carried away by lust?" He chuckled. "Shock and surprise can be as effective a deterrent as a bucket of cold water, *gatinha* . . . I was brought up short. Stunned, actually. Suddenly, I was making love to a virgin instead of the experienced woman I thought you were . . ."

"And if you make love to a virgin, your gentlemanly code of honor demands that you *marry* her. Isn't *that* what really dashed cold water on your ardor?"

"Perhaps . . . As I've just stated, marriage isn't possible just now . . . Surely, *you* would not consider it either. In Brazil, married women lead lives that are every bit as sheltered and protected as the

212

lives of young virgins . . . You would *hate* being a Brazilian wife."

"Not if I were married to a man who let me be myself, instead of trying to force me into a stupid confining mold that doesn't really fit any woman."

"You see? We'd never suit, *gatinha*. When I marry—*if* I marry—I want a traditional Brazilian wife, while *you* want a husband that hasn't yet been invented—not even in the *Estados Unidos*."

"My brother, Jordan . . ." she started to argue, but he cut her off with a sharp laugh.

"Doesn't approve of half the things you want to do! He tolerates more than most men, but doesn't buy your whole program . . . and anyway, he's your brother and already married. Show me a man who approves of the same things you do, and I'll eat my leather *vaqueiro's* hat."

"There's Padre Osmundo!"

"I mean a man who's free and able to marry you— not some poor priest who would agree to anything if it meant you would teach his poor *caboclos*."

Renewed anger was fast edging out Tory's hurt. "You're right," she snapped. "We wouldn't suit. I don't know why I came out here on this midnight ride with you . . . Or let you do the things you did to me . . . I don't know why I'm standing here talking to you . . . Where's Renegade? I want to go back to the ranch right now."

"*Gatinha* . . . Don't be angry. I said I was sorry. Truly, had I known you were a virgin, I would have treated you far better . . . If we can't be lovers, we can at least be friends, can't we?"

"I'd rather be friends with the devil himself!" she spat. "At least with the devil, I'll never be surprised by the depths of his wickedness. You are the most

213

despicable man I've ever had the bad fortune to meet."

She whirled away from him, searching for Renegade who was munching grass not far off. A moment later, she felt Sebastian's hand on her arm. "Don't touch me!" she shrieked. "Don't you dare touch me ever again!"

His hand fell away. "No, *gatinha* . . . That I promise you. I'll not touch you again. But it will be very hard to keep that promise, because despite all you have said, I still burn for you."

"Then I sincerely hope you go up in flames! I hope your flesh melts from your bones, and your eyeballs bleed down your face."

"*Cristo!* You sound as if you really do hate me."

"Hate is too mild a word for what I feel for you right now . . . At the moment, I wish you were dead."

She strode away from him and went to get Renegade, keeping her head ducked so he couldn't see the tears that threatened. They were tears of sorrow, shame, and bitter disappointment. What had nearly been the best, the most wonderful and exciting night of her life had turned out to be the absolute worst.

They rode back to the ranch in strained silence, a far more subdued ride than the mad gallop Tory had relished earlier. As soon as she dismounted, Sebastian reined Renegade around and took off again across the *sertão*, headed God knew where at this late hour. Tory watched until he disappeared, then she went into the house and climbed the stairs to bed. Only after she had buried her head beneath the pillow did she allow the tears to start; they flowed like the silvery river beside which she had almost lost her damned, unwanted virginity!

Chapter Fourteen

Sebastian spent the rest of that long night rustling cattle and destroying property. His unexpended sexual energy demanded fierce physical activity, and the demons in his mind drove him to new heights of recklessness. He stole cattle from beneath the noses of the guards Cerqueira had posted, then doubled back and set fire to a row of huts used for shelter, and finally, tore down a corral built to contain stock during branding.

All the while he was doing these things, Sebastian conducted a ruthless interrogation of himself. Why had he pursued Victoria King so relentlessly? Why hadn't he interpreted the signs of her innocence correctly? Granted, he had never before met such a woman, had little experience with Americans, and possibly understood the American culture less than he thought he did . . . Still, he ought to have realized that she knew next to nothing about love-making from her shy kisses and timid caresses. He was deeply chagrined. All his life he had taken care not to woo women who could trap him into marriage; now he had nearly bedded a female who would make the worst possible wife for him!

Oh, he wouldn't mind the hours spent in bed with her—but he would certainly mind her outspokenness, her tendency to meddle in everything, her unconventional behavior, her outrageous liberalism, and most of all, the way she distracted him from long-cherished goals. Much as he hated to admit it, she was causing him to take time from more important activities. Lately, he had been neglecting his role as the Falcon . . . Why, Tory even had him wondering what it would be like to live normally, concerned only with his ranch and family, instead of being obsessed by the need for revenge against Mundinho Cerqueira!

He could not help wondering what would it be like to have children with a woman like Tory. She would undoubtedly breed strong, independent-minded offspring infused with her own stubbornness and tenacity, as well as, perhaps, her tenderness of heart toward the poor and downtrodden. These were qualities he wouldn't mind seeing in his children. He also had to admit that it was about time he started thinking of producing legitimate heirs to his growing empire, as Padre Osmundo was continually urging him to do. He had always been sorry that his two little bastards had died so young, without ever knowing that they had a father, much less one who was prepared to claim and love them. All Brazilians doted on children, even those born out of wedlock, and he was no exception . . . But he had definitely *never* imagined his future children having a rebel for a mother!

Thoughts roiled in his brain like ocean waves being tossed by a storm, so that he felt compelled to ride madly across the *sertão*, herding his enemy's cattle before him. Teodoro, Miguel, and his other *vaqueiros* could hardly keep up with him. It was dawn when they reached the dilapidated ranch in the

216

state of Sergipe where a fellow *cangaçeiro*, Ramiro Bastos, kept a large corral for the purpose of receiving stolen animals and disposing of them. Bastos had once had his own band of thieves, but old age and ill health had finally caught up with him; now he contented himself with buying and selling cattle and horses stolen by others.

Bastos was delighted to see Sebastian and came out of his daub-and-wattle hut to welcome him. *"Bom dia,* old friend!" he called out. "It has been a long time since you've visited the humble abode of Ramiro Bastos."

Observing the old man's scraggly gray beard and hair, filthy leather chaps, dirt-encrusted face, and blood-shot eyes, Sebastian could easily guess what Bastos had been doing since the last time he had brought cattle to sell to him. Fumes of *cachaça* radiated from the old bandit, reminding Sebastian that this was how *cangaçeiros* usually wound up—if they weren't shot or hanged first. That Bastos still lived was a tribute to his wily ways; he was a sly old vulture, quick to seize opportunities and just as quick to flee when danger threatened. Sebastian both pitied and admired him; Bastos had taught him much about survival on the *sertão*.

"Bom dia, you old drunk ... Are you sober enough to conduct business—or should I leave and return another day?" Sebastian taunted.

Bastos grinned and bowed low at the waist. "I am always prepared to serve a man of *your* reputation, Senhor. Bastos is the humble *empregado* of *Sebastião Prêto,* or should I say of the most esteemed and renowned *Falcão?*"

Sebastian glanced around uneasily. The place looked deserted, but he could never be sure who might be listening nearby, and the fewer who knew

217

his real identity, the better. To the casual observer, he resembled the part he was playing. He was as dust-coated and filthy as any of his men, but if the name Sebastian Black were bandied about in the same breath with the Falcon, it might reach the ears of someone who could blackmail or expose him.

"I have never heard of this *Sebastião Prêto,*" he grimly announced, dismounting and leading a weary Renegade to a water trough beside the corral. "You must be thinking of another man ... In any case, it would be better not to mention names at all, Bastos, if you value our long-standing and mutually profitable relationship."

"There's no one here but me," the old man said testily. "And I am your friend. You know that Ramiro Bastos would never betray you."

"Ah, but would he cheat me when it comes to buying my fine, fat cattle?"

The old man chuckled. "That remains to be seen, Senhor ... Come into my house ... We will eat and drink while we discuss those skinny, flea-ridden beasts. To me, they look like they are hardly worth the effort it took to bring them here."

Sebastian handed Renegade's reins to Teodoro and followed the old thief into the hut, which was littered with *cachaça* bottles and furnished with a raggedy hammock, a three-legged table, and two chairs. Bastos's poverty was typical for the *sertão*, but Sebastian inadvertently wrinkled his nose against the stench and dirt. He resolved to allow the old man to cheat him outrageously, worse than usual, for it was obvious that few cattle had been stolen recently. Possibly none had arrived since the last time Sebastian himself had brought a consignment.

"You must forgive this mess, esteemed Senhor. Business has been very bad lately—so bad in fact that

I am going back to raiding myself. I cannot survive on what is being brought to me." Bastos kicked a few bottles out of his path and righted a toppled chair for Sebastian to sit on.

"Where will you get men to join you?" Sebastian sat down on the rickety chair without examining it too closely. Miraculously, it didn't collapse. "You can't go raiding on your own, my friend. You need at least a half dozen reliable *vaqueiros*."

"I have found them, Senhor . . . The greed and cruelty of the *fazendeiros* never fails to replenish the pool of men eager to take what they cannot gain any other way . . . But don't worry. We'll stay out of Bahia; I intend to concentrate all of my activities in Sergipe, and you can continue to bring your cattle and horses here as usual . . . Also, you need have no fear that I will compete with you when it comes to feeding and clothing the poor peasants. I am no *Falcão*, my friend. My first loyalty is to my own belly . . . But if ever you should need extra men to ride along with you on your raids, do not hesitate to call upon me. I have not forgotten how to sit a horse or shoot straight, and I owe you for keeping me alive this long with your business."

"Thank you for your offer, Bastos. Someday, I may need a few extra guns to protect my back . . . Now, about the cattle I brought today . . ."

An hour later, Sebastian emerged from the hut with his business concluded. In a week's time, he planned to return for the money Bastos would make from driving the cattle across the *São Francisco* River and selling them in the neighboring state of Alagoas. Bastos would get a cut for each head and probably cheat Sebastian out of a cow or two, but that was to be expected—and Sebastian wanted him to do it, anyway. Next time, Sebastian promised himself, he would bring some good horses for the old man's band to ride. Without good horses, Bastos would not last long out on the *sertão*.

Before mounting Renegade to return home, Sebastian took one last look at the sleek, plump, silver-gray cattle with the distinctive humped necks that had once been the property of Mundinho Cerqueira. These were Brahman cattle, a breed that survived well on the dry *sertão* and had cost a great deal of money to import. Cerqueira would be furious, as he was always furious to lose prime stock to the Falcon. Eventually, Cerqueira's fury would force him to do something rash. It was for such a moment that Sebastian had been waiting these many years, and from all accounts, the moment was close at hand.

No, Sebastian sternly lectured himself, he didn't need to be involved with a little blonde *Americana* who might make him forget what he had been working for all his life. From now until she left for Espirito Santo with Padre Osmundo, he must stay away from Tory King. No more starlit rides or tumbles on grassy river banks! No more imagining what it would be like to make love to her all night long. He could not afford to be distracted. Too much was at stake. Thus decided, he swung aboard Renegade and rode away without sparing another thought for Tory.

Tory was glad when Sebastian did not return to the ranch on the day following their awful encounter on the river bank. She had convinced herself that she would be far happier if she never saw Sebastian again. Determined not to mope about like a love-sick schoolgirl, she spent her time teaching the *caboclos*, blatantly disregarding Sebastian's ridiculous orders.

When he didn't return that night either, she sat with Amâncio until very late, patiently showing the black man over and over how to make the letter A. On the following day, Tory again conducted classes in the morning, lunched with Padre Osmundo, and then set out to sneak a ride on Percy before Sebastian's anticipated return for the evening meal.

She waited until Padre Osmundo retired for his afternoon nap and the entire household was occupied elsewhere. Then she donned a skirt she had altered to permit riding astride and went downstairs. Before she could slip out through the cookshed to the corral, a heavy knock sounded on the front door. Dona Guilhermina had left the big house and gone home to her own little *casa* with Carmelita in tow, and Quinquina was somewhere upstairs dusting and cleaning, so there was no one nearby to answer the summons.

Tory wondered who could be knocking on the front door in the middle of the afternoon; there were no neighbors for miles around, and no visitors expected—at least none that she knew of. Tucking a stray blond wisp into the single long braid she had fashioned to restrain her unruly hair, she walked to the front door and opened it. A tall, swarthy, imposing-looking gentleman dressed in elegant, but dusty, riding clothes stood on the verandah.

His black eyes widened appreciatively when he saw her, and the thin, bloodless lips beneath the black mustache curled into a tight smile. *"Boa Tarde,* Senhorita . . ." He bowed slightly, and removed a black brimmed hat. "My name is Mundinho Cerqueira. Will you please tell Senhor *Prêto* that I have come calling?"

Tory politely returned his greeting. "Good afternoon, Senhor. I'd be delighted to give your message

221

to Mr. Black, but he's not here at the moment . . . I myself am a guest, along with my good friend, Padre Osmundo. Is there something either of us could do to help you?''

The elegantly attired gentleman brushed at the dust on his impeccably cut jacket, then gestured behind him to a group of mounted *vaqueiros.* "Would it be all right if my men went around back to water their horses? My business with Senhor *Prêto* is most urgent, so I will wait for him as long as necessary.''

Tory noticed that Senhor Cerqueira didn't ask if it would be convenient if he waited; he assumed he had the right and merely requested hospitality for his men. "You are a friend of Senhor *Prêto's*?'' she inquired, not about to let a perfect stranger into the house, even if he did seem to be a gentleman and an acquaintance of Sebastian's.

"My land adjoins his to the southwest, Senhorita . . . I'll gladly tell you all about myself, if you will kindly permit me to enter. It has been a long, hot journey, and I would appreciate some refreshment, no matter how modest.''

"Of course!'' Tory guiltily exclaimed. It was rude of her not to have thought of the thirst the poor man must be suffering. "Please come in . . .'' She opened the door wide. "I'll send for refreshments for both you *and* your men.''

As Senhor Cerqueira entered the house, Tory crossed to the stairwell and called for Quinquina. Then she ushered the visitor into the front room set aside for entertaining guests. The tall gentleman— he was almost as tall as Sebastian but not as young, lithe, or fit—tossed his leather gloves and hat onto a round table in front of an unshuttered window, then pivoted to study her.

"Whom do I have the pleasure of addressing, Senhorita?" he inquired in his cultured tones. "Your accent and coloring tell me you are not Brazilian; I'm most curious to discover who you are and where you come from."

Mundinho Cerqueira's manner was that of a man accustomed to being obeyed. He exuded the same infuriatingly casual arrogance as Sebastian, and for a moment, recalling how much she disliked that quality, Tory considered telling Senhor Cerqueira nothing. But then she remembered that he was Sebastian's guest, and in Sebastian's absence, she must do her best to make him feel welcome.

"I'm an American," she informed him, seating herself on the leather sofa where he soon joined her. "And I came to this country to teach for a year in Padre Osmundo's new school in Espirito Santo . . . Are you acquainted with Padre Osmundo? He suffered an injury recently and is resting, but I've no doubt you'll meet him before you leave. I don't expect Senhor *Prêto* to return immediately, so your wait will probably prove quite lengthy."

At the mention of Padre Osmundo's school, Senhor Cerqueira's black eyes hardened. Or maybe it was Padre Osmundo's name that caused the change in the man's expression. "I am well acquainted with that trouble-making priest, Senhorita, and deeply distressed to hear that you are going to teach in his school . . . Again, I ask you: What is your name?"

Tory was taken aback by Cerqueira's haughty attitude and his reference to Padre Osmundo as a troublemaker. "Victoria King . . . and *I* am distressed that you think of Padre Osmundo as anything but a walking saint."

Mundinho Cerqueira leaned back in the deep sofa and regarded her with cold amusement. "Forgive me,

Senhorita, for offending you ... But you cannot know the depths of anguish that cause me to label as a troublemaker any man who stirs up the peasants."

"You are experiencing some difficulties, Senhor?" Tory tactfully inquired.

"*Sim*, Senhorita, grave difficulties, and that is why I have come here today to seek the help of Senhor *Prêto*. I don't normally bother my neighbors with my personal problems, but finally, I have been driven too far."

"Tell me about these problems," Tory urged. "I have nothing better to do right now than listen ... and I wish to learn everything I can about your country."

So Mundinho Cerqueira told her. He cited one incident after another in which his cattle or horses had been stolen, and his property destroyed by the brazen, lawless bandit known as the Falcon. The latest incident involved prize cattle who were part of a breeding experiment Cerqueira had been conducting. He claimed that the theft would push him over the brink into financial ruin, as the animals were irreplaceable. Tory doubted that this arrogant *fazendeiro* could be that close to disaster, but she listened with cautious sympathy to his tale of woe, hoping to discover a reason why he should bear ill will toward Padre Osmundo because of crimes the Falcon had committed. When Cerqueira had finished, and she still hadn't found such a reason, she said as much.

"Ah, but Senhorita, you do not understand!" Senhor Cerqueira set down the *cafèzinho* Quinquina had served them during his long diatribe. "Your friend, Padre Osmundo, *is* the reason why rogues like the Falcon rise from the masses of the poor, illiterate *caboclos*. Padre Osmundo encourages the poor to rebel from their natural station in life—then they run

MORE PASSION AND ADVENTURE AWAIT... YOUR TRIP TO A BIG ADVENTUROUS WORLD BEGINS WHEN YOU ACCEPT YOUR FIRST 4 NOVELS ABSOLUTELY *FREE*
(AN $18.00 VALUE)

off and join the bands of *cangaçeiros* roaming the *sertão*. What he *should* be doing is preaching humility and obedience—assuring the poor wretches that their reward for living a just life will be an eternity spent in heaven, and their punishment if they seek to overstep their boundaries will be the everlasting fires of hell."

"You can't mean that religion should be used as a tool to control the masses and keep them in a state of poverty so that the wealthy never need share their wealth!" Tory burst out, horrified.

"I don't claim anything so radical as that, Senhorita . . . On the contrary. I myself am known to be a religious man. My own cousin is an archbishop. I attend mass on all the feasts and holy days, give alms regularly to beggars on the church steps, and support many other charitable works. What I am saying is that a priest should not use his influence over simpleminded people in order to lead them into waywardness or make them dissatisfied with their lot in life . . . This Falcon was obviously once a peasant. Just as obviously, he was provoked into stealing by the intemperate exhortations of some misguided cleric such as Padre Osmundo . . . It's very doubtful that this base-born criminal, whoever he is and wherever he comes from, would have thought of rebelling against the present social order all by himself. *Caboclos* are not that smart."

"But maybe the present social order isn't all that wonderful, Senhor Cerqueira! Have *you* ever thought of what your life would be like had you been born a *caboclo*, instead of a *fazendeiro*?"

Mundinho Cerqueira curled his patrician lip. "No, never, Senhorita . . . We are what God makes us. We cannot change that, nor should we try. By teaching the dirty little peasant children to read and write, you will only make them restless and unhappy ... I am surprised that Senhor *Prêto* doesn't agree with me. As a member of the ruling class, he knows the dangers of raising hopes too high for people to ever attain them. I would not have thought him supportive of this latest scheme of Padre Osmundo's."

"He *doesn't* fully support it, Senhor ... Though I've never heard him criticize it to the extent that you do, I'm happy to say. Indeed, he helped to ...''

"So we have company!" A voice suddenly boomed from the doorway.

Tory looked up to see Padre Osmundo advancing into the room on his crutches. "Quinquina told Dona Guilhermina, who told Carmelita, who finally told me, that Paraíso has a most distinguished visitor ... and so it does. Senhor Cerqueira, I am honored to see you again—and how is your exalted cousin, the archbishop?"

Senhor Cerqueira rose to his feet almost reluctantly, Tory thought, but he did suffer Padre Osmundo to embrace him in the typical Brazilian fashion indicating affection between old friends.

"My cousin is extremely busy as usual. It isn't easy bearing the burdens of high office ... As a parish priest living in isolation on the *sertão*, you have no idea of the challenges facing him every day, Padre."

"Oh, I quite agree. I haven't the faintest idea ... Sit down, sit down," Padre Osmundo urged, taking a seat opposite Tory. "No, I'm sure it's a terrible cross to bear, being an archbishop these days. Managing the Church's lands and its wealth in this part of the country must be a thankless, arduous task, indeed ..." He shook his head. "Fortunately, as you point out, a humble parish priest living in isolation on the *sertão* only has to worry about whether or not his peasants

226

are starving, or otherwise dying from obscure, untreatable illnesses."

"No one is starving these days, Padre," Senhor Cerqueira scoffed. "If they are, my cousin could do little to help . . . You know as well as I that the Church's wealth is tied up in gold, silver, and land. There would be nothing left for future generations if he squandered that wealth on the poor every time we have a drought on the *sertão*."

"Oh, I understand perfectly why no funds are ever forthcoming from the diocese to help my poor *caboclos* in Espirito Santo . . . The Church's treasures must be safeguarded, no matter what the cost in mere human lives. But do not worry yourself into a state of sleeplessness over the problem, Senhor Cerqueira. I look elsewhere for the assistance I need."

"And undoubtedly receive it—since you yourself hardly appear half-starved. You're much stouter than I remember, Padre. Still, I'm glad to see you in such good health even if you've suffered some mishap or ill fortune." Senhor Cerqueira glanced down at Padre Osmundo's crutches and wrapped ankle.

"A minor inconvenience only," Padre Osmundo assured him. "It won't delay my work for long, Senhor Cerqueira. The school is almost ready to open, and the teacher eagerly awaits her students."

The two men silently appraised each other, their hostility palpable. Padre Osmundo's barely civil attitude surprised Tory; she had never known the good-natured little priest to be rude or discourteous. Obviously, his relationship with Mundinho Cerqueira had been a stormy one, and he had ample reason to dislike and mistrust the arrogant *fazendeiro* every bit as much as he himself was disliked and mistrusted by him.

"Senhor Cerqueira, you must stay for dinner if

227

Sebastian hasn't returned by then," she said, bowing to the inevitable.

"I intend to," Mundinho Cerqueira replied. "And if he hasn't returned by dark, I also intend to spend the night."

Tory sat up straighter in astonishment and dismay. She caught Padre Osmundo's eye and realized that the priest was no more pleased by the information than she was. But Padre Osmundo at least had the presence of mind to respond graciously, with a sly twinkle in his eye.

"Well, if it becomes necessary, I'm sure we can find a place in the barn for you and your horse to bed down . . . I'm truly sorry," he explained to the tight-lipped rancher. "But all of the rooms in the house are occupied."

Tory very well knew that such was not the case, but it gave her great pleasure to hastily agree. "Yes, it's a shame . . . We haven't a spare bed to offer you."

"Whatever the accommodations," Cerqueira snapped. "I am remaining here until I speak with Senhor *Prêto*."

Chapter Fifteen

Sebastian did not return in time for the evening meal, and it turned out to be a strained affair in which Senhor Cerqueira and Padre Osmundo verbally sparred with each other, then became openly hostile when Cerqueira made a disparaging remark to Carmelita about how much sugar he preferred in his *cafêzinho*. Padre Osmundo immediately demanded that Carmelita bring the sugar pot and allow Senhor Cerqueira to sweeten his own coffee and even to remake the coffee itself if it did not meet his standards.

"You needn't serve this gentleman so graciously, Carmelita," Padre Osmundo scolded. "He's not your *patrão*. Why don't you send Dona Guilhermina or Quinquina to remove the dishes, and you go get your own dinner. It's growing late, and you must be hungry."

Carmelita was embarrassed. "It's all right, Padre," she whispered. "Don't trouble yourself over so small a matter . . . I will make more coffee, since my first effort did not please Senhor Cerqueira. Dona Guilhermina and Quinquina are busy feeding Amâncio and the senhor's *vaqueiros*. I doubt that either of them can come right now."

"I'm surprised that you defend this incompetent female, Padre," Cerqueira snidely observed. "Even the lowliest peasant knows how to make coffee. She is also impertinent . . . No one asked her opinion of anything. *Caboclos* should not have opinions."

"I am *not* a *caboclo!*" Carmelita protested, black eyes flashing. "I was born and raised in Salvador, not on the *sertão.*"

"You have the look, indeed, the very smell of one," Mundinho Cerqueira sniffed. "However, you don't have a *caboclo's* humility. I am shocked that Senhor *Prêto* tolerates servants who put on such airs."

"She is not a servant on this ranch; she is my house-keeper," Padre Osmundo corrected. "More than that, she's my friend!"

"She rises above her station." Cerqueira wagged a finger at Padre Osmundo. "You have taught her to be impertinent. I suspect you've also encouraged that thieving Falcon to steal my best cattle."

Padre Osmundo quivered with indignation. "I encourage no one to rob or steal! I've never laid eyes on the Falcon. His identity is a complete mystery to me."

Senhor Cerqueira sat back in his chair and smoothed his mustache with one tapered finger. "It is said that he gives you money."

"Indirectly, perhaps," Padre Osmundo admitted, red-faced. "But I can't really be certain, since I don't keep track of who contributes every *cruzeiro* in my collection basket. If he does leave generous dona-tions, he should be praised, not criticized."

"Not when it's *my* money he's donating. You aid and abet the Falcon by your supportive attitude, if nothing else, Padre. I should mention this to my

230

cousin, the archbishop. As you already know—or *should* know—he takes a dim view of the clergy interfering in secular affairs."

"Gentlemen, please," Tory intervened. "The dinner table is no place for arguments or threats. Neither constitutes good manners . . . We are all guests in this house and should not be hurling accusations at each other when Sebastian—Senhor *Prêto*—is not even present."

"You're quite right, Senhorita . . ." Mundinho Cerqueira flashed a cold, reptilian smile. "Why don't you show me around the ranch before it gets dark?"

"I'd be happy to do so . . ." Tory rose to her feet, glad for any reason to separate the two men. "Excuse us, please, won't you, Padre, while I assume the role of hostess and entertain Sebastian's guest?"

Padre Osmundo nodded petulantly, more out of sorts than Tory had ever seen him. She couldn't blame him; Mundinho Cerqueira was worse than she had imagined rich, conceited *fazendeiros* could be. Sebastian was beginning to look like an angel in comparison! She decided to show him the corral out back, which, among others, contained the three horses taken from the *cangaçeiros*. Maybe Cerqueira's mood would lighten when he learned that he was not the only one to be harassed by thieves and bandits.

She took him through the center courtyard and met Quinquina coming out of Amâncio's room with a tray of dirty dishes. On impulse, Tory stopped. "Senhor Cerqueira, look in here . . . I want you to meet one of Sebastian's servants who was wounded during an encounter *we* had with *cangaçeiros* on our way here from Salvador."

Mundinho Cerqueira's brows shot up. "You were attacked by the Falcon?"

"No, it was a small band of men led by a man named Porco. Sebastian later went after him, killed three of his men, and took their horses to teach him a lesson."

"I've never heard of this Porco. He must be a minor outlaw, hoping to become a major one, like the Falcon." Bypassing Quinquina as if she didn't exist, Cerqueira stuck his head in the open door, then withdrew with an exclamation of surprise and indignation. "Why is that fellow in the house? You deny *me* a room, but allow the lowliest of servants the luxury of his own bed."

"That man is injured, Senhor Cerqueira. Not only was he shot, but he broke his leg. It's easier to nurse and keep an eye on him when he's nearby." Tory stuck her own head inside the door and waved at Amâncio who was propped up on pillows in the narrow bed with a linen napkin still tucked under his chin.

Cerqueira's face grew black with anger. "This would never happen in *my* house . . . A man of his lowly station would lie in the barn or some out-of-the-way hut, where my family and guests would not be subjected to the stink of him."

Tory started. "What do you mean, the stink of him? He washes daily; I myself have toted water for him to bathe."

"Surely, as a woman and an *Americana,* your senses are refined enough to detect his odor . . . His sort doesn't belong in the fine house of a *fazendeiro.* I'd never allow it—and in a bed, yet! The ground is good enough for him, or if not that, at least a hammock."

Tory felt such overwhelming fury that for a moment, words failed her. When she finally found

232

her tongue, she had to exert every ounce of willpower she possessed to keep from telling this bigoted jackass exactly what she thought of him. "Senhor Cerqueira, I've changed my mind about enduring another moment of your unpleasant company . . . You may wait for Sebastian as long as you wish, but you'll have to do it on the verandah, not in the house. I can't tolerate the stench of your conceit any longer. I'll accompany you back there, but then I'm retiring to my room for the night."

"As you wish, Senhorita . . ." Cerqueira inclined his head. "If you find my company so distasteful, I shall not inflict it upon you any further. However, I find your attitude extremely puzzling."

"Why puzzling?" she challenged, leading him back through the house.

"Why does an attractive young woman such as yourself come to Brazil to teach illiterate peasants? And why does she wear a skirt sewn shut straight down the middle?"

Tory had forgotten about the skirt she had donned earlier to go riding. "The latter is an American fashion," she lied. "As to the former, you would never understand."

"There is much I do not understand in this house, Senhorita," he responded ominously. "And you are only one small part of it."

It was very late that night by the time Tory heard Renegade's whinny out in the corral, and Sebastian's voice soothing and quieting him. Quickly, she rose from her bed and hurriedly threw a dressing gown over her nightdress. She was halfway down the stairs, when Sebastian's startled greeting made her pause and listen.

"Mundinho Cerqueira... This is a surprise. You're the last person I would expect to find on my doorstep at this hour of the night."

"Good evening, *Sebastião*... I was beginning to think you were never coming home. Your guest, the very lovely and outspoken Senhorita *Rei*, banished me to the verandah to await your return... It seems she disapproves of me, as does your other guest, Padre Osmundo."

"You mustn't mind them, Mundinho... They are two dewy-eyed idealists with a penchant for judging people by distorted views of right and wrong... They disapprove of me, too, you know. I only tolerate them because they amuse me."

"Then you have a strange sense of humor, Senhor... They would not spend a single night at *my* ranch; I would feel compelled to drive them off my land the moment they set foot upon it."

Sebastian laughed—too heartily, Tory thought. She had been hoping that when Sebastian arrived, he would waste little time showing Mundinho Cerqueira the track out of Paraíso. Instead, to her disappointment, he sounded calm and friendly, *much* too friendly.

"I can understand why, Cerqueira. My own hospitality is wearing thin—but they'll be leaving soon for Espirito Santo... Did they at least feed you? Come into the house and have a brandy with me... I'm anxious to discover what brings you here... I'm also thirsty. I've been chasing *cangaçeiros* all over the *sertão*, and my throat is as parched as the land itself."

"Ah... Did you catch them, Senhor? The *cangaçeiros* are why I am here."

"No, more's the pity. I tracked that rascal, the

Falcon, halfway to Alagoas, but lost him when he crossed the *São Francisco* River."

"No doubt with *my* cattle in his possession! I would give anything to cut off his head and mount it on a pike on the road to Salvador. His severed head might serve as an effective warning to all other would-be thieves and murderers."

"*Your* cattle and *my* horses are what he took . . ." Sebastian said. "I had a band of mares and promising young colts turned out to graze, and now, they are missing . . . If I want to keep an animal, it must stay in my corral . . . The situation is growing intolerable."

"Which is precisely why I am here . . . But I'll wait until you refresh yourself before telling you of my plan to apprehend the villain and rid ourselves of him, once and for all."

As the two men entered the house, Tory dashed back up the stairs. She didn't want to be caught eavesdropping; what she had already heard greatly disturbed her. Padre Osmundo would certainly want to know that plans were afoot to capture and kill the Falcon. Would Sebastian even tell him? The two disagreed over the bandit. Padre Osmundo thought him a great hero, but Sebastian condemned him as a criminal . . . In his anger over the theft of a band of horses—was Renegade's colt among them?—Sebastian might do anything. He probably wouldn't hesitate to hang or shoot the thief!

Tory stayed out of sight at the top of the staircase until Sebastian and Cerqueira went into the library, then she crept silently down the steps and tiptoed toward the room. The door was ajar, and the men's voices carried easily to her ears. Sebastian was saying: "All right, Cerqueira, now suppose you tell me

235

about this plan of yours to catch the Falcon . . ."

As Sebastian listened to Cerqueira and sipped his brandy, he could hardly keep from gloating. This was the long dreamed-of moment! Cerqueira was finally seeking his help and obviously didn't suspect Sebastian of anything except being too tolerant of Padre Osmundo's coddling of the peasants. Now he must pretend that he really had lost all patience with the priest and was as anxious as Cerqueira himself to rid the *sertão* of the Falcon.

"I wish to lay a trap for the *Falcão*," Mundinho Cerqueira was saying. "I intend to make it impossible for him to resist coming to *us*, instead of us having to search for him. The *sertão* is, after all, his element, the place he knows better than any other. That is why we always lose him there."

"The idea sounds reasonable," Sebastian commented. "But what could possibly make him come to us?"

"First, we must infuriate him—threaten something or someone he values . . . He must be so angry that he will risk capture in order to rescue that which he cares about."

"We don't know the Falcon well enough to guess what he values," Sebastian pointed out.

"I disagree . . . We know that he cares about the peasants—and that he contributes to causes that benefit them."

"I've heard that," Sebastian cautiously admitted. Cerqueira was watching him closely, as if gauging the effect of every word.

"It is no mere gossip. The *Falcão* has contributed heavily to Padre Osmundo's new school. The priest conceded as much at dinner, but even if he had not, I

236

know it to be true . . . My cousin, Guedes Figueiredo, the archbishop, confirmed my suspicions when last I mentioned it to him . . ."

"I know your cousin's name . . ." Sebastian growled, disliking where the conversation was leading.

"Well, Guedes says that the Church has contributed nothing to Padre Osmundo's work . . . The good Padre is most independent and prefers doing everything on his own, he says . . ."

"I'm sure that's true," Sebastian drawled. "Naturally, he would never take money from the Church when it has so many other, more pressing needs . . ."

"Exactly why Guedes hasn't offered any . . . You know how expensive it is to build schools and hire foreign teachers, so where is the money coming from, if not from the Falcon? The peasants could not accomplish such feats with the few, paltry *cruzeiros* they have to spare."

"Obviously not, since they're barely a step above starvation, which is exactly where we *fazendeiros* prefer to maintain them."

Mundinho Cerqueira smiled an unpleasant smile. "I'm glad you understand the necessity for keeping them hungry, *Sebastião* . . . I must admit, I sometimes doubted your loyalty to our class. Your friendship with Padre Osmundo is no great secret, and he and his new teacher are guests beneath your roof this very minute."

"I have found that it's always better not to alienate the defenders of the poor," Sebastian explained. He waved his brandy negligently, as if it were no problem whatever to keep himself from smashing the face of this unpunished murderer, right then and there. "You adhere to the same policy in Salvador, don't you? Or is there no truth to the rumors of your generosity to the Church there?"

"Of course, I support my cousin's pet projects . . ."

"And I, of course, support Padre Osmundo's, though I never contribute as much to his projects as he would like. I give just enough that he sends me workers whenever I need them."

Mundinho Cerqueira's brows rose. "Really? What a unique idea. I've never thought of *currying* the man's favor, in order to gain reliable workers who are always so hard to find."

"You should try it sometime," Sebastian advised. "It takes very little to get poor, dumb peasants eating out of the palm of your hand. They'll do anything for you, if you but show them an occasional trifling generosity."

"You're not saying *you* built that school of Padre Osmundo's!"

"No," Sebastian hastened to deny. "That would be entirely too much generosity . . . But what has all this to do with trapping the Falcon?"

"It has everything to do with it. Before I tell you my plan, I must know where you stand on this matter of Padre Osmundo's school . . ."

Sebastian frowned. He did not want to say the wrong thing and send Cerqueira fleeing for cover— but neither did he want to jeopardize the school. "I think it's harmless enough, don't you? No matter how hard the old priest tries, he'll never succeed in teaching *caboclos* to read and write. They are far too stupid and undisciplined."

"Oh, I quite agree. But the school *will* stir up the peasants and raise their expectations. Soon, they'll be demanding better wages and doctors to treat their many disgusting illnesses. I predict that as soon as they learn to print their names, they will start to think that they are as good as any of us, and then they will want what we have . . . Literacy for the masses is a dangerous thing. A few peasants might actually become educated and start to read newspapers and books—and where will that lead? They won't want to work in the cane fields or herd cattle, I can assure you of that."

"Amazing!" Sebastian exclaimed. "I've argued the very same point with Padre Osmundo and his new teacher . . . We don't see eye to eye, naturally, but I still think you and I have nothing to worry about. The experiment will eventually fail. It can't help but fail."

"I want to make certain it fails," Cerqueira snapped. "My plan has a two-fold purpose: to catch the Falcon and to stop this nonsense of educating *caboclos*."

"So tell me what you intend to do."

"You mean what I intend for us *both* to do . . . First, we must destroy the school and kidnap Padre Osmundo . . . When the Falcon hears of it, he'll attempt to rescue the priest, giving us the opportunity to capture *him* and destroy his band."

"I see . . ." Sebastian muttered, surprised and disturbed. He had never imagined that Padre Osmundo and the new school might be threatened—yet otherwise Cerqueira's plan had all the right ingredients.

Thinking that Sebastian had joined him on his mission to destroy the Falcon, Cerqueira wouldn't discover until too late that Sebastian actually intended to destroy Cerqueira himself. Cerqueira's death could then be blamed on the Falcon, who would mysteriously disappear. Thus, Sebastian would gain his vengeance, while at the same time protecting his future. Once Cerqueira was dead, Sebastian could buy back the land that had once belonged to his parents. He could also openly assist Padre Osmundo to help the peasants . . . and marry and have the family he wanted.

But Sebastian could agree to none of this, if he couldn't keep Padre Osmundo from being harmed. "Do you plan to murder the priest as well?" he asked, concealing his concern in a tone of casualness.

"Murder a priest? Not I. In matters of this kind, murder is sometimes necessary and unavoidable, but I don't want the sin of killing a cleric on my conscience . . . No, I've made other arrangements for that meddlesome old man. Guedes agrees with me that it's time for Padre Osmundo to retire to a monastery . . . The priest need not be present when we dispose of the Falcon. In fact, it would be better if he weren't there, so he can't witness what happens . . . I think we should take him straight away to the monastery . . . We'll tell him he's being confined as a consequence of disobeying Church orders to cease meddling in civil, non-religious affairs. My cousin *has* warned him in the past not to enflame the peasants against the landowners."

So murder is sometimes necessary and unavoidable, you bastard, Sebastian thought furiously. He struggled inwardly to restrain himself. He dared not throttle the man in his own living room, or he himself would have to pay the consequences. And he had not waited this long for such a golden opportunity, to throw it all away on a whim.

"But why destroy the school, if Padre Osmundo will be out of the way anyway?" he calmly asked. "Perhaps the building could be utilized for some other purpose."

He was thinking that after the whole thing was

240

over, and he rescued Padre Osmundo from the monastery, his old friend could continue his work as before—this time with Sebastian's whole-hearted approval and support. Cerqueira shook his head in protest.

"I can think of no good use for a building that will only serve to remind the peasants of the champions they've lost in Padre Osmundo and the Falcon . . . Then, too, that new teacher may decide to stay and teach, even without the priest . . . No, it must be destroyed and crumbled into dust."

"Destroying it is likely to rouse the anger of the *caboclos* against *us*," Sebastian argued, worried now that Tory's presence was indeed a good reason for Cerqueira to tear down the school—and what about Tory herself? How was he going to keep her from interfering in all these events?

"You're right," Cerqueira said thoughtfully. "Perhaps we should hold the priest hostage inside the building itself. Or, better yet, take him to the monastery but make everyone *think* that we're holding him hostage inside the school . . . The school stands on the outskirts of town, I'm told. We must force the Falcon to go there to negotiate the priest's release. Then we can kill him when he comes and make sure the school is badly damaged during the fight. If the building is damaged, we have a good excuse for finally tearing it down . . ."

"That's true . . ." Sebastian agreed, hoping the building wouldn't be *too* badly damaged. He would have to lure Cerqueira out into the open somehow, before the shooting began, because he didn't want to kill him inside the school itself. The superstitious peasants would refuse to set foot inside the door of a place where a man had been murdered.

"Maybe we could make the whole fight appear to be a confrontation between rival bands of *cangaçeiros*," he suggested. "Then we can't be in any way connected with the Falcon's death or blamed for it."

"An excellent idea!" Cerqueira exclaimed excitedly. "Wasn't there a large band that used to roam the area of Espirito Santo some years ago? I haven't heard much of them lately, but it seems logical that they would be angry with the Falcon for taking over their part of the *sertão*."

"Ramiro Bastos," Sebastian said. "That's the name of the man who led the band you're thinking of . . . I don't know what happened to him, but yes, people will believe anything of the *cangaçeiros*, even that they fight among themselves. A battle between bitter rivals would surprise no one."

Remembering the help Bastos had offered, Sebastian decided to enlist Ramiro's aid in the battle against Cerqueira's *vaqueiros*. Bastos would find it all a huge joke; he wouldn't mind taking the blame for killing the Falcon *or* Cerqueira. Maybe the Falcon should "die," not just disappear. Then no other *fazendeiros* would be tempted to lay a trap for him following Cerqueira's death. Sebastian smiled to himself. It might all work out better than he had dared dream.

"Then it's settled!" Cerqueira announced. "As soon as Padre Osmundo returns to Espirito Santo—you must let me know when he leaves—we'll put our plan in motion. I'll take care of kidnapping Padre Osmundo and escorting him to the monastery my cousin has designated, and . . ."

"I'll take care of getting word to the Falcon that Padre Osmundo is being held captive in the school," Sebastian volunteered. "I'm sure that Carmelita,

Padre Osmundo's housekeeper, will know how to contact him through the peasants. She'll send any message I tell her."

Cerqueira smiled with dark satisfaction. "Your *vaqueiros* can hole up in the school and wait for the bastard's arrival . . . You and I and my men will hide in town until the Falcon comes. It should not be too difficult to trap him in the crossfire from both sides when he approaches the building. He'll never know what struck him."

"A fine plan," Sebastian agreed, all the while refining his own plan. He decided to keep half his men with him, and put the other half inside the school with Ramiro's band. At his signal, they would all open fire on Cerqueira's men—saving Cerqueira himself, of course, for Sebastian.

With Padre Osmundo safe inside a monastery, the only other person Sebastian had to worry about was Tory . . . He was sure he could think of some way to detain her elsewhere until the shooting was over. If he had to, he would tie her up in Padre Osmundo's house, along with Carmelita!

He poured himself and Cerqueira more brandy, then raised his glass in a toast. "Here's to getting rid of our worst enemy, a man I have hated for many years . . . a vicious monster who's stolen far too much and must now pay for his heinous crimes . . ."

"You can't know how pleased I am to drink to that," Cerqueira said, grinning. "I'm delighted that you've consented to join me in this endeavor . . . I wasn't sure you would when I came, especially when I met that little blonde *Americana* and started tangling with Padre Osmundo."

"Ah, well . . ." Sebastian sighed. "I have tried hard to be his friend over the years, but even I can see that it's time for Padre Osmundo to retire to a quieter life . . . As for the little teacher, I've already told her that she doesn't belong here. The Falcon's death and the school's destruction will force her to go back where she came from . . . Do you know that in America, women are fighting to gain the right to vote?"

"Meu Deus! What is the world coming to?" Mundinho Cerqueira laughed and lifted his glass. "To the preservation of our class and sex! May we always triumph!"

Sebastian drank deeply, as if in complete agreement, but in his head, he was debating which rifle to use to kill the man who now shared his brandy.

Chapter Sixteen

Tory didn't sleep a wink all night. She lay awake wondering what she was going to say to Padre Osmundo in the morning. The priest would be devastated when he learned of the evil plans for him and the Falcon; she herself was devastated. There could be no further proof of the kind of man with whom she had fallen in love than the conversation she had overheard between him and Mundinho Cerqueira.

Sebastian cared nothing for the peasants or his long-time friend, Padre Osmundo, and even less for her. He was plotting to kill a man whose only real crime was that he stole from the rich to give to the poor. Padre Osmundo claimed the Falcon was innocent of all the other sins of which he was accused—and Tory believed it. She also believed that Sebastian Black and Mundinho Cerqueira were more wicked than she or Padre Osmundo had ever suspected in their worst moments of doubt. She dreaded telling Padre Osmundo the truth but knew she must. They had to warn the Falcon and find a safe hiding place for both the bandit and Padre Osmundo.

At breakfast, Sebastian did not appear, and neither

did Mundinho Cerqueira, though Tory surmised he must have spent the night at Paraíso. Padre Osmundo was his usual cheerful self, inquiring after her plans for the day and expressing satisfaction that Amâncio's injuries seemed to be healing nicely. Neither mentioned the previous night with its disastrous dinner, and Tory said nothing about Sebastian's arrival, for she was determined to hold her tongue until privacy could be assured. Rising on his crutches at the meal's end, Padre Osmundo beckoned for her to follow him.

"Come, child... You look as if you didn't get much sleep last night... Let's walk out to the corral to check on my new horse, and you can tell me what is bothering you this morning."

It was a perfect opportunity to unburden herself, but Tory followed with a heavy heart, not speaking until they were out of earshot of anyone in the house. She leaned against the top rail of the corral, watching Percy and brooding, working up her courage to begin. "Padre," she finally said. "It grieves me to tell you what I learned last night, but I don't think I have a choice..."

She told him everything, leaving nothing out, except for the impact the revelations had upon her own emotions. Padre Osmundo didn't need to know that she had foolishly offered her heart and her virginity to a man who scorned them and couldn't wait until she left the country.

"So you see, Padre," she sighed in closing. "We can't possibly stay here, but neither can we go to Espirito Santo. As soon as you get there, Cerqueira intends to kidnap you, and Sebastian will go along with it in order to trap and kill the Falcon."

"Dear me..." Padre Osmundo shook his balding head and pursed his full lips. "I suppose I should be

246

surprised, but somehow I'm not ... I've always known that *Sebastião* fears poverty above all else. However, I never dreamed he would go this far to protect his financial interests.''

''Why should Sebastian fear poverty, when he's as rich as he is?''

''Because, my child, he hasn't always been rich. I've told you this. Before *Sebastião* came to me, he experienced great deprivation among the poor peasants. It was a harsh lesson he never forgot ... At the monastery where he received his schooling, when other boys took time from their studies to run, laugh, and play, *Sebastião* would retreat with a book and couldn't be persuaded to participate ... He said he didn't have time for such foolishness ... He wanted so much to make something of himself and to succeed in life ... How do you think he became a *fazendeiro?* He worked, schemed, and struggled for it—so naturally, he doesn't want a thief like the Falcon to take what he has sacrificed so much to gain.''

''That doesn't mean he has to betray *you* or kill a basically good man! If anything, Sebastian should sympathize with the poor peasants, precisely because he's been poor himself ... To side with a cruel bigot like Mundinho Cerqueira is inexcusable. He should be ashamed of himself. I'm ashamed for him, and so should you be!''

''Oh, I am, my child ... I mourn for him, but I cannot condemn him. I know too well the demons that are tearing him apart. They are the same ones that have plagued and tortured him all his life.''

''You needn't be so understanding! Sebastian wants to see *you* confined in a monastery, prevented from continuing your work—and all that *after* he destroys your new school!''

247

"I know, my child ... I know. For me, the monastery would not be so terrible, but killing the Falcon and destroying the school are two crimes I would indeed find it difficult to forgive—especially killing the Falcon. Murder is always a sin ... Are you certain they mean to shoot, not merely capture him?"

"They specifically discussed trapping him in the crossfire between two groups of *vaqueiros*."

"You mean *pistoleiros* ... Mundinho Cerqueira's men have better reputations as *pistoleiros* than they do as *vaqueiros* ... They will not miss. They are good marksmen."

"So is Sebastian. And he thinks nothing of killing bandits. The Falcon will be a prestigious name to add to his list. Another notch on his gun, if that's how he keeps track."

Padre Osmundo suddenly banged a crutch against the fence, startling the horses. "Perdition! I wish I were not still incapacitated. We must leave here as soon as possible, go to Espirito Santo, and tell the peasants to warn the Falcon ... We must also organize a defense of the school. I want the building to remain intact, if at all possible. There's no money to repair costly damages ... And of course, no murders must take place in or near it."

"But after we get there and take all of these precautions, you must hide, Padre, or else you'll be kidnapped."

"No, I won't be. My *caboclos* will conceal me ... If I cannot be found and the school building is guarded by innocent peasants, what can *Sebastião* and Cerqueira do? Their plans will fail."

"But what if they harm the peasants? Cerqueira might insist upon destroying the school and the peasants along with it, as a warning to the Falcon to leave his horses and cattle alone."

248

"*Sebastião* will not permit a single *caboclo* to suffer; on that, I would stake my life . . . He hates the Falcon, but he'll protect the peasants—and the school, too, if the peasants are in it."

"I wish I had your confidence, Padre. I don't understand how you can still defend him."

"Because I have seen the good in him, my child . . . I wish you could have seen it, too. When I first noticed the way he looked at you—and you looked at him, I had hoped . . . Well, never mind what I hoped. It isn't to be . . . *Sebastião* is not yet ready. He may never be ready, though I pray every day that he opens both his eyes and his heart . . ."

"His heart is made of stone," Tory said, more bitterly than she intended, but she couldn't help herself. "He's incapable of love or tenderness."

"Perhaps you are right, my child . . . in which case there's nothing either of us can do but pray. It will take a miracle from God to change him."

Tory did not see Sebastian all day. She deliberately avoided him, for fear that her face might reveal her feelings. Not only did she despise him for rejecting her on the night they made love, but now she hated him for being a deceitful, two-faced traitor plotting to betray his best friend and murder the Falcon. She couldn't wait to leave Paraíso and hoped that Padre Osmundo would soon be ready to travel. Her mood demanded the distraction of hard physical labor, so she spent the day helping Quinquina do laundry, much to Dona Guilhermina's and Carmelita's disapproval.

Fortunately, Tory didn't encounter Mundinho Cerqueira either. He rode out early with his band of *vaqueiros*, a bunch of hard-eyed, foul-mouthed men

249

who had made indecent propositions to several of the women, including Quinquina. Tory took her evening meal with Amâncio, leaving Padre Osmundo to keep Sebastian company at the dinner table. She wondered what they would find to talk about but knew she needn't worry about the priest mentioning their conversation. She and Padre Osmundo had agreed on complete secrecy. When they left the ranch, they would do so at a time when Sebastian was away from Paraíso. That would give them a head start to warn the Falcon before Sebastian could inform Cerqueira that they were gone.

After the evening meal, Tory wandered out to the corral to visit with the horses. Their presence comforted her, though she was painfully reminded of her reckless gallop with Sebastian on Renegade. If only she could mount Percy and ride off by herself, she was certain she would feel much better. As it was, she could hardly feel worse. How and why had she ever allowed herself to become emotionally involved with Sebastian?

It was the worst mistake of her life. Yet she couldn't blame Sebastian for hurting and disillusioning her; he had never claimed to be a gentleman—which he was in his own singular, twisted way. How ironic! When she was finally willing to surrender herself to a man, he didn't want her because she was still a virgin!

Renegade ambled over to the split-log fence and whinnied a greeting, prompting Tory to extend her fingers and stroke his velvety-soft muzzle. The horse's ears pricked, alerting Tory that she wasn't alone. Slowly, she turned. Sebastian stood behind her, his face in darkness but his eyes discernable by their liquid shine.

"Is this how you spend *all* your time, *gatinha?*" he asked. "Watching the horses?"

"There isn't much else to do . . . Since you've forbidden me to ride or to teach."

He drew nearer, close enough that she could see the wry grin curving his lips. "I can think of other ways you might entertain yourself and pass the time. Would you care to chance another wild gallop across the *sertão?*"

"No!" Tory cried, too quickly and too vehemently, considering that she had resolved to never again betray her emotions to this man. "I'm sorry I took the last one . . . I'll regret it for the rest of my life."

His grin disappeared. "I regret it, too, *gatinha.* You are not the sort of woman with whom a man should trifle. I'm ashamed that I did so."

"Well, what sort of woman am I then—the kind you should disappoint and walk away from?" Realizing what she was saying, Tory spun back to the horses. Sebastian must never know how much he had hurt her; she had to pretend relief that he had stopped in time.

His fingers gently stroked her shoulders, igniting a treacherous fire deep in her belly. "You're sorry that I didn't take your virginity, aren't you?" he softly inquired. "How strange! I thought you would be furious that I tried. I thought your anger was the reason you have been avoiding me ever since."

"It *is* the reason. I *am* furious that you tried . . . I've also been avoiding your despicable friend, Senhor Cerqueira. No woman in her right mind would desire the company of either of you. You are two of a kind—arrogant, bigoted, conceited . . ."

"I don't much like him either . . ."

"Narrow-minded, cruel . . . You don't like him

251

either?" Tory spun to face him. "Did I hear you correctly? Did you just say you didn't like him either?"

"I abhor him . . . He's everything you say—and worse. I've hated and despised him for years."

Tory searched his face in the darkness. Incredibly, he seemed sincere. He could *not* be faking the contempt she saw so clearly in his eyes. As a teacher, she had learned to read her students very well; few people were such accomplished actors that they could hide what was in their eyes.

"If you hate him, then why do you welcome him into your home?" she bluntly inquired.

"For business reasons . . . Our land abuts, and there are times when I must cross his territory with my horses and cattle. Fortunately, I have my own water and don't need to borrow his—but it would still be unwise to alienate him. Mundinho Cerqueira is a powerful *fazendeiro* with connections in all the right places . . . He's not a man you want for an enemy, so I go out of my way to be civil to him . . . That doesn't mean, however, that I *like* him . . . I'd sooner shoot him than pretend to be his friend. However, it's something I must do."

Sebastian's eyes now looked haunted, and his tone conveyed a deep, startling hatred. Tory was astonished. It suddenly occurred to her that Sebastian Black was a man at war with himself. Contradiction and conflict surrounded him. There *must* be good in him; Padre Osmundo and Amâncio couldn't be wrong about that—but a broad streak of cruelty and violence also existed . . . What did he want from life? Who were his friends? Why was he still unmarried?

Above all else, Sebastian Black was a man of mystery—and Tory ached to draw him out, to become his confidant, to discover his secrets. Maybe then she could understand why he did the things he did . . . why he conspired with a man he professed to hate. Behind the facade he so carefully presented, there existed a man no one really knew, not even Padre Osmundo.

"How long have you known Mundinho Cerqueira?" she asked quietly.

"Forever," Sebastian answered, gazing past her at the horses. "I've known him since I was a child . . . and he's never been a person you would desire for a friend."

Tory pondered this a moment, wondering where a son of starving peasants would have had the opportunity to meet a *fazendeiro* of the upper class. Not wanting to give Sebastian a reason to end the conversation, she didn't ask, but instead cast about for a safer topic that would at least keep him talking about himself. "Were you a precocious child? It seems to me you must have been."

Unexpectedly, he laughed. "No, I was a hungry one—hungry for everything. Food, education, land, wealth, security . . . You name it, I wanted it."

She laughed too, easily imagining him coveting anything and everything. She herself had been that kind of child—eager for every new experience, certain she would triumph over every challenge. Then she had discovered that she was a female, and females couldn't aspire to the same things as males.

"What did you want most as a child?" she queried.

"Revenge . . . I wanted revenge." His response was instantaneous, without thought or hesitation.

The answer chilled her. His eyes sought hers, and he repeated it, as if the statement encompassed everything he stood for and all that he desired. "I wanted revenge, *gatinha*. It was what I lived for, what I still live for."

"Revenge for what?" she whispered, afraid to ask.

"That is a question I refuse to answer . . . I've never told a living soul, so I shall not tell you . . . But rest assured I will have it one day. Nothing on this earth matters more to me than obtaining revenge."

A brief silence followed, during which Tory wrestled with her own conflicting emotions. She was torn between shock and censure. "Then you must be very lonely," she finally said. "And you will always be lonely. Revenge, I suspect, makes a cold bedmate."

"My bed has rarely been cold, *gatinha*," he said wryly. "As I'm sure you know by now."

"Undoubtedly, women have stood in line to keep it warm for you . . . I'm not talking about your body, but about your heart, soul, and mind . . . Don't you wish for someone to share your thoughts, not just your passion? Don't you want a friend with whom you can talk, argue, laugh, weep, and play? Don't you want a . . . a life-long companion who will care for you as deeply and fully as you care for yourself?"

"*Cristo!* No, never! . . . For I despise myself, you see. If I wanted someone to love me as I love myself, I would have to sleep with a pistol beneath my pillow for self-defense."

He grinned at her in the darkness, but she did not return the grin. This was no joking matter. It must be awful to live like Sebastian—to believe as he did, to be as alone as he was. A wetness gathered in her eyes. "I'm so sorry for you, Sebastian . . ."

When he saw her tears, his expression softened. He touched a finger to her cheek and gently captured a glistening drop. "Don't weep for me, *gatinha*. I'm not worth it." He tilted up her chin and gazed into her eyes. "Women have wept *because* of me, but never

254

for me . . . This is a new experience; I'm not sure how I should react."

She said nothing—what *could* she say? She was weeping for a man she hated . . . No, not hated, *pitied*. Obviously, he had never experienced love, never loved, or *wanted* to love. She could not imagine such a bleak, depressing existence! Even though she had lost her parents at a young age, she had always had the affection of her brother, Jordan, and her sisters to rely upon. She had known that someone in the world cared about her and would grieve if something happened to her . . . But who had ever provided that kind of security for Sebastian?

Padre Osmundo had done his best, but for some reason, it hadn't been enough. Sebastian carried a heavy load of bitterness; no wonder he had never married!

Sebastian's mouth hovered just above hers. Her glance fell to his lips—those sensuous, full lips that knew exactly how to enflame a woman's passions. Yes, they knew how to kiss, all right . . . But they weren't acquainted with tenderness. She could teach *him* a thing or two that *he* didn't know. Standing on tiptoe, she brushed his lips with her own, tentatively at first, then with more confidence.

He drew back in surprise, his eyes scanning her face as if looking for the meaning of the gesture. She raised her hands and captured his jaw, noting the prickle of beard on it and the warmth of his skin. She held his face steady so she could kiss him again. All of her longing and her feelings of confusion, mistrust, and sympathy poured into her next kiss . . . If she couldn't find the words to touch his heart, maybe she could find the right motions.

Again he withdrew, his eyes bright with amazement and slightly dazed with desire. *"Gatinha,"* he rasped in a shaky voice. "What are you doing?"

In answer, she pressed herself against the hard length of him and wrapped her arms around him. "I'm holding you, Sebastian—loving you, if you will allow it . . . For all your supposed carnal experience, you don't seem to realize when a woman wants you, do you?"

His hands slid over her buttocks and clamped her to him. His mouth sought hers, and he kissed her as a drowning man might gulp down water. She opened her lips and gave him her tongue. He crushed her in his embrace, then suddenly let go long enough to sweep her off her feet and cradle her in his arms.

It didn't matter where he was taking her. She didn't care if they encountered someone on the way into the house or not. He could take her wherever he chose. Her love flared stronger than her hate, so strong that she believed it capable of conquering his indifference and toppling the defenses he had built to protect his innermost self. Before the night was over, Sebastian would tell her why he wanted revenge, why he felt he must betray Padre Osmundo, why he conspired with a man he professed to hate, and why he intended to kill a man who was only trying to help poor peasants . . . Her love was strong enough to work miracles and her desire too compelling for him to resist.

Chapter Seventeen

Sebastian carried Tory to his room, not her.s. Tory registered that fact when he deposited her upon a bed twice as wide as her own and three times as hard. They had met no one upon entering the house, and she was glad he had kicked shut the door behind him. It was dark, but her eyes soon adjusted to the soft glow of starlight—and the light of a new moon—that spilled through the tall, open windows.

She felt no shyness. She had chosen to give herself to this man. By doing so, she was taking a great risk, but she had always been a risk-taker, gambling everything on what she believed to be right . . . And this felt right to her. Nothing had ever felt so right and good. In Sebastian's arms, she had the unnerving sensation that she had found some lost part of herself that she hadn't known was missing—and now could not do without. It had to be the same for Sebastian, she thought, only he was more determined to fight it.

With typical lack of modesty, he stripped in front of her; she did the same—wiggling out of her clothing with an eagerness that once would have shocked and mortified her. Desire did strange things to a woman, she mused. It gave her a reckless courage totally at odds with the more reticent facets of her personality. She who had always been so prim and proper now longed to be completely naked and seductive, tantalizing this man who so tantalized her.

He uttered a low growl as he fell upon her, rolling her over with her skirt still tangled around her knees. When she lay skin to skin, sprawled full length on top of him, he began to kiss her hungrily, hardly caring if his kisses landed on her lips. Being the one above gave her a sense of power, and she devoured him as her own urgings prompted. She tasted his skin with a relish usually reserved only for the finest of foods. Never having realized she possessed such an appetite, she wanted to kiss, caress, stroke, and taste every inch of him. His body was a feast for her starved senses, and she could not get enough of him.

But he didn't allow her to dine at will. Again rolling her over, he pinned her beneath him while he conducted his own devastating explorations. Her breasts became succulent fruits from which he seemed determined to suck the last drop of juice. She moaned as his lips traveled over her abdomen, then back up to her throat . . . He was eating her alive! And she reveled in it. He consumed her, as she also consumed him.

She wanted him inside her—wanted their union with a fiery desperation that drove every other thought from her mind. He turned her sideways and fitted himself around her spoon-wise, then proceeded to inflict tender torture on her breasts, belly, thighs, and between her legs. She could feel his iron hardness pressing against the back of her thighs, and opening them, squeezed down upon him, so that he groaned into her hair.

"*Cristo, gatinha* . . . Do not do that."

She squeezed harder. "I want you, Sebastian . . . I *need* you."

Releasing him, she tried to turn over and face him, but he held her fast with his arms and one leg thrown across her hips. "*Gatinha,* I want you, too . . . As I have never wanted any woman. But let me love you like this for awhile . . . Lie still and relax. Open your legs . . . Why must you always be rushing? There's more pleasure to be had in going slow and enjoying the journey . . ."

She sighed and did as he requested. His fingers slid into the core of her and worked a glorious magic that soon made her forget everything but the nuances of exquisite sensation he so effortlessly wrought. Her entire being centered on the burgeoning fullness in her nether regions. With one hand he stroked her breasts and pulled at her nipples, while with the other, he titillated the tiny bud of flesh between her thighs that throbbed so hard it felt as if it might burst.

Dimly, she perceived him moving against her from behind—slicking her buttocks and probing between them. She was too far gone in her own cresting pleasure to realize what he was about, but suddenly, he gripped her tightly and spasmed against her, calling out a ragged: "*Gatinha!*"

Too late, she realized that he had brought her to shuddering fulfillment and taken his own release— but they had yet to be joined together. She lay still until her thundering heartbeats faded away, and her breathing returned to normal . . . A marvelous satiation filled her body, but a coldness had invaded her heart. Sebastian had rejected her again. He hadn't truly taken her, hadn't spurted his seed into the welcoming recesses of her body, hadn't gazed into her eyes and committed himself as he finally made her his own. He was so much more experienced than she, that he had been able to control the whole thing, from beginning to end. She was a virgin, still—if virginity meant only the retention of a small, meaningless barrier.

Her body still throbbed with delightful tremors, but she wanted more . . . She wanted the heart and soul of the man, and he had denied them. Curling into a ball, she began to weep hot, silent tears . . . Why did she keep reaching out to him, while he kept retreating and backing away? Why did she surrender everything, when he withheld the most vital part of himself?

He cuddled her while she wept. "*Gatinha,* don't cry . . . It destroys me to see you cry."

"Don't say that!" she sniffled. "It's a bald-faced lie. Nothing destroys you, reaches you, touches you . . . You never lose your head even when you're making love to me."

"That is not true, *gatinha* . . . No woman has made me burn as you do. I adore you, my small, blonde wildcat . . . my feisty *Americana.* However, since we don't intend to marry, I dare not make you pregnant . . . But that does not mean we cannot enjoy this mutual madness we have for each other."

"Madness is all it is!" Tory sobbed. "I don't even like you . . . I don't trust you. I abhor what you are and what you do . . ."

He turned her around and gathered her into his arms. "Hush, kitten . . . You're not to blame for what has happened between us. This is your first experience with passion. It has overwhelmed you . . . You think you can control and conquer it. Instead, it controls and conquers you. That is the nature of passion."

"I don't want to be in love with you! I don't want to want you!"

"I know, my sweet . . . No one intends to sin, but when the opportunity arises, the temptation is just too great."

He kissed her tear-flooded eyes, her cheeks, then her forehead. With great tenderness, he kissed her mouth. Incredibly, she felt the first stirrings of renewed desire and was shocked at herself. She made a feeble attempt to pull away, but he pressed her back into the pillows, leaned over her, and bestowed soft, swollen kisses all over her face—then lower, between her breasts. He circled her nipples with his tongue, drew one into his mouth, and suckled it.

A sob died in her throat as her body came alive again beneath his skillful ministrations. He took her hand and guided it to his own nipples. She caressed and explored them, pausing when she heard his sharp intake of breath. He was as much a captive of passion as she; they were both trapped, unable to resist the need and hunger they felt for each other.

Her hand wandered down his flat belly and became entangled in the crisp hair that curled around his sex. She boldly fondled him, amazed when he swelled beneath her caresses and grew strong and hard.

"You see what passion does to me, *gatinha?* You see what *you* do to me?"

His questions did not require an answer, so she gave him none. She had an overwhelming urge to kiss him where she held him—as if by doing so, she might finally, actually know him. Succumbing to the urge, she rolled over and climbed on top of him. Then she squirmed lower, dipped her head, and tasted him. He did not repulse or revolt her; nothing

261

about Sebastian's body revolted her—only his character did so, but she could no more stop herself from loving him, than she could have stopped breathing.

Barely had she satisfied her intense, wanton yearnings, when he grabbed her hair and pulled her head away. *"Cristo!* Stop, *gatinha* . . . You must stop, or I'll lose control . . ."

Feeling sly and feline, she smiled a secret smile. That was what she wanted—for Sebastian to lose control. Sliding her body along his, she sat astride him, in which position he was powerless to deny her anything she wanted . . . and what she wanted was all of him, penetrating her fully. She raised herself on her knees, seeking the proper position, uncertain what that position might be.

"No, *gatinha!*" He bucked beneath her, twisted sharply, and threw her off. Just as quickly, he seized her from behind, dragged her down onto the bed, and clamped her to him.

She started to struggle, but it was useless. Sebastian knew too well how to conquer her totally. After a few brief moments of resistance, she submitted once again to his sensual expertise . . . Once again, he loved her without really loving her. He made her moan and thrash helplessly, call his name, beg him to take her . . . He pleasured her senses without pleasuring her soul. He didn't belong to her and never would . . . This was only an exercise in the power of passion, which ruled her utterly, but without giving any real joy or happiness.

When Tory awoke the next morning, Sebastian was gone. His bed was empty and his clothes missing from the floor where he had tossed them the previous night. She rose, dressed, and crept down the hallway to her own room, where she mussed the bed to make it look as if she had slept there. Then she washed herself, changed into clean clothes, brushed out her hair, and descended the stairs to find Padre Osmundo. In the mornings, he could usually be found in the courtyard, saying his prayers.

He was there when she arrived and glanced up to give her a smile as warm as the sunshine streaming into the courtyard. "How are you, my child? I missed you last night at dinner . . . *Sebastião* accused me of being a very poor conversationalist, but I couldn't very well tell him what was on my mind, now could I?"

"Where is Sebastian?" Tory asked casually, seating herself on the stone bench beside the priest.

"He rode off and said he would be gone all day, maybe even overnight . . . There is always a great deal to do on a ranch, and his cattle are scattered all over the *sertão*."

"Then it would be a perfect day for us to leave for Espirito Santo, wouldn't it?"

Padre Osmundo nodded. "If I were up to traveling, it would . . . But I can't sit a horse yet."

"I have been thinking about that, Padre . . . Why should you have to sit a horse? How did you plan for Carmelita and me to get there?"

"You and Carmelita were going to ride in the ox cart . . . But we can't all three ride in the cart. Aside from being woefully crowded, one of us should be on horseback. If we run into trouble with *cangaçeiros*, someone must be able to ride off in search of help."

"Then why don't you and Carmelita ride in the cart, and I'll ride horseback."

Padre Osmundo frowned. "Oh, I don't know, my

child . . . Originally, I had counted on *Sebastião* accompanying us. Even if I wasn't still hobbling about on crutches, it's a long, dangerous journey to Espirito Santo . . . Of course, I changed my mind about him going with us, when all this came up about the Falcon . . . Even so, I am the man in the party. I should be the one riding lookout."

"I don't see why, Padre. I can ride lookout as well as you. Aren't you anxious to leave here as soon as possible? I certainly am . . . Please, Padre. I find it most difficult to remain in the same house with a man I've come to despise . . . Besides, the cart is still packed with most of my baggage and the supplies you wanted from Salvador. We could leave within the hour."

Padre Osmundo stared long and hard at her. She felt guilty and had to drop her gaze. What would this good priest think of her if he knew how she had spent the night? Of course, there was no reason for him to know; she needn't fear being pregnant, but instead of relief, she felt a wretched sorrow and wanted to weep again. Had Sebastian planted his seed in her and made her pregnant, she would have carried the child proudly, her head held high. She could find no shame in such blatant proof of a man's love and devotion. Sadly, such was not the reality in her case, so she lowered her eyes and blushed, too embarrassed to meet Padre Osmundo's searching eyes.

"If you feel so strongly that we must depart Paraíso today, I will do my best to accommodate you, child— though in truth, I had rather we waited another week or two."

"Good . . . I'll tell Carmelita that we're leaving as soon as possible."

"If you insist, my dear . . . But could we not have

breakfast before we go? I hate to travel on an empty stomach."

"Of course, we'll eat first. We'll also take along plenty of food. That way we won't have to stop to cook—only to rest. With the moon on the rise, we can travel after dark. The *sertão* will be bright enough for us to see our way."

"You *are* determined to get to Espírito Santo as quickly as possible, aren't you, my child?"

"The faster we get there, the faster we can warn the Falcon and the peasants—and the faster you can go into hiding, Padre."

"That's true . . ." he sighed. "I only wish all this were not necessary."

"So do I, Padre. But it is necessary, so let's get started."

Even with Tory rushing about and prodding Carmelita and Padre Osmundo to hurry, it was noon before they were ready to depart. Disturbed by the shortness of notice, Carmelita grumbled unceasingly under her breath, while Quinquina begged to accompany them. Sadly, they had to refuse Quinquina's request without revealing the reason why. Amâncio also questioned the urgency of their departure, but neither Tory nor Padre Osmundo wanted to take the chance of exposing the truth of the matter. All they could do and did was cite Tory's eagerness to begin teaching the peasants and Padre Osmundo's desire to return home.

Tory left Amâncio and Quinquina a copy of the alphabet, so they could acquaint themselves with all the letters, hugged each one in farewell, then helped Padre Osmundo climb into the ox cart.

"Senhor *Sebastião* isn't going to like this," Dona Guilhermina warned as she watched from the verandah.

The woman's thin mouth slanted downward in disapproval, but it wasn't until she saw Tory mounting Percy that her ire finally exploded. *"Meu Deus,* Padre! How can you permit Senhorita *Rei* to ride your horse—and astride yet? Surely, it's a sin for a woman to expose her limbs like that! Why, it's totally indecent!"

Tory calmly draped her divided skirt over her ankles. "I don't see any exposed limbs, do you, Padre? . . . If you must carry tales to Senhor Sebastião when you see him, Dona Guilhermina, be sure and get them straight. Tell him that riding was *my* idea, not Padre Osmundo's. He disapproves almost as much as you do."

"Let us go now, before an argument erupts," Padre Osmundo wisely counseled, clucking to the oxen. "Carmelita, hold onto your shawl."

"Good-bye, my friends!" Carmelita called out as the cart lurched forward.

Surrounded by women and children waving and wishing them well, Tory, Carmelita, and Padre Osmundo departed Paraíso. Tory's relief expanded with each step Percy took to carry her away. If she stayed much longer, she would surely lose all respect for herself, because all Sebastian had to do was crook his little finger, and she would fall into his arms again and let him do whatever he liked with her.

Putting distance between them was the only possible cure for her shameful addiction; if she couldn't see him, she couldn't succumb to him. In time, she would forget the wonderful, but frustrating intimacies in which they had so recklessly indulged. At least this was what she told herself as she left Sebastian's ranch, and together with Carmelita and

Padre Osmundo, headed north toward Espirito Santo.

They stopped and made camp that night long after dark, when everyone, including Tory, was too exhausted to travel any farther. After a brief meal of cold rice, beans, and bread, they stretched out on rudimentary pallets beneath the stars. Carmelita and Padre Osmundo promptly began snoring, but Tory lay awake tossing and turning for what seemed like hours. Her muscles were stiff and sore from the unaccustomed hours in the saddle, and her body longed for the feel of a bed beneath it—Sebastian's bed. To her utter disgust, she craved the warmth and security of his arms around her.

Several times, she sat up itching and slapping at unseen insects, and once she dreamed that Sebastian was lying beside her, making passionate love to her, so that she moaned aloud and woke herself up again. Toward morning, she finally fell into a fitful sleep, but her relaxation was rudely shattered when a man's voice jolted her awake.

"Mamãe de Deus! What do we have here, my friends? Is this not one of the horses stolen from our three unjustly murdered companions?"

Tory sprang to her feet, gazing wildly about—only to find herself staring down the barrels of three Winchesters held by mean-looking men on horseback. "Padre Osmundo . . . Carmelita . . . wake up. We have visitors."

One of the men—the largest and meanest-looking of the trio—grinned and shoved back his leather *vaqueiro's* hat, so he could get a better look at her. Morning sunlight illuminated his bearded, dirty face, which had a flat, pug nose and cheeks as round as apples. He reminded her of something or someone, and in a moment, she realized what it was—a pig. He had the face—and the stench—of a barnyard pig.

"Bom dia, Senhorita," he greeted her. "I am called Porco, for reasons which must be obvious . . . and these are my fellow *cangaçeiros.* Their names will mean nothing to you so I'll not bother to mention them . . . We were passing by, saw your camp, and decided to investigate . . . and then we recognized that horse." He pointed to Percy who was cropping grass at the end of a rope Tory had tied to the back of the ox cart.

"Do you know the animal?" Tory innocently inquired. "We just bought him and have no idea where he originally came from."

"From whom did you purchase him, Senhorita?"

"Why, we got him from a friend of mine," Padre Osmundo said, using the cart wheel to brace himself as he got to his feet and reached for his crutches. "I needed a horse, so my friend sold him to me. Of course, I don't know where *he* got him, but I can assure you there was no foul play involved in how *we* obtained him."

Porco narrowed his eyes and studied Tory, Padre Osmundo, and Carmelita, who had awakened and was staring at the intruders, wide-eyed and trembling. "I recognize you women, as well as that horse . . ." Porco said. "You were in a group we attacked on the *sertão.*"

"I recognize them, too, Porco," one of the other men asserted. "I'd never forget that pretty *loura* with the long, gold hair . . . I wonder if she's got gold hair anywhere else on her body . . . We'll soon find out, won't we?"

He laughed harshly, stripping Tory with his eyes. She took an involuntary step backward and wished she had thought of taking turns guarding the camp throughout the night. They had a rifle in the cart, but she wasn't sure if Padre Osmundo knew how to use it. She and Carmelita certainly didn't. How foolish they had been not to have taken precautions against just such a surprise as this!

"Don't you dare think of laying a hand on these women!" Padre Osmundo cried, limping forward on his crutches. "Have you no fear of hell? You endanger your immortal souls indulging in such wicked thoughts."

"It's not the women we want, Padre," Porco snarled. "But if I did want them, the threat of damnation is not enough to stop me from taking them . . . What I most desire is revenge against the man who killed my *pistoleiros* and stole their horses. We have been riding all over the *sertão* looking for him— waiting to catch him unawares. There is no sense lying about who he is—we know his name. It's *Sebastião Prêto*, and he owns a big ranch about a day's ride from here."

"Whatever *Sebastião* did to you, you aren't justified in raping and killing these innocent women—*or* in killing *Sebastião* himself," Padre Osmundo argued. "Such violence is a mortal sin. Why don't you take back your horse and be gone? Our oxen will get us to Espirito Santo where I have my church and a school for the peasants . . . We are en route to do God's holy work, and if you harm us, you will suffer all the torments of the damned when you finally die."

Porco's two friends shifted uneasily in their saddles and exchanged glances with each other. Padre Osmundo's warnings were causing them to reconsider, but Porco only grunted and spat a huge wad of spittle on the ground near the priest's feet. "You don't scare me, Padre . . . I had rather get my revenge on the man who killed my friends. I think I'll take the lot of you back to his ranch and threaten to kill you in front of his very eyes, unless he agrees to fight me himself."

"I'm afraid it wouldn't do you any good to return us to Paraíso, my son," Padre Osmundo advised him. "We left there yesterday, and he wasn't in residence. Nor did he leave a message of when he intended to come back . . . No, the wisest thing would be to forget your quest for vengeance and permit us to continue peacefully on our way."

Porco squinted at the priest. "He's not there, you say?"

Fearing that the bandit might decide to destroy the ranch in Sebastian's absence, Tory hastened to assure him that Sebastian would soon return. "Senhor *Prêto* said he wouldn't be gone long though, and when he returns he's bringing all his *vaqueiros* with him. The ranch will be swarming with men—all good shots with a rifle."

Porco's lip curled in a sneer. "You just don't want me to go there. That's why you're telling me these lies."

"They aren't lies," Tory insisted. "Three men don't stand a chance against fifty. You might as well let us go . . . Besides, if you harm us, Senhor *Prêto* will hunt you down like dogs, just as he hunted you down before—only next time, he won't make the mistake of leaving anyone alive."

"She's right, Porco . . ." the third man grunted. "Whatever we do, he'll take his revenge on us just like he did the last time . . . Of course, if we rape the women here and now, then kill all of them including

270

the priest, nobody will know who did it. It'll be days—maybe weeks—before their bodies are found, and by then, the *urubus* will have made it impossible for anyone to identify them."

"If you kill us, I shall personally see to it that you roast in hell for all eternity," Padre Osmundo staunchly threatened. "As a priest, I possess the power to do this . . . Such a sin would be beyond forgiveness."

All three men lowered their rifles in indecision.

"I must think about this . . ." Porco growled.

"We'll surely be damned if we kill the priest," the other two men muttered among themselves.

They wheeled their horses around in the dust, rode a short distance away, and commenced arguing in low, ominous voices. Tory debated whether or not to make a grab for the rifle hidden in the cart. Padre Osmundo saw where she was looking and shook his head.

"Don't, my child . . . We stand a better chance of outwitting them than we do of killing them."

"Oh, Padre Osmundo, I'm so frightened!" Carmelita wailed.

"Be brave . . . We shall survive this threat and soon be on our way again," Padre Osmundo soothed, but his brow was furrowed with worry.

Carmelita took out her rosary beads and began twisting them in her pudgy hands. "Aren't you frightened, *Professôra?* I'm old woman; they will kill me quickly . . . But you are young and beautiful. They will keep you alive a long time to serve their lust and degrade you."

"Hush, Carmelita!" Padre Osmundo scolded. "We must not show fear, or they will feel contempt for us and kill us more easily."

271

No sooner had he finished speaking than the trio came trotting back to them.

"I have decided," Porco announced. "My two companions will remain with the priest and the fat old woman, while I take the pretty young one and go to Senhor *Prêto's* ranch . . . If he is there, I will demand satisfaction for the wrong he has done me in killing my men and stealing their horses. If he refuses to fight me, then I will kill the girl then and there . . . He will not, of course, dare to shoot *me*, because I will tell him that if I have not returned here in three days' time, my men have orders to rape and kill the old woman, then leave you, Padre, to wander alone on the *sertão*, and die or be saved as God wills . . ."

"But what if he is *not* there?" Tory demanded. "What will you do then?"

Porco grinned a porcine, evil grin. "Then I will wait for him, *moçinha* . . . If he has fifty *vaqueiros* riding with him, he has probably left few at home. I will enter his house, tie up his servants, and wait for him in his own bedroom, in his own bed . . . We shall enjoy ourselves while we wait, eh? And what a surprise he'll have when he opens the door and I cut him down where he stands! . . . After that, we'll return here, so my men can enjoy you, too. The padre and the old woman will die quickly, but you, my pretty *loura*, will live for a very long time . . . providing you please us, of course. We shall teach you how to please us."

"That is a vile, ungodly plan, and you damn your souls for having thought of it!" Padre Osmundo bellowed. "Get off those horses, get down on your knees, and beg God's forgiveness at once!"

Porco's response was to spur his horse into a gallop and ride straight for Tory. She tried to elude

272

him, but he bent down, clamped his arm around her waist, and easily lifted her off her feet. Then he dumped her face down across the saddle in front of him. The saddle horn gouged her mid-section, nearly breaking her in two, but Porco didn't stop to make her more comfortable. He set off across the *sertão* at a full run, and Tory had all she could do to keep from falling or being impaled on the horn.

In the midst of her agony, she had a bitterly ironic thought: Had her virginity survived this long only to be lost to a man like Porco?

Chapter Eighteen

It seemed like hours but was probably only minutes before Porco finally slowed his horse and allowed Tory to assume a less precarious position. He made her sit in front of him, wedged between his body and the saddle horn, in which position he could fondle her while they rode. She had ridden in a similar position with Sebastian on Renegade, but then they had been riding bareback, and Tory hadn't minded being so close to the man behind her.

This time, she minded terribly. Trapped by the horn used to dally cattle, she couldn't squirm away from Porco's groping hand, and so had to content herself with slapping it whenever he became too bold. Her resistance only made Porco laugh and squeeze her tightly around the waist, all the while murmuring obscenities into her ear—lurid descriptions of what he intended to do to her as soon as time and circumstance permitted.

Tory was already feeling nauseated from the jouncing she had suffered, and Porco's filthy mouth did nothing to resolve the problem. Unable to stop herself, she leaned to one side and was violently, explosively sick to her stomach. Porco swore when her dinner from the night before soiled the toe of his boot, but the incident did dampen his ardor for a time, giving Tory the opportunity to take stock of her situation and think about how she might change it.

Appealing to Porco's better instincts did not appear to be a possibility, and she doubted that tears or pleading would get her anywhere either. Maybe she could convince Porco that she was on *his* side, she finally decided, and once he dropped his guard, could gain the upper hand. She mulled over the idea for several miles, as the day grew hotter, and she grew thirstier. Just as she was beginning to think she might not make it back to the ranch—she would die of thirst, first—Porco slowed the horse to a walk and reached for a leather canteen fastened to the side of his saddle.

He took a long swig, then offered the container to her. Hating to put her mouth where his had just been, she nonetheless drank deeply of the warm, brackish water and sighed appreciatively.

"It's good, eh?" He laughed in her ear. "And maybe you are feeling better now, are you not, *moçinha?*"

She wished he wouldn't call her by the name Sebastian had first used when he met her; coming from Porco, it sounded sacrilegious. "My name is Victoria King," she informed him. "But almost everyone calls me *Professôra*, because that's what I do—I teach."

"You, a mere female, are a teacher? What do you teach—lace-making?"

He roared with laughter, as if he had made a fine joke. When he finished, Tory said with dignity: "No, I teach reading, writing, and simple sums . . . I'm going to teach in the priest's new school. That's why I came to this country . . . I'm really not a friend of *Sebastião Prêto's*. And I wish you weren't taking me back to his ranch, for I thoroughly despise the man and hope never to see him again."

"You are not his friend, little *Professôra?* How can that be, when you and the other lady were traveling with him and his servant on the *sertão?*"

"Senhor *Prêto* was only escorting me to Padre Osmundo, who couldn't come get me in Salvador because of his broken ankle. However, after I got to the gentleman's ranch, we had a severe disagreement and parted the worst of enemies . . . If you're really going to kill him, I won't be that sorry to see him die. The man stole my horse, and we had no choice but to take your friend's old nag in his place."

"What horse are you talking about, *Professôra?* The chestnut was the best of the three that *Sebastião Prêto* stole from us . . . Surely, the animal he stole from you could not have been a better one."

Tory paused a moment to give herself a chance to think. She was improvising as she went along and didn't want to say anything too implausible. For all he disgusted her, Porco seemed an intelligent man. Sometimes, he almost sounded like a gentleman, though his manners and intentions were anything but gentlemanly. She must try to win his sympathy without enraging him.

"That big bay he rides is mine. I owned him in America and brought him with me, thinking that I could use a good beast to provide transportation while I'm living here . . . When Senhor *Prêto* saw how excellent he was, he asked to borrow him, then wouldn't give him back . . . He said that in Brazil, women don't ride horses."

"They do not, Senhorita . . . That is the truth."
Porco seemed somewhat astonished by her declarations. "They especially do not ride or drive powerful stallions like that big *baio*."

"Nevertheless, the bay horse is mine, and Padre Osmundo agrees that Senhor *Prêto* should return him to me. The priest intervened on my behalf, but Senhor *Prêto* still refused. After that, we no longer wished to avail ourselves of his hospitality . . . That's why we set out for Espirito Santo before Padre Osmundo's ankle was even healed."

"Such a sad tale, little *Professôra* . . . But what difference do your troubles make to me? Senhor *Prêto* killed three of my men—friends and companions of many years—and then stole their horses. For that I must kill him, or my shame would be too great to bear . . . I must protect my reputation, you see. It's not as great as some men's, but to lose it would greatly distress me."

"Then kill him," Tory said carelessly. "I hate him as much as you do! My horse means as much to me as your three friends and your reputation do to you."

They rode in silence for another few miles, while Porco digested this new information. He seemed to be weighing it in his mind and coming to some decision. Suddenly, he said: "What would you be willing to give me if I returned your horse to you after I kill Senhor *Prêto?*"

"Why, I don't know . . . I would have to think about it," Tory responded with far more calm than she was feeling. At least, she now had Porco thinking about something other than raping her! "I left some funds with friends in Salvador and would be happy to pay you handsomely for the horse's return . . . But, of course, I would only do that if you spared Padre

Osmundo and Carmelita as well."

Porco's hand moved abruptly to her breast and squeezed it hard. "Will you also demand that I forego the pleasure of raping you?"

Tory fought the urge to scream and claw his hand from her body. "Do you enjoy rape more than a woman's willing participation, Senhor Porco?"

The pain in her breast eased as he slowly released it. *"Não,* little *Professôra.* No man enjoys forcing a woman, if he can persuade her to grant her favors freely . . . Do you love this horse so much then?"

"That horse is . . . is all I have left of my family's fortune. When my father died, I lost everything," Tory pouted, embroidering the truth only slightly. "Do you think I would have come here to teach if I still had my home, the big ranch I lived on in America?"

"Did you not have relatives to look after you—or a handsome suitor to offer for your hand in marriage?"

Tory didn't dare mention that she had a brother and two sisters. "I had nothing, Senhor. My mother died before my father, and when my father's creditors took everything we owned, I became less desirable on the marriage market . . . To escape the shame of my lack of prospects, I fled to Brazil."

"A very sad tale, Senhorita . . . So sad it almost makes me weep."

Tory wondered if he was being sarcastic, but she couldn't risk turning around to look at him for fear he would see in her eyes that she was spouting lies. "The horse means everything to me, Senhor Porco . . . So the answer is yes, I would be willing to do almost anything to get him back again, even grant my favors to a man who means nothing to me."

"Never have I met such a blunt-spoken, deter-

278

mined woman, *Professôra*. Meeting you is a rare experience for a man of my humble background. I will think about what you have said, and maybe we can reach a bargain before we arrive at Senhor *Prêto's* ranch."

"Maybe we can," Tory agreed. "I would be happy to help you gain revenge on Senhor *Prêto*, if you will only help me get back my horse."

His hand suddenly found her breasts again. "Oh, I won't need you to assist me in obtaining revenge, little *Professôra*. It's the other things—the money and your sweet cooperation—that interest me more."

Tory gritted her teeth and pushed his hand away with less of a show of revulsion than she was actually feeling. "You will have both, I swear it, Senhor Porco—but not until my horse is once again in my possession."

Again, he laughed. "Suit yourself, *Professõra*. I am a patient man; I can wait for what I want—at least, until I kill Senhor *Prêto*."

"You will have to wait, or else I won't yield a thing to you. Instead, I'll fight you tooth and nail."

"You drive a hard bargain, Senhorita."

"I do indeed, Senhor Porco."

They arrived at Paraíso about two hours before dark. Porco rode boldly toward the front verandah of the house. One of his dirty, hairy hands encircled Tory's waist and held the reins, while the other gripped a long-nosed pistol. Tory could see at a glance that Sebastian wasn't home. Neither Renegade nor the horses ridden by Teodoro and Miguel were in the corral out back. Probably the only man on the place was Amâncio.

279

To Tory's dismay, Quinquina immediately ran out of the house and stared at them with curious, frightened eyes. *"Professôra,* what has happened? Where's Padre Osmundo and Carmelita? Who is this man?"

"Quinquina, this is Senhor Porco, a *cangaçeiro* who waylaid us on our journey to Espirito Santo . . . Padre Osmundo and Carmelita are all right, but I must see Senhor *Prêto* immediately. Is he here? His horse—rather, *my* horse—doesn't appear to be in the corral."

"No, *Professôra* . . . Senhor *Prêto* has not yet returned. Shall I go and fetch my aunt?" Quinquina took no notice of Tory's slip of the tongue. The girl's mouth was quivering. Nervously, she smoothed down her skirt. Although Tory couldn't see where Porco was looking, she guessed that the ugly bandit was thoroughly examining the pretty young girl.

"You! Go fetch everyone who's here on the ranch," Porco ordered. "Tell them to get out here on the verandah where I can see them—and if they try anything, I'll put a bullet through the *professôra's* head."

"Oh, please, Senhor! . . . Do not hurt her . . . Must I fetch everyone? One man cannot walk; he has a broken leg and a bullet wound."

"Ah . . ." Porco growled in satisfaction. "That must be Senhor *Prêto's* servant. I wondered if I had wounded him that day when I first attacked."

"You did, and he's confined to bed. He can't possibly come out here on the verandah," Tory reasonably pointed out.

But Porco was in no mood to listen to reason; his voice held a harsh note of threat and authority. "Then I want him carried out in his hammock!

Everyone must come to the verandah immediately, or else I'll start shooting.''

His tone made his horse side-step skittishly. As Porco tightened the reins to keep the animal under control, Tory reached for the pistol. Before she could grab it, Porco raised the weapon and rapped her smartly on the wrist.

"Ow!'' she yelped in sudden pain.

"That is not the action of a *partner,* is it, little *Professôra?* You disappoint me.''

"I merely thought to steady the gun, in case you let go of it in your effort to control the horse,'' Tory breathlessly explained. Her wrist felt as if it might be broken. Gingerly, she moved it and was relieved that she could still do so. "You didn't have to react so violently,'' she scolded.

"Violence is the only thing I know and trust, *Professôra* . . . But perhaps you will soon teach me tenderness, eh, my little blonde temptress?''

"I will teach you nothing if you hurt me again—or if you harm any of these poor people. They didn't kill your men or steal your horses. You have no cause to treat them cruelly.''

"I'm not going to harm them, *Professôra.* I'm only going to make certain that they don't alert Senhor *Prêto* to my presence . . . Girl! Go do as I said. Warn everyone to remain calm and not to oppose me, and I will let them and the little teacher live.''

Twenty minutes later, everyone—women, children, and one old man Tory had never seen before who could barely walk—had gathered on the wide front porch of the house. Even Amâncio was there; Dona Guilhermina had employed three women to help her carry the black man's small narrow bed out onto the verandah.

"We're all here," Dona Guilhermina irritably announced. She glared at Tory, as if, somehow, this was all her fault. "What do you want with us?"

Porco instantly deduced that Quinquina's aunt was the woman in charge. "*Moça*, is there an underground storage place on this ranch—a place used to preserve food from the hot sun?"

"*Sïm*, Senhor . . . There is a small cellar underneath the house."

"Then that is where I want all of you to go—and you can take the injured man and the old fellow with you."

"Senhor!" Dona Guilhermina started to protest, but Porco waved his pistol at her.

"If you argue, I will shoot you in the head! Get moving! I have a very short temper and don't like to be kept waiting!"

Sliding off the horse, Porco dragged Tory with him, then forced her to tie the animal's reins to the railing while he watched Dona Guilhermina and the women struggle to move Amâncio's bed down the front steps and around the back of the house. Amâncio had been silent all this time, but as he was thumped and bumped around, he found his tongue.

"Senhor *Prêto* will not like this, Senhor . . . You will regret what you do here today."

Porco pistol-whipped him, striking a single, vicious blow across his face. To everyone's horror, the black man collapsed unconscious upon the pillows, blood streaming from his mouth. "Stop it!" Tory screamed, throwing herself at Porco and trying to wrestle the gun away from him. "Don't you dare hurt these people!"

Porco only laughed and jammed the pistol into her ribs. "He did not show me the proper respect, *Profes-*

sôra—a mistake I urge the rest of you not to make."

His threat silenced the whimpering children and frightened women, who hurried faster to do his bidding. Carrying Amâncio's bed, they descended meekly into the cellar, too frightened to do anything but trudge down the shallow flight of stone steps and disappear through the huge wooden double doors. When all but Tory and Porco were inside the dark, dank enclosure, Porco made Tory close the doors and slide the heavy, wooden bolt into place to secure it.

Porco grinned widely, his large yellow teeth chipped and broken, his breath fetid as it blasted her face. "Now, we will hide my horse in the barn, and you will then show me Senhor *Prêto's* bedroom . . ."

Tory's gorge rose in her throat. "What if he doesn't come home soon?"

"Then I will find it most difficult to keep our bargain, *Professôra*. Much as I would like your money in Salvador and your willing participation when I finally take you, I don't know if I can wait that long . . . I lied when I claimed to be a patient man, you see. If anything, I am known for my *im*patience."

"I'm not worried about *my* fate," Tory haughtily informed him. "I'm worried about the people we just locked in the cellar. They can't be left there in the dark without food or water. The children, especially, should not be deprived of basic necessities."

"I *may* permit you to give them some," he responded with a sly smile. "If you ask me as sweetly as you know how . . . Come, *Professôra*. I wish to test the comfort of Senhor *Prêto's* bed before he arrives."

I've got to overpower him somehow, Tory thought to herself, but how?

She didn't have much time to figure out a way of doing it. If Sebastian returned tonight, Porco would coldly kill him—and if he didn't, Tory's virginity would be long gone by morning.

Sebastian arrived at Paraíso just as the sun was setting. He was hot, thirsty, and tired after his long, unrelenting ride, but determined to make it back tonight—so determined that he had left Miguel and Teodoro behind when their horses could not keep up with Renegade. He hadn't wanted to leave Paraíso and Tory in the first place, but it had been necessary to lay the groundwork for his plan to bring Mundinho Cerqueira to final justice.

Both his trusted *vaqueiros* and Ramiro Bastos were now informed of what was to happen, and Sebastian couldn't wait to see Tory again. He intended to bathe, eat, and then make love to her all night long, as he had done before he left. His need for her burned like a fever in him; it was a worse torment than he could remember suffering *before* he had taken her to his bed. This had never happened to him with a woman; in the past, he usually became bored after possessing one and could go for days, if not weeks, before he wanted her again. But then he hadn't really *possessed* Tory—so maybe that was why he still craved her so desperately.

Her virginity tantalized him. Coupled with the passions that smouldered just beneath the surface, waiting like a banked fire to blaze into an inferno, her innocence was a forbidden treasure shimmering just beyond his reach. He dared not deflower her, thus incurring instant marital obligations, but he could do everything short of it, and his imagination had been taunting him with all sorts of fascinating possibilities.

284

However, he must be careful that no one else in the house found out what they were doing, especially Padre Osmundo. Other than that, he had until the priest's ankle healed before Tory had to leave, and he wanted to make the most of that precious, limited time. He refused to think about what he would do or feel after she left; first, he must settle the problem of Mundinho Cerqueira, and then he would be free to seriously consider marrying Tory King—if she would have him, which by no means could he take for granted.

He himself found it difficult to imagine her in the role of his wife. However, since he had met her, he couldn't seem to imagine anyone else in that role, either. Nor was it easy to picture himself in the role of a husband—tied to one woman, prohibited from seeking other females, subjected to all the silly whims that one woman might harbor . . . Yet he did want children, and yes, as Tory had once suggested, he wanted to share his life with someone—a friend, lover, and confidante all rolled into one. The idea had taunted him ever since she had mentioned it. For some reason, he had never before thought of marriage as a kind of intimate partnership where two human beings cared about each other before all others.

Tory's version of marriage seemed simultaneously unique, challenging, wonderful, and frightening. If the woman was someone as intelligent, beautiful, and feisty as Tory, he could perhaps accustom himself to the necessity of conjugal faithfulness. Tory might exasperate him beyond endurance, but she would never bore him . . . Each morning, he would wake up wondering what the day might hold and relishing the uncertainty of it. Once he gave up being the Falcon, he would need something challenging to amuse and entertain himself.

Taking almost no note of his surroundings, he cantered up to the corral, dismounted, hastily unsaddled Renegade, and put him inside the corral with the other horses. The big bay was too hot and sweaty to be watered or fed; Sebastian decided to do that later, after he himself had bathed and eaten. Renegade promptly rolled in the dust, nickering with relief and pleasure, then got to his feet and shook himself. After that, he greeted his mares, nosing them one by one, evidently satisfied to be home again.

For a moment, Sebastian envied the big horse. Renegade had everything a stud could want—plenty of food, exercise, and the companionship of as many adoring females as he could service. Perhaps that was why he now behaved with such perfect manners; he was relaxed and happy. Every man should be so lucky, Sebastian thought, starting to walk away.

A shrill angry whistle stopped him in his tracks. He turned back to see Renegade prancing and snorting, then racing up and down, snorting challenges. Only the presence of a strange, unknown horse—possibly a mare in heat or another stallion—could cause such behavior. But all the horses in the corral were familiar. Then Sebastian noticed the closed barn door, which was normally kept open except in severe wet weather, an infrequent occurrence these days on the *sertão*.

An answering whinny from inside the barn confirmed Sebastian's suspicions: Someone was here. But why would a visitor confine his horse out of sight in the barn, instead of turning it out with the other animals? Sebastian cocked his head, listening, and noticed the unnatural silence. No one had come out to greet him, and the usual sounds of women's and children's voices coming from the servants' quarters were missing.

Unsheathing the long-nosed pistol he kept strapped to his hip, Sebastian started for the house. It stood dark and quiet, apparently empty. Where could everyone be at this hour? Apprehension twisted Sebastian's gut. He had left Paraíso unprotected, never dreaming that anyone would dare raid his home or threaten his people. Other than the incident involving his parents so many years ago, direct attacks on the big ranches were unheard of. *Cangaçeiros* never aspired to such boldness, because they could never be certain when a *fazendeiro* might be in residence with all his *vaqueiros*.

Raiding always occurred away from the *fazendas*, on the broad stretches of *sertão* where cattle and horses roamed at will, and few bystanders were present to witness the crimes. Yet Sebastian suddenly had a sick feeling in the pit of his stomach. He *knew* something had happened—and whatever it was involved Tory. Tory's slender, blonde beauty might be reason enough to produce courage in even the most cowardly of *cangaçeiros*, men like Porco and his cohorts.

He began to walk faster toward the house, then broke into a run. He mounted the steps of the verandah and threw open the door. Silence and darkness greeted him, fueling his fear. Belatedly recalling caution, Sebastian stepped inside the house as silently as a cat. Whoever or whatever awaited, he still had the advantage of surprise; his arrival might not have been noticed. He searched the entire ground floor and found no one, not even Amâncio or

Amâncio's bed. Despair knotted Sebastian's stomach, but he refused to give in to it until he had searched the upstairs as well.

Face it, he told himself, as he headed toward the staircase. You may find only dead bodies—one of them Tory's.

Oh, God, if anything had happened to Tory, he would tear the man—or men—apart and force them to eat their own entrails!

Chapter Nineteen

"You make a sound, *Professôra*, and you'll be teaching the angels, not the peasants, how to read and write." Porco finished stuffing a torn section of bed linen into Tory's mouth, then turned back toward the window.

With her hands tied to the bedstead and her mouth full of linen, Tory could not have made a sound if she tried. She lay perfectly still, torn between relief that Porco's attempted rape had been interrupted by Sebastian's arrival, and fear that Porco would manage to kill Sebastian as soon as he opened the door to the bedroom.

Her plans to keep the bandit at bay had failed not long after they reached Sebastian's room. For awhile, she and Porco had maintained a vigil beside the open window looking out over the corral, but as the sun set, and darkness crept across the landscape, Porco had decided that Sebastian wasn't returning—at least, not tonight. He had then ordered Tory to undress. She refused, and they struggled, with Porco quickly overpowering her. Tying her to the bedstead, he had started to rip off her clothes when they heard approaching hoofbeats.

Standing beside the bed and peering cautiously out of the window, Porco had muttered under his breath. "*Silêncio*, you damn horse! I should have put a bullet between your eyes instead of shutting you up in the barn to keep you quiet."

Now, Tory could hear Renegade whinnying and snorting, and an answering response from Porco's horse inside the barn, but from her position on the bed, she could see nothing of what was happening outside in the corral. From her perspective, the only things visible were the stars beginning to shine in the bluish-purple sky. The room lay in shadow, and Tory drew a deep breath. She *must* succeed in making a warning sound before Sebastian burst into the room.

Sensing what she was thinking, Porco kept his pistol leveled at the closed door while he drew a long-bladed knife from a sheath at his waist. With his free hand, he pressed the blade into her throat. "Not one sound, *Professôra*," he hissed.

Tory squirmed helplessly against her bonds. She didn't care what happened to her, as long as Sebastian didn't get hurt. The thought of Sebastian's broad, muscled chest being shattered by a bullet was more than she could bear. Scalding tears spilled from her eyes and dripped down into her hair; she must truly love Sebastian, she realized, for lust had nothing to do with how she felt at this moment. She would cheerfully give her life to save him.

Groaning through her gag, she arched her body on the bed and attempted to jiggle the mattress. It made a rustling sound, and Porco swore and jabbed the knife blade into her neck. She felt a stinging pain and a spurt of wetness. Just then, the door slammed open, and something white and fluffy sailed through the air into the room. Distracted, Porco whirled and shot at it. The noise was deafening, and feathers flew everywhere. A second blast of gunfire sent Porco spinning round and round.

He caught at the doorjamb to keep himself from falling. His eyes gleamed whitely, and his mouth hung open. Shaking his head in surprise, he glanced down at his chest, where a dark, liquid stain was rapidly spreading across his shirt and leather vest. He dropped the pistol and knife, then staggered out into the hallway, bellowing in pain and anguish. As he stumbled out of sight, a man's figure suddenly loomed beside the bed, startling Tory who had yet to see anyone enter the room or shoot at Porco.

A muffled scream died in her throat as she recognized Sebastian. In a single savage motion, he tore the gag from her mouth. *"Gatinha!* What did he do to you? . . . There's blood on your neck. Oh, *Cristo,* he tried to slit your throat!"

"Sebastian," she managed to gasp. "I'm all right. Go after him . . . Make sure he's dead."

Before Sebastian could say or do anything, they heard a loud crash followed by a thump-thumping, as if a body were tumbling down a staircase.

"If he's not dead yet, he soon will be . . . I got him in the chest . . . It is *you* who worry me, *gatinha."*

Sebastian untied the knots securing her hands, and while she chaffed her wrists to restore the circulation, he lit a lamp on the table nearby and brought it close to her. "Let me look at you."

His eyes widened as he took in her torn clothing. The amber light in them darkened to a deep, muddy brown. "The bastard! If he isn't already dead, I'll make him suffer before I finally end his miserable life."

Tory tugged the edges of her torn bodice together. Porco hadn't quite succeeded in stripping her naked, but he had managed to bare all the essentials. She was suddenly, acutely embarrassed. Sebastian had seen and caressed her entire body in the throes of passion, but this time was different. This time, she felt vulnerable and defenseless, more exposed than she had ever been in her life.

She grabbed the sheet and drew it up to cover herself, but Sebastian wouldn't permit her to shield her nakedness from his gaze. "Let me look at you!" he demanded, sounding angry as he bent over her. Taking the edge of the bed sheet, he gently wiped the blood from her neck. "The cut is a small one, *graças a Deus* . . . There's a little blood, but no real harm done. What about the rest of you?"

"I . . . We . . . He didn't have time to really hurt me," she stammered.

But no, that wasn't entirely true, she realized. He *had* hurt her, inside, where the wounds didn't show. She no longer had a shred of pride or innocence. In those few moments when she had known herself to be utterly helpless and incapable of escaping his lust, Porco had destroyed something fragile and precious. She wasn't the same person she had been only an hour ago . . . He had taught her fear and humiliation. Suddenly, she doubted that she would ever again be able to trust any man; weren't all men, including Sebastian, lust-driven brutes who could hardly control their base appetites? They cared nothing for a woman's feelings, as long as they could have her body!

Tears gathered in her eyes again, and Tory

struggled futilely to suppress them.

"Wait here a moment," Sebastian barked. He departed the room only to return several moments later. "I was right; he's dead . . . He'll never bother you again, *gatinha*. No man will bother you. I won't permit it."

A sob caught in Tory's throat. The last thing she wanted was to weep in front of Sebastian, but she couldn't seem to stop herself. She felt so violated—so degraded. On the one hand, she rejoiced that Sebastian had arrived in time, apparently rolling into the room on his belly while Porco was busy shooting at a pillow, and then shot the beastly *cangaçeiro*. On the other hand, she couldn't quell the tremors erupting inside her. The anxiety she had not felt before now clutched her in its icy grip and wrung her very heart and soul.

"*Gatinha* . . ." Sebastian said softly. He sat down on the bed and gathered her into his arms.

She didn't want him to touch her, but he wouldn't let her pull away. Instead, he wrapped his strong arms around her and lifted her onto his lap, then held and rocked her while she wept on his shoulder. "I w—wasn't scared when it was happening," she sobbed. "I d—don't know why I should be scared, now."

"It's all right to be scared, *gatinha* . . . You try too hard to be strong and brave, but that is not the nature of women . . . Regrettably, it's not the nature of men, either. I always thought it was—until tonight. Tonight, I learned that men can be afraid every bit as much as women."

Tory leaned back and gazed at him through her tears. "Don't tell me you were afraid, too!"

He gently kissed her forehead. "Yes, my sweet,

courageous wildcat . . . I was afraid. Tonight, I discovered the true meaning of fear. Fear is when you know you've lost—or are about to lose—everything that is precious and dear to you."

"But you didn't lose anything, Sebastian . . . All of your people are safe; they're locked in the cellar . . . Oh, we must let them out! And then we have to rescue Carmelita and Padre Osmundo. They're being held captive by two of Porco's men."

Worrying about the others gave Tory a new boost of energy and confidence. She started to squirm out of Sebastian's arms, but again, he held her too tightly. "Wherever Carmelita and Padre Osmundo may be, we can't do anything to help them until morning . . . and my people can survive another few moments in the cellar . . . I can't let you go just yet, *gatinha*. Somehow, I must convince myself that you are still alive."

Tory lifted her teary-eyed gaze to meet his. Emotion shimmered in the amber depths of his eyes, evoking a flood of sensation all through her body. A sensual awareness crept into her consciousness; she ceased to be embarrassed by her nakedness and instead felt a quiver of anticipation. Sebastian smiled lazily and traced the curve of her cheek with his fingertips.

"*Gatinha*, I think I must be the world's greatest fool to have denied myself the pleasure of union with you . . . When I thought I had lost you, I realized the many mistakes I had made—especially when it came to you. No woman has ever touched me as you do, has ever meant so much to me, has forced me to rethink all that I've ever believed . . ."

"Dear Sebastian," Tory sighed, reveling in his admissions. Maybe now he would admit how wrong he had been to conspire against Padre Osmundo, plot the Falcon's death, and consent to the destruction of the school. "There's so much we have to talk about . . ."

"Yes," he murmured, leaning forward to kiss her throat and trail kisses along her collar bone. "I have not been honest with you, *gatinha*. In truth, you know little about me . . . Even my good friend Padre Osmundo doesn't know me as well as he thinks he does."

His kisses made her shiver. Desire unfurled in her belly and flashed like quicksilver along her nerve endings. "We must tell each other everything, Sebastian . . ."

"We will, *gatinha* . . . This I promise you. But right now all I can think about is correcting my worst mistake . . . I want to make you *mine*—completely, wholly mine. I would have cursed myself forever if Porco had taken what I refused. When I think of his hands on you, his mouth upon yours . . ."

"*Your* hands and mouth are all I desire, Sebastian . . . Don't mention any others. I think I belonged to you from the day we met . . . I never wanted to yield to you; I fought it as long and hard as I could. But what we feel for each other is too strong. It's more powerful than the moon pulling back the tide . . ."

She trailed off as he bent her back upon the bed and tenderly removed her torn garments. She helped divest him of his clothing, and they came together with a sweeping urgency. He still teased and tantalized her, skillfully stoking the fires of her passion, and she still demanded the same liberties with him, but this time, everything was different . . . Their love-making had a purpose to it, a sense of commitment that made each touch an exquisite surrender, an affirmation of tenderness and caring.

He gave to her as he never had before, and she responded with a joy and willingness missing in their previous encounters. The knowledge that either one of them might have been grieving, instead of loving, lent a special poignancy to the already momentous occasion. His hands and mouth beguiled every inch of her, and Tory felt herself being swept toward a bottomless abyss of sensual delight—yet it was the mental and emotional union she craved as much as the physical. She strained toward him, kissing, caressing, and hugging him, desperately wanting him inside her.

When at last he poised above her, positioning himself for the first glorious plunge, she opened her eyes and gazed deeply into his. "Now, Sebastian . . . Come into me, now," she whispered.

She felt the insistent nudge of his hot, rigid flesh and opened herself to the piercing invasion; it came a moment later, startling her with a momentary discomfort that quickly faded as he sheathed himself completely. They were one! She almost laughed out loud with the exhilaration of it. Never taking his eyes from hers, he began to move . . . backwards and forwards, in and out. He drove deeply into her, paused, withdrew, then drove again.

She matched his rhythm with small thrusts of her own, each one creating a delicious friction in the burgeoning fullness of her female passage. She had never known such pleasure or happiness.

"You are mine!" Sebastian growled exultantly, slamming her hips into the mattress with the force of his thrusting.

"Yes! Oh, yes . . ." she murmured. "And you are now *mine*."

She raked her fingernails possessively along his back. A fury came over them both. Tory closed her eyes and concentrated all her energy on their wild, frantic mating. The tension spiraled to unbearable proportions. She squeezed him between her thighs, summoning every ounce of her female strength to hold and possess him. As she shuddered with the final ecstasy, so did he. Tremors of satisfaction shook her from head to foot . . . and she was still spasming when he collapsed on top of her, sighing her name in a ragged whisper.

They floated in a warm, sunny wash of peacefulness—utterly content and fulfilled, and then Sebastian said: "I want to love you like this every night, *gatinha* . . . I want the right to love you in the mornings before the day begins, in the afternoons when I catch you alone—whenever and wherever it pleases both of us to do so . . . I want to fill your womb with my sons and daughters, and later, to hear you teaching them their letters and laughing over their small mistakes . . . I want to laugh with you, and weep when tears are warranted . . ."

Tory pushed him back with a gay, happy cry. "Sebastian! Are you asking me to marry you?"

A dark shadow fell across his face. "*Não, gatinha*, not yet . . . But I am asking you to wait for me, until I can offer you a life with no secret, hidden valleys where pain and sorrow wait to trap the unwary."

His words confused and perplexed her. She cupped his face between her hands. "You can never offer me a life guaranteed to be free of pain and sorrow, Sebastian. None of us can foretell the future or predict cruel twists of fate."

He seemed to be debating whether or not to tell her something—something he thought she didn't know.

It was long past time to tell him what she had discovered. "Sebastian, I overheard you plotting with Mundinho Cerqueira to trap and kill the bandit, the Falcon. I know that you intend to betray Padre Osmundo, have him locked up in a monastery, and destroy the precious school he's worked so hard to build."

She waited for his reaction, which wasn't long in coming. He gazed at her in utter stupefaction. "And you don't hate me for it?"

"Oh, my darling, I disapprove with all my heart. I despise these things you want to do, and think you are truly misguided if you believe revenge is the way to solve all your problems . . . But I don't hate *you*. I've tried and found I couldn't do it . . . At first, I blamed that failure on lust. But my feelings go far beyond lust. I could no more hate you than I could hate myself . . . Does that make sense to you?"

"You believe that I could betray my only friend in the world, Padre Osmundo, and still, you want me— *love* me?"

Tory had to smile at his incredulity. "Perhaps love is composed of three parts forgiveness, two parts hope, and only *one* part lust . . . Yes, I love you even though I despise many, if not most, of the things you do. Somehow I can't convince myself that you are intrinsically wicked and evil. Somewhere inside you," she tapped on his naked chest, "is a good man fighting to get out. To be free at last. Padre Osmundo believes it, and so do I, Sebastian."

To her great astonishment, moisture welled in his amber eyes. They shone with unshed tears. "What have I ever done to deserve your faith, *gatinha*, or Padre Osmundo's? . . . I can't explain everything yet, because you might try and stop me from doing what I must . . . But I nonetheless beg you to guard that faith. The day will come when it will be justified, and I can be the man you deserve, the one who will cherish you all the days of your life and never disappoint or fail you."

"Why can't you be that man now, Sebastian? Why can't you at least explain why you intend to deprive the poor peasants of their only champions, Padre Osmundo and the Falcon?"

"That I *can* explain, *gatinha* . . . I *don't* intend to betray Padre Osmundo, as you mistakenly believe. But what do you think will happen if I refuse to participate in Mundinho Cerqueira's plan to trap the Falcon?"

Tory pondered this a moment. "I don't know . . . I suppose he'll go ahead with it anyway."

"Precisely . . . You must trust me, *gatinha*. I give you my word that Padre Osmundo and his precious school will come to no harm."

"And the Falcon? Will you shoot him down like a mad dog, just because he stole a few horses and cattle that you can probably well afford to lose?"

"How do you know what I can afford to lose, *gatinha?*" He dropped a light kiss on her forehead. "The Falcon cannot continue as he has been doing . . . Surely, you realize that. Sooner or later, someone will kill or hang him; that's what happens to *cangaçeiros*. It's a well-known risk of their profession."

"But it doesn't have to be *you* who kills him, Sebastian!"

"Trust me, *gatinha* . . . That is all I can or will tell you." He kissed the tip of her nose. "One day soon, everything will be made clear to you."

"Oh, you are so infuriating!" Tory cried, pummeling his shoulders with her clenched fists.

"Ah, but you love me anyway! You said so yourself." Laughing, Sebastian defended himself by grabbing her hands and pinning her beneath him on the bed. Then he grew abruptly serious. "I know it is much to ask, little one, but I ask it anyway, for I have no choice . . . *Trust me*. I will not disappoint you."

She saw by his expression that she could beg, plead, and weep, but it would make no difference. He wouldn't tell her anymore. "I'll try, Sebastian, but you demand a great deal of me. If, as you are implying, you only agreed to help Mundinho Cerqueira so that you could rescue Padre Osmundo and save the school, why won't you just come out and say so? Why all this mystery?"

"It is necessary to my survival, *gatinha* . . ." He levered himself off her and reached for his trousers. "Now, we will speak of it no more. Instead, we will dress, free my workers from the cellar, and dispose of the body at the foot of the steps . . . And tomorrow, I will rescue Padre Osmundo and Carmelita."

"You mean *we* will rescue them . . ." Seeing his frown, Tory added: "You can't do it without me; I'm the only one who knows where they are."

Sebastian's frown became a scowl. "Where *are* they, *gatinha*? . . . And how do *you* know where they are, if Porco's men took them away from the ranch?"

"I know because all three of us—Carmelita, Padre Osmundo, and I—had already left the ranch when Porco and his men found us . . . We were headed for Espirito Santo in the ox cart. Porco only brought me back here because he wanted revenge on you for having killed his friends and stolen their horses. He didn't bring the others because he intended to use

300

them as hostages, in order to force you to face him alone."

"Then the three of you departed with no escort, without even bothering to say good-bye," Sebastian growled. *"Cristo!* You deserved to be waylaid by Porco! What was Padre Osmundo thinking of—going off alone in his condition, and without protection?"

"He was thinking exactly what I was thinking—that neither of us wanted to spend another night beneath your roof. We were—and still are—going to warn the Falcon of Cerqueira's plans for him, and also organize a defense of the school. Then Padre Osmundo will disappear, so that Cerqueira can never find him no matter how long and hard he searches."

"I can see that I'm going to have to have a little talk with Padre Osmundo, as soon as I rescue him . . ."

"Yes, you'll have to give him the same 'trust me' speech that you gave me . . . I wonder if it will work as well without the added persuasion of relieving him of his virginity."

He slanted her a crooked grin that she found completely irresistible; it dissolved her irritation almost instantly. "I'm glad to see that our loving has not deprived you of your rapier tongue, *gatinha* . . . I shouldn't want you to become so docile that you lose all the fire that first attracted me to you."

"You needn't worry that I'll ever become meek, Sebastian. There isn't a morsel of meekness in my character—nor will there ever be."

He burst out laughing and tossed her chemise to her. "Come! Let's get dressed and free my workers. This evening's revelations have given me an enormous appetite."

"I'm not nearly so hungry for food as I am to learn the truth about you," Tory reminded him. "For me, there haven't been enough revelations."

"Patience . . ." Sebastian chided. "Patience and trust, *gatinha* . . ."

Tory heaved a huge sigh. She could perhaps convince herself to trust this enigma of a man, but, like Porco, she had *never* possessed patience.

Chapter Twenty

The following morning, Sebastian attempted to sneak out of the house and leave the ranch without Tory accompanying him. Having anticipated just such treachery on his part, Tory was ready and waiting. As he rode off at dawn in the company of Miguel and Teodoro who had returned the previous night while she and Sebastian were freeing the workers in the cellar, Tory cantered up beside him. Dressed in a clean blouse and an embroidered linen vest of Quinquina's, Tory also sported her divided riding skirt, the one she had been wearing when Porco had captured her, Padre Osmundo, and Carmelita. A tight coronet of braids confined her hair beneath a leather *vaqueiro's* hat borrowed from a *guarda roupa,* and the horse she rode was the handsome animal Porco had ridden.

Miguel and Teodoro gaped in surprise when they saw her—and gaped even more when they noticed how well she could handle Porco's horse. Sebastian only shot her a fulminating glance, then proceeded to ignore her and behave as if she hadn't suddenly appeared at his side, dressed like a female *vaqueiro,* and riding as proficiently as any one of them.

"Take no notice of any strange riders joining us," he counseled Miguel and Teodoro. "I have heard that there is a mad *Americana* loose on the *sertão*. She thinks she can ride, shoot, and fight bandits as well as any man, but then she had ridiculous notions about the abilities of women before she ever arrived in Brazil."

"Senhor, she'll get herself killed," Miguel protested, slanting a sideways glance at Tory. "And us along with her."

"She is setting a very poor example for the other young women at the ranch," Teodoro complained. "First, she tried to teach them to read and write, and now, she's riding a horse and toting a pistol. Her behavior will encourage all sorts of improprieties."

Tory had taken one of the guns adorning the wall in Sebastian's library, and tucked the weapon in her waistband in hopes that this time, she would at least be able to defend herself. Sebastian glanced down at the pistol under discussion and said calmly in English: "That gun is loaded, *gatinha*. Be careful you don't shoot yourself in the thigh as we ride. I would hate to see such a tender, succulent portion of your sweet anatomy all bloody and blown to bits."

Tory quickly snatched the pistol—it had been thumping against her leg—and handed it to Sebastian, nose first. "Then perhaps you had better take it, Senhor *Cochorro*. But don't think to convince me to turn around and go back. I won't do it . . . As I said last night, you need me to show you the way."

Sebastian chuckled dryly. "I assure you, *gatinha*, that I am perfectly capable of following the trail of an ox cart, even in the dark of night. I also know the way to Espirito Santo."

"But you need me for back-up assistance."

"I have Miguel and Teodoro for that. You said

304

there were only two bandits. The three of us out-number them as it is."

"Ah, but you most definitely require moral support . . . I wouldn't be surprised if Padre Os-mundo encourages the bandits to shoot you as soon as he sees you . . . After all, he's suffering from the same misconceptions I was, before you so graciously enlightened me—or should I say mystified me, worse than ever. I'm the only one he trusts, you see. He thinks that *you* have gone over to the enemy."

Sebastian sighed deeply. "God help your country if women ever win the right to vote . . . I don't see how politicians will survive. You and your ilk will badger them to death with illogical opinions, demands, and exhortations, until they are driven half mad with frustration and anger. You women will probably even try to tell them what to wear on the street."

"Which is no more than what men do to women all the time," Tory retorted. "Deceitful politicians undoubtedly won't survive . . . We women will demand honesty and accountability from public offi-cials. We won't swallow lies or half-truths. And if they belittle or ignore us too much, we may decide to run for public office ourselves."

"*Cristo!*" Sebastian exclaimed. "You are far more dangerous and radical than I thought."

"I'm not really all that dangerous or radical, Sebastian . . . I simply refuse to believe that I'm stupid just because I don't have a big fat worm dangling between my legs."

Sebastian's head jerked, and he swiveled in the saddle to stare at her. She could see that she had shocked and upset him with her blunt speech and unorthodox views. But he might as well realize right now that she did not intend to change her beliefs

305

should they ever marry. She was what she was and couldn't possibly redesign her entire philosophy in order to please him . . . and she suddenly realized that he couldn't alter his, either. He was what he was, too.

His gaze swept down her body, noting the divided skirt and the way she sat her horse . . . He had already indicated his disapproval of women riding or dressing as she was now dressed; would he ever be able to accept her idiosyncracies as normal and natural? And would she be able to accept all the strange quirks in *his* character? . . . Trust . . . He had begged her to trust him, and she was trying hard, but it wasn't easy. The wonderful rapport they shared in bed had yet to transfer to all other aspects of their relationship.

They were one, and yet they were divided—in their goals, plans, and expectations. Innumerable decisions and compromises still faced them.

"Gatinha," Sebastian finally said. "Do you think we can postpone debating whether or not females are equal to males, until *after* we rescue Padre Osmundo and Carmelita? I don't wish to be fighting for my life while my mind is distracted by hopelessly muddled female thinking."

"Of course . . . It was thoughtless of me to raise the issue, Sebastian. If it gives you confidence to think of me as an idiot simply because I was born a female, then go ahead and think it . . . Of course, I consider you a god simply because you were born a male. No mere woman could ever hope to match your wit, intelligence, flawless judgment, and grasp of complex subjects . . . I confess I am amazed that such a lowly creature as myself could possibly rattle your composure enough that you would suggest she cease arguing with you . . . But if it bothers you so much, I . . ."

"*Gatinha!*" he thundered, causing the horses to jump, and Miguel and Teodoro to eye him warily.

"I mean it. I'm truly sorry, Sebastian, so I won't say another word."

Tory smiled, and gathering up her reins, cantered ahead of him. She did not have to look back to know that she had stirred up a dust cloud that enveloped the three men in her wake. So let them eat dirt, she thought triumphantly, and see how *they* like it for a change!

They caught sight of the ox cart, the two bandits, Padre Osmundo, and Carmelita in mid-afternoon. While the two bandits were shielding their eyes to get a good look at them, Carmelita prudently climbed under the ox cart, and Padre Osmundo took shelter behind a wagon wheel. Neither precaution proved necessary. As soon as the bandits recognized Sebastian—or maybe it was Porco's horse with someone besides Porco riding it—they uttered loud cries and fled for their own horses.

Moments later, they were galloping full tilt across the *sertão* as if the devil himself were pursuing them.

"Shall we go after them, Senhor?" Miguel inquired. "Teodoro and I would be happy to chase and kill them, if that is your wish."

"No, let the poor bastards go . . . Without their leader, they'll die soon enough as it is. Porco was the only smart one among them. Unless they find a respectable leader in a hurry, they'll get themselves shot or hung within a week or two."

"Maybe they'll join forces with the Falcon," Tory

mused aloud. "Though they didn't seem to have the Falcon's bent for charity."

Sebastian snorted disdainfully. "The Falcon wouldn't have them. From all accounts, he chooses only fearless men to ride at his side."

Miguel and Teodoro exchanged smug, amused glances, though Tory couldn't understand what they found humorous in Sebastian's comment. Again, she rode out ahead of the men, for she was anxious to discover if Padre Osmundo and Carmelita were really all right.

"*Professôra!*" Carmelita cried, crawling out from beneath the wagon. "*Graças a Deus*, is it really you?"

"Of course, it's me, Carmelita . . . Don't let this old hat fool you. I only wore it to keep the sun out of my eyes." Quickly, Tory dismounted and embraced the plump, little woman and then Padre Osmundo, who was limping around the corner of the ox cart.

"My child! My child . . . It's a great relief to see you again. I had such terrible fears when Porco rode off with you! I doubted we would ever lay eyes on you again this side of heaven."

Tory was almost crushed against the priest's rotund, roly-poly figure, but then he pushed her away and started toward Sebastian. "*Mon filho*, I demand a word with you! None of this would have happened if you hadn't succumbed to greed and the desire for revenge against the Falcon for stealing your cattle. We never would have left Paraíso until my ankle was healed, and you could have accompanied us. Because of you, Jordan King's sister fell into the clutches of that evil bandit, and Carmelita and I were stuck out here under the broiling sun, with nothing to do but pray and imagine the worst happening to our poor *professôra* in Porco's wicked hands."

Sebastian dropped his reins across Renegade's neck and regarded the scolding priest with a look of disgust. "Is this the thanks I get for saving Miss King's life, not to mention rescuing *you?* Had I known you were going to deliver a tirade, I would have left you out here to fry beneath the broiling sun."

Arms folded across his belly, Padre Osmundo glared at the tall man still seated on the big bay horse. "You should be ashamed of yourself, *mon filho.* Where is your repentance? After all I've done for you, I don't deserve such shabby treatment as being whisked away to a monastery and shut up there until Kingdom come . . . And how could you agree to destroy my school? You yourself have contributed a great deal of money toward it, though not as much as you *should* have. I have the Falcon to thank for that school, and if you plan on killing him, then you will surely deserve the hellfires awaiting you when you finally die . . . I'll look down on you from heaven and mourn your sad end, but I won't send an angel with even a single drop of water to ease your torments. In truth, you will have *earned* your suffering."

Sebastian made a great show of yawning in boredom. "Why, Padre, I thought the Church always taught that God is merciful, but you make Him sound vindictive."

"Don't try and distract me, *Sebastião.* As I recall, you were always trying to distract—or confuse—the good friars who taught you and tried so hard to eradicate your pride and arrogance. God *is* merciful, but He is also just . . ."

"A contradiction in terms, Padre. How can He be both?"

309

"If you two can cease debating theology for a moment," Tory interrupted. "I would like to say something, Padre."

Padre Osmundo glared at her. "Well, what is it, my child? Can't you see that I'm trying to convince this sinner to acknowledge the error of his ways before it's too late? . . . As I recall, you were less willing to forgive him than I was, the other night."

"Padre, Sebastian has told me that he doesn't really intend to destroy the school or force you to enter a monastery against your will; he only said that so Mundinho Cerqueira thinks he supports him and will confide in him and reveal all his plans."

Padre Osmundo blinked. "*Sebastião* actually said that?"

"Not in so many words, perhaps, but he did strongly imply it . . . He wants us to trust him. He says he can't tell us everything yet, but when we know the whole story behind his cooperation with Mundinho Cerqueira, we will approve of his actions."

Padre Osmundo turned back to Sebastian. "Is that true, *mon filho?* . . . Ah, I *knew* it!" he exulted without waiting for an answer. "I *knew* you couldn't really do all those wicked things! Then the Falcon has nothing to fear, does he? You'll stand up for him and defend him . . ."

Sebastian cleared his throat, again drawing the priest's scrutiny and attention. "The Falcon's days are numbered, Padre. I never told Tory that I would help the Falcon, and indeed, I won't. With or without me, Mundinho Cerqueira means to destroy the man. I think it's better if he does it *with* me, because at least I can make certain no one else gets hurt in the conflict . . . Whereas, if he does it without me, I'm almost positive that innocent bystanders will suffer."

Padre Osmundo sorrowfully shook his head. "No,

mon filho. Do not tell me that . . . You mustn't side with Cerqueira against the Falcon. I know that the Falcon has stolen from you, but he is a good man. I know this in my heart, and it will be a great loss to all of us, if he dies. Besides, you will be endangering your immortal soul."

"Aside from my soul, which is already damned, I'm sure, the Falcon's death will be no loss to me," Sebastian argued.

"Oh, but it will!" Padre Osmundo insisted. "Because then I will have to come to you for *all* the money I need to support my work among the peasants."

"One way or the other, whether it comes from me or the Falcon, it's still *my* money, isn't it, Padre?"

"No, some of it is Mundinho Cerqueira's and the other *fazendeiros* from whom the Falcon steals. But if the Falcon dies, then it will all have to come from you. Cerqueira certainly won't donate funds of his own accord."

"Forgive me, Padre," Sebastian murmured somberly. "But in this, I cannot accede to your demands. I cannot promise you that I'll defend the Falcon."

"Then you leave me no choice, my son . . . I thank you for rescuing Carmelita, Miss King, and me, but now we'll continue on our journey to Espirito Santo . . . If there's any way we can do it, *we* will save the Falcon."

"*Cristo!* You are a stubborn old fool, Padre . . . All right, go to Espirito Santo. But at least permit me to accompany you and make sure you come to no more harm on the rest of the journey."

"We would be pleased to have you accompany us, *mon filho.* You, Miguel, and Teodoro are most welcome."

Sebastian inclined his head. "Good. But once we

311

get there, we won't remain for long. And after we leave, you certainly *must* go into hiding, Padre."

"Perhaps I will, and perhaps I won't," Padre Osmundo stubbornly retorted. "I must think and pray on the matter."

"You'll have plenty of time to pray if Cerqueira kidnaps you and locks you in a monastery."

"Monasteries have locks to keep people out, not to keep them in," Padre Osmundo corrected.

"Such subtleties make no difference, Padre, when archbishops are giving the orders. If Cerqueira's cousin tells you to stay put, you will. You have always had far too much respect for ecclesiastical authority. I don't think you are capable of disobedience."

"If there's no respect for authority, there will be nothing but chaos in this world, *mon filho* . . . Shall we get moving? My ankle is once again starting to pain me. Give me a hand with the oxen, Teodoro. We still have several hours before it gets dark."

The journey to Espirito Santo was an arduous one over difficult terrain, and Tory had no opportunity to be alone with Sebastian—not that Padre Osmundo tried to keep them apart. Rather, it seemed to Tory, the priest did a complete about-face. He actually tried to create opportunities for the two of them to be alone together—opportunities that Carmelita, Teodoro, or Miguel was always interrupting.

Tory suspected that the priest had come to some decision regarding her and Sebastian and was now doing everything he could to encourage their relationship. Perhaps he thought she might have a softening effect on Sebastian, but she herself saw no evidence of this; Sebastian steadfastly refused to discuss the possibility of sparing the Falcon and even declined to discuss how he meant to save the school and keep Cerqueira from kidnapping Padre Osmundo.

Instead, he seemed satisfied with Padre Osmundo's plan to "disappear" among the peasants, which left Tory feeling quite dejected and on edge. She longed for Sebastian to bare his soul to her; that he should insist on keeping secrets deeply wounded her, however much she tried to overlook it. She herself was too forthright a person to be able to understand another's need for reticence, and in her darkest moments, she wondered if Sebastian might not be lying about his intentions. Maybe he really was on Cerqueira's side. He continued to exude strong vibrations of inner conflict and turmoil; even when she caught him gazing at her hungrily, tenderly, or with silently shared amusement. He seemed to be fighting or resenting the unspoken communication; it was as if she were distracting him from more important goals . . . But what those goals might be, she could not imagine.

She only knew that she wanted and needed him, as much as she needed air or water, and it was agony to be near him, yet so far apart. She dreaded their arrival at Espirito Santo, because then Sebastian would leave her and return to the ranch, and she probably wouldn't see him again until he and Cerqueira returned in pursuit of the Falcon. All too soon, it seemed, they reached the outskirts of the small, dusty town of Espirito Santo, and as they rode down the single main street, Tory could not help wishing that she and Sebastian could spend one more night in each other's arms before they parted. Only in Sebastian's arms could she subdue her fears and suspicions . . . But we've run out of time, she thought sadly, and with a great effort of will, concentrated her attention on the village where she planned to spend the next year of her life.

Espirito Santo, Padre Osmundo had told her, was like a hundred or a thousand other small Brazilian towns, but to Tory's eyes and nose, everything was a revelation. First came the distinctive odor—a not unpleasant combination of animals, flowers, baking, garbage, dust, and primitive civilization.

Next came the visual impact. The town had one unpaved street which led to a large cobblestoned square surrounded by the most important buildings and the homes of the wealthiest inhabitants. There were several small shops, a bakery, an open-air market, a public stable, and of course, the church, the *Igreja de Santo Antônio*. Padre Osmundo's church was the largest structure of all, though quite modest and plain compared to the churches in Salvador.

As in Salvador, the nicest homes were pastel-colored with red-tiled roofs and inner courtyards hidden behind high walls with wrought-iron gates. Tory counted a half-dozen nice homes as Padre Osmundo pointed out the residences of important local government officials, most of whom lived on nearby ranches but maintained houses in town as a means of convenience and to demonstrate their importance as leading citizens.

Down narrow, dusty side streets, there were less impressive abodes—shacks, really, with crumbling walls and broken-tiled roofs, or mud-and-daub huts with roofs of thatch. Scrawny chickens, pigs, dogs, and an occasional donkey, cow, or horse roamed at will, freely mixing with the people spilling out of nearly every structure to welcome them and call out greetings to Padre Osmundo. When they saw Sebastian and Tory, they surrounded them, laugh-

314

ing, chattering, and asking questions, which Tory was hard put to answer in the din of shrieking children and barking mongrels.

The first thing that struck her about the town's people was their poverty. Everyone was barefoot and wore clothing that must have seen a thousand washings; nearly every man, woman, and child bore some evidence of disease—emaciation, yellowish, unhealthy pallors, and the big bellies and stick legs of inadequate nutrition. Compared to the workers on Sebastian's ranch, these people were barely a step above starvation.

But they seemed to take little note of their heart-rending poverty. Their joy at Padre Osmundo's return was genuine and effusive, no less so than his. The plump little priest exchanged *abraços* with everyone who hopped onto a cart wheel or begged him to lean down for the customary embrace. And all the while he hugged, he talked, inquiring about this one's health, that one's new baby, or another's yield from his banana tree.

Padre Osmundo was the peasants' St. Nicolas, their *patrão*, their Santa Claus father-figure, Tory thought, moved to tears by the display of warmth and mutual affection between Padre Osmundo and his beloved *caboclos*.

"Come, Padre!" the people cried as they neared the church. "You must go at once to see the new school. It is finished, and it is beautiful."

So instead of stopping in front of the church with its small attached parish house, the ox cart rumbled down an alleyway and headed out of town behind the church. The school did indeed stand off by itself in a copse of swaying palm trees, and Tory could immediately understand why the peasants were so proud of it. The building was by far the newest in town. Built of whitewashed stucco with a red tile roof and red double doors to match, it stood on the very edge of the *sertão* as if defying the dry, thorny cactus to overtake it. Several small boys raced each other to the post out front which held a shiny new bell, from which dangled a long cord. They took turns ringing the bell, adding to the joyous clamor.

Glancing toward Sebastian, Tory saw that he was smiling at the gay, happy scene and seemed quite pleased by it . . . Surely, this meant that he did not intend—and never had intended—to destroy the school.

When the ox cart finally stopped in front of the school doors, Padre Osmundo rose from the seat and leaning on his crutches, addressed the assembled peasants. "Oh, my friends, for more than twenty years, I have waited for this day . . . Now that it has come, I hardly know what to say. I can only weep tears of joy and thanksgiving . . . Not only do we have this fine new school, but today I have brought home the *professôra* who will teach here . . . She is a wonderful young woman who has left her home and family in order to enlighten you. I pray that you will welcome her warmly, take her to your hearts, and ease the *saudades* she must feel for her own country so far away."

"What are *saudades?*" Tory whispered to Sebastian.

"Longings for home," he answered. "What you would call homesickness."

"But I'm not homesick," Tory denied, *unless perhaps it's for the feel of your arms around me*, she added silently.

Sebastian grinned. "I'm glad, *gatinha* . . . Tonight, the peasants will probably hold a big *festa* in your honor. If they do, will you dance with me?" His amber eyes held a promise of something more than dancing.

"Yes," she gladly assented, and again, added a silent message: *And I'll do anything else you desire as well.*

"Then let's dismount and inspect the new school, shall we?"

Sebastian slid off Renegade and held up his arms to help her down. He lifted her to the ground as the peasants began cheering her arrival. She wondered what they really thought of her—arriving on horseback and dressed so strangely, but they seemed so happy to have a teacher that they would have cheered even had she arrived in town wearing nothing but a corset and possessing two heads and four pairs of legs. Arm in arm with Sebastian and thronged by cheering peasants, Tory started toward the school and her new life in Espirito Santo.

Chapter Twenty-One

The music of Brazil had an irresistible beat. Using anything they could find that possessed the remotest possibility of making music, the peasants created a cacophony of sound. Primitive whistles, flutes, rattles, drums, and tin pans produced a hypnotic rhythm that demanded a response from the listener. At the *festa* that evening, Tory could not stop herself from joining the long line of swaying bodies dancing to the beat of the drums.

"This is wonderful! It's marvelous . . . fantastic!" she called out to Sebastian as she passed him in the line. "I never knew people danced like this."

"Oh, this is nothing, *gatinha*. Wait until you see Carnival . . . For three days and nights before Lent starts, men, women, and children dance almost non-stop to the whistles and the drums." Sebastian danced past her, and Tory marveled at the way the lower half of his body moved, as if it didn't belong to the rest of him but had a life all its own. He displayed a sensual grace that made her cheeks flame, and she quickly looked away from his hips and focused her attention on something else.

All around them, the peasants were laughing and

dancing, their cares and poverty forgotten. Occasionally, one of them would sway up to Sebastian and exchange some bit of news. He seemed to know most, if not all of them, and he laughed easily and often, showing genuine interest in what they were saying. It struck Tory that he really cared about these people. The young girls flirted, the boys teased, and the older folks told ribald jokes, none of which seemed to bother or embarrass Sebastian. He was at ease with them in a way Tory had not seen him at ease with anyone, even his own workers.

One woman pushed her young daughter into his arms, and dancing closer, Tory could hear the woman thanking him for the medicine and hair ribbons he had brought the child the last time he came to Espirito Santo.

"Hush!" Sebastian scolded. "Do you want the entire community to hear you?"

Tory looked more closely at the little girl Sebastian held as if she were a dance partner. The child had black hair and olive-colored skin. Suddenly suspicious, Tory edged nearer and saw with relief that the girl's eyes were black, not amber. Even so, there was no mistaking the invitation in the eyes of the child's mother, a thin but pretty woman dressed in a faded red blouse and skirt.

"I am indebted to you, Senhor *Prêto,* for saving my daughter's life," the woman said before retrieving the child from Sebastian's arms. "If there's any way I can repay that debt, please let me know."

He can have any woman here that he wants, Tory thought dejectedly. None would refuse or deny him.

Disturbed by her own jealousy, she let herself be carried away in the crowd, but Sebastian doggedly pursued her. "What is it, *gatinha?* Are you tired of all this dancing? If so, we can stop and eat."

319

A table had been set up in the torch-lit square in front of the church where the *festa* was taking place. It held big kettles of cooked rice, black beans, and bowls of *farofa,* the ground manioc root Brazilians sprinkled over their food.

But Tory wasn't hungry, at least not for food. "Let's just walk and rest a bit," she pleaded. "It's so warm tonight, isn't it?"

"No warmer than usual," Sebastian commented, falling into step beside her as she headed away from the dancers. "Obviously, you aren't used to so much exertion at one time," he teased.

"I am amazed that the peasants can keep this up for as long as they do. Many of them look too weak to be able to walk, let alone dance . . ." Tory fanned herself with her hand as they strolled the plaza. "I'm also amazed by their . . . their carefree acceptance of their lot in life. They appear to be such a happy people."

"They *are* happy, *gatinha.* Nowhere in the world can you find people as joyful as Brazilians. They are also the most hospitable, willing to share whatever they have. I have been in peasant homes where everyone was starving, but still they offered me food—the last morsel of bread or fruit . . ." He broke off abruptly, and Tory sensed that he had revealed more than he intended.

"You love these people, don't you?" she probed. "Yes, you do, I can see it in your face. You've helped many of them . . . You also help the poor in Salvador. I no longer believe that Carmelita and Amâncio were feeding the beggars without your permission—or giving them money before we left."

Sebastian laughed ruefully and, she thought, uneasily. "So my meagre generosity has been discovered, has it? Well, don't make it bigger than it is, *gatinha.* I'm no Padre Osmundo, sacrificing his life for the downtrodden . . . And don't think to change my mind about killing the Falcon either. He must be stopped, no matter the good he does. Men like Mundinho Cerqueira have taken a stand, and I agree with them. The Falcon does as much harm as good."

"How can you say that?" Tory demanded. "What harm does he possibly do?"

Sebastian faced her beneath a torch that illuminated his amber eyes, dark hair, and handsome face. "For one thing, he teaches people to depend on charity, instead of upon themselves . . . and he encourages the peasants to rebel against authority."

"Nonsense!" Tory cried. "You can't mean that."

"I do mean it," Sebastian calmly disputed. He resumed walking, and Tory followed suit, leaving the noisy plaza behind. "The peasants have made a hero out of a bandit," Sebastian continued. "And every little peasant boy now wants to grow up to be a thief . . . Many probably will become *cangaçeiros*, only they'll be more like Porco than the Falcon."

"Hah! You're just jealous because they don't want to be more like *you*."

"Oh, some of them do want to be like me—but the chances of a poor peasant becoming a *fazendeiro* are probably a million to one."

"You did it." Tory paused and gazed up at the stars.

Away from the torch-lit plaza, she could see them better; they were as brilliant as twinkling jewels, shedding a lovely light that reminded her of what she would rather be doing besides arguing with Sebastian. After studying them a moment, she lowered her eyes to meet the gaze of the man she wanted to kiss instead of correct.

"You were able to do it because someone taught you to read and write at a tender age, proving to

Padre Osmundo that you were quick-witted enough to benefit from an education . . . Who was that, Sebastian? Who taught you? It could not have been peasants, because none that I have met know how."

"I don't remember . . ." Sebastian suddenly seemed as fascinated by the stars as she was; his deeply etched frown suggested that he did not want to discuss this particular subject and therefore welcomed any distraction.

"I think you do remember," she whispered. "But for some reason, don't wish to tell me."

He grinned and slid his arms around her waist. "Isn't it enough that I can hardly concentrate on anything but you, and that you've made me want you more than I have ever wanted anyone? . . . Must you also probe and dissect my past, seeking to discover every boring detail about my life before I met you?"

"I want to know all there is to know about you, Sebastian," Tory answered honestly. "I want to understand why you think and behave as you do. But how can I ever comprehend the man you are today, if I know so little about the boy you once were?"

Sebastian pulled her to him and embraced her. "Restrain your curiosity awhile longer, *gatinha* . . . All I ask is that you . . ."

"*Trust* me," Tory finished sarcastically, beginning to hate the word.

"Yes, *gatinha*, trust me."

"But don't *you* trust *me?*" She leaned back to look at him. "If you do, then why can't you tell me why you're so set on destroying the Falcon? . . . Sebastian, I don't like the similarities I see between you and Mundinho Cerqueira. Something about Cerqueira frightens me. He's a dangerous, ruthless man who doesn't care at all for the peasants; he's greedy and selfish, devoted only to himself."

322

"Cerqueira and I are both landowners," Sebastian reminded her. "So of course, we share many points of view. That is inevitable, *gatinha*. But you must try to understand *our* side of things, as well as Padre Osmundo's. If you and I marry and have children, our first born son will be a *fazendeiro* and our daughters will marry *fazendeiros*. In Brazil, there is no middle class of people such as you have in America. Here, you are either rich or you are poor . . . If you are rich and want to stay rich, you must protect your kingdom against marauders, bandits, and thieves like the Falcon."

"But what good is laying up treasure on earth if in the process, you lose your immortal soul?"

"*Cristo!* Now, you are beginning to *sound* like Padre Osmundo."

"He wasn't the first to say that," Tory pointed out. "And anyway, it's true. Plotting to kill a person is a terrible crime, a sin for which there's no forgiveness."

"Then I guess I'm damned, *gatinha* . . . Can you love a man who will probably spend eternity in hell, while you are fluttering merrily about heaven?"

"Oh, Sebastian!" Tory gulped back an involuntary sob. "How can you treat this so lightly? How can you . . . ?"

She trailed off miserably, knowing that it was useless to argue any further. There was no reaching him. Try as she might, she could never seem to penetrate the barriers that stood like a stone wall between them.

"Don't, *gatinha* . . ." Sebastian pleaded, drawing her into his arms again. "Let's not quarrel on our last night together for what may be a long time. Quarreling is such a waste of time."

Tory clung to him, burying her face in his shoulder. "Then you'll be leaving in the morning?"

"Yes, little one, but before I go, I have something

most important to ask of you."

"What?" Tory demanded, sniffling into his shirt front.

"Promise me you won't let Padre Osmundo endanger himself trying to save the Falcon or the school."

"He said he would hide."

"Ah, but he may change his mind . . . I know him well—and he isn't one to seek safety for himself when danger threatens those he cares about."

"Well, what can I do if he suddenly refuses to hide? I can't force him to keep out of sight."

"No, but you can outwit him, using that clever, devious mind of yours. I will send word with Teodoro or Miguel, telling when Cerqueira's men are about to kidnap Padre Osmundo. Then all you have to do is manufacture a fake emergency to lure our little priest friend out of town."

"What sort of emergency? I'm not too good at lying and faking things, Sebastian."

"I don't know, but you'll think of something . . . Remember his weaknesses; he'll go anywhere to save a soul—and he can't refuse the sacrament of absolution or the last rites to anyone who requests them."

"I suppose I can find a dying sinner somewhere. That should be no problem at all," Tory quipped facetiously. "But it would be a lot less bother if you simply persuaded Cerqueira to abandon his wicked plans."

"Cerqueira will carry out these plans with or without me, *gatinha*. Why won't you accept that?"

Tory refused to answer; Sebastian's complicity with Cerqueira bothered her terribly. She did not want Sebastian to have anything to do with the man. Their relationship frightened her. She had seen nothing in Cerqueira's behavior to indicate any gentleness of heart beneath that arrogant, vengeful exterior. Cerqueira was a bad influence on Sebastian; as *fazendeiros*, they had too much in common, and in time, no matter how much Sebastian claimed to dislike his neighbor, he might begin to adopt more and more of Cerqueira's attitudes as his own.

"*Gatinha* . . . Come here a moment." Sebastian had stopped in front of a small lean-to behind the church. He held out his hand, and when she took it, led her toward the shadowy, black interior of the little structure.

"Where are we going? What's in there?" she asked tremulously.

She saw the white flash of his teeth and knew that her trepidation amused him. "Only a horse or two. There are three stalls inside, at least one of which I'm sure is empty. Miguel and Teodoro hobbled our horses and turned them out on the *sertão* to graze. Padre Osmundo's horse, the one you call Percy, is probably the only one inside."

"Oh . . . Is there something wrong with him? I didn't notice him limping or anything on the journey here."

"There's nothing wrong with *him*. The trouble is with *me*. I want to hold and kiss you where no one can accidentally discover us, thereby ruining your reputation on your first night in town."

"Oh . . ." Tory repeated, aware that she sounded dim-witted, but unable to think of another thing to say. The prospect of being alone with Sebastian in the dark took her breath away and set her heart to pounding.

She followed him willingly into the lean-to. No sooner had she entered, when he took her in his arms and began kissing her with an urgency that turned her knees to water. Dimly, she heard Percy munching hay contentedly nearby, then came the soft rustle of straw or hay as Sebastian paused long enough to kick open a bale and spread it on the ground in a corner away from Percy's stall.

He drew her down on the prickly, sweet-smelling mass and resumed kissing her. He kissed her until her blood sang, and her body became a quivering receptacle of yearning and desire. She tugged at his clothes, and he at hers, but they were too quickly and desperately aroused to take time to completely undress. Instead, they shed only those garments that impeded their union and ignored the rest.

Sebastian entered her with the enthusiasm of a young bull at his first mating. Plunging and rearing, he was wild and magnificent in his desire to possess her. She responded with equal ferocity, never having known such instant, compelling passion. The lack of time prohibited the tender, seductive caresses at which Sebastian excelled; now, there was only explosive, soul-searing desire, a need that consumed them utterly.

Locked together, they writhed in a primeval struggle to attain the unattainable—perfect unity. When the moment of fulfillment came, it shook them both as if they stood alone in a hurricane, buffeted by the strongest winds imaginable. Tory had the sensation of dying and being reborn in another time and place. Slowly, she returned to consciousness in Sebastian's arms.

"*Cristo,*" Sebastian sighed against her hair. "I do not know what you do to me, *gatinha*. Never has it been like this for me with a woman. As you already know, I am no stranger to carnal pleasure—but *this*, this is more than that. There are no words to describe it . . . You are my heart and soul. Each time we come together, more of me dies and something new takes its place . . . I hardly know who I am anymore . . ."

"You're mine," Tory whispered. "That's all you need to know. I love you . . . With every breath I take, I love you more . . ."

They held each other tightly, loathe to break the connection between bodies and spirits. Then Tory succumbed to the temptation to test their togetherness by asking Sebastian a question that wouldn't go away, but kept returning to threaten her peace and confidence. "Sebastian . . . do you have children? Here in Espirito Santo, or at Paraíso? Indeed, do you have them anywhere?"

He tilted back his head, apparently studying her, but it was too dark for her to see his face. "Would it make a difference in how you feel about me if I did?"

She swallowed hard. "It might . . . I'm sure I wouldn't hold it against *them*, but . . . but I . . . I'm afraid I might hold it against you."

"Why, *gatinha*? You can't be angry because I wasn't celibate before I met you, so long as I am faithful to you now."

Tory laughed nervously. "Oh, I know it's not rational—but I want to be the only woman who ever gives birth to your babies. I want *our* babies to be the only ones with a claim on your affections."

Sebastian was silent for a moment, so that she dreaded his answer and wished she had not asked the question. "I have fathered two children that I know of, *gatinha*, and both of them died, one at birth and the other soon after."

Tory shriveled a little inside. "Were they . . . from the same woman?"

"No . . . They had different mothers. Are you now going to ask me how many women I've known intimately? Or if I knew them in the same soul-shaking fashion that I have known you?"

"I don't think I want to know that," Tory answered in a small voice, shriveling more inside with every word he spoke.

"Good, because I don't remember . . . Most were not very memorable. In my youth, especially, I craved a variety of women in much the same way that I wanted more to eat than just rice and beans . . . I wished to sample everything available."

Tory pushed against him, trying to dislodge him. "And now? Do you still crave variety?"

He laughed and wouldn't budge an inch. "No, little one . . . When a man has finally tasted ambrosia, he has no need of other sustenance. I only crave you. You *are* variety, after all. From day to day and moment to moment, I never know what to expect next . . . You are a hundred women rolled into one fascinating, irresistible package . . . more than enough female to satisfy my lustful nature and command my attention for the rest of my life."

Tory still sought reassurance. In America, she would not have looked at a man who had fathered two children with two different women and didn't find it in the least unusual or alarming. Here in Brazil, she was actually considering marrying one—a man not only promiscuous, but a murderer as well! When she didn't say anything but lay stiff as a board beneath him, he began to tickle her. With a loud shriek, she attempted to evade his hands and fingers, but he attacked her relentlessly.

She started laughing and couldn't stop. She laughed until the tears came, followed by a spate of hiccups. Only then did he desist. He nuzzled and stroked her until she grew quiet again, and then he said: "*Gatinha*, I am sorry about the children . . . I regretted siring them, regretted their deaths, and regret even more that you will not be the first woman to bear my offspring . . . Please don't let my youthful mistakes come between us. If we look for reasons to be angry with each other, can we not find enough in the present, without searching the past?"

Tory threw her arms around him and cradled him against her breasts. "I'm sorry I ever brought it up, Sebastian . . . What really worries me isn't the present or the past, but the future . . . Whatever it holds, I don't want to lose you."

"You won't lose me, *gatinha,* not if you trust me . . ."

"Oh, will you please stop blathering about trust! I'm sick to death of the word."

"But if you don't trust me, we have nothing. There will be no future," he pointed out reasonably.

"All right, I trust you! I trust you totally!"

"Good . . . Because there's one more thing I want you to do for me, *gatinha.*"

Tory grew suddenly suspicious and wary. "What?"

"When you convince Padre Osmundo to leave Espirito Santo, I want you to accompany him . . . Tell only Carmelita where you are going, and when it is safe again, I'll come after you."

"You don't want me to watch you and Cerqueira kill the Falcon," Tory accused.

"I want you out of harm's way," he corrected. "Promise me you'll do as I say."

"I'll promise no such thing!"

He held her tightly, trapping her beneath him and rubbing his body sensuously against hers. *"Promise me."*

"You can't make me . . ."

"Oh, yes, I can, *gatinha* . . . Shall I prove it to you?"

He began to move against her. She could feel him swelling, hardening, elongating . . . as his passion reawoke. It made no difference what she did or didn't promise, did or did not intend. He could force her to say or do anything.

He thrust inside her, drew back, and thrust again. "Do you promise, my sweet, stubborn angel? You will do as I ask?"

The fire in her belly flared to life again. Desire crested hotly, and passion swept over her in burning waves. "Don't make me promise, Sebastian," she pleaded. "Someone should be here in case the peasants need help or decide to fight Cerqueira, even without Padre Osmundo's leadership."

"I will be here . . . There's no need for you to stay in town . . . *Promise me."*

His thrusts came harder, his body transforming itself into a battering ram capable of destroying all reason and logic. She strained to take more of him into her. "I'll do anything you ask . . . anything . . . only don't stop! I promise . . ."

Having gained her assent, Sebastian rewarded her as only a man can reward a woman. She wept while he did so, castigating herself for her weakness. How was it possible that a woman who had always wanted equality between the sexes, had allowed herself—shamelessly, wantonly, knowingly—to be totally dominated to the point of enslavement?

Chapter Twenty-Two

Sebastian left Espirito Santo the following day. After his departure, Padre Osmundo lost no time in spreading the word that the Falcon was in danger. With Tory an uneasy witness, he organized the women and children of the village to keep watch for strangers approaching on horseback from any direction. He then instructed the townspeople on what must be done if and when a large group of *pistoleiros* arrived in town.

Speaking to them from the pulpit of the church which also served as a town meeting hall, Padre Osmundo advised everyone—young and old—to meet at the school.

"But you are not to bring arms or weapons of any kind—no pitchforks, staves, or clubs," Padre Osmundo warned. "This will be a peaceful demonstration against whatever violence or destruction may be planned. We will simply occupy the school and surround it until the *pistoleiros* go back where they came from."

Tory noted that Padre Osmundo said "we," not "you." She shifted uncomfortably in the front pew. Obviously, the priest did *not* intend to go into hiding, though he knew he risked being kidnapped. He probably thought that the Falcon would heed his warnings and not show up in town to save him. He could thus take the chance of staying and trying to protect the school, alongside his beloved peasants. It was exactly what Sebastian had feared his old friend might do.

"But why do we need to do anything, Padre?" one man worriedly challenged. "The Falcon will not allow our school to be destroyed . . . And neither will Senhor *Prêto*. Without rifles or pistols to defend ourselves, we ought not to anger the *pistoleiros*. When the shooting starts, too many of us could get hurt or killed."

"I don't think Mundinho Cerqueira will fire on innocent women and children, my son," Padre Osmundo answered. "And we cannot depend upon others to protect that which belongs to us. The Falcon's life is the one in danger; I have told you this. We don't *want* him to come here at the risk of his life . . . As for Senhor *Prêto*, he has his own quarrels with the Falcon and has decided to support Senhor Cerqueira's campaign against the bandit. We must not expect him to save our school, either. It is entirely up to us."

An old woman in a lace mantilla stood up and glanced angrily around her. "This is not our affair!" she announced shrilly. "Always the Church has taught us to live quietly and mind our own business, and our reward will come when we die and go to heaven . . . Why do you now counsel us to enflame the tempers of the *fazendeiros*, Padre? If angered, they need not kill us to take their revenge. There are many ways to make us suffer. They won't hire our menfolk to cut cane or herd cattle. Our women will not be asked to do laundry, cook, and clean their houses . . . How will we eat when the bad times come? We dare not make enemies of Senhor *Prêto* or Senhor Cerqueira. They will tell the other *fazendeiros,* and no one will give us work or feed us during the dry season. When the drought comes, we will all die."

"What you say is true, Dona Maria, but only partially," Padre Osmundo sadly countered. He had not, it seemed, anticipated any resistance to his plan. Tory was also surprised by it.

"Normally it is a bad policy to make trouble and meddle in the affairs of others," Padre Osmundo continued. "However, this is a special case. Our new school is threatened, and we must show that we value it and will protect it as best we can—in a nonviolent manner, of course."

"If God wants the school to stand, it will stand," muttered the old woman. *"Se Deus quiser . . .* If God wills . . . Isn't *that* what the Church always teaches?"

The phrase was repeated around the church. *Se Deus quiser.* Tory was suddenly reminded of what Sebastian had told her—that poor *Sertanejos* were governed by superstitions, taboos, and religious beliefs from the cradle to the grave. It was hard to believe that the peasants would use God as an excuse for refusing to take a stand, but fear apparently did strange things to people. Padre Osmundo was asking them to do something they had never done before— challenge authority. She had witnessed the same uncertainty in the faces of women back home; they wanted the right to vote, but were afraid of angering their menfolk in order to get it.

Throwing off the yoke of oppression is always a risky, scary business, she concluded. And here, as at home, religion had sometimes been used to keep the peasants in their places, just as it had been used in past centuries by male-dominated churches around the world to keep women ignorant and subserviant.

Tory felt compelled to say something. Disregarding her promises to Sebastian, she signaled Padre Osmundo, rose to her feet, and faced the people congregated in the church pews. "My friends," she began, choosing her words carefully. "I came here all the way from across the sea to teach you and your children how to read and write, so that you will no longer be ignorant and at the mercy of those who are literate . . . Now, I discover that you really don't care if you learn or not. You aren't even willing to protect your new school . . . Padre Osmundo can't defend it by himself. He needs your help. How can you refuse him, when he does so much to help you, and he is the man who made the school possible in the first place?"

The peasants exchanged guilty glances, their faces red with shame. But many of the older people still muttered among themselves. No matter what arguments were offered, they feared the power of the *fazendeiros* and rightly so, since their survival depended upon the rich landowners. Tory wondered if the people might be more willing to fight for the school if classes started, and they could see for themselves what they would lose if the school building was destroyed.

"Tomorrow, I will begin teaching in the new school," she informed them. "The bell will signal the beginning of classes for all those under twelve years of age. Later in the afternoon, I will ring the bell again, and anyone over the age of twelve who wishes to learn to write his or her name and read, may come for a one hour period, and I will teach them also . . . It makes no difference if you are male or female, young or old. I will teach anyone who wishes to learn. The children will also be taught other subjects, and if there is a demand for more learning among the adults, I will hold classes in the evening as well . . . Then you will realize the importance of the school and can decide whether or not you wish to defend it in the peaceful manner Padre Osmundo has suggested."

"If God and the *fazendeiros* don't want it, there will be no school!" the shrill-voiced woman shouted.

Studying her more closely, Tory saw that she was blind; a milky-white substance filmed both her eyes, which perhaps accounted for her lack of enthusiasm for learning to read and write.

"If *you* don't want it, there will be no school," Tory corrected. "Don't blame God or the *fazendeiros* if the new building is destroyed; blame yourselves for not preventing it."

"When the *pistoleiros* come, there will be enough people at the school to show support," Padre Osmundo said quietly and confidently. "We have all worked too hard and too long to abandon our dreams without a fight. Nor will we permit the Falcon to be harmed . . . Again, I beg those of you who know how to contact him to do so and warn him to stay away from Espirito Santo no matter what happens here— no matter what is done to lure him out of hiding . . . If he comes, for whatever reason, he will be killed . . . Now, let us end our meeting with a prayer to the Almighty that we may respond courageously to the challenges set before us . . ."

Two weeks later, Tory was in the middle of a geography lesson in the new school when Teodoro suddenly appeared at the doorway and motioned for her to meet him outside. The children didn't see him at first; their backs were turned toward the open double doors. They sat on long wooden benches facing a big map hung on the wall. Tory had been trying to show them where she came from in the United States, but the children had never seen a map before and could not grasp what it represented.

"Children, take out your slates and practice writing the letters of your names again . . . You must excuse me for a moment. Don't worry; I'll be right back."

Twenty-two heads swiveled to watch Tory hurry to the double doors and step outside to see what message Teodoro had brought. So much for secrecy, she thought, accompanying Teodoro around the side of the building and out of the children's sight.

Teodoro looked dirty and tired, but excited. Quinquina might not have recognized her attractive young suitor; reddish-colored dust covered him from head to foot. His horse looked as filthy and exhausted as his master; he was also lathered, having been ridden hard. Appreciative of the effort the young man had made to get there quickly, Tory wasted no time on pleasantries. "Well, Teodoro . . . I know why you're here. How much time do I have before Cerqueira and Sebastian arrive?"

"They'll be here by tomorrow afternoon, *Professôra*. I'm to give you my message, then return and slip back into camp tonight, while everyone is sleeping."

Tory thought she already knew the message: *Get Padre Osmundo out of town.* But she waited politely for Teodoro to deliver it.

"Senhor *Prêto* says that you and the priest must leave immediately. Tell no one but Carmelita where you are going. When you depart, do not lock the school building, and on no account should you alert the peasants that anything is wrong. Senhor *Prêto* fears that Cerqueira's men will shoot anyone who interferes with Cerqueira's plans or appears to have knowledge of them. That includes the peasants, so it is most important that no one be near the school."

Tory chewed her lower lip in consternation. Now was the moment of decision. This was the strongest warning Sebastian had given her, and she must decide whether or not to trust him. If she did nothing, Padre Osmundo and the peasants would gather at the school to defend it as soon as they saw riders approaching. Padre Osmundo might be taken captive and sent to the monastery, and the peasants might actually be goaded into fighting when they saw their beloved priest being manhandled by Cerqueira's men. The situation could easily explode into violence.

If, however, she did as Sebastian asked, the peasants would probably do nothing to defend the school without Padre Osmundo there to encourage them. The priest could not be used as a lure to entice the Falcon out of hiding. Thwarted in his efforts to trap the Falcon, Cerqueira might decide to destroy the school anyway, but at least no one would be hurt.

Did she really have any choice? Tory could think of only one possible alternative to either of these two scenarios. What if she contrived to send Padre Osmundo away, discouraged any peasants who still had an idea of resisting, and she herself hid in the school? That way, if Cerqueira did decide to destroy the building out of malice or disappointment, she could emerge and perhaps shame him into sparing it. She doubted that he would go as far as killing a lone *Americana*, and in any case, Sebastian would be there to defend her . . . At least, she *hoped* he would defend her, despite his anger at her disobedience.

Tory eyed the two pistols strapped to Teodoro's

slim hips. "Teodoro, I think I've conceived the perfect plan for persuading Padre Osmundo to leave town, but I'm a bit nervous about the two of us venturing out onto the *sertão* again without any means of protecting ourselves. Some other *cangaçeiros* might happen upon us and cause trouble as they did before . . . Do you suppose you could lend me one of your pistols and quickly show me how to use it?"

Teodoro grunted in surprise. "You want me to give you one of my pistols, *Professôra?*"

"Oh, I'll be sure and give it back the next time I see you . . . I just don't want to be completely defenseless. I suppose I could obtain a rifle somehow, but I don't want to alert Padre Osmundo that I expect any trouble when I lure him away from Espirito Santo. I intend to keep the pistol a secret unless I need to use it."

Teodoro glanced down at his two pistols and gave a small sigh; clearly, he didn't want to part with either.

"If you tell Senhor *Prêto* why I want one, he'll surely agree that it's a good idea. Maybe he'll replace the one I'm borrowing with another from the wall of his library, until I can return yours," Tory pressed. "All I need is for you to show me how to fire it . . . Not that I plan on firing it. But I think I should know, just in case."

"There's really no trick to it," Teodoro said grudgingly. He pulled out one of the pistols and gave her a brief demonstration on how the gun worked. "Then all you have to do is squeeze right here," he said, indicating the trigger. "And she'll blow a hole in whatever she's aimed at . . . Do you want me to show you again how to load it?"

"No, I'm sure I won't need to load it," Tory demurred. "As I said before, I'm not planning to shoot anyone. I just want to have the gun in my possession in case we're threatened."

"It's a good pistol, *Professôra* . . . The kick isn't too bad when it fires, but you should expect one, all the same. It could possibly knock down a small woman like you."

Tory shook her head in annoyance. Did all Brazilian men think women were inferior, weak creatures? "I'll keep that in mind, Teodoro . . . Thank you for lending me the weapon." She slipped it into a deep side pocket of her sensible linen skirt. "Now, you may hurry back to Sebastian and assure him that I'll do everything in my power to keep Padre Osmundo and the peasants away from the school for the next few days."

"I'll do that, *Professôra*. He'll be glad to hear that you didn't argue about it . . . He said if you did, I was to make sure you and the priest left town at pistol-point, if I had to."

"Oh, he did, did he?" Tory's irritation compounded; damn Sebastian, anyway! She ought to have guessed that he would act in such a high-handed, imperious manner. "How fortunate you can tell him that I'm as meekly obedient as a little lamb . . . By the way, how is Quinquina? I miss her terribly. When you get back to the ranch, please give her my warmest regards."

Teodoro frowned. "Quinquina isn't talking much to me these days . . . All she does is practice writing the letters you taught her. I don't understand it . . . You would think she would be more interested in finding a husband than in learning something as useless as reading and writing."

"Teodoro, let me give you a word of advice . . . Women want to be wooed, not ordered about as if they were mindless slaves. Why don't you show some interest in what she's doing? You'll never win her if you keep treating her as if she hasn't got a brain in her head."

"But it's not natural for a woman to be so stubborn and rebellious! You have been a bad influence on her, *Professôra*. Once, I thought she wanted to marry me, but now, she pretends I don't exist."

"Do you love her, Teodoro?"

Teodoro flushed and glanced away, too embarrassed to admit it. Sheepishly, he nodded. In that instant, Tory forgave him and pondered what she could say or do to aid him in his quest to win Quinquina. The girl did need a husband, and Teodoro was a nice enough young man, despite his typical male conceit and his misconceptions about women and learning. He wouldn't mistreat Quinquina, Tory felt certain, and Quinquina herself had expressed more than a passing interest in the young man.

"You're afraid if Quinquina learns to read and write that she'll be smarter than you, aren't you?" Tory guessed.

Again, Teodoro's deep flush gave him away.

"Well, there's no need to worry on that score . . . After this affair with Cerqueira is over, I'd be happy to teach *you* to read and write. Then you can surprise Quinquina with your new found knowledge and maybe even share the joy of learning."

Teodoro immediately brightened. "Perhaps I could surprise her with a thing or two that she doesn't know."

"Perhaps you could—if you apply yourself diligently and outstrip her efforts. You'll have to work hard just to catch up with her."

"I never thought I would have much use for book learning," Teodoro grumbled. "The truth is, I was

340

always afraid of it. But I'm willing to try anything if it means Quinquina will notice me again."

"I'm sure she will." Tory chuckled softly, so as not to appear that she was mocking him. "The only other man at Paraíso who shows any inclination toward reading and writing is Amâncio. Other than Senhor *Prêto* himself, that is. As you may have noticed, a literate man commands respect wherever he goes."

"Then I'll do it! If a woman can learn something, so can a man."

Tory patted the pistol in her pocket. "And if a man can learn it, why can't a woman?"

Teodoro blinked at her in surprise. "Maybe she can," he said wonderingly. "Just maybe she can."

Tory smiled in satisfaction. At least, she was making progress somewhere. "I had better get back to my class, now, Teodoro, and you must return to Senhor *Prêto*."

He sketched an awkward bow in her direction. *"Bom dia, Professôra,"* he said respectfully.

"Bom dia, Teodoro."

An hour later, having dismissed the children early, Tory was trying to convince Carmelita that she must lie to Padre Osmundo about a relative living in the distant village of Jacobina. They stood arguing in Carmelita's neat-as-a-pin little house that was only a three minute walk from the church and Padre Osmundo's attached residence. Tory lived with Carmelita, but while she spent most of her time at the school, Carmelita passed a good part of the day at Padre Osmundo's—cooking, cleaning, and keeping his vestments in good order.

"On several occasions, I have heard you discussing

your uncle with Padre Osmundo," Tory pointed out. "And I know he's anxious to get the old man to quit drinking and make his peace with God before he dies. Claiming that your uncle is dying would be a perfect excuse for convincing Padre Osmundo to go to Jacobina."

"But he isn't dying, *Professôra!* I've received no such word of him being ill and asking to see Padre Osmundo. How can I convince Padre Osmundo that I have?"

"How do you usually obtain news of your uncle, short of journeying to Jacobina yourself?"

"*Tio* Bruno himself never sends news. *I* am the one who inquires after *him,* whenever I hear of anyone passing through Espirito Santo who has come from the vicinity of Jacobina. Once when I needed to tell him something, I had Padre Osmundo write a letter, and a traveler took it to the house of a government official, and a servant of the government official fetched my uncle, and the government official read the letter to *Tio* Bruno."

"Then that's how you can claim that you received news of your uncle's illness. I'll write a short note, and you can say it came from a traveler who carried it from the government official who wrote it at *Tio* Bruno's request . . . There's no priest in Jacobina, is there?"

"No, *Professôra* . . . The priest died last year, and the archbishop has yet to replace him. Jacobina is as remote and poor a town as Espirito Santo. I don't think any priest wants to go there except Padre Osmundo, who occasionally performs baptisms, weddings, funerals, and administers the other sacraments."

"Then what better excuse could we think of! I'll write the note immediately."

"But, *Professôra,* I cannot lie to Padre Osmundo. He will know it's a lie as soon as he gets there and discovers my uncle is in good health—or drunk on *cachaça,* more likely."

Tory took Carmelita by the shoulders and gently shook her. "Carmelita! Do you want Padre Osmundo to be shot and killed? That's what's going to happen if we don't find a way to get him out of town. Afterwards, you can claim it was all a mistake . . . You can say anything you like. But today we have to convince Padre Osmundo that your dying uncle is finally ready to ask God's forgiveness for his wretched life of drunkenness."

Carmelita's black eyes filled with tears. *"Tio* Bruno will also be furious with me. Padre Osmundo has talked to him before, and *Tio* Bruno threw him out of his hut and told him never to come back . . . And Padre Osmundo promised he wouldn't, unless *Tio* Bruno was on his death bed and begging for him . . . Oh, they will both be so angry, *Professôra."*

"Better they should be angry than Padre Osmundo dead. Dry your tears, Carmelita, and I'll write the note. Then you can take it over to the parish house and give it to Padre Osmundo."

Padre Osmundo was ready to leave early the following morning. He sat uneasily in Percy's saddle, having had a difficult time mounting the horse. The priest's ankle had healed enough for him to give up his crutches, but climbing on the horse had been an awkward, uncomfortable matter. Still, it was the easiest way to travel such a long distance, and Padre Osmundo's main worry was that Cerqueira might come in his absence.

"I'll only be gone for three days," he told Tory and

343

Carmelita. "One day to get there, another to pray with your poor uncle, and a third to travel back again. I hope nothing happens while I'm gone."

"Don't worry, Padre . . . Nothing has happened in the past two weeks, so maybe Cerqueira has abandoned the plan. If he does come, I myself will gather the peasants to defend the school," Tory assured him.

"That's what worries me, child. I don't like to think of you confronting Cerqueira without me. Whatever the man's feelings for the Falcon and the poor peasants, he would never dare shoot a priest."

"No, he'll only kidnap you and shut you up in a monastery—with his cousin's consent."

"I think I could talk him out of that—at least, I could try," Padre Osmundo sniffed, full of his own pride and arrogance.

"Just hurry back," Tory begged with a false heartiness.

"And tell my poor uncle that I am praying for him day and night," Carmelita added.

"You should be going with me, Carmelita, but I suppose you must stay and keep our little *professôra* out of trouble. Besides, we haven't another horse, and you wouldn't ride if we did. It's too bad I sent the cart and oxen back to Paraíso."

"You can travel faster without me, Padre."

"Then good-bye, my children . . . I should be happy to have this fine animal available to me, but somehow I'm quite nervous about this journey . . . Ah well, I have no choice so I had better stop complaining." Padre Osmundo raised his hand and traced a cross in the air over their heads. "God bless you and keep you."

"Good-bye, Padre . . . Good luck with Carmelita's uncle!" Tory watched as the priest departed. When he was well on his way, she turned and started back

344

toward Carmelita's house with long, quick strides.

"What shall we do now, *Professôra?*" Carmelita quavered, walking beside her.

"I'm going to prepare a small store of food and water, and then I'm going to lock myself in the school," Tory stated. "When the *pistoleiros* come, you must tell the peasants to stay inside their homes and keep as far away from the school as possible."

"For most of them, that will come as good news . . . But what if some refuse to obey?"

"You must convince them that Padre Osmundo has changed his mind and wants no interference whatever. The peasants are to leave everything to Senhor *Prêto.*"

"But, *Professôra*, what will *you* do? You should stay here with me, where it's safe."

"I won't do anything I don't have to, Carmelita. Trust me. I've no wish to get myself shot. However, if it appears that anything I might say can stop the destruction of the school, then of course, I'll say it."

"Oh, *Professôra*, you are the bravest woman I have ever known!"

"Either that, or I'm the dumbest, Carmelita. I guess we'll find out which this afternoon."

Chapter Twenty-Three

As Sebastian galloped alongside Mundinho Cerqueira toward Espirito Santo, a sense of elation and dread swept over him. Cerqueira didn't know it, but he was rushing to meet his death. Everything should be in place by now. Teodoro had returned during the night, having safely completed his mission to tell Ramiro Bastos to hide himself and his men in the school, and to warn Tory to leave town with Padre Osmundo. All should be ready. When they arrived at the school, Sebastian and his small band of trusted *vaqueiros*, those who had ridden with him as the Falcon, would surround Cerqueira and his *pistoleiros*, trapping them in front of the building.

At long last, the man who had stolen the Falcon's land and gunned down Sebastian's parents would meet justice. The son of Manuel *Falcão* would have his revenge . . . So also would the poor peasants and small landowners who had suffered at Cerqueira's hands or been driven off their modest holdings so that Cerqueira could add to his ever-expanding empire of land and cattle. Over the years, Sebastian had kept track of his enemy's crimes. Few besides himself had survived to seek revenge, and many times, the Falcon had been blamed for the atrocities Mundinho Cerqueira had committed.

Sebastian felt no remorse for what he was about to do. He had already instructed Bastos to shoot as many of Cerqueira's thieving, murdering *pistoleiros* as possible; but no one was to kill Cerqueira. Sebastian wanted that pleasure for himself. He had waited half his lifetime to obtain it, and before he put a bullet through the monster's black heart, he wanted Cerqueira to know exactly who was killing him and why.

Then Sebastian thought of Tory, and for a moment, his resolve wavered; would she condemn him for this cold-hearted murder? Surely not when she learned what Cerqueira had done! But she was an American, and the concept of vengeance was distinctly foreign to her; Sebastian had learned that much during the years he had lived in her country. In America, disputes were usually settled in the court-room, and Sebastian had often wondered if American men didn't long for a more personal means of obtaining justice. In some parts of the country, he had heard, there still existed a lawlessness that caused men to carry guns wherever they went, but in the more civilized areas, firearms were rarely seen anymore.

Sebastian touched one of the pistols strapped to his side; without them, he would feel undressed. Even when he didn't wear the big pistols or carry his Winchester, he was never without a weapon hidden somewhere on his person. Danger could erupt at any time, and he had learned that the only means of staying alive was to be prepared. Soon, he mused, one or the other of the pistols he wore today would kill the man who rode beside him. He couldn't help darting Cerqueira a surrepticious glance that his nemesis intercepted.

Grinning, Cerqueira patted his own Winchester. "It won't be long now," he crowed. "Before sunset, the Falcon will lie dead."

Sebastian nodded. "Soon," he agreed, "a long-standing debt will be paid."

About midafternoon, they caught sight of Espirito Santo shimmering in a haze of heat and sunshine. The sleepy little town appeared more quiet than usual. As they approached, Sebastian happily noted that the school stood still and silent on the fringe of the *sertão*. Cerqueira rode unerringly toward it. "We'll take possession of the school before we go looking for the priest," he called over his shoulder to Sebastian. "If there are children inside or that outspoken *Americana*, I'll detain them there until we catch Padre Osmundo . . . He'll come running when I tell him he's needed at the school."

"A good plan," Sebastian assured him. "It doesn't look as if anyone's here. The door is closed and the windows shuttered."

He cast a sideways glance at Miguel and Teodoro. No other signal was needed; Sebastian's men immediately began to close ranks and bunch together, forming a protective horseshoe to protect each other and Sebastian himself. He had eight good men with him today, men who had ridden many a hot, dusty trail at his side. When they weren't raiding, most of them stayed out on the *sertão*, herding and guarding cattle; only a few such as Miguel and Teodoro spent much time at Paraíso. All had sworn a blood oath, sealed by gashing the palms of their hands and allowing their blood to mingle with Sebastian's, to never reveal his identity as the Falcon, or discuss the raids they had made under his leadership—not even to their wives and children.

In exchange for their years of loyalty, each man had a sizable cache of money hidden in a secret place in Sebastian's cellar. Sebastian had promised all of them that when he finally avenged himself against his parents' murderer, they could take that money and buy their own land, cattle, horses, or whatever else took their fancy. Miguel and Teodoro had been mere boys when they first started riding with him, and Sebastian had always made them wait out on the *sertão* until whatever stock had been stolen was driven toward them. Amâncio had been with Sebastian the longest, and Sebastian was sorry that the quiet, loyal black man wasn't with him today—on this last and final ride.

They arrived at the school in a cloud of dust, which set horses and men to coughing and snorting. As the dust settled and the noise died down, Sebastian furtively reached for his pistol, at the same time kneeing Renegade in front of Cerqueira's horse, to block him from escaping. A flash of silver shone in Cerqueira's hand. It was a drawn pistol, and without saying a word, Cerqueira leveled it at Sebastian's chest. Sebastian stared at him questioningly, his fingers poised above his weapon.

"What's the meaning of this, Cerqueira?" he growled into the sudden, breathless silence, but he feared he already knew the meaning.

Cerqueira's thin, colorless lips curved upwards beneath his mustache. His black eyes sparkled. "I should think you would have guessed by now, Senhor *Prêto*—or should I say, Senhor *Falcão* . . . That is your *real* name, is it not? *Luis Sebastião Falcão*."

Sebastian felt his heart stop beating. "How did you

discover it?" he asked in a voice that sounded distant and deceptively calm, considering that he had just received the second greatest shock of his life—the first being the deaths of his father and mother.

"Oh, I have known it for some time . . . I would have to be very stupid not to have suspected a connection between the bandit called the Falcon and Manuel *Falcão*, who died at my hands over twenty years ago . . . Eventually, it occurred to me that perhaps Manuel *Falcão* had another son besides the one I killed that day—or thought I had killed. But I checked all the birth and baptism records, and could find no mention of other children . . . Then I wondered if he might have had a younger brother. My research again revealed no other man with the same last name. At last I realized that you must not have died that day when your parents did . . . Do you know that I searched your geneology all the way back to the Falcons who originally came from the *Estados Unidos*, following that country's Civil War? . . . You are actually an *Americano*, and your grandfather did not go by the name *Falcão* in your native country, but rather by the name Falkner."

"That's a foul lie!" Sebastian blurted out. "I assure you I know my family's name—just as I know that you are the one who killed my father and mother in order to steal their land."

"Your name is Falkner, but when your grandfather came to Brazil he changed it. We Brazilians found it easier to say and to remember *Falcão* . . . Also, the name had a more romantic connotation, signifying as it does, a proud bird of prey."

"All lies!" Sebastian shouted, enraged that Mundinho Cerqueira would try to take his name away, on top of everything else.

"You could have learned all this for yourself in

350

Salvador. The original deed for your grandfather's *fazenda* was made out in his legal name—and that name was Falkner. Later, when your father was born, your grandfather attached an addendum saying that thereafter, he and his family would be known as *Falcão*." Mundinho Cerqueira smiled a cruel, satisfied smile. "Unfortunately, you will have to take my word for all of this. You cannot check it yourself, because I can't permit you to live."

"I'll never take your word for anything, you pit viper. You're the lowest, most debased of God's creatures."

Mundinho Cerqueira's mouth twitched at the insult, but he did not drop his guard. Sebastian could make no move with Cerqueira's pistol aimed straight at his heart. Neither could his men. From the corner of his eye, Sebastian could see their stricken faces. They had waited too long to draw their pistols, unlike Cerqueira's *pistoleiros* who were ready and waiting. Cerqueira had planned better than he had, and it was a bitter pill for Sebastian to swallow. His last hope was Ramiro Bastos, hidden inside the school—but Bastos couldn't do much either, until he had a clear shot.

Cerqueira jerked his pistol in the direction of Sebastian's men. "Tell your followers to remove their weapons and toss them into a pile in front of the school, along with yours. Thomas! Since the school appears deserted, take a couple men and go get the priest and the little blonde teacher. Escort them to the church, and stay there with them until I send someone for you."

"And just what do you intend to do with all of us, Cerqueira?" Sebastian sat very still, making no move to remove his gunbelt. "We won't be so easy to kill as you might imagine."

351

Cerqueira snorted with laughter. "You'll be easy enough! You see, I have it all planned. I may even emerge a hero. No one will fault me for eliminating a dangerous bandit and his loyal followers—and not until you're dead will it be discovered that you are the man known as *Sebastião Prêto*. Of course, having rid the *sertão* of a terrible menace, I will be rewarded with all the Falcon's riches; everything you own will pass to me."

"By whose permission?"

"My cousin, the archbishop, has promised to speak to the proper government officials . . . There has already been discussion among them of offering a suitable reward to anyone who apprehends the Falcon. I will, of course, offer to make a generous donation to the Church, and then no one will dare refute my claim."

"Your plan could possibly work, Cerqueira, were it not for one tiny but significant detail."

"What detail is that, Senhor *Falcão?*"

"There's a large band of men hidden inside the school awaiting my signal to open fire on you and your friends."

Cerqueira's eyes widened, and his nostrils flared; he glanced worriedly toward the school, and Sebastian chuckled. "Why do you think I agreed to accompany you here and participate in your plan to kill the Falcon?"

"To avert suspicion from yourself, naturally!" Cerqueira snapped. "Knowing what we would find, which is precisely nothing, you could afford to act as outraged as I am over the Falcon's thefts."

Sebastian slowly shook his head, savoring every moment of his own revelations. "For years I planned this, Cerqueira. I robbed and stole from you every chance I got. I knew that eventually you'd be driven

352

to act—and that you would come to me, begging my help. You're too much of a coward to take on the Falcon all by yourself. All I had to do was wait. Now the waiting's finally over. *You* will be the one to die in a confrontation with the famous bandit."

"You're bluffing!" Cerqueira scoffed. "There's no one at all inside that school."

"Bastos!" Sebastian called out. "Cerqueira needs proof of your presence."

As Cerqueira wheeled around to watch, one of the shutters of the school building slowly swung open. An unseen pistol spat a streak of fire into the air overhead. The noise made all the horses except Renegade jump and mill about. As his mount went crazy, Cerqueira lowered his gun and fumbled for his reins. Sebastian grabbed for the weapon, but Cerqueira grimly held on. The pistol discharged into the air, completely panicking his already spooked horse. As the horse reared, the pistol spun away into the dirt and was trampled and lost from sight.

Sebastian flung himself atop Cerqueira, and they tumbled to the ground in a welter of arms, legs, and prancing hooves. Sebastian came up swinging, his fists making solid contact with Cerqueira's chin and chest. But Cerqueira had more guts and strength than Sebastian had expected. Ignoring the blows, he stumbled to his feet, and the two adversaries warily circled each other, while men from both sides reined back their horses to give them room.

"Let the two of them fight it out!" exclaimed one of Cerqueira's men. He spat on the ground and shoved his pistol back into his gun belt. "Why should the rest of us shed blood over an old dispute that doesn't involve any of us? . . . If the Falcon wants his vengeance, let him take it. Senhor Cerqueira must stop him as best he can."

There was a low murmur of approval from both sides. Then Sebastian heard Teodoro's excited cry. "Now you bastards will see how the Falcon fights! He is the greatest bandit of all time," the young man boasted to the onlookers. "His name will go down as legend . . . Who wants to wager on the outcome of this fight?"

Sebastian groaned to himself; Teodoro was going too far. As the men eagerly began making bets, Sebastian glared into Mundinho Cerqueira's black eyes. "So, Cerqueira . . . It's come down to you and me. That's the way it should be; why must anyone else have to die for a wrong committed before some of them were even born?"

"I will kill you with my bare hands," Cerqueira hissed. "Then I will take your land, cattle, and horses, just as I took your father's before you. Only this time, there will be no fledgling falcon left to avenge the deed. I will have it all, *Falcão*. And after I kill you, I'll get rid of Padre Osmundo and send the little teacher back where she came from . . . No one will stop me then; I'll rule the *sertão* forever. *My* name will become legend."

"Quit talking and start fighting, Cerqueira. I accept your challenge. We fight to the death . . . and it will give me great pleasure to fight as the peasants do, using only my feet in the ancient art of *capoeira*." Sebastian kicked out suddenly, grazing Cerqueira's ear with his boot.

He grinned at Cerqueira's suddenly alarmed expression. As Cerqueira well knew, *capoeira* was the method employed by the lowliest slaves in Brazil's colonial times to settle disputes among themselves, when fighting was forbidden to men of their class. The intricate, agile footwork had been born in

354

the dark recesses of Africa, and to the onlooker appeared as a kind of strenuous, athletic dance between two well-matched opponents. But it was actually a means of killing an enemy, and rarely did both men walk away with their lives.

Mundinho Cerqueira had probably witnessed many demonstrations of *capoeira*, but as a white man of the upper class, he had most certainly never fought that way nor expected Sebastian to be proficient at it. Sebastian had honed his techniques as a young boy living among the peasants, and Amâncio had continued his education. It was a sport they regularly practiced in order to keep agile and fit. Sebastian had never killed a man using the method, but he knew all the points of the body where a properly placed blow could cripple or maim . . . And he intended to make Cerqueira suffer before he dealt him the final death blow.

Sebastian laughed with the sheer exhilaration of the moment. Fear had crept into Mundinho Cerqueira's eyes. "I do not know *capoeira*," Cerqueira complained in a wooden voice. "This will not be a fair fight."

"Then I'll make it easier for you." Sebastian tore off his shirt, then quickly tugged off his boots and tossed them to one side. "Like the slaves, I'll fight barefoot and bare-chested . . . Come, Cerqueira, let us begin—unless you prefer Bastos to shoot you first, and be done with it."

With the shouts of the onlookers ringing in his ears, Sebastian circled his wary enemy, and he wasn't the least bit daunted when Cerqueira furiously snatched a knife from his own boot. "This makes things a bit more equal!" Cerqueira waved the knife under Sebastian's nose. "Do your worst, *Falcão*.

First, I'll slice your feet to ribbons, then I'll cut off your balls as you die."

Peeking through a crack in the closed double doors, Tory heard and saw everything. She wasn't sure which of the astounding revelations shocked her the most. Yet, despite the surprises, everything had finally fallen into place. It was almost embarrassing that she hadn't suspected the true identity of the Falcon before this; the clues had all been there, but she had ignored them . . . *Of course, Sebastian was the Falcon*. That explained his secret charity, his rapport with the peasants, his frequent, mysterious absences from Paraíso . . . and his inability to marry and devote himself to a wife and family.

Trust me, he had said, and someday, you'll understand.

Well, now she understood. It had all been for the purpose of gaining vengeance against the man who had killed his parents and stolen their land. Yet Tory supposed that vengeance hadn't been the only motivating factor. No, Sebastian also cared about the peasants—and cared deeply. He had tried to repay them for keeping him alive after Cerqueira had supposedly killed him, along with his parents. By aiding the poor, both here and in Salvador, Sebastian had proven that at heart he was kind and good, even if he had been planning a murder for more than twenty years.

As she watched the fight unfolding before her, Tory gripped the wooden doorjamb with one hand and Teodoro's pistol with the other. *Capoeira* was a strange way to attack a villain or defend oneself. Using his arms for balance, Sebastian kicked, jumped, and leaped into the air. Striking out with his bare feet, he personified masculine grace and strength, Tory thought, while Cerqueira reminded her of a cornered rat, fighting for its life. He kept slashing the air awkwardly with his knife, missing Sebastian's toes by inches.

Despite Sebastian's impressive agility, Tory wished he had chosen a more conventional means of vanquishing his enemy. She wished that Bastos—whoever he was—had indeed arrived at the school and was waiting to shoot Cerqueira and his men if anything went wrong. She had been there all day by herself, and no one had appeared. Fortunately, Cerqueira and his followers hadn't yet discovered this, and she hoped Cerqueira was dead by the time they did.

Riveted to the scene taking place outside, Tory wondered why Teodoro and Miguel would allow the fight to take place with Cerqueira wielding a knife and Sebastian at the disadvantage of being barefoot. Then, suddenly, she understood; Sebastian delivered a stunning blow to Cerqueira's shoulder that sent the knife twirling through the air to land in the dirt as the pistol had done before it. Cerqueira swore and gripped his shoulder.

"Did I break anything?" Sebastian inquired silkily. "No matter. Next time, I will. I intend to break bones all over your body, Cerqueira. I'll show you no mercy. You showed none to my poor mother . . . First, you shot my father, then killed my mother as she ran outside to save him. Like a hunter stalking small game, you flushed them both out into the open by setting fire to the dry grass in front of the house."

"I've used that method many times . . ." Cerqueira sneered breathlessly, rubbing his shoulder. "It always

357

works. Peasants or rich men like your father. Makes no difference. They all run like rabbits when they smell smoke."

Sebastian kicked, and Cerqueira sprawled backward, clutching his stomach. Then he scrabbled for something lying in the dust beside him. Horror crashed over Tory as she saw that it was a pistol. Cerqueira raised himself on one knee and aimed it at Sebastian. A scream welled in Tory's throat. Yanking open the school door, she ran outside.

Sebastian and Cerqueira both saw her at the same time. Before either could react, she raised Teodoro's pistol and pointed it at Cerqueira. "Don't shoot, or I'll shoot you!" she cried.

"Gatinha," Sebastian said impatiently. "He doesn't understand English." Turning to Cerqueira, Sebastian repeated the threat in Portuguese.

Tory struggled to remember a single word of the language she had worked so hard to learn. "Get up," she commanded shakily. "Get up and drop the gun."

Cerqueira took an absurdly long time rising to his feet. He behaved as if he were gravely injured, but he did leave the gun on the ground. She stepped closer, holding the pistol out in front of her, determined to shoot if he made any move toward Sebastian. He never did. Instead, he suddenly lurched toward Tory. Thinking he was falling, she instinctively reached out to save him. Too late, his deviousness revealed itself. One hand snaked around her waist, and the other grabbed the pistol out of her grasp.

A cry of warning burst from her throat. Something cold and hard jammed into her neck. "Don't anyone move!" Cerqueira snarled in her ear. "If you do, I'll kill her."

"Where's Bastos?" Sebastian angrily demanded of Tory. A muscle spasmed in his jaw as he gazed at

Tory with mingled exasperation and fear for her safety.

"I—I don't know," Tory quavered. "I've no idea who he is. There's been no one here but me all day."

"*Cristo!*" Sebastian swore. "Shoot *me* if you want, Cerqueira, but leave the *professõra* out of this."

Cerqueira laughed harshly. "Oh, no, Senhor *Falcão*. I cannot do that, for I've just thought of a most interesting way to gain everything I want from you without having to share it with the Church or persuade reluctant government officials to let me have it."

"What is your price, Cerqueira? I'll do whatever you want. Just let the woman go. I'll even turn myself over to the authorities in Salvador."

"Why would I want you to turn yourself in, *Sebastião?* That would ruin my plans to kill you one day, after all . . . No, what I want is for you to go to Salvador and deed all your lands and property over to me, as if you had sold them to me . . . In a way you have; the price will be this lady's life. When the papers are legally and properly filed, I will send word where you can find her . . . Until then, she is my prisoner."

"Sebastian, no! Don't do it!" Tory screamed. "Look! There's someone coming—probably that man, Bastos, that you've been waiting for."

A cloud of dust on the horizon indicated a large number of horsemen approaching. But Cerqueira did not seem in the least worried. He moved the pistol so that its nose pressed a spot right below her ear. "I swear to you that I will kill her if you do not do as I demand," he growled at Sebastian. "I will give you two weeks from this day to file the papers. If they are not on record by then, the authorities will discover the naked, beaten body of a blonde woman down on

359

the docks, somewhere in the worst part of Salvador. No one will be able to prove who did it . . . I, of course, will deny everything and have excuses you cannot invalidate."

Cerqueira shoved Tory in the direction of his horse. "Climb aboard, *Professôra* . . . Hurry. I wish to be gone . . . And don't think to follow me, Senhor *Falcão*, or the *professôra* will die that much sooner."

Trembling, Tory stumbled, but two of Cerqueira's men grabbed her by the arms and swung her astride the horse. Cerqueira quickly mounted behind her. Jamming the pistol into the small of her back, he signaled for a canter, and the horse surged forward. The only sound was Sebastian's anguished, *"Cristo!"* exploding like a pistol behind them . . . and then Tory heard Cerqueira's cruel laughter. She felt the vibrations of his mirth shaking the very saddle beneath her. She herself was too numb to do anything but keep her balance and ride.

Tears blinded her as they galloped away across the *sertão,* and her lips formed a silent plea: *Dear God, let Sebastian think of some other way to rescue me without giving up everything he loves.*

Chapter Twenty-Four

Two weeks later, at the courthouse in Salvador, Sebastian transferred ownership of all his property and assets to Mundinho Cerqueira. As he walked down the courthouse steps in the heat of late afternoon, he reflected that becoming a poor man wasn't as bad as he had thought it would be. At least he had saved Tory's life. Soon, he would find out where Cerqueira had hidden her. He had torn apart the city searching, and offered a substantial reward, but no one had come forward with information. She might have fallen off the face of the earth.

Sebastian had not been able to eat or sleep for worrying; a thousand times he condemned himself for putting her life in danger. He ought to have known she wouldn't go into hiding with Padre Osmundo. He should have guessed that she would try to interfere. Her appearance at the school was so typically Tory that he wanted to kick himself for not making certain she was out of harm's way.

At first, he had behaved like a mad man—cursing his men and berating poor Bastos for showing up late. Bastos had done the best he could considering his many problems: colicky horses and an irate *fazendeiro* from Alagoas who had come in search of the thieves who had stolen his best horse. Through all of his suffering and anxiety, Sebastian had clung to one certainty: Cerqueira wouldn't dare harm Tory for fear that he wouldn't get the deed to Paraíso, after all. And if Cerqueira did touch a hair of Tory's blonde head, Sebastian would skin him alive, inch by agonizing inch.

Thinking of the satisfaction to be gained from watching Cerqueira die, Sebastian headed toward home to await word of Tory's whereabouts. No sooner had he arrived at his house when a child in tattered clothing and bare feet ran up to him and thrust a folded sheet of paper into his hand. *"Bom dia*, Senhor . . . a gentleman told me to wait here and give this to you when I saw you."

"What gentleman?" Sebastian's eyes searched the street, but he didn't see anyone he recognized.

"He did not tell me his name, Senhor. But he said you would reward me handsomely for delivering this important message to you."

Sebastian swore under his breath. Cerqueira knew his weaknesses only too well. He dug into his pocket, extracted a handful of *cruzeiros*, and stuffed them into the child's dirty hands. "Good thing you caught me when you did, *mon filho* . . . Soon, I'll have no money left, not even to pay for messages from enterprising young rascals like you."

I'm not lying about my poverty, Sebastian thought, as he watched the boy take the money and happily dart down a nearby alley.

He had never had much cash. Most of his wealth was tied up in land, cattle, and horses—and the part that wasn't went to Padre Osmundo. Now, his land, cattle, and horses—except for Renegade, stabled here in town, and several good mares sent off with

362

Bastos—belonged to Cerqueira. He had kept only the title to his house in Salvador, but without money or servants to keep the place going, he was faced with having to close it up. To each of his faithful employees had gone the savings set aside for them in the cellar. On his advice, most were moving to Espirito Santo to escape serving a new master at Paraíso. All but Dona Guilhermina had chosen to leave. Quinquina's stubborn aunt had decided she preferred working for Cerqueira to starving in that poor little village. Not so Quinquina; the girl had run off with Teodoro to get married, and the two of them planned to settle down near Padre Osmundo.

Amâncio had also gone to Espirito Santo in the ox cart, accompanied by Miguel, with instructions to tell Padre Osmundo that both oxen and cart were now his. It was the last gift Sebastian could give his old friend for a very long time—if the priest would even accept it. Padre Osmundo was so angry with Sebastian that he had not spoken to him since the day they had argued upon Padre Osmundo's return from Carmelita's uncle's house. Sebastian had told the priest everything, and Padre Osmundo had listened in pained, disbelieving silence, then blasted him with all the criticism he was capable of so eloquently delivering.

As Sebastian opened the message the boy had brought him, Padre Osmundo's parting words rang in his ears. "You mean you have been deceiving me all these years? Oh, my son, you should not have done that . . . I don't know if I'll ever be able to forgive you. God is punishing you for your wickedness by allowing Cerqueira to win, after all . . . Go to Salvador and do as he demands. You do not deserve better. You are a liar and a would-be murderer. You have rejected and sinned against everything I've taught you, so it's only just that you lose your wealth to your greatest enemy."

Sebastian stared down at the words his wealth had brought him—the knowledge of Tory's whereabouts. The script seemed to waver and crawl across the page. There wasn't much to read—only a short, brief instruction. *You will find her at the Igreja de São Francisco.*

How ironic! He crumpled the paper and laughed out loud. How had Cerqueira known that the church was where he had first seen Tory in his own country and feared that he was falling in love with her? His attraction to the outspoken little blonde had begun in the United States, but it wasn't until he had watched her in the flickering gold light of the darkened church that he felt the awakening flutters of something more than mere lust. She had turned her lovely green eyes on him, and something had wrenched and shattered in the region of his heart.

He recalled blaming the feeling on the fish he had eaten at lunch, but it had not been indigestion that made his insides quake, and he had realized it even then. Only Tory made him feel that way. He was quaking now, knowing that soon he would be with her and could once again gaze into her beautiful eyes. Unfortunately, he wasn't at all certain that Tory would welcome him when he went to get her. She had to be feeling the same contempt for him that had struck Padre Osmundo. And there was nothing he could say or do to overcome it. He *had* behaved contemptibly.

Worse, he now had nothing to offer her—no home, no future, no proud Brazilian heritage. It was all gone. He owned little more than Renegade, a roof over his head, and the clothes on his back. He could barely afford to feed himself, let alone a wife and family!

His only consolation was that at least he would get to see her one more time before he had to say good-bye forever. This time, he must convince Tory to forget about teaching in Padre Osmundo's school. Surely, she now realized that life in Brazil was much too dangerous. He intended to persuade her to return to the United States if it was the last thing he ever did. Only after she was safely out of the country could he join forces with Bastos and spend the rest of his life making Cerqueira pay for his many crimes. Some-day, Cerqueira would come after him again, and one of them would finally die.

But not today . . . Today belonged to him and Tory. Swept with an eagerness he could no longer contain, Sebastian tossed the paper into the street and set off at a run for the *Igreja de São Francisco*.

Tory sat in the same pew of the church where once before she had sat waiting for Padre Osmundo. Everything looked exactly the same in the darkened interior: the same gold walls, flickering candles, and old women praying at the side altars. Yet everything was different, too. Tory felt as if she had aged ten years in the relatively short time since that first day in Salvador. Would Sebastian appear as he had then, on a day that now seemed so long ago?

She knew nothing of what had happened during the last two weeks. She had spent them in a convent not far from the church, where Cerqueira had turned her over to the mother superior, warning that the good sisters would not believe a word she had to say to them. The nuns had been told that she was mad—

subject to fits of insanity in which she fabricated preposterous tales—and that a renowned physician in Salvador had prescribed a period of total seclusion, claiming it as her only possible hope for a cure.

Sympathetically but silently, the nuns had led her to a small, spare cell, from which she was released twice daily—once for mass in the morning, then again in the late afternoon for exercise in the convent gardens. No one spoke to her the whole time, nor would they listen. Instead, they scurried away, performing many small acts of kindness, but otherwise refusing to converse with her for any reason.

In the face of such stalwart discipline, Tory had finally given up. The nuns could maintain silence for days. Their eyes conveyed that they really did think she was mad, especially when she began singing to herself so she could hear the sound of a human voice, even if it was only her own. The experience had taught her much about her unexpectedly strong needs for social discourse and small luxuries.

Glancing down at herself, Tory smiled ruefully; it felt wonderful to be dressed in her own clothes again after two weeks spent wearing a drab, scratchy habit the nuns had lent her. She was glad they had returned her clothing clean and intact. Despite her past avowals of disinterest in current fashions, she had no desire to meet Sebastian dressed as a nun! At the thought of seeing him again, her heart constricted . . . What if this was all a cruel joke, and she *wasn't* going to get to see him again? What if Cerqueira had killed him? But if he had, then why had the nuns brought her to the church and told her to wait there for "a close friend" to come for her?

She decided that Sebastian must have met Cerqueira's demands and signed over all his property.

That was why she was finally being released. Two weeks had passed without Cerqueira returning to abduct and kill her. That could only mean that Sebastian had capitulated and was on his way to find her.

Tory straightened her skirt and patted her braided hair, hoping she didn't look too haggard and thin after the regimen of sparse meals she had not been able to eat. She knew by the fit of her skirt and shirtwaist blouse that she had lost weight, and Sebastian would probably accuse Cerqueira of deliberately starving her. In actuality, the odious man had done her a favor. Having nothing to do but think for two weeks, she had figured out what she and Sebastian should do.

Now that he no longer owned property in Brazil, he would be free to start over someplace else. Sebastian could return home with her to America, and once she told her brother how good Sebastian was with horses, Jordan would hire him in a minute. They could make a new life together in the United States, even search for remnants of Sebastian's original family—the Falkners.

There was nothing in Brazil to hold Sebastian any longer; without Paraíso, he had nothing. Tory understood what the ranch meant to him—not only wealth and power, but identity. Sebastian measured himself by what he owned; it was the measure of all men in Brazil. Only in a country like the United States did other standards apply. In America, people would respect him for the knowledge he possessed and the kind of man he was. With his awesome ability to train horses, he would soon be able to live comfortably, if not perhaps luxuriously.

She hoped he would listen to her. She prayed that he was finally ready to leave Brazil. Staying meant eventual disaster, because someday he would meet Cerqueira again, and one of the two men would die. Too much hatred flourished between them; as big as Brazil was, it was too small a country to contain both of them . . . Tory felt that she *had* to make Sebastian see that a new life was possible, and it could be a happy, fulfilling one . . . If he loved her as much as she loved him, he should be willing to go home to America with her. He was an American, after all, *not* Brazilian, and he belonged in the United States.

Immersed in her thoughts, Tory did not at first see the tall figure approaching from a side altar. When she looked up, her breath came faster, and it seemed as if the walls began to shake. Sebastian was coming toward her just as he had the first time when she had sat waiting for Padre Osmundo. . . .

Without thinking, she leapt to her feet and called his name. Then she was running toward him, arms outstretched, overjoyed that he was alive and whole. He caught her and crushed her to him, holding her so tightly that her ribs were in danger of cracking.

"Gatinha!" he murmured. *"Cristo!* Half way here, I grew afraid I would never see you again—terrified he might have killed you and only brought me here to raise my hopes and then dash them, inflicting the tortures of the damned upon me."

"Sebastian . . . Oh, my darling! I was afraid *you* might be dead! Did you do it? Did you deed all you own to him?"

"Yes . . . Yes, I had to. I tried everything I could think of to find you. I offered rewards, I searched throughout the city . . ."

"I was locked up in a convent," she breathlessly explained. "Unless you're a relative of one of the nuns—or the cousin of the archbishop—you can't get past the gates."

"I should have thought of that . . . Ah, sweetheart, you have grown so thin!" Sebastian ran his hands up and down her ribcage. "The flesh has all melted from your bones. Didn't the nuns feed you?"

"The food was plain but adequate. I just wasn't hungry." She explored the contours of his torso. "I'm not the only one who's skinny. You've lost more weight than I have."

He took her hand. "Come . . . We'll go to my home, where our reunion won't scandalize these poor old women." He nodded toward two old ladies who were eyeing them indignantly.

"You still have a home in town? Thank God for that. I was afraid Cerqueira had taken everything."

"He *has* taken everything. My house in town means nothing to me without the land to provide for its upkeep . . . I won't be able to maintain it for long."

"Let's wait until we get there before we talk. I've so much to say, Sebastian."

"So do I, *gatinha.*" He hugged her close once more, his lips on her forehead, then drew her after him. "Come . . . let's hurry. Until I have you locked behind my own strong doors, I still fear for your safety."

And until I've taken you across the sea to America, I still fear for your safety, Tory silently added.

By the time they arrived at Sebastian's house, neither was in the mood for talking. Sebastian's yearning eyes convinced Tory that any discussion of the future could wait until later, when hopefully, a more relaxed frame of mind would enable him to consider her proposal carefully, not reject it outright. They stood in front of the life-size cross hanging on the wall in the main room and embraced each other hungrily. To Tory, it seemed an eternity since they had last kissed and hugged.

She clung to him in a fever of longing, her hands seeking to touch as much of him as possible. She accidentally tore his shirt trying to get to his chest, then gave up and clasped his face in her hands while she kissed him long and deeply. He broke away laughing.

"Little wildcat, we'll go to my room . . ."

"That's not necessary," she murmured. "I don't need a bed. There's a perfectly good floor right here."

His eyes strayed to the huge, ominous cross, as if it signified a disapproving presence in the room. "Padre Osmundo would say that what we're doing—or about to do—is a grave sin."

"I don't believe it. Loving you can't be a sin," Tory gasped as his fingers brushed across her breast. "It's the closest to paradise I've ever come."

Stroking her, Sebastian nibbled her ear, while at the same time, nudging her toward the hallway. "Some people believe sex is evil, even sex between husbands and wives."

"Pooh! God was the one who created these feelings. So they *must* be right and good. It's only when we . . . when we . . ." Sebastian distracted her by pausing long enough to remove her blouse, untie the ribbons on her chemise, then push it down to the level of her waist.

"When we what?"

"I can't remember what I was going to say," she complained, distracted by Sebastian lifting her in his arms so that her breasts were level with his mouth.

He nuzzled the cleft between the tingling mounds. "This is worth whatever punishment I must endure

370

for enjoying it," he sighed. *"Cristo,* but I love you, *gatinha."*

"Prove it to me, Sebastian . . ." she whispered. "We've been separated far too long. I want to be one with you . . . I want there to be nothing in this world but you and me."

He carried her to his bedchamber and lay her down on the cool linen sheets. She wriggled out of the rest of her clothes while he tossed his garments left and right. Then he joined her, and they rolled together in joyous passion. They traded kisses with feverish abandon, rediscovered the familiar, beloved terrain of each other's bodies, and tantalized themselves into near delerium. Craving union, Tory would not permit Sebastian to prolong the final ecstasy.

Straddling his hips, she guided him into her, then savored the delicious friction of moving up and down on his body. He groaned from the sweet agony. Her release came with a sudden explosiveness that left her gasping. Wave after wave of sensation crashed over her, while Sebastian lay perfectly still and unmoving beneath her. Dimly, she perceived that he was holding back from taking his own release.

Abruptly, he rolled her over on her back, plunged into her several times, then suddenly unsheathed himself. A wet stickiness spurted across her thighs, leaving no doubt in her mind that he had deliberately wasted his seed again, denying her the ultimate joining.

"Oh, Sebastian . . . why?" she whispered, as she cradled him in her arms. The answer came to her in a rush of pain and disappointment. Before he opened his mouth to tell her, she already knew the reason.

He leaned back and smoothed away the tendrils of

hair that clung to her damp cheek. "*Gatinha*, forgive me, but I dare not make you pregnant. I wish with all my heart that you could be the mother of my children; no other woman will ever bear them, I swear it. But I think we both know that marriage between us can never take place."

Tears gathered in Tory's eyes, but she made a valiant effort not to shed them. "Sebastian, it doesn't bother me that you've lost your land. I never loved you because of your wealth . . . I'm sorry I was the reason you had to sign everything over to Cerqueira, but I don't regret that you're now free of encumbrances . . . Now, you can come home with me to America. My brother, Jordan, will beg you to help train his horses once he hears my glowing accounts of Renegade's behavior. We'll have enough to live, and maybe one day, we can buy our own farm in America, and raise and train our own horses . . . I've thought it all out, Sebastian, and I know it can work!"

Even as she babbled, Tory could tell that Sebastian flatly rejected the idea. His amber eyes darkened, and his face hardened. Finally, he levered himself off her and reached for his trousers. "No, *gatinha*," he said without looking at her. "It could never work. I can't leave Brazil while Mundinho Cerqueira still lives, enjoying the fruits of *my* labor. Even were that not so, I doubt I could stomach the humbling experience of working for another man."

"Then you admit it; you're too damn proud!" Tory raged. "And too conceited to recognize that there can be pride and honor in a task well-done, whether it is performed for yourself or for another. I never realized that being Brazilian meant you scorn humble labor; now, I'm glad *I* don't have to live here for the rest of my life. At least in America, the lowliest street cleaner or school teacher can take pride in his or her profession. Self-esteem isn't determined by who a person's parents are and whether or not they owned any land."

"You don't understand," Sebastian murmured in a tone of deep regret. "Only another Brazilian would understand."

"You're at least half American!" Snatching the sheet from the bed, Tory wrapped it around herself to cover her nakedness while she argued. "Don't you want to find out if any of your relatives still live in America?"

Having finished putting on his trousers, Sebastian sat on the edge of the bed and ran his fingers distractedly through his dark hair. "Of course, I would like to do that, someday. But it may be years before I get another chance to eliminate Cerqueira . . . He surrounds himself with *pistoleiros*, and I have no doubt that from now on, they will be instructed to shoot me on sight."

"But, Sebastian, what will you do now? You can't waste your entire life trying to get even with this man, hoping to draw him into another fight. Where will you live? How will you eat?"

Sebastian turned burning eyes upon her. "I will become the greatest bandit of all time," he said simply. "The Falcon is already quite renowned; with a bit more effort, he can become a legend."

Tory was horrified. She knew that Sebastian could—and would—become a famous criminal. "They will put a price on your head . . . Eventually, the *fazendeiros* will hunt you down like a mad dog and shoot or hang you."

"I prefer to think that I'll live a life of unrelenting adventure. Such a life does not, of course, allow for a wife and family. That would make me too vulnerable, not to mention how vulnerable *they* would be . . ." he smiled the wry smile that always caught her off-guard and wrung her heart. "Look what happened to my beautiful, blonde lover. She got locked up in a convent. The next time, she might fare worse."

Tory got on her knees on the bed, clutching the sheet to her bare breasts. "Sebastian, I beg you . . . Please come home with me. Haven't you lost enough? Will you keep fighting Cerqueira until you lose your life too? . . . Forget about him! He's an evil man who will come to his own bad end. The world doesn't need you to hasten it along."

"No, but *I* need to keep fighting until I regain some portion of what I've lost . . . I am a man, *gatinha,* and all I have is my pride. I could not live with myself if I permitted Cerqueira to get away with all he's done to me and mine."

"He *won't* get away with it! God will ultimately decide his punishment. Leave Cerqueira in the hands of a higher authority."

"I cannot, *gatinha.* I'm sorry. I never meant to hurt you. You are the one good thing that has happened in my life . . . You and Padre Osmundo. He has finally turned his back on me; it would be better for both of us if you now did the same . . . You must strive to forget me, *gatinha.*"

"Sebastian, I can't! I love you too much!" She threw her arms around him and tried to hold him, tried to pull him back down on the bed. "You are my heart, my life, my breath! Don't ask me to give you up. I'll die if I do!"

Gently, he disentangled himself and set her aside. "You will die if you don't—and that I will not permit. This very day I am booking passage for you on a ship leaving for America. I cannot force you to

374

board it, but I can certainly show you that you've lost me whether you go or stay . . . We will not do this again, *gatinha*. It does nothing but frustrate us both; we shouldn't have done it this time . . . It was only that I . . . I wanted to say good-bye and . . . and make a memory to cherish always."

"I don't want to cherish memories, spending my life looking backward!" she cried. "I want to live each day in the present, waking up each morning relishing what lies ahead . . . Forego your vengeance, Sebastian, and come home with me to America."

His eyes held the bleakness of winter, and his features seemed carved from granite. Without responding, he gathered up his remaining clothes and boots, and went to the door. "Good-bye, *gatinha*. I will let you know when and from where the ship will be leaving. Miguel came with me to Salvador. At the moment, he is visiting relatives, but he will look after you and see to your needs . . . I think it would be better if we did not see each other again."

She was hurting too much to argue. The pain was so great she could hardly speak. "If that is your wish . . ." she mumbled. "Good-bye, Sebastian . . ."

She waited until he left the room before flinging herself across the bed and hiding her face in her hands. This time, she did not permit herself to weep. She had shed too many tears over Sebastian already, and she, too, had her pride. She would not, she decided, weep for him again. He had chosen what he wanted, and now, she must choose what *she* wanted . . . and decide how she was going to get it.

Chapter Twenty-Five

"What are you doing, Miguel?" Tory stepped into the main room where the sound of pounding had awakened her from an exhausted sleep. Now she could see what he was doing—nailing boards across the window openings so that if someone broke through the wooden shutters, they could not gain access to the house.

"*Bom dia, Professôra* . . . I apologize for making so much noise so early in the morning but Senhor *Sebastião* and I are leaving soon to go back to the *sertão*, and he wanted me to close up the house first, and make it ready for a long absence."

"When are you leaving?" Tory inquired, walking over to a nearby table where her name scrawled across a brown packet had just caught her eye.

"Very soon . . . perhaps this afternoon . . ." Seeing where she was headed, Miguel pointed to the packet. "Senhor *Sebastião* left that for you. It is your embarkation ticket for a ship leaving tonight for the *Estados Unidos*. You must be on it by four o'clock this afternoon. He also left a small sum of money with me, and I am to help you purchase anything you might need for the journey, since your belongings are

376

still in Espírito Santo. Then I must see you safely to the ship."

"Where is Senhor *Sebastião,* now?" Determined to conceal the inner turmoil his words caused her, Tory studied Miguel more closely than she ever had before.

Like Teodoro, Miguel had an earnest face and typical Brazilian coloring—dark hair, eyes, and skin the color of tanned leather. She guessed him to be about five years older than Teodoro. Now, however, he flushed a ruddy shade and seemed boyishly reluctant to answer. "I am not certain, *Professôra,* but I think he spent last night in a certain house he used to visit often before you came to Brazil."

Tory reeled inwardly from the pain of that informational blow. Where else would Sebastian spend the night but in the arms of one of his old paramours? Only another woman could make him forget everything he had shared with *her.*

"I see . . ." she murmured, keeping a tight grip on her emotions. "He expects me to be gone by tonight, and then the two of you will go back to the *sertão.*"

"*Sim, Professôra* . . . When we get there, I hope to spend some time in Espírito Santo. My wife, Filomena, and my two children have gone there to live. I wish to see them comfortably settled before I . . . before we . . ."

"Take up a life of banditry," Tory finished for him. "Because of your loyalty to the Falcon, you're willing to risk making your wife a widow and your children orphans, aren't you?"

Miguel's flush deepened. "It is the only life I know, *Professôra.*"

"It *wouldn't* be the only life you know had you gone to school when you were younger, Miguel . . . I'm sorry there was no school back then, but what I don't understand is why you've condemned your

377

own two children to the same bleak existence."

Miguel shrugged and dropped his gaze. "I *may* allow my children to attend Padre Osmundo's new school," he conceded. "That is, if the priest can find a new teacher after you leave."

Tory lifted her chin. "We haven't yet established that I *am* leaving, Miguel. It may be Senhor *Sebastião's* intention that I go, but I haven't yet made up my mind. *I* may decide to stay."

Miguel stared at her with horror. "Oh, no, *Professôra,* you cannot! You are the Falcon's only weakness. For you, he would do anything—as he has already demonstrated. If you stay, he will be easy to catch and eventually to kill. You must leave this country, or Senhor *Sebastião* is as good as dead."

Tory had never viewed the matter in this light, but now that she thought about it, she decided that Miguel was right; Sebastian could still be manipulated through her . . . and maybe Miguel himself could be manipulated through his devotion to the Falcon.

"Miguel, I think I would feel better about leaving if I could just get a message to Padre Osmundo . . . I hate to leave without any explanation or even saying goodbye. I wonder if you would consent to deliver a letter to him when you see him."

"Of course, *Professôra!*"

"Good. I'll write the letter immediately, but the first thing you must do is take this embarkation ticket, and hurry down to the docks with it." She picked it up and handed it to him.

Miguel looked puzzled. "But, *Professôra,* what should I do with it down on the docks?"

"Why, you must exchange it for a ticket on a ship leaving in about three weeks time."

Miguel's eyes widened, and he started to protest, but she stopped him with an upraised hand. "No, Miguel . . . I'm not returning home until I see Padre Osmundo again. In my message, I'll ask him to come here to Salvador. Only *after* I speak with him face to face will I consent to go aboard *any* ship."

"*Professôra*, Senhor *Sebastião* will be furious. More than that, you will be endangering his life, as I just said. He will surely insist on staying here in the city to look after you, and he might encounter Senhor Cerqueira, and . . ."

"Then you see why you mustn't tell him that I'm still in town. Go ahead and leave with him for the *sertão*. I'll stay here in his house and live quietly until Padre Osmundo arrives. Everyone will think that the house is deserted."

"But, *Professôra*, you will have to go out to the market to get food to eat."

"Not if you find a little *empregada* to do the marketing for me . . . I promise you, Miguel, no one will know. I'll pay the girl extra to keep my presence here a secret. She can sneak in through the back gate in the second courtyard—the one the beggars always use. And I won't have to stick my nose outside the house until I leave to go to the ship . . . As private and sheltered as this house is, no one will suspect that it is occupied."

"That is true," Miguel grudgingly admitted.

"Then please do this for me, Miguel . . ." Tory pleaded. "My business with Padre Osmundo *may* actually help Senhor *Sebastião*. That's the *real* reason I don't want to go yet."

Miguel chewed his lower lip doubtfully, then sighed, and pocketed the embarkation ticket. "All right, *Professôra*. I'll do it, but I still think it would

379

be better for everyone if you returned to your own country with no fuss or arguments."

"Doesn't Filomena ever argue with you, Miguel? If she doesn't, she should. Women have worthwhile ideas, too, you know . . . Sometime, you ought to sit down and listen to what your wife has been thinking while you're off terrorizing the countryside."

Miguel frowned. "She doesn't like it, *Professôra*. She would prefer that I find a less dangerous way of making a living."

"Oh, well . . ." Tory said airily. "When you finally get shot and killed, your wife will undoubtedly find herself another husband . . . She's an attractive woman, and your children are adorable. Some other man will come along to warm your wife's bed and raise your offspring."

Miguel's frown deepened. "She had better not allow anyone else into her bed!"

"You can hardly prevent it if you're dead, now can you? No, it would be far better if you stuck around to take care of her and the children yourself."

"I suppose it would . . ."

By now, Miguel was glowering like a wounded bear. Tory smiled smugly to herself. She enjoyed sowing seeds of discontent among Sebastian's loyal *vaqueiros*. If, by some miracle, what she had in mind actually worked, then she wanted *all* of Sebastian's followers to be anxious to try some other line of work. Maybe Miguel would mention their conversation to other husbands with wives and children. She hoped he would. Did these men really think they would live forever? The life expectancy of a bandit had to be very short—and that was why she was willing to try anything to cut short Sebastian's career.

"Please let me know when you find an *empregada*

380

for me, Miguel. Now, you had better hurry down to the docks and see about exchanging that ticket."

Padre Osmundo arrived in Salvador two weeks later, just as Tory was beginning to despair that he was ever coming. She heard someone banging on the back gate of the second courtyard and knew immediately that it must be him. Gabriella, the little *empregada* Miguel had found to do her marketing, never knocked. She just scurried inside the unlocked gate, left the food in the cookshed and hurried out again, as if the place was haunted. Of course, Tory had taken pains to maintain the appearance of the house being deserted; superstitious, little Gabriella didn't like to linger in such a gloomy, silent place.

The ground floor shutters were all boarded and nailed shut, and Tory only opened the second story windows overlooking the inner courtyard after dark, for fear that someone walking by in the alley might see them and wonder who was living there. She spent most of her day reading in the darkened library, did her chores and cooking at night, and kept the outside gate locked, except for the time when Gabriella was due to arrive. Such a solitary existence was beginning to get on her nerves; therefore, the loud knocking sent her flying to the gate to open it. Once there, however, she remembered caution and peeked through the slats to see who was there.

"Senhorita *Rei!*" a familiar voice boomed. "If you are in there, please let me in . . . Poor Percy is about to expire from thirst."

Tory gladly threw the gate wide open, and Padre Osmundo led the tired, limping beast into the courtyard. "My goodness, what happened?" she exclaimed. "You both look terrible."

Padre Osmundo waved a hand impatiently. "Never mind me . . . See to poor Percy. It's a long way from Espirito Santo, and neither of us particularly relishes each other's company. I don't like to ride, and he doesn't like to carry me."

"How is your ankle?" Tory fussed, taking the animal's reins. "I hope it's in better shape than Percy's hoof. He must have picked up a stone or bruised himself to be limping so badly."

"Oh, my ankle still hurts every now and then, but it's much better. I'll go find a patch of shade while you tend to the poor beast. You must excuse me, but I have reached the end of my strength."

As Padre Osmundo limped into the courtyard, Tory shook her head in sympathy. She had not realized what a sacrifice she had demanded of the priest and the horse. She led Percy back out into the alleyway to the lean-to where Renegade was usually stabled. Fortunately, Sebastian had left some forage and a clean bed of straw for the next time he came to town. Percy whinnied plaintively at the sight of such luxury, and Tory hurriedly unsaddled him, rubbed him down, fed, and watered him. Then she confined him in the lean-to and hurried toward the house.

Padre Osmundo was waiting for her in the cool, dark library. He lifted a large glass of brandy and smiled ruefully. "I hope you don't mind. I helped myself. After that long, dusty journey, I needed something to soothe my parched throat."

"It's not up to me to mind, Padre. That's Sebastian's brandy, but I'm sure he wouldn't begrudge your enjoyment of it."

"Then enjoy it I shall." Padre took a large swallow, then sighed appreciatively as he leaned back in the large leather chair. "Oh, my child . . . I'm quite put out with both you and Sebastian, you know. Carmelita, too. You should have told me the truth, not fed me a pack of lies to get me out of town on short notice. Not only was Carmelita's *Tio* Bruno not dying, but he held a pistol to my head and threatened to shoot me, if I ever set foot in Jacobina again. I was lucky to get out of town alive."

"Please forgive me, Padre. We only did it to protect you . . . Had we told the truth, you would have gone to the school and played right into Cerqueira's hands."

"Well, Cerqueira got what he wanted anyway, didn't he? . . . And there's no way you can teach in my school now. Miguel is right when he says that your continued presence in Brazil threatens *Sebastião's* safety . . . Not that I'm speaking to *Sebastião* these days. That boy has broken my heart . . . All those years he lied to me and deceived me!"

While sympathizing with the priest, Tory felt compelled to defend Sebastian. "Yes, but he also gave you every spare *cruzeiro* he had and then some. He's not entirely wicked and vengeful, Padre. You of all people must realize that . . . Why, he regularly feeds the beggars here in Salvador, too, not just your poor peasants. If you don't believe me, ask Carmelita."

"Oh, I don't need to ask Carmelita anything . . . She is his greatest champion. She positively dotes on *Sebastião* and won't listen to a bad word about him. In any case, I didn't come here to discuss that subject. Why did you send for me, child? Why didn't you just get on that ship and go home? There's nothing you can do here now . . . Your grand adventure has ended. I regret all the unpleasantness you have suffered; I never meant for any of this to happen. When I heard how you were locked up in a convent, held captive against your will, I broke down and wept . . . It's inconceivable that a holy place such as a convent should be converted to a prison! . . . But I guess I cannot depend on anything anymore. The man I thought of as a son is actually a would-be murderer, and the heirarchy of Holy Mother the Church is guilty of more crimes than I care to enumerate."

Padre Osmundo took another deep swallow of the brandy, then sat gazing down at it with a self-pitying, woebegone expression. Tory wished that she knew how to comfort him. He had lost all the linchpins of his beliefs, and no one could restore his faith in them.

"Padre . . . I sent for you because I can't leave this country without trying one last time to save Sebastian's land. What Cerqueira has done to him is monstrous. He murdered Sebastian's parents in front of his eyes, then tried to kill Sebastian himself. He thought he had killed him . . . You can hardly blame Sebastian for wanting revenge; Cerqueira also stole his inheritance, and now, he's finally taken everything Sebastian owns . . . Why are you so hard on Sebastian, when Cerqueira is not just a would-be murderer, but a murderer, in fact?"

"Because I taught Sebastian better! Because he knows that violence and murder are not the answer."

"Then what *is* the answer, Padre? What do you suggest we do to make Cerqueira return even a small portion of what he has stolen?"

Padre Osmundo plunked his glass down on a nearby table. "I don't know! God help me, I'm supposed to know, but I don't! . . . However, I'm damned well certain that killing Cerqueira *isn't* the answer."

"Well, I have an idea, Padre . . . and that's why I sent for you. If it works, Sebastian will get back Paraíso, and I can stay longer and teach in your school, after all . . ."

"No, no—you can't teach there, no matter what

happens. Being responsible for you has made an old man of me . . . I committed a terrible mistake accepting your offer to come here. What I want in a teacher now is an ugly old Brazilian that no man in his right mind would look at, much less decide to kidnap, rape, or harm in any way. I want an educated Dona Guilhermina."

"If that's how you feel, then I *won't* teach there, even if my plan succeeds. Of course, if it fails, I won't be teaching, anyway. I'll be on a ship leaving Brazil in nine days' time. Miguel tried to book passage on a vessel leaving sooner, but there were no departures scheduled. It's still cold in the United States, and the shipping season isn't yet in full swing."

"It grieves me to admit it, my child, but that's how I do feel. I want an old dragon for my next teacher . . . So tell me about this plan, and define precisely how you expect me to help you."

"Padre, I want to see the archbishop, Cerqueira's cousin, about whom I've heard so much."

"You want to see Guedes Figueiredo? Whatever for, my child? He is not a man who makes himself accessible to any but the wealthy and influential."

"I expected as much. And I didn't want to make a public fuss about getting in to see him. Actually, I would prefer to meet him in secret. That's why I need *you* to obtain an audience for me. He probably would not see me on the strength of my own request, but I doubt he will say no to you."

Padre Osmundo shook his head. "I doubt he will say yes to me. Nor am I certain I wish to make such a request. If Figueiredo believes everything Cerqueira has told him about me, then the man has reason to confine me in a monastery . . . The last time I saw him privately—some fifteen years ago—we did not see eye to eye on things. He warned me not to incite

385

the *caboclos* to violence or rebellion in my quest to better their lives. I am charged with their spiritual needs only, not with improving their minds or cleaning up the filth and squalor in which they live, or anything else . . ."

"You mean to say that you have not discussed your work with him in the last fifteen years?"

Padre Osmundo gave a short, sharp laugh. "Dear child, I was hoping he had forgotten that I exist! Apparently, Mundinho Cerqueira has repeatedly reminded him . . . My illustrious superior did give me a rather piercing look the last time I attended him during the high mass at Pentecost . . . Feast days are the only times I usually come to Salvador, when the priests all gather to celebrate special liturgies. We take turns attending the archbishop. Few of us have much direct, personal contact with him, a fact that distresses many of my fellow friars—but for myself, I prefer it that way."

"Padre, I *must* get in to see him," Tory insisted. "He is our only hope."

Padre Osmundo flashed her a questioning glance. "You intend to appeal to his conscience—is that it? You hope to convince him to exert pressure on his cousin? I fear that will never work, my child. It is Mundinho Cerqueira who controls Guedes Figueiredo, not the other way around. That is what I have always heard, and I have never witnessed anything to convince me otherwise."

"Don't worry over what I shall say to him, Padre . . . Just worry over how I can obtain an audience."

Padre Osmundo leaned forward, extending one hand in mute supplication. His hand, she noticed, was dimpled and pudgy—endearing like the rest of him. "My child, why do you care so much what happens to Sebastian? He has charted his own course and obviously cares nothing about you. If he did care, he would be here—preventing you from leaving. Better yet, he would be accompanying you back to America, planning to build a new life with you there."

Tory swallowed hard against the lump in her throat. "I love him, Padre . . . and I understand why he has rejected me. He believes that he has no other choice. I tried to offer him alternatives—such as returning with me to America—but he could not accept the idea of walking away, defeated and humiliated. He has nothing left, Padre, except his pride."

"No, my child. That is where you are both wrong. He has *you*. He has your love for him. He has the life you two can share together."

"I tried to tell him that, Padre, but he couldn't see it! And now I find that I cannot bear the thought of walking away defeated and humiliated, either. I'm going to fight for him, Padre. I'm going to use every weapon at my disposal in order to win him . . . What other woman understands him as I do? What other woman really *wants* him, flawed as he is? . . . On the other hand, what man wants me, flawed as I am?"

Padre Osmundo patted her hand. "Any man who gets you, my child, will be getting a rare treasure indeed."

Tory smiled tremulously. "Perhaps, Padre, but it will take a man with a great deal of pride, arrogance, and conceit to tolerate me . . . I intimidate most men. They feel threatened by women who speak their minds and invade exclusively male territory . . . Sebastian himself complains and lectures, but in the end, I think he likes it. My audacity stimulates him, just as my sister-in-law's stimulates my brother . . . Sebastian is my one, true mate, Padre. Or so it seems to me."

Padre Osmundo sighed. "Then I suppose I must risk contacting the archbishop if you think it will somehow help things . . . I would not want to be responsible for depriving you of your one, true mate, my child."

Tory looked to see if he was teasing, but he only smiled at her affectionately.

"Promise me one thing," he said.

"What's that?" Tory inquired.

"If you somehow succeed in getting *Sebastião* to the altar, I want to be the one who performs the ceremony, and later, baptizes all the little *Falcãos*."

Tory's throat clogged with emotion. "I wouldn't have it any other way," she vowed. "No, dear Padre Osmundo, I wouldn't have it any other way."

Chapter Twenty-Six

Three days later, Tory and Padre Osmundo went to see Archbishop Guedes Figueiredo, who was residing at the monastery beside the *Igreja de São Francisco* until renovations were completed at his regular quarters.

"But I thought women were not permitted inside the monastery," Tory said as they approached the walled compound with its high wooden gate.

"Normally, they're not, but because the archbishop is staying here, several rooms and a portion of the monastery garden have been set aside for his use," Padre Osmundo explained. "That means that anyone who has the archbishop's permission can enter to conduct business, but may not, of course, intrude into other areas of the compound."

"I confess to being curious about how an archbishop lives," Tory continued. "Does he keep the same vows of poverty, chastity, and obedience as the monks?"

"Yes, but he doesn't practice them to quite the same extent. In his exalted position, he cannot remain secluded behind four walls, praying the entire day and night; he must oversee temporal matters as well as the spiritual welfare of the Church in his jurisdiction."

"I see," Tory responded thoughtfully. Remembering the gold-leafed walls of the nearby *Igreja de São Francisco*, she wondered if they reflected Figueiredo's taste for the ostentatious. She was trying to decide the best way to approach the man, but without having met him, couldn't commit to a definite plan. She would have to wait and see what occurred to her upon first impression—and hope that her first impression proved correct.

She also hoped that she herself made a good impression; to that end, she had groomed herself to squeaky-clean perfection. Not a mote of dust or trace of grime remained on her well-worn shirtwaist blouse and skirt. Her shoes shone like polished ebony, and her hair had been washed, brushed until it crackled, and arranged neatly and primly on top of her head. The *sertão* had long ago ruined her straw bonnet, but Carmelita had left behind a gauzy, black lace mantilla, which Tory wore over her head to give herself the appearance of a devout woman who regularly attended church.

Padre Osmundo gained immediate access to the compound by ringing the bell beside the entrance. The massive gate swung open to reveal a charming courtyard where flowers bloomed in a riot of red, pink, white, and gold. Enchanted, Tory stepped inside and followed Padre Osmundo and a silent, cowled monk down a flagstone path into one of the thick-walled buildings. It was dark and cool inside, and they were ushered into a small spare room that reminded Tory of a cell. It held three straight-backed chairs and a plain wooden table upon which a red clay pot was the only ornament. A single crucifix adorned the wall, and bars covered the solitary window.

As the cowled monk left the room and closed the door behind him, Padre Osmundo motioned for Tory to sit down. "We must wait here until the archbishop comes . . . I hope you know what you are going to say, because there's nothing *I* wish to discuss with His Grace . . . In view of how he has always felt about me, the sooner we are gone from here, the better."

"You shouldn't be nervous about meeting with your superior," Tory chided. "After all, you've done nothing wrong."

"I hope the archbishop doesn't disagree with you." Sitting down on the straight-backed chair, Padre Osmundo nervously thumbed the large brown rosary beads hanging from a rope around his ample waist. "I have always admired this monastery, but I'm not cut out to live a cloistered life . . . Barred windows and high walls make me feel uncomfortable. Give me the broad, open spaces of the *sertão* and the friendliness of my little parish house in Espirito Santo any day."

Tory hid a smile behind her hand. More than just high walls were bothering Padre Osmundo. Considering his fondness for good food and drink, she could not imagine him residing in an austere place like this where they probably served only bread and water for dinner. The monk who had admitted them had practically been a walking skeleton. His habit hung on his thin, bony frame like a sheet draped over a starvation victim.

Hearing a sound outside the door, Tory shot to her feet, as did Padre Osmundo. She wiped her moist palms on her skirt. Suddenly, she couldn't remember the proper etiquette for greeting an archbishop. Did one kneel and kiss his ring? Did he even wear a ring— or was that some other member of the Church hierarchy? How was she to address him?

The door opened, and a short, corpulent gentleman dressed in a black cassock trimmed with gold and purple waddled into the room. "Your Grace," Padre Osmundo said, sinking down on one knee.

"Now, now . . . we don't stand on ceremony in this humble abode, Padre Osmundo. Rise and be seated . . . You also, young woman. Take that chair over there. They are all equally uncomfortable. It's a penance just to sit down in this place. There's not a decent chair in the entire monastery. I know, I've tried them."

Tory gratefully resumed the seat she had been occupying. "Thank you, Your Grace. I'll try my best to suffer silently."

She hadn't meant the comment to sound disrespectful, but somehow, it did, causing Archbishop Guedes Figueiredo to look at her more closely. She in turn studied his round, puffy face. Folds of fat encased his tiny black eyes and thick lips. He bore little family resemblance to Mundinho Cerqueira, sporting no mustache or indeed little hair at all. Like Padre Osmundo, he was almost completely bald, except for a few tufts of wispy gray.

While Padre Osmundo made the proper introductions, she silently appraised the precious stones winking from several rings on the archbishop's pudgy fingers. The large crucifix hanging from a gold chain around his neck held an enormous glowing ruby, which, if sold, could provide enough money to feed all the beggars in Salvador for the next ten years. Tory grimaced in disgust . . . Padre Osmundo's excesses had always charmed her, but this man's gluttony seemed grotesque and sinful.

Marks of dissipation and over-indulgence ravaged the archbishop's fat face, leaving his eyes inscrutable but worldly-wise . . . She thought she detected a glint of humor in them, but could not be certain. In all likelihood, she had made a mistake by coming here, but she would give it her best try and also put in a good word for Padre Osmundo who was now watching her with an almost terrified expression. Obviously he was thinking the same thing; Archbishop Guedes Figueiredo would *not* be sympathetic to their cause.

"Thank you for agreeing to see us, Your Grace," she began calmly, seizing the initiative. "But before I tell you why I've come, I would like you to hear my confession."

The archbishop blinked. Padre Osmundo looked startled. Then the archbishop spoke. "Daughter, is that really necessary? I'm sure Padre Osmundo would be happy to assume the duties of your confessor . . . My time is limited and most valuable. I thought you had important business to discuss with me."

"Excuse me, Your Grace, but I was under the impression that no priest—not even an archbishop— could refuse to hear a person's confession. What business could you possibly have with me or anyone that is more important than absolving sin and saving an immortal soul?"

A shadow of anger crossed the archbishop's face. He glanced at Padre Osmundo, blaming *him* for this inconvenience. "All right, Senhorita *Rei*. Since you insist, I'll gladly administer the sacrament of penance. Do you prefer we go into the church and use a confessional, or will you be comfortable right here?"

"Here will be fine."

"Leave us a short while, Padre Osmundo. I trust this won't take long . . . unless, of course, the young lady is guilty of more sin than I judge by looking at her. She hasn't lived long enough to be a truly *great* sinner."

Tory chose not to respond to that; instead, she bowed her head, folded her hands, and closed her eyes in anticipation. As soon as Padre Osmundo departed, she slid off the chair, sank to her knees, and began. "Bless me, Father, for I have sinned . . . and these are my sins. First and foremost, I have all but lost my faith . . . I am clinging to it by a mere shred, and I seek your guidance and advice in this delicate, disturbing matter."

She paused, waiting, until Guedes Figueiredo finally responded. "What advice can I give you, daughter, when I don't know the source of your conflict? How is it that you are losing your faith?"

"Well, Your Grace, since my arrival in this country, I have witnessed the most horrible miscarriages of justice. In my naivete, I trusted that representatives of Holy Mother the Church would speak out about them and do all they could to stop them . . . Instead, other than Padre Osmundo, they have maintained a grievous silence, and by doing so, contributed to these heinous crimes."

Tory heard the creak of the chair as the archbishop shifted his weight. She didn't dare open her eyes and look at the man she was accusing. "To what exactly do you refer, daughter? I am a representative of Holy Mother Church, but I have no knowledge of any such vile crimes."

"Then you must not be very observant, Your Grace. I have seen children scavenging in the garbage and forced to steal in order to eat. I have observed beggars sitting on the church steps, in dire need of more than just a paltry handout. I have known a good man to embrace a life of crime, because the murders of his parents go unavenged and his lands have all been stolen . . . And I have seen a fine priest despair that he has made a difference, when he has spent his entire life working to aid the poorest of the poor . . ."

"The poor will always be with us, daughter," the archbishop interrupted. "Even Our Lord said that. There's little you or I or anyone can do in the face of dire poverty—except pray. As I have told Padre Osmundo in the past, prayer is always the best remedy."

"Perhaps, Your Grace, but I don't believe people should ask God to alleviate misery they themselves have caused or could eliminate . . . The poor *can* be helped. Indeed, the men I just mentioned—the priest and the-good-man-turned-thief—have been helping the poor a great deal, but with no assistance or encouragement from the Church in Salvador. That is what I find so incredibly disheartening."

Tory opened one eye and caught the archbishop fingering the huge ruby on his crucifix. Rather than looking indignant—or defending himself—as she had expected, he seemed subdued, as though he hadn't the nerve to deny it and might even be ashamed of himself.

"In fact," she continued, "I find it so disheartening that when I get home to America, I am going to visit the archbishop there and tell him all about it. I may even write the Pope. My family has always been on extremely good terms with His Holiness in Rome."

Archbishop Figueiredo abruptly dropped the crucifix. "Your family knows His Holiness, the Pope?"

"Of course . . . and we regularly entertain a well-known cardinal for dinner. Church authorities in my own country are ill-informed of the gross injustices in Brazil, but I intend to tell them everything I've discovered about the shocking laziness of the Church in Salvador."

"Lazy, are we? Are you sure we are not simply ignorant?" Figueiredo inquired. Both his hands and his voice had begun to tremble. "This good man that you say has turned to a life of crime . . . Tell me about him, if you will, daughter."

"Certainly . . ."

So Tory told him, leaving out very little except the actual names of the people involved. She had no doubt that Figueiredo knew who she was talking about . . . She mentioned Mundinho Cerqueira's personal connections to the Church at least three times, and each time she did, Figueiredo grew a little paler.

"Now you understand, Your Grace, why my faith has been so severely tested . . . I never dared imagine that evil men could exert such influence over a sacred institution founded by Christ. I never thought they could manipulate the clergy into helping them line their own pockets. I certainly never anticipated that they could hide behind the Church's authority, thereby protecting themselves from the dire consequences of their wickedness . . . Now that I have discovered how naive and foolish I was, I feel compelled to root out this cancer, and I will go to any lengths to do so."

Figueiredo bowed his head in an attitude of shame and defeat. He sighed deeply. "As well you should, daughter . . . As well you should."

When he lifted his chin, Tory was struck by the deep sorrow shimmering in the archbishop's black eyes. In that moment, he appeared both vulnerable and sincere.

"It is *I* who have sinned, daughter, not *you*," he said miserably. "For I suspected that these things were happening, but I ignored my own suspicions . . . You see, as a young man, I was pressured into becoming a priest when I did not really feel the calling. I was the second oldest in an influential family, and everyone knew that if I entered the priesthood, one day I would become a bishop or archbishop and control vast amounts of wealth and riches, far more than I could hope to inherit . . . I could not say no. It was my duty."

"But you could have stopped your family from taking advantage of your position," Tory pointed out.

Again, Figueiredo sighed. "I am not a rebel like you, Senhorita King. I am a peace-maker. I go along with things. I enjoy my little luxuries and the prestige my office brings me, and for the rest . . . I rarely think of it. Nor does anyone dare call these crimes to my attention. I assure you that I have received a very different version of the events you just described."

"Then I must tell you everything, Your Grace, and leave no doubt in your mind as to whom we are discussing. Your cousin, Mundinho Cerqueira, is the murderer I mentioned . . . And he has lied to you about Padre Osmundo as well. Padre Osmundo does not stir up the peasants and incite them to violence. He only wants to educate them so they can escape the poverty that entraps them. His little school will harm no one . . ."

"He has built a school for the *caboclos*?" Figueiredo sounded surprised—and interested. The school was a minor detail Tory had left out in her recitation of

Sebastian's and Cerqueira's history. "Who is teaching in this school?" he inquired.

"I came here to be the teacher," Tory admitted. "But before I even got started, your cousin threatened to destroy the building. He kidnapped me and held me prisoner in a convent in order to force *Sebastião Prêto*—his real name is *Sebastião Falcão*—to sign over his lands. Rather than endanger Senhor *Falcão* any further, I must now return home and fight this battle from a safer vantage point."

"Daughter . . ." Guedes Figueiredo took her hand as she knelt at his feet. "Your courage and dedication—and yes, your faith—shame me. For many years, I have been living in a dark hole of my own making, wishing I could see the light. Believing myself unworthy to be an archbishop, knowing *how* I came to be one, I have done nothing but augment the Church's wealth and administer my diocese . . . I have lived like a king in a gilded palace. Now, as the end of my life draws near, I find that I am sorely afraid . . . I have not lived as Our Master taught us. *He* never wore rubies the size of hen's eggs, and His best friends were thieves and murderers . . . When I face Him, what will I say? How can I justify the failures of my stewardship? I am not such a fool that I believe archbishops should only guard the gold on the walls of the *Igreja de São Francisco* . . . They must also shepherd the flocks entrusted to them."

The archbishop's face crumpled, and Tory feared he might burst into tears. She had thought to threaten and blackmail him, not shatter his composure and destroy his self-esteem. If he fell apart, she might not be able to put him back together again. "Your life isn't over yet, Your Grace," she soothed, almost feeling sorry for him. "There's still time to change its direction and right a few wrongs."

Figueiredo sniffed loudly. "I don't know . . . I wish I could. Do you think it's possible? Only yesterday, I was treated for a stomach ailment, and the doctor said I must mend my ways or die an agonizing, premature death . . . I must stop eating rich foods, walk long distances daily, and deny myself the fruit of the grape—*me*, an archbishop, forbidden to drink wine! Can you imagine it? . . . Why, I am much better at drinking wine than hearing confessions. I haven't heard anyone's confession in years, but I indulge my craving for wine everyday!"

Tory bit back a grin. "No one said it would be easy, Your Grace, but if you want to have time to accomplish some good in your life before you die, then you must follow the doctor's advice."

Figueiredo hung his head. "Yes, I must, mustn't I? . . . And I will start my personal reformation with *this*. Do not ask me how I shall do it, daughter, for I don't yet know. But somehow, I will make things right for *Sebastião Falcão*, Padre Osmundo, and you yourself . . . Will your faith remain strong if I can accomplish all that?"

"Oh, yes, Your Grace! My faith will be strong enough to . . . to move mountains."

"If I can accomplish all you ask, it *will* be moving mountains." Figueiredo chuckled. "Come now, tell me where I can reach you several days from now . . . I'll need at least that long to do anything. Then I shall give you absolution, unless you have other sins you wish to confess."

"Padre Osmundo can deal adequately with my other sins, Your Grace."

Figueiredo broke into a hearty laugh. "Yes, I'm sure he can," he chortled. "You saved the most

399

serious one for me, however, and that's only as it should be. An archbishop was meant to deal with the *big* sins."

"Thank you for hearing my confession, Your Grace."

"Thank you for insisting that I do so, daughter. You've opened my eyes as they haven't been opened in a long, long time."

"It was my pleasure," Tory demurred.

"I can see that . . . Beware the sin of pride, daughter. Speaking from experience, I can tell you that it is capable of cancelling out all other virtues and blinding you to your own faults."

"I'll try to keep my pride in check, Your Grace."

"Do you mean to tell me that you and the archbishop laughed together and parted *friends?*" Padre Osmundo demanded upon their return to Sebastian's house.

"Yes, we did, Padre, and he's actually a very nice man. All these years, you have simply misunderstood him . . . What he needs is a confidant, not a critic."

"*I* need a confidant, not a critic! This is unbelievable . . . I've known the man for twenty years and never gotten along with him, and you spend five minutes in his company and become his boon companion. How do you account for this?"

Tory arched her eyebrows coquettishly. "It must be because I'm a female, Padre . . . I don't know how else to explain it."

"*Cristo!*" Padre Osmundo exploded, using Sebastian's favorite epithet.

"Tut, tut," Tory scolded. "You should be ashamed of yourself for taking the Lord's name in vain. That

400

doesn't set a very good example for a poor sinner like myself."

"I was merely calling upon Him for wisdom and patience," the priest responded with wounded dignity. "Anyway, if I were you, I wouldn't rely too heavily upon Figueiredo's promises. He has been weak and vacillating all his life—always bending to his cousin's influence, among others within that powerful family. It's quite possible you'll never hear from him again . . . Just what are you expecting— that he'll return the deeds to Sebastian's lands?"

"I'm not *expecting* anything . . . I'm simply hoping. I believe I came along at the right time in the right place to encourage him to take control of his life and reform. I don't think he likes himself very much—at least, he doesn't like what he's permitted himself to become . . . This is his chance to regain his self-respect. It's an opportunity to do something good and defy his manipulative cousin all at the same time."

"Well, I hope you won't be disappointed, my child . . . Now, what are you planning to have for dinner? I would be delighted to help with the cooking."

Smiling, Tory led him to the cookshed and put him to work peeling onions.

Chapter Twenty-Seven

On the morning of the second day after her visit with the archbishop, Tory heard a timid knock on the front door of the boarded up house. She hurried into the courtyard, climbed on a stout wooden box, and peered over the wall to see who it was. A tall, cadaverous-looking monk stood on the doorstep. With a little cry of excitement, Tory jumped down from the box and dashed to the front door, arriving there the same time as Padre Osmundo.

"I thought I heard someone knock," the priest said. "Shall I open the door and see who it is? Or should we maintain the pretense that the house is deserted?"

"Open it!" Tory cried. "It's someone from the monastery."

They unbolted the door and threw it open, then motioned for the monk to come inside. He resolutely shook his head, then reached into one of his voluminous sleeves and withdrew a packet of papers. "These are for you, Senhorita, from His Grace, Archbishop Guedes Figueiredo. He sends warm felicitations along with his personal blessing."

Tory accepted the packet with shaky hands.

"Please tell him thank you . . . Are you sure I cannot persuade you to come inside and refresh yourself with a *cafèzinho* before you return to the monastery?"

The tall, skinny monk shivered, as if repulsed by the very idea. "No, Senhorita. I must hurry back where I belong. Whenever I leave the monastery walls, I become nervous and can't wait to return . . ."

Tory and Padre Osmundo exchanged glances of amusement. "Then I thank you for mustering the courage it must have taken to bring this to me." Tory indicated the packet with a nod. "I deeply appreciate it."

"God's blessings upon you both, Senhorita, Padre Osmundo . . . I doubt we shall see each other again." With a slight bow, he turned and hurried away, disappearing in the traffic along the street.

Closing the door on any curious onlookers, Tory whirled with the packet clutched tightly to her breast. "I hope this is what I think it is! Let's go see, shall we, Padre?"

"I hope it is, too," the priest said, following her into the main room. "But you must not be too upset if it isn't. I still don't believe the archbishop can reform that rapidly; it would be like a leopard suddenly changing its spots."

Tory went to a table near the life-size cross on the wall and began opening the packet and spreading documents out on the tabletop. "Look at these, Padre, and help me identify them . . . I don't read Portuguese as fluently as I speak it. Wait! . . . Here's a letter from His Grace."

"Give it here . . . I can read it more quickly," Padre Osmundo took the letter and briefly scanned it. Eyes alight, he began reading in a breathless voice. *"I hope the documents contained herein are what you wanted, daughter. I threatened my cousin with excommunication and everlasting torment in hell in order to obtain them. I have further insisted that he don sack cloth and ashes and join the beggars on the church steps of the Igreja de São Francisco for a period of forty days. His penance is to beg his bread as they do, and during that time, to reflect upon his many sins and ask God's forgiveness.*

"I myself have donned sack cloth and ashes, and for the remainder of my time on earth will live a life of true sanctity and humility . . . At least, I will try. You will note that some of these documents do not concern Senhor Falcão, but will be of great interest to Padre Osmundo. Please tell him that hereafter I expect an annual report of his accomplishments, coupled with a detailed list of his most pressing needs. He has been most lax in providing such information, and if he refuses to do so in future, I shall be forced to recall him to Salvador for a period of prayer and reflection, such as my cousin and I are undertaking . . . We are all subject to a higher authority, and I trust you will remind Padre Osmundo of that fact."

Padre Osmundo glanced up and caught Tory's eye. "You needn't remind me *yet*," he snapped. "I'll do anything to keep from being locked up in a monastery."

"Is that all he has to say?" Tory asked. "Or did you just read the important sections?"

"The rest consists of his best wishes for your continued good health and for a safe and pleasant journey back home to the United States."

"Well, then, put it down, and let's tackle these documents."

They were silent for several moments, during which the only sound was the crackle of parchment as they opened yellowed papers stiff with age.

"My God," Tory finally sighed. "It's . . . it's more than I ever dared hope for . . ."

"The deed to Paraíso," Padre Osmundo said reverently, placing a paper gently on the table. "The bill of sale for all of *Sebastião's* horses and cattle . . . and this . . . the most precious of all."

He handed Tory the oldest and stiffest of the documents. She took it with trembling fingers, knowing how much Sebastian would value it. It was the deed to the *Estância de Falcão*, the land, the house, and the assets that had once belonged to Sebastian's parents.

"He will be so happy!" Tory exclaimed. "This is what he wanted all those years—what he struggled so hard to obtain and mourned for so long, why he became the Falcon in the first place . . ." Tears of joy spilled down her cheeks, but she was barely conscious of them. "He's got it all back, Padre! Everything he ever lost to Mundinho Cerqueira has now been returned to him."

"Not quite, my child . . . Figueiredo cannot restore *Sebastião's* parents—nor the innocence he possessed before he saw them murdered. Nor his faith in God and the goodness he eschewed in order to dedicate his life to revenge . . . You must also be aware that half the assets listed on this deed to the *Estância de Falcão* no longer exist. The cattle and horses were either sold or assimilated into Cerqueira's own herds, and the house is no longer habitable. When Sebastian finally told me the story of his parents, he admitted that the house fell to ruin years ago . . . It was the land Cerqueira wanted, not the house. As a grown man, Sebastian visited the crumbling, abandoned structure, removed personal items from it, and brought them here to Salvador, I believe—or else he took them to Paraíso."

"No, he doesn't have everything he lost," Tory agreed, instantly sobered. "Sebastian will never regain all the things Cerqueira stole from him . . . But at least, he'll have the land that once belonged to the Falcons . . . Well, how are we going to tell him about this, Padre? What shall we do next? . . . Wait, before we decide, tell me what is in the documents the archbishop sent to *you*."

Grinning widely, Padre Osmundo waved one of them under her nose. "Well, my child, this one authorizes the annual salary for a teacher the diocese will now provide for my school . . . and this one," he picked up another, "is the deed to a piece of land on which a health post will eventually be built . . . and this last one certifies the creation of a special fund to build that facility. Donations will be solicited here in Salvador and at every church across the diocese, with the idea that the health post will serve the medical needs of *caboclos* all across the *sertão*."

"My goodness! Can one outpost really do that? The *sertão* is such a big place."

"No, but it can serve as a model for health posts in other places." Padre Osmundo's eyes glowed with enthusiasm. "It is more than this poor priest ever dreamed of . . . and I owe it all to *you*, my child."

"I can hardly claim credit," Tory denied. "I didn't really *do* anything."

"Oh, yes, you did . . . While the rest of us assumed that the archbishop was as much an enemy as Cerqueira, you kept an open mind and decided to confront him. You gave him the benefit of the doubt and in so doing, achieved a near miracle . . ."

"It wasn't quite like *that*, Padre . . ."

"At this point, what does it matter *how* it happened? The important thing is that it *did* happen . . . Oh, we must celebrate! I'll buy a bottle of wine for our dinner. We can invite that little *empregada* who's been doing the marketing—and we can prepare *feijoada,* and buy fresh bread . . ." He smacked his lips in anticipation. "I wish Carmelita were here to give us a hand with the cooking; she makes the best *feijoada* in the country . . ."

"You don't think we ought to fast and abstain in thanksgiving?" Tory teased. "I'm sure I can find some sack cloth and ashes around here somewhere."

Padre Osmundo pulled a long face. "God forbid we should do anything so foolish as that. This will be a night of gladness and celebration. I'll say a mass first. And we'll take the boards down from the windows in the dining room, to admit fresh air and make it less stuffy."

"If you insist, Padre . . . and tonight at dinner, we'll decide the best way to get word to Sebastian that he doesn't have to become a bandit on a permanent basis, after all."

Intoxicated with happiness, Tory did a little jig around the room. Laughing and cheering, Padre Osmundo joined her, and they danced to a tune only the two of them could hear. They didn't stop until Padre Osmundo suddenly tripped and stumbled backwards against the wall, nearly toppling the huge wooden cross that hung there.

"Gracious," he said, reaching out a hand to right it as it dipped crookedly. "I must be careful. This cross is so heavy, it would crack my head in two if it fell on me."

"Here, let me help." Tory assisted him in straightening the cross, which seemed much heavier than it looked. The wood was solid and dense, about six inches thick, from some tree Tory didn't recognize.

It was meant to call to mind Christ's death and glorious resurrection, but instead, it seemed to symbolize dark despair and oppressiveness. Tory decided to ask Sebastian to remove the cross if she came to live here as his wife . . . if he now asked her to marry him . . . if she said yes . . . and if they spent much time in Salvador. Would he now be willing to think about making a new life in America? She still wanted to get him as far away as possible from Mundinho Cerqueira.

In any case, the cross was simply too huge, taking up the entire wall space and dominating the room. She hoped he wouldn't mind giving it up, but resolved not to fight him if he refused. She was thrilled to be able to contemplate the thought of marrying Sebastian and soon forgot about the cross as she and Padre Osmundo made plans for their celebration dinner.

Tory was on her second glass of wine and Padre Osmundo on his third when a commotion on the doorstep brought their dinner to a sudden halt. The little *empregada*, Gabriella, stared at Tory with frightened eyes. The girl had accepted the dinner invitation with some trepidation, obviously unaccustomed to sharing elegant meals with employers. As yet, she had ventured only a sip or two of the wine—a fine Portuguese red that Padre Osmundo had bought in the marketplace.

"Should I see who is there, Senhorita?" she timidly inquired.

"Could it be Sebastian, do you think?" Tory asked Padre Osmundo. "Miguel said he wouldn't be returning to town for a long, long time."

"We'll never find out who it is unless we open the door," Padre Osmundo sensibly pointed out. "The two of you wait here. I'll be right back."

But Padre Osmundo did not immediately return. From the hallway came the sound of male voices—one slurred and angry, the other gently cajoling. Tory became alarmed. "Finish your dinner, Gabriella. I'll see what's keeping Padre Osmundo."

She rose from the table and hurried into the hallway, but Padre Osmundo and the unexpected visitor had already moved into the main room. Entering it, Tory felt her heart sink. The unexpected visitor was none other than Mundinho Cerqueira, and from the look and smell of him, he had been heavily drinking. He wheeled around, staggered, and almost collapsed as she called his name. "Mundinho Cerqueira, what are *you* doing here?"

"Oh, don't look so surprised to see me, Senhorita King . . ." Cerqueira said in the precise tones of a man finding it difficult to pronounce his words properly. "You know very well why I am here. I want thosh—those—deeds back. I never should have surrendered them to my cousin, but he shamed and bullied me so badly I had no choice . . . Not only did he threaten excommunication, but he alsho—also—vowed to turn our entire family against me . . . Me! The one who has worked, schemed, and slaved all these years to increase our wealth and add to our prestige and influence! . . . It'sh a little late to embrace holiness, now, I told him; I've had a pact with the devil for far too long . . . So that is why I am here, *Professõra*. Give me back the documents that my cousin gave you, and I shall leave you in peace—but resist me, and I'll kill you both!"

He waved his hand to include Padre Osmundo. Tory moved protectively nearer to the priest. Cerqueira's eyes were wild, his usually impeccable clothing disheveled, and she had never seen him so distraught. It must have taken a great deal of liquor to

409

put him in this dangerous state, and Tory knew she must act with caution, so as not to inflame him further. Mundinho Cerqueira was dangerous when sober; drunkenness had made him doubly menacing and unpredictable.

"We don't have them, Senhor Cerqueira. We . . . we hid them in a safe place until Senhor *Sebastião* arrives to take possession of them."

In point of fact, the papers were in a wooden box in Tory's bedchamber, but she thought it best to pretend that they were inaccessible.

"Where are they?" Cerqueira demanded, lurching toward her. "Tell me where they are, Senhorita, and we will go there and retrieve them."

"I . . . ah . . . left them with your cousin at the monastery. The monks locked them up in . . . wherever it is they keep their own valuables."

"You lie!" Cerqueira shrieked. "Guedes told me he sent them to you earlier today, and you accepted them. He thought to convinsh—convince—me that all was finished; I would never see them again . . . He had no right to do that! I told him so. We exchanged bitter words. I was so angry that I took a jeweled dagger he keeps on his desk to open important letters, and I . . . I . . ."

"You *killed* him with it?" Padre Osmundo gasped in a horrified tone.

Cerqueira nodded. His eyes were like burning coals. "I drove the dagger deep into his fat belly. He shquealed like a stuck pig and fell across his desk. Blood poured out of him like a fountain . . . I think he was dead when I left him. I do not know. After that, I came here . . ."

It was then Tory noticed the dark blotches on Cerqueira's garments. Blood had dried on his hands and splattered his elegantly-creased trousers. "You've

410

murdered your own cousin," she murmured. "There's blood on your hands and clothing."

"This can all be washed away. No one will believe I did it . . ." He reached into his coat pocket and extracted a gold chain from which hung a crucifix that Tory recognized by the enormous red ruby in its center. "There were no witnesses. The monks were all at prayer. They will think a thief broke into the monashtery in search of treasures, but all he found wash thish—this—gem my cousin always wore . . . Who knows? Maybe they will think it was the Falcon. I always warned people that one day the Falcon would go too far . . . I will insist upon leading a search to bring him to justice . . . But first, I will regain thosh deeds to his property."

Cerqueira reached into his pocket and withdrew a pistol, then waved it at them in vicious triumph. "Get me thosh documents!"

"But we can't!" Tory protested. "I swear to you— they are not here!"

Cerqueira raised his arm so that the pistol was aimed straight at her forehead. "I am going to count to three, *Professôra*. If you don't tell me where to find them, I will shoot you where you shtand—stand."

Tory hoped he was bluffing; surely, he must realize that if he shot her he would never get the documents. "I won't tell you . . ." she insisted.

"One . . . two . . ." Cerqueira counted.

As he reached the fatal number, Padre Osmundo made a sudden motion. From the corner of her eye, Tory saw the priest charge Cerqueira head-first and butt him squarely in the center of his chest. The pistol discharged as Cerqueira flew backward and banged against the wall, dislodging the huge, heavy cross that hung there. It teetered and swayed above him for a single spine-tingling moment. Mesmer-

411

ized, Tory watched as it came crashing down, the crossbeam striking Cerqueira squarely across the head and landing atop Padre Osmundo. Eyes widened in shock, Cerqueira slid down the wall and collapsed like a puppet with its strings suddenly cut. As he did so, the pistol fell near her feet.

A brief space of thunder-struck silence followed, and then Padre Osmundo complained in a breathless voice: "*Cristo!* This thing is heavier than I thought!"

The priest was struggling to get out from beneath the section of cross that pinned the lower half of his body to the floor. Tory helped lift one arm of it. As they worked together, breathing heavily from their exertions, a section of wood fell out of the back of the cross, and something bright, gold, and heavy clattered onto the parquet floor and lay gleaming in the lamplight.

"A gold ingot!" Padre Osmundo exclaimed. "Look! There are more ingots inside the cross. All we have to do is pry away the back of it. The entire thing is lined with gold bars!"

"Now we know why it's so heavy," Tory grumbled, lowering the cross beam as soon as Padre Osmundo had crawled to safety.

Wincing, the priest rubbed his legs. "Did I do it? Did I knock him out?"

Tory hurried to examine Cerqueira. Leaning over him, she picked up his hand and felt for a pulse, then put her head to his chest and listened for a heart beat. Life fluttered in him still, but the beat was very faint. Before she could do anything to save him, it faded and was gone. She straightened and somberly regarded Padre Osmundo.

"He's dead. That blow on the head must have killed him."

"God have mercy!" Padre Osmundo breathed a

long drawn sigh, then knelt by the dead man's side, took his hand, and began praying in Latin. It was the prayer for the dead and dying, but Tory feared that nothing could help Mundinho Cerqueira now. He had gone to meet the judgment of his Maker.

Feeling suddenly weak and shaky, Tory stumbled into the hallway where Gabriella met her with a stunned, disbelieving expression. "Oh, Senhorita," the girl said. "I heard everything . . . What will you do now? My brother carves beautiful caskets. Shall I go and tell him to make one and bring it to the house?"

"Mundinho Cerqueira doesn't need a beautifully carved casket," Tory responded. "A plain one will do . . . However, the monastery may require something fancier for the archbishop. Tell your brother to go there and ask the monks if he may supply it."

"*Sim*, Senhorita. I'll go at once. I don't wish to remain in a house where the devil has just claimed a man's soul . . . Beware that gold! It is probably cursed. If I were you, I would not touch it."

Tory accompanied Gabriella through the first courtyard and into the second, where the girl bade her good-bye at the back gate. As Gabriella disappeared into the night, Tory saw a light in the lean-to where Percy was stabled. Was someone trying to steal the animal? she wondered, starting toward it. A man suddenly emerged from the shed and headed in her direction.

She recognized the broad-shouldered, lean-hipped figure even in the darkness. Her heart jolted in her chest, and she felt a soaring sensation. Wings sprouted on her feet, and she broke into a run. "Sebastian! Oh, Sebastian!"

He caught her half-way, crushing her to him. "*Gatinha!* . . . I should have known you would disobey me and refuse to leave Salvador. Miguel finally admitted that you had stayed and sent for Padre Osmundo, so I returned as quickly as I could . . . What have the two of you been up to? What trouble are you causing now?"

Throwing her arms around him, Tory hugged him hard before she answered. The alley was no place to tell him everything that had happened, and anyway, joy at seeing him again had momentarily rendered her speechless. Releasing him after a long, wonderful moment, she gazed up into amber eyes that looked as glad to see her as she was to see him.

"Come into the house, Sebastian," she said at last. "Come into the house, and we'll tell you everything."

Chapter Twenty-Eight

"Confide in us, my son. Share with us what you are feeling," Padre Osmundo encouraged Sebastian when all the explanations had been completed, including how Mundinho Cerqueira had wound up dead on the floor of Sebastian's house.

Sebastian, Padre Osmundo, and Tory were seated in the dining room with the door closed, so they would not have to look into the main room and see Cerqueira's corpse still lying where Padre Osmundo had left it, covered with a clean sheet. The only thing they had done since Sebastian's arrival was haul the heavy cross out of the room, so they could remove the gold ingots inside it. The ingots now stood stacked on the table in two gleaming rows, each of them ten bars high.

"I know all of this must come as a great shock to you," the priest continued. "Given your penchant for hiding your feelings, even from yourself, I caution you not to deny the emotions of this incredible moment. It would be better for you in the long run to get them out into the open, now."

"I'm glad that Mundinho Cerqueira is dead," Sebastian admitted. "But I feel no great satisfaction that he finally got what he deserved. If anything, I am relieved that I don't have to be the one to kill him . . . I have carried the burden of that responsibility far too long. I'm happy to be free of it. As for the rest . . ."

Sebastian struggled to express his ambivalence. He did not honestly know how he felt about everything else. It was hard to summon any sympathy for Guedes Figueiredo; the archbishop could have stopped Cerqueira years ago, had his own greed not blinded him to his cousin's crimes. Naturally, Sebastian was elated to have Paraíso and his parents' property returned to him. As for the discovery of the gold ingots, that was nothing short of miraculous, more than compensating for the loss of the stock he would never recover from Cerqueira.

However, his elation was somehow anti-climactic. Of far more importance to him personally was the fact that Tory had come through everything in one piece. Had he lost her, nothing else would have mattered—not the land, cattle, stock, or gold ingots.

Finally, at long last, he was able to ask her to marry him, but he could not bring himself to say the words while Mundinho Cerqueira's body still lay in his house. Its mute, grisly presence effectively deterred all mention of romance; how could he pledge passion, love, tenderness, and commitment to a woman, while the body of his worst enemy polluted the very air he breathed?

"I want to get him out of here as soon as possible," he told Padre Osmundo. "This very night, I will find someone to make a coffin. In the morning, we'll transport the body to the *Igreja de São Francisco*. The monks can inform Cerqueira's family of his death; they can also make all the arrangements for a joint funeral for him and his cousin."

Padre Osmundo nodded. "As good an idea as any."

416

"I know someone who would be delighted to make the coffin," Tory volunteered. "Gabriella's brother. She already left to tell him about the archbishop's death."

"Gabriella?" Sebastian questioned. "Who is she?"

"The young woman who's been doing my marketing." Tory smiled at him. "However, I no longer need her services now that my presence here in your house need not be kept secret any longer."

Sebastian allowed himself a long, lingering look at the woman he loved, the woman who had restored to him all that he thought he had lost and more. Having sent her away, he did not feel deserving of all she had done for him. He had rejected her, but instead of leaving, she had stayed and convinced Guedes Figueiredo to repudiate his cousin.

Admittedly biased, he thought Tory was angelically beautiful. She had regained some of the weight she had lost while incarcerated in the convent, but she was still on the thin side, her fragile bone-structure almost transparent. Her blonde delicacy had always had the power to wring his heart, but now, coupled with the new maturity she exhibited, it took his breath away. No longer was she a child-woman, a charming combination of innocence and sensuality; Tory King had become *all* woman—confident and sure of herself and what she wanted.

Her shimmering gray-green eyes met his without any coyness or pretense. They told him that she was waiting for *him* to make the first move. She had done all she could, and now it was his turn. He longed to take her in his arms and lead her upstairs, but would not shame her in front of Padre Osmundo. The next time they made love, it must be as man and wife. He wanted *nothing* to stand between them; his commitment would be total and irrevocable. Never again

417

would he debase their love-making by trying to avoid pregnancy. He could imagine no greater joy or pride than one day holding a child born of their passion.

Since he could only satisfy his longing by gazing at Tory, he gazed long and hard. A small, gentle smile played about Tory's tender mouth, as if she knew precisely what he was thinking. He felt himself blushing like the greenest schoolboy at the transparency of his thoughts . . . What he wouldn't give for one of her sweet, delicious kisses! When Padre Osmundo glanced the other way, she blew him one, and he had all he could do to keep from jumping up and carrying her out of the room.

Afraid that Padre Osmundo would realize what they were both thinking, Sebastian tore his glance away from Tory and concentrated on the matter at hand—getting rid of Cerqueira's body. "I will handle everything," he told Padre Osmundo. "I'll hire a cart and driver to haul the coffin to the church. You and I should be able to carry it into the sanctuary. Then I'll go next door and inform the monks of what has happened."

"No, that should be *my* job—telling the monks," protested Padre Osmundo. "You needn't seek to spare me the ignominy of admitting that I was the one who killed Cerqueira. I did, you know. I butted him in the chest, and he fell back against the wall and knocked down that huge, heavy cross—which reminds me, how did all those gold ingots get into the wood, in the first place?"

"I have no idea," Sebastian said. "But if you had *not* done what you did, he might have killed you both, and I never would have known they were there."

"Where did the cross itself come from?" Tory quizzed. "And why did you hang it on your wall? The

418

weapons I can understand, but the cross always did puzzle me."

"The cross belonged to my parents," Sebastian informed them. "And before them, probably to my grandparents. It was one of the mementoes I took from our house when I returned to Brazil after completing my schooling in America. The cross and the silver rosary were still hanging on the walls of my parents' house, though the house itself was crumbling . . . The cross always hung in the main room, but the rosary was displayed in the dining room. Cerqueira took everything of value—the furniture and so forth—but he touched nothing of a religious nature . . . I suppose I will never learn who sealed the gold into the cross, but I suspect it must have been my grandparents. Perhaps, when they came to this country, they sought to hide their wealth and then died before they could tell my father about it . . . They did die suddenly, I recall, but how or why escapes me."

"You could not have been very old when your own parents died," Tory observed. "I am amazed that you can remember the cross and the rosary . . . Wait a minute!" Her eyes lit like glowing emeralds. "If your grandparents hid something in the cross, maybe they also concealed items of value inside the rosary!"

Sebastian leaped out of his chair at the suggestion. "Wait here," he said. "You needn't enter that room again until Cerqueira's body is removed. I will go and get the rosary."

He departed, went into the main room, and sparing only a glance at the sheet-shrouded figure, lifted the rosary from the pegs that held it on the wall. The rosary was nowhere near as heavy as the cross had been, but it did seem weightier than he would have expected. He carried the rosary into the dining

419

room, shut the door, and spread the silver beads out on the table.

The beads were intricately and beautifully carved, each the size of a ball that might fit a child's small hand. However, the silver was badly tarnished. No one had cleaned it since Carmelita had taken it upon herself to polish the fine old sterling. "Help me check the beads," Sebastian invited Padre Osmundo and Tory. "If you find one that is heavier than the rest, let me know . . . I don't want to destroy the rosary needlessly."

"That would be a desecration," Padre Osmundo agreed. "The rosary may have been blessed, not merely used for decoration. We must handle it reverently."

No one spoke for several moments, while they carefully examined the individual beads. Tory discovered the first that felt different from the others. "This one," she said, gently shaking it. "Do you hear the rattle? There's something inside this bead."

Sebastian took the bead and twisted it. Both sides were joined to the other beads by a short, silver chain. The chain on one side suddenly popped out, leaving a small hole in the bead. Sebastian tapped the bead on his palm. A half dozen small round objects fell out through the hole and lay glittering in his outstretched hand.

"*Meu Deus!*" Padre Osmundo cried. "What are they?"

Sebastian lifted one and turned it in the light; it sparkled with a radiant fire. "Diamonds, I believe . . . small, perfect diamonds."

"Oh," Tory breathed. "They're beautiful!"

"They will look lovely set into a necklace or ear bobs for a certain woman I know."

His suggestion made Tory blush furiously. That's

exactly what he would do with them, Sebastian decided. And he would insist that she wear them when they made love—the diamonds and nothing else.

He set the diamonds on the tabletop. "Let's check the rest of the beads, shall we?"

They examined each one, and before they were finished, discovered small caches of emeralds, more diamonds, several rubies, and a handful of gorgeous sapphires. Sebastian's grandparents must have converted everything they owned in America into jewels and gold ingots, keeping out only what they needed to start a ranch in their new country . . . Unfortunately, they died before they had a chance to spend any of the treasure, or else they were using it bit by bit, as the need arose.

Sebastian suddenly recalled his father talking about a patrimony set aside for him, the first-born son. "This must be the inheritance my father once mentioned to my mother," he said wonderingly. "I recall my mother begging my father to use some of it to buy land with water rights, so our cattle would not have to cross Mundinho Cerqueira's land to get to the river . . . and I remember my father shouting: *'No! Never! . . . This drought will be over soon, and then we will have all the water we need from our own wells. We must not touch the boy's patrimony. His grandfather charged me with holding it in trust for our little* falcão.'"

Sebastian had forgotten that conversation until now. He had locked it away in a corner of his mind with all the other painful, half-forgotten memories. He glanced first at Padre Osmundo and then at Tory. "All this time, while I was scheming and struggling to build my empire and destroy my enemy, I had wealth and riches right beneath my nose. I could have bought anything I wanted . . ."

"And built schools without resorting to thievery," added Padre Osmundo. "My . . . my . . . It was here all the time."

"But you didn't know it," Tory reminded both of them. "Oh, Sebastian, what will you do now? You are richer than you ever dreamed you could be."

Yes, Sebastian thought to himself, but his wealth did not lie in the gold ingots or the glittering jewels spread across the tabletop. His wealth lay in the love of the blonde-haired woman gazing at him from across the room. The gold of her hair far outshone the ingots, and her eyes shamed the diamonds and emeralds. Her shining, precious love was priceless, worth more than all the treasures a man could steal or inherit.

"I will think on the matter and tell you tomorrow, *gatinha—after* we dispose of Cerqueira's body. What *I* want to do depends upon what *you* want to do, so you had better be thinking seriously about your own future."

"I will," she answered breathlessly.

Smiling to himself, as if he had a great idea, Padre Osmundo picked up one of the sapphires and held it near the light. *"Sebastião,* if you grant me this one small treasure, I promise you I will make good use of it."

"For what, Padre? I thought Figueiredo already made arrangements for you to pay a teacher and build a health post. What more could you possibly want?"

"I want to buy land . . ." the priest said, his eyes dreamy.

"Don't tell me you are growing greedy like the archbishop!"

"No, *mon filho."* Padre Osmundo gave Sebastian

a wounded look. "I am not greedy, not for myself, but this sapphire could buy land that my poor peasants in Espirito Santo could use to grow their own crops and raise their own cattle. They could jointly share in the labor and ownership, and benefit from the rewards . . . When the rains come, they can grow a surplus of food to tide them over during the season of drought, and never again will they fall victim to the neglect and cruelty of the big *fazendeiros*."

"You never quit, do you, Padre? . . . Go ahead. Take two or three sapphires, but leave the diamonds alone."

"Thank you, *mon filho*." With a wide grin, the priest bent over the gems to make his selection. "I do not know how God feels about it, but it seems to me that your ever-abundant generosity is fair retribution for all the sins you have committed in the past."

"What sins? Do you mean my secret life as a bandit? You, Padre, are a better bandit than I ever was. What retribution do *you* intend to make?"

"I will think of something," Padre Osmundo sniffed. "Perhaps I will force myself to continue being your devoted friend. You need all the friends you can get, my son."

Sebastian could not help laughing. "Indeed, I do, Padre!"

Again, he caught Tory's eye. She mouthed a silent message to him; *I love you*. He mouthed it back, and they grinned at each other, like two silly, love-sick fools. Tomorrow, he thought. Tomorrow cannot come soon enough.

Early the next morning, immediately after the church doors opened, Sebastian, Padre Osmundo, and two men Sebastian had hired, carried Mundinho

Cerqueira's casket up the center aisle of the *Igreja de São Francisco*. Tory followed several steps behind the little procession and slipped into a pew near the back of the church. She did not know how long this would take, but she was anxious for the whole thing to be over.

Today, she and Sebastian would decide how to spend the rest of their lives. Today, they would make plans and dream dreams. Today, she would hear the words she had been waiting to hear since the day she first met Sebastian: *I love you. I want to marry you. Will you marry me?*

She would say yes, and they would live happily ever after . . . or would they?

Tory had not been able to sleep last night. She had lain in bed, hugging herself in anticipation, wishing that Sebastian were there in bed beside her. At the same time, she had been glad of his sudden discretion; she had no desire to shock Padre Osmundo or rush Sebastian into anything. She and Sebastian still needed to discuss several vitally important issues, such as where they would live, how they would live, and what sort of husband he intended to be.

The latter gave her the most worry. That he would be faithful, she had little doubt, for they had already settled that issue between them. What bothered her now was the question of what he expected of her as his wife. Would he demand that she stay at home all of the time, wherever home was, and never teach again, never work to advance women's rights, never ride horses or bicycles, never wear knickerbockers, never argue politics or religion . . . ?

Tory loved Sebastian with all her heart, but if he tried to prevent her from being herself, she foresaw a great deal of unhappiness ahead for both of them . . .

Now was the time to confront these issues, before they married and said or did things to hurt each other. She had tossed and turned all night in a desperate attempt to resolve matters in her own mind and decide what was most important to her—and by this morning, she was more confused and upset than ever.

Sebastian meant more to her than anything. Loving him meant complete and total surrender; therefore, she was willing to compromise and sacrifice certain things in order to appease and make him happy. But she could not help dreading what he might demand. No such fears and doubts had assailed her earlier; when it came time to confront the archbishop, she had never hesitated. Why was she so afraid and hesitant now?

Moving to kneel instead of sit, Tory bowed her head and prayed that she and Sebastian would do the right thing and make the right decisions. She prayed for inspiration to say what was in her heart without angering or provoking Sebastian. The greatest barrier to their love, Mundinho Cerqueira, no longer existed. God—or fate or chance—had removed that barrier, and Tory now hoped that God—or fate or chance—would intervene again to help her and Sebastian forge a commitment strong enough to last a lifetime.

She also prayed for the souls of Cerqueira and the archbishop. Cerqueira's was probably damned, but that was God's judgment to make, not hers. For the archbishop, she felt pity and grief; it seemed a shame that Figueiredo had to die when he had only just begun to live a worthwhile life.

So engrossed was she in her prayers that she did not hear anyone enter the pew beside her. But suddenly, she felt a hand on her arm. *"Gatinha,* come outside with me. I want to talk to you while we wait for Padre Osmundo to visit the monastery and speak to the monks."

Glancing up at Sebastian, Tory nodded. Her mouth suddenly went dry, and her heart thumped a loud tatoo. Wordlessly, she followed Sebastian out of the church. He led her to the wagon they had used to transport Cerqueira's coffin, then nodded to the man who owned it.

"Let me borrow your horse and wagon for a short while, will you? We won't be gone long."

The man gave his assent, and Sebastian helped her onto the seat and sat down beside her. Then he took up the reins and clucked to the tired-looking beast in the traces.

"Where are we going?" Tory asked.

"To a beautiful, private spot I know that overlooks the *Bahia dos Todos Santos.*"

"Why are we going there?" Tory persisted.

He slanted her a warm, amused glance. "Do not tell me you cannot guess, *gatinha.* We're going there to have that talk I mentioned yesterday . . . You are ready to talk, aren't you?"

"I suppose so," Tory answered.

Her lack of enthusiasm drew his attention. "Do not look so scared . . . I thought you would be happy to finally have this little talk."

"I thought so, too." Tory nervously twisted a portion of her skirt between her fingers. "But now, I'm reconsidering."

Sebastian hooked an arm around her waist and pulled her closer to him on the seat. "Smile, *gatinha* . . . I am hoping this will be the happiest day of both our lives."

Tory tried to smile but found she could not.

426

Despite the warm sunlight, her face suddenly felt frozen.

"*Cristo*," Sebastian muttered, frowning at her expression. "This is not starting out very well."

He snapped the reins on the horse's rump, and the wagon lurched forward and rumbled down the cobblestones.

Chapter Twenty-Nine

Tory maintained a grim silence as the wagon creaked noisily through Salvador's narrow streets, then climbed steadily upwards until it reached a winding road that ran alongside a cliff overlooking the sea. The view of brilliant blue sky and water far below was breathtaking, drawing her eyes to the curve of white sand beach and lush, green palm trees that rimmed the beautiful Bay of All Saints.

Tory would have been enchanted, had she not been so miserable. Sebastian drove the poor horse relentlessly until they reached the very end of the road. It stopped abruptly at a lonely, deserted spot in the middle of a circle of palm and banana trees. The trees shielded the wagon from view, had anyone been there to view it. No one was, for the road had no destination, save this quiet, sheltered spot overlooking the bay. Still, it was a place of rare beauty and tranquility, where land, sea, and sky came together in perfect unity.

"Where are we?" Tory asked. "Why is there a road leading up here, but nothing to see when you arrive? I mean, nothing built here . . . The view itself is magnificent."

"This is a little piece of property I own," Sebastian said. "I was always going to build a house up here one day, but never did. Probably because I never found the right woman to share it with me."

"I s—see," Tory stammered. "It's . . . um . . . very isolated, isn't it?"

Sebastian set down the reins and climbed out of the wagon. "It's not nearly as isolated as Paraíso. With servants and a half-dozen youngsters running around, it would not seem at all isolated. It took us less than a half hour to get here from the city . . . You should see the view at night, when the town's lights can be seen . . . You would swear it is the most beautiful spot on earth."

He came around to her side of the wagon and held out his arms to lift her down. But he did not let go of her when her feet hit the ground. "Would you find it so terrible to live up here when we come to Salvador?" he growled, clamping her tightly against his big body.

"No," she whispered. "It is indeed beautiful . . . Do you envision us coming to Salvador often?"

"We'll come as often as you like," he purred in her ear. "I have been thinking, *gatinha*. With all the land and money I now possess, we can do anything we want. Our children can be citizens of the world, raised both here and in the *Estados Unidos*. We can buy land near your brother, if that would please you, and start our own horse farm in your country. We could live there for part of the year and spend the other half in Brazil, either here in Salvador or at Paraíso . . . What do you think of that idea?"

Tory was overwhelmed. "Oh, Sebastian! There's nothing I would love more! Do you really mean it? You would be willing to spend time in America as well as here in Brazil?"

429

He leaned back and regarded her with a puzzled expression. "Why wouldn't I mean it? I intend to search for my roots, *gatinha,* and how can I do that if we never spend any time in the country where my grandparents once lived?"

"But who will look after Paraíso and your horses and cattle here?"

"Miguel, Teodoro, and the rest of my *vaqueiros* . . . and in America, we will have your brother to keep an eye on things for us. We will find good people, I am sure, both here and there. We'll offer our workers good pay, pleasant surroundings, and education for their children."

"Education for their children . . . What do you mean by that, Sebastian?"

Again, he regarded her in surprise. "Well, you are a teacher, aren't you? So why should we not have schools on our farm and our *estância?* We will need good schools for our own children. You will have to be in charge of that; I know nothing about schools."

Tory could hardly breathe for excitement. "You will let me teach, if I want, for as long as I want?"

"Of course, if you have time, considering all the help I will need in riding and training our horses in two different countries."

"Riding and training!" Tory gasped.

Sebastian shook his head in exasperation. "Perhaps you prefer that I buy a bicycle for you to ride in the *Estados Unidos,* but I thought you would choose horses over bicycles."

"I already have a bicycle! . . . I also have a cat and dog that I'll want to keep."

Sebastian cocked an eyebrow at her. "What next? Please don't tell me you also have an elephant; that would be going too far, I think."

430

"Oh, my dearest, darling Sebastian!" She flung her arms around his neck. "I can't believe you will let me do all those things—ride and teach and live half of every year in the United States!"

He held her tightly, as if she were the most precious thing in all the world to him. "Do you think I do not know what will make you happy, *gatinha?* Did you really believe that I meant to make you suffer for the rest of your life? . . . Little one, I cannot promise that we will never disagree, or that everything you want will always meet with my approval . . . But I *can* promise to try and see your side of things. Already, you have forced me to revise my entire philosophy regarding women."

"I have?" She tilted her head to look up at him. "And what have you learned about women since meeting me?"

"I have learned that women are . . . brave, courageous, capable, and intelligent. Those are qualities I once associated only with men."

"Then you now admit that we are *equal* to men."

"I did not exactly say that . . . You are not as strong as I am. You are not as tough . . . You are not as stubborn."

She stiffened slightly and stared him down until he chuckled sheepishly. "Well, maybe you are all those things, too—but in a different way. That is something we can argue about forever, something to keep us occupied when there is nothing else to do."

She leaned into him, rubbing against him like a cat wanting to be stroked and petted. "Will there ever be a time when there's nothing else to do but argue differences and similarities between men and women? Somehow, I don't see too much chance for boredom in our busy future."

"I don't either," Sebastian smugly retorted. "That's

431

why I decided not to fight you about how you spend your time. A busy woman is a contented woman . . . and above all else, I want you to be content, *gatinha*."

"I will be," she sighed. "And maybe not so hard to get along with as you think. Before you offered me the gift of your willingness to let me do all those things, I was willing to forego some of them in order to please you."

"Which ones?" he demanded.

"I won't tell you. It's better that you never know."

"Cristo!"

"Shhhhh . . ." she soothed. "Don't be angry, Sebastian. You've taught me a few things about men, too."

"Such as?"

"I have learned that men can be tender, gentle, generous, affectionate, giving, and romantic—qualities I once associated only with women."

"Maybe love is the great equalizer between the sexes," Sebastian mused. "It strengthens women and gentles men. It enables both sexes to conquer their weaknesses and discover new dimensions in their characters and personalities."

"That's very profound! I never knew you could be so profound."

"I can be anything you want me to be," Sebastian whispered. "Just say that you love me and intend to marry me."

"You haven't asked me to marry you," Tory pertly reminded him.

"Gatinha, will you marry me?"

"Yes, Sebastian, I most definitely will."

"Then let's go back to Salvador and collect Padre Osmundo and have him do the thing immediately, this very day."

"Today? Immediately? But . . . but I always wanted

to have a big wedding at Castle Acres with my brother and my sisters present . . ."

"We'll do that, too," Sebastian assured her. "That will be our *second* ceremony, but today will be our *first* . . . I promised myself I would not make love to you again until you were my wife; you don't want me to *break* that promise, do you? Not now, when I am getting so proficient at being good . . ."

"All right," she agreed, knowing that Sebastian would never be able to wait months before they made love again—and neither would she. "We'll have him perform the ceremony as soon as possible, but then we'll renew our vows at Castle Acres in front of my entire family."

"An excellent plan . . . Let's leave now."

They climbed into the wagon and hurried back to Salvador. At the monastery, a jubilant Padre Osmundo awaited them. "He isn't dead! The archbishop isn't dead! Figueiredo will recover, the monks tell me. Cerqueira didn't succeed in killing him, after all, and he's more determined than ever to make the Church the servant of the poor and downtrodden."

"That's wonderful news, Padre," Tory said. "And we have some wonderful news of our own."

"Don't tell me; let me guess." The priest eyed them speculatively. "You two are going to get married!"

"Were you, perhaps, hiding in the wagon, spying on us?" Sebastian growled.

"*Sebastião, mon filho,* you must show more respect for me and my sacred office, or I shall refuse to perform the ceremony."

"Must I grovel at your feet, Padre? We want to get married today."

"What? Today? But that is impossible!"

"That's what I told him, Padre," Tory cut in. "But he wouldn't listen."

433

"Not today, *Sebastião*. It cannot be done. The bans haven't even been posted. And who will be your witnesses? You know what they say. Marry in haste; repent at leisure . . . No, you cannot get married today."

"It will be today, or I'll never give you another *cruzeiro!*" Sebastian snapped.

"It will be a month from now, or I'll ban you from all the sacraments!" Padre Osmundo threatened.

"The longest I'll wait is until tomorrow," Sebastian shot back.

"Three weeks from now!" the priest insisted.

"*Two* days, and not a minute more."

"Two weeks!"

"*Four* days!"

They finally settled on one week, while Tory stood by, tapping her foot in mortification and annoyance. "Have you two finished shouting at each other and arguing right in the middle of the street?"

Both men regarded her with some surprise, apparently having forgotten she was there.

"I would like to have my first wedding ceremony in Espirito Santo," she haughtily informed them. "With Quinquina, Carmelita, Teodoro, and Amâncio as witnesses and attendants—and also, Miguel. We will have a grand *festa* and invite everyone in town. Then Sebastian and I will go home to Paraíso for a one week honeymoon, and then return here to Salvador and board a ship leaving for America . . . We would like you to go with us, Padre, and perform the second ceremony at my brother's home."

Padre Osmundo blinked owlishly. "But *two* ceremonies are unnecessary, my child."

"It is what I want," Tory announced. "What Sebastian and I both want . . . Besides, if Sebastian has to repeat his vows a second time, they will tend to sink into that thick head of his and remind him that he is really married."

"I won't need to be reminded, *gatinha*. I know very well what I am promising . . . However, I wish you would rethink your desire to have our first ceremony in Espirito Santo. It will take us a week or more just to get there."

"Perhaps, but we can be patient awhile longer, can't we?" Tory gave Sebastian her most winsome smile. "I do so want all of the peasants to attend our wedding, too . . . and what about Ramiro Bastos? He should certainly be invited."

Sebastian sighed. "You win, *gatinha*. So let us leave at once for Espirito Santo."

"This very day," Tory promised.

Padre Osmundo could only groan. *"Cristo.* I hope Percy is up to this journey. I'm not sure I am!"

Tory's and Sebastian's wedding took place precisely twelve days later, longer than Sebastian wanted, but shorter than Padre Osmundo would have liked, and absolutely perfect timing for Tory. They spoke their vows in the little church, and then retired to the school for the evening's celebration. There were music, dancing, toasts, and tables piled high with food. Tory danced until blisters popped out on her feet, and then Sebastian picked her up and danced her all around the school building, to the laughter and shouts of the peasants. The celebration lasted through the wee hours of the morning, until Tory could hardly keep her eyes open.

"Sebastian," she complained. "Isn't it about time we retired to Carmelita's house?"

They had decided to spend that first night in town and depart for Paraíso in the morning. Carmelita had made plans to sleep at a friend's house and leave her cozy little nest to the newlyweds. Watching the surprise creep across Sebastian's face, Tory realized that she had underestimated Sebastian's zest for *festas*, which was typically Brazilian. Apparently, as long as a party was in progress, he could restrain his eagerness to take her to bed.

"I'm sorry, *gatinha*. I did not realize it had grown so late."

"I'm the one who's sorry, Sebastian; I'm afraid I've grown quite sleepy," she apologized, yawning despite herself.

"My poor little kitten; you really are exhausted, aren't you?" Sebastian swept her into his arms and insisted upon carrying her back to town. A handful of noisy *vaqueiros* and giggling young ladies accompanied them, Teodoro and Quinquina among them.

"I doubt she is as sleepy as she pretends," Quinquina brazenly teased.

Teodoro had kept his arm around the young girl's waist all evening, Tory had noticed. The two were obviously supremely happy in their marriage and delighted that Tory and Sebastian were embarking on the same joyful journey.

"When will you begin my reading lessons, *Professôra*?" Teodoro inquired. "How about tonight? You haven't forgotten that you promised to teach me, have you?"

"There will be no reading lessons, tonight," Sebastian firmly stated. "And the *professôra* is going to be quite occupied for the next several months. If you want to learn to read so badly, Teodoro, you will have to start with the new teacher Padre Osmundo intends to hire for the school."

"But I will help you as soon as we return to

Paraíso, after our trip to the *Estados Unidos*," Tory promised.

"Hah! You'll be too busy," Sebastian snorted. "I doubt you'll have time even after we return."

"Now, don't start sounding like . . . like a *brioso* cretin," Tory warned. "You agreed to let me teach, remember."

In the light of the torch Teodoro was carrying, Quinquina's pretty face looked puzzled. "What is a *brioso* cretin, *Professôra?*"

"Well, a cretin is a person with extremely limited intelligence," Tory explained. "And *brioso* means vile, wicked, and terrible."

"It does?" Quinquina questioned. "I always thought it meant brave, proud, courageous, and generous. Indeed, I often thought that Senhor *Prêto*, your new husband, is very *brioso* . . . and Teodoro, too, of course."

"I *am brioso*," Sebastian affirmed, his lips twitching with silent laughter.

Tory recalled the day that he had supplied the term in response to her request to find a bad word to call him. "Sebastian! You *lied* to me," she accused. "All this time when I used the word *brioso*, I thought I was insulting you—and now, I find out I was giving you a compliment."

"No, *gatinha*, you were only telling the truth."

Everyone around them roared with laughter, and the laughter followed them all the way to Carmelita's house. When they finally reached it, Sebastian turned to the small assembly. "Goodnight, my friends . . . I trust you will leave us alone now, so the *professôra* can get some sleep."

"Then perhaps she should come home with me," one of the men called out. "If she stays here with

437

you, she'll get no sleep."

"Don't worry. I'll see to it that she gets plenty of rest." Sebastian's dark glower abruptly ended the laughter.

He is still the master, the powerful Falcon, the rich *fazendeiro*, Tory thought. These people love and respect him, but fear him, too—an emotion I will have to work hard to eradicate.

"Goodnight, everyone . . ." she said into the sudden, awkward silence. "Thank you for making our wedding a truly special, memorable occasion. When we return from the *Estados Unidos*, we will have another grand *festa* . . . And at the next one, I promise not to get sleepy before the sun rises."

Someone chuckled, restoring the convivial mood, and the peasants gathered around them, wishing them well. "Goodnight, *Professôra!* Pleasant dreams! . . . Goodnight, Senhor *Sebastião*. Pleasant dreams to you, also."

Still carrying her, Sebastian entered the house and closed the door behind them. "At last . . . alone with my new bride," he said, his eyes warmly caressing her.

Carmelita had left a lamp burning on the table, and the tiny house gleamed with cleanliness. Tory glanced around appreciatively. The little house-keeper had even set out the clothes they would need tomorrow for their journey to Paraíso. Her garments hung over the back of a chair, and Sebastian's leather chaps and vest were folded and stacked on the seat, with his hat on top of them.

"Put me down, Sebastian," Tory directed. "There's one other thing you must do before I'm ready to go to bed with you."

Sebastian warily set her on her feet. "What might that be?"

Tory doubted that he would remember the challenge he had issued so long ago. She crossed to the table where Carmelita had thoughtfully provided bread, cheese, fruit, and wine for a snack, all neatly laid out, with plates and cutlery, should they be needed. Picking up a plate, knife, and fork, Tory retrieved Sebastian's leather *vaqueiro's* hat, placed the hat on the plate, with the silverware beside it, and handed it to him.

He looked at her as if she had suddenly lost her mind. "What's this?"

"Your hat. Have you forgotten? You said that if I ever found a man who approves of the same things I do, meaning the same freedoms for women, that you would eat your leather *vaqueiro's* hat ... Well, I found one, and he approves so much that he up and married me. So now you must make good on your promise ... Would you care for a swallow of wine to wash it down with? ... Or how about a bite of bread?"

"Gatinha ... I am *not* going to eat this hat." Sebastian set the plate back down on the table.

"Then I can't trust a word you say, can I? I'll have to find another word besides *brioso* to describe you. How do you say liar? Deceitful? Untrustworthy?"

"Come here!" Sebastian roared.

She eluded his grasp and put the table between them. "Not until you eat that hat!"

"Whatever I put in my mouth tonight, it won't be that hat!"

He chased her into the bedchamber, where Carmelita had already turned down the sheets. Tory ran around the other side of the bed, but Sebastian flung himself across it and succeeded in grabbing her arm. He dragged her down on top of him, where she struggled futilely to escape his hands and mouth. Finally,

439

he rolled over, pinning her beneath him and grinning triumphantly.

"I will gladly devour your lips, breasts, belly, and thighs . . . but I will not eat that hat. Is that clearly understood, *gatinha?*"

It sounded like a fair compromise to Tory. Besides, she knew that however much Sebastian might yield to her, he would *never* be completely tamed. He was a beautiful, masculine, proud, arrogant lion of a male . . . and she really didn't want him any other way. He was everything she had learned to crave in a man—masterful, demanding, powerful, passionate . . . unrelenting in his desire to possess her.

She wrapped her arms around him and drew him down to her. "Whatever you say, my darling husband," she demurely whispered. "Whatever you say."

Epilogue

"So you are my grand-nephew," the old man said, leaning back in the leather chair and examining Sebastian with an eagle eye. "And you changed your name from Falkner to Falcon, or rather your grandfather, my elder brother, changed it."

"Yes, sir," Sebastian responded, exchanging glances with Tory. "You are my great uncle, in so far as we can determine."

"Oh, I am, all right . . . You look just like my brother, Bartholomew. You've got the same color eyes, the same swagger, and the same way of looking down your nose at people."

"I do?" Sebastian questioned, frowning at Tory's smile.

Tory had also noted a strong resemblance between Sebastian and this snowy-haired, distinguished-looking gentleman, but she thought it best to wait until they knew him better before pointing it out. Both men exuded the same straight-backed pride, stubbornness, and sense of self. If this was how Sebastian would look in his nineties, she hoped they would both be around to enjoy his old age.

"Yes, you do . . ." Marcus Falkner said. "I always

wondered what happened to Bartholomew and his family . . . I received a letter from him saying that he and his wife were sick with fever and dysentery, and then I never heard from him again . . . Your father, Manuel, was never much for writing. Of course, he didn't know me from Adam, since he was born in that god-forsaken country and grew up more Brazilian than American."

Sebastian stiffened. "Brazil is a fine country, Senhor. I take it you have never been there."

"No . . . never had time for travel. My brother left me with a heavy load for a young man to pull on his own; I was only in my teens when he took what was left of his inheritance after our disastrous War between the States, married his childhood sweetheart, and lit out for Brazil to make his fortune . . . I was mad as a hornet at him—and stayed mad for years. I couldn't understand how he could leave our beloved state of Kentucky, and go someplace wild and unsettled like Brazil . . . About the time I was ready to forgive him, I realized it was too late. I had lost contact with him, and couldn't find hide nor hair of him or his son."

"He abandoned you when he left for Brazil?" Tory asked, fascinated by this ancient family history.

"Oh, he left enough money to tide me over until I could finish my education and find work, but the bulk of our parents' estate he converted into gold and precious jewels, and then hid them in a cross and a rosary, to deter thieves."

"I found the treasure only recently," Sebastian informed the old man. "My father died when I was a child, and I never knew that it existed, much less where it was hidden."

Marcus Falkner snorted. "I'm surprised you found

it at all. My brother didn't intend to spend it right away. He wanted it saved for 'future generations,' so that none of his grandchildren would have to suffer the deprivations he and I experienced after the war, when our family lost so much . . . He thought of the gold and jewels as a stake in the future of the Falkners."

"It has provided security and comfort for me and mine," Sebastian assured the old man, drawing Tory closer to him, and fondly glancing down at her rounded belly. "And it will continue to provide the same."

Heavy with child, Tory moved slowly and awkwardly into the circle of Sebastian's arm. The baby was due any day now, which was why she and Sebastian were in the United States, so that Spencer could help with the delivery. The past several months had given them the opportunity to concentrate on searching for Sebastian's relatives, and it had come as an amazing surprise that the Falkners lived only a half-day's journey from Castle Acres and even less than that from Paradise Farms, their own new home in Kentucky.

"I hope you don't mind us coming here like this, catching you by surprise," she apologized. "We certainly didn't mean to stir up unpleasant memories."

"On the contrary, my dear . . ." the old man protested. "I'm damned glad to discover what happened to my brother and his family."

"And we are pleased to meet you, Senhor . . . You are my only living blood relative," Sebastian told him.

Marcus Falkner laughed. "Not quite, young man. I sired a whole passle of children, and my children are themselves good breeders . . . Now, let me see." His brow furrowed. "If memory serves correctly, you have thirty-two first and second cousins, give or take a cousin or two."

Sebastian's amber eyes widened. "Thirty-two!"

"Children are the only wealth worth having, son—you can take all your gold, precious gems, horses, houses, land, and cattle, and dump them off a cliff somewhere, and you can still be happy . . . so long as you've got a good woman by your side, and a bun baking in the oven . . ." He eyed Tory's stomach with sly amusement. "Oh, yes, I knew you were a Falkner, as soon as you swaggered in here . . . All I had to do was feast my eyes on your little lady's swollen figure."

Tory felt her cheeks turning crimson. "You don't mince words, do you, Uncle Marcus?"

His head jerked at the familiarity of her address. "No, I don't . . . and I see that you don't, either. I suppose that you're one of those trouble-making females who think women should have the right to vote."

Sebastian laughed. "She's not only one of 'those trouble-making females,' she's a leader among them. You had better prepare yourself to see major changes in this country; sooner or later, women will win that right."

"I'll probably be dead by then," the old man scoffed. "And I can't say I want to live to see it . . . Too old-fashioned, I guess. I want women to be women and men to be men."

Just then, the door to the old gentleman's library flew open, and a child ran into the room. "Grandpa! Grandpa!" she cried. "You've got to come quickly! Queenie just had her new foal."

Marcus Falkner scowled at the pretty, dark-haired little girl in her starched blue and white pinafore and ruffled apron, which was deplorably stained and dirty. "What do you mean, bursting in here like a young ruffian, when I'm busy entertaining guests? You should be ashamed of yourself, Amanda . . . You haven't even curtsied and said hello . . . and look at your dress! You've got horse dung on your apron!"

Any normal child would have been intimidated, but Amanda Falkner simply stopped in her tracks and stared up at her grandfather. "You *said* to tell you when Queenie had her foal . . . Well, she just had it, and if you don't hurry, you're going to miss seeing the colt take his first few steps."

"Well, ah . . . ahem," the old man glanced sheepishly at Sebastian and Tory. "I don't suppose you would mind a short visit to the foaling barn, would you? . . . When Amanda commands, we all obey. As you can see, she's a regular tyrant."

Again, Sebastian and Tory exchanged glances of amusement. Noticing them for the first time, the child made a futile attempt to straighten her mussed clothing. "Please, excuse me," she chirped. "I don't mean to be rude, but Grandpa and I have been waiting for Queenie to have this foal for an awfully long time. He's going to be *my* horse, you see, my very own horse. Grandpa promised, didn't you, Grandpa?"

It was obvious that Amanda Falkner had her grandfather wrapped around her little finger. Seeing Tory's smile, Marcus Falkner sought to reassert his crumbling authority. "Really, I shouldn't have done it," the old man grumbled. "But the child talked me into it . . . Next thing you know, she'll probably be talking me into supporting the female right to vote . . . Of course, if all females were like Amanda, I wouldn't mind them having the vote. She's smart as a whip, that girl. I don't doubt she could run the whole country if she put her mind to it."

He rose from his chair. "Well, come on . . . let's go see the new colt. And then I'll introduce you to the rest of the family. You must stay for dinner, of course, and come to visit often, now that you know where we live . . ."

As Tory and Sebastian followed the old man out of the room, Sebastian took Tory's hand and whispered in her ear. "If our babe turns out to be a girl, I hope she's exactly like you and Amanda. If she is, I might even join your battle for womens' rights."

"Oh, Sebastian . . . would you really?"

"I said *might, gatinha*. That means *maybe* . . . At least, I'll give it serious consideration." He squeezed her fingers. "On the other hand, it would probably be easier to eat my leather *vaqueiro's* hat, than to admit I've been wrong all these years about the aptitude of women."

"I've still got the hat," she reminded him.

"And if you press the point, I'll do what I did last time."

Tory made a mental note of that, deciding that she would, indeed, press the point, as soon as her condition permitted. She might even press it *before* she had this baby. Sebastian was being ridiculously over-protective and refusing to do anything but hold her in his arms at night, a situation she was finding more and more intolerable. As a matter of fact, tonight would be a perfect night for getting out Sebastian's hat and making him put up or shut up.

Smiling to herself, thinking of the night to come, Tory accompanied Sebastian out to the barn to see Amanda's colt.

446

Afterward from the Author

Were it not for a reader of one of my previous
books, WILDLY MY LOVE, this book would not
have been written. The reader suggested that I write
the story of Jordan King's sister, Victoria, who never
actually appeared in WILDLY MY LOVE, but was
mentioned several times. Tory had captured *my*
interest, as well . . . All I needed was a hero strong
enough to handle her and a setting I was eager to
write about.

Jordan had met Spencer in Brazil's Amazon
region, a place my husband and I had briefly visited
twenty years ago. Yet it was the *sertão* we knew better,
having lived there for two years while in the Peace
Corps. I knew I would enjoy researching a time and
place that has tantalized my memory for more than
half my lifetime.

I derived Sebastian's character from a real-life,
Robin Hood hero who roamed the *sertão* a few years
later than the period of this story. His name was
Lampião, and he is one of Brazil's most notorious
cangaçeiros. In a museum in Salvador, we saw
Lampião's severed, preserved head. *Lampião* and his
love, a young girl named Maria Bonita who often

447

rode with him, met a sad, tragic end. I didn't want such an ending for Sebastian and Tory, so of course, I wrote the story to suit myself . . . That's the fun of fiction for the writer and also, I hope, for the reader.

My next book will take you to the Abaco Islands in the Bahamas during the post-Revolutionary War period, when British sympathizers were forced to wreck and plunder passing ships in order to survive . . . My heroine is the daughter of a wrecker, and my hero is one of their victims, come to the islands in search of his ship-wrecked brother . . . Until then, I wish you happy reading and all the joy of romance, real and imagined.